GUIDES TO VILLAINY AND LOVE
BOOK ONE

THE DARK LORD'S GUIDE TO DATING
(AND OTHER WAR CRIMES)

TIFFANY HUNT

SCARLETT PRESS

SIMON & SCHUSTER

London   New York   Amsterdam/Antwerp   Sydney/Melbourne   Toronto   New Delhi

First published in Great Britain in 2025 by Scarlett Press,
an imprint of Simon & Schuster UK Ltd

Text copyright © 2025 Tiffany Hunt
Previously published in 2025 by Tiffany Hunt
Illustration copyright © 2025 Fernanda Suarez
Cover designed by Greg Stadnyk

This book is copyright under the Berne Convention.
No reproduction without permission.
All rights reserved.

The right of Tiffany Hunt to be identified as the author of this work has been asserted by her in accordance with sections 77 and 78 of the Copyright, Designs and Patents Act, 1988.

1 3 5 7 9 10 8 6 4 2

Simon & Schuster UK Ltd
1st Floor, 222 Gray's Inn Road
London WC1X 8HB

For more than 100 years, Simon & Schuster has championed authors and the stories they create. By respecting the copyright of an author's intellectual property, you enable Simon & Schuster and the author to continue publishing exceptional books for years to come. We thank you for supporting the author's copyright by purchasing an authorized edition of this book. No amount of this book may be reproduced or stored in any format, nor may it be uploaded to any website, database, language-learning model, or other repository, retrieval, or artificial intelligence system without express permission. All rights reserved. Inquiries may be directed to Simon & Schuster, 222 Gray's Inn Road, London WC1X 8HB or RightsMailbox@simonandschuster.com.

www.simonandschuster.co.uk
www.simonandschuster.com.au
www.simonandschuster.co.in

Simon & Schuster Australia, Sydney
Simon & Schuster India, New Delhi

The authorised representative in the EEA is Simon & Schuster Netherlands BV,
Herculesplein 96, 3584 AA Utrecht, Netherlands.
info@simonandschuster.nl

A CIP catalogue record for this book
is available from the British Library.

PB ISBN 978-1-3985-5897-7
EB ISBN 978-1-3985-6216-5

This book is a work of fiction. Names, characters, places and incidents are either the product of the author's imagination or are used fictitiously. Any resemblance to actual people living or dead, events or locales is entirely coincidental.

Printed and Bound in the UK using 100% Renewable Electricity
at CPI Group (UK) Ltd

For Nicole

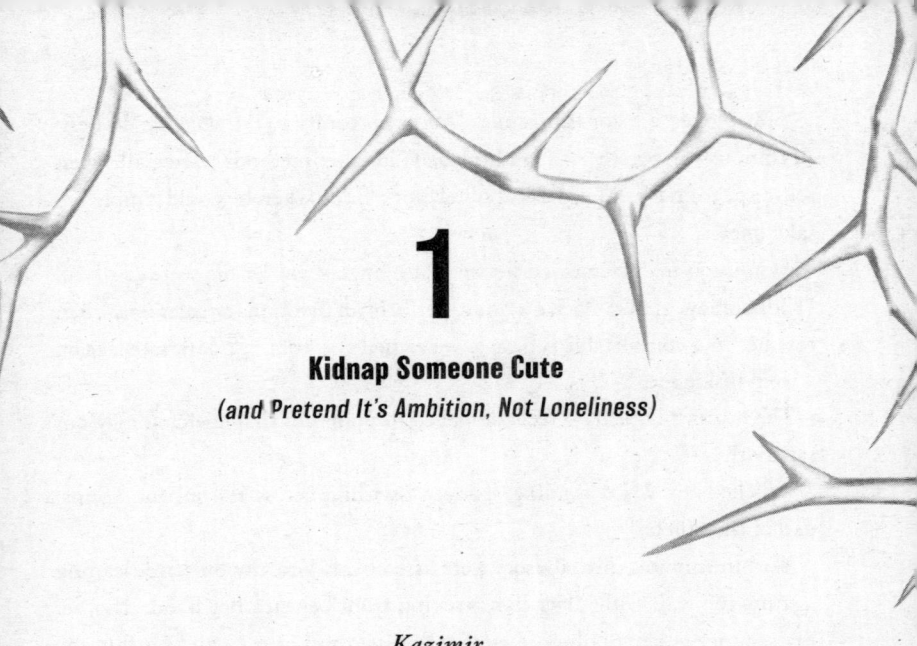

1

Kidnap Someone Cute

(and Pretend It's Ambition, Not Loneliness)

Kazimir

"No." I slammed my fist on the obsidian table. "Absolutely not."

The mirror's surface rippled as it spoke. "The terms are nonnegotiable, Lord Blackrose. The Heirloom requires a marriage bond with one of heroic bloodline. Without it, the artifact is basically an ancient hunk of metal."

Behind me, maps covered the war room's walls, each one marked with careful notes for future conquests. Etched tracking spells flickered across the table, charting movement throughout my domain. And there, on its black marble pedestal, rested the Heirloom of Dominion, a deceptively simple circlet of gold.

"My lord?" Sims cleared his throat. He was a thin, meticulous strategist, the kind of man who told me the truth whether I wanted it or not. "Perhaps we should consider the requirements as an opportunity?"

I rounded on him, letting shadows curl in the corners of the room. "An opportunity for what, exactly? To parade around, courting some vapid princess?"

Sims offered a razor-thin smile. "An opportunity to do what we do best. Accomplish it by, ah . . . traditional villainous methods. After all, what self-respecting Dark Lord asks politely for a bride when he could simply . . . take one?"

Dominion magic crackled between my fingers as I let his words sink in. "Kidnapping," I said. "Seize a bride, perform an involuntary ceremony, then toss her in a comfortable cell once we've tied the knot." A dark satisfaction stirred inside me.

The mirror bubbled. "I feel compelled to point out that coercion may not satisfy the—"

I flicked my wrist, sending shadows swirling across the mirror. "Sims, gather the others."

Within minutes, my advisors were assembled: Vex, my Steward, leaning against the wall with silver hair peeking from beneath her hood; Thorne, my security chief, a human fortress of muscle and grunts; and Griffin, my slightly problematic enchanter, wearing robes several inches too short for his unnaturally stretched frame.

I pressed both palms on the table. "By now, you all know the situation. I need a highborn descendant of the First Hero, someone who'll survive proximity to my dark magic without keeling over." I pulled a dagger from my belt, testing its edge with my thumb. "Preferably someone who won't try to stab me in my sleep, though that's negotiable."

Griffin, half distracted, said, "What about Princess Marigold of the Summer Court?"

I spun the dagger idly. "That poet who writes odes to butterflies? She'd faint at the sight of my breakfast spread."

"Lady Rosamund of the Western Isles?" Thorne offered.

"Already betrothed to three different princes." I drove my dagger into a stack of maps. The blade quivered. "Too messy politically."

Sims tried next. "The Duchess of Thornhaven?"

"Too old," I dismissed.

"She's thirty-eight."

"Practically ancient," I said, wiggling the dagger free. "And I hear she collects unicorns. Living ones." I suppressed a shudder.

Griffin spoke up, fidgeting. "Princess Violet of—"

I paused mid-spin. "Which Violet? The pacifist who started a goblin peace coalition?"

"No, the other Princess Violet."

"The one who breeds rabbits?"

"No, the *other* other Princess Violet."

"How many Princess Violets exist in this cursed realm?" I snapped.

Griffin paled behind his glasses. "Seven, my lord. Popular name twenty years ago."

"Absolutely not. I refuse to spend eternity clarifying which Princess Violet I kidnapped." I hurled the dagger across the room, embedding it in the front of a desk. "Any suggestions that might save me from losing my dignity?"

Griffin brightened. "What about Lord Sebastian from the Northern Peaks?"

The entire room went still. Even my shadows seemed to freeze.

"Lord Sebastian," I echoed, voice dangerously soft, "the imbecile who invited the Bone Witches to last year's Winter Solstice ball?"

Thorne snorted. "I heard about that. Half the court of Solandris was cursed with speaking in rhymes for a month."

"Well, yes, but—" Griffin pushed his glasses up. "He *does* have the First Hero's blood. He's gorgeous. And his scones are allegedly—"

My shadows erupted from beneath the table, plunging sections of the war room into darkness. Everyone wisely shut up.

I let the tension hang before I spoke again. "I need someone with a modicum of self-preservation, or my enemies will never stop laughing."

"Oh." Griffin's face fell. "I just thought . . . since you mentioned the stabbing thing . . . he's quite pacifist—"

"Moving on," Sims cut in quickly. "What about—"

"If you say 'Violet' again, I'm throwing you all off the battlements."

Vex slid forward, producing a slim folder from within her cloak. "I keep a record of all significant nobles within a hundred leagues. The heroic bloodlines . . . well, they're dwindling. But I found a possibility. Lady Arabella Evenfall of Solandris."

I plucked the page from her hand. "Suitable how?"

"She's of marrying age. The only daughter of Lord Evenfall, who's currently out of favor at court—her disappearance might not cause much of a stir. And she has direct hero-blood lineage on her mother's side."

I eyed Vex. "What's the catch?"

"She's known to be, ah, accident-prone," Vex said, sounding far too pleased with herself. "She's driven three suitors away, possibly by setting fire to one's cravat. Once, she convinced an entire Summer Court delegation she could speak to ghosts—"

"Could she?" Thorne asked.

"No. It was complete nonsense, but it worked a little too well. Her father's kept her out of major court functions since." Vex tapped a silver-painted nail against the table. "The betting pools in Solandris have her either burning down her father's estate or being shipped to a remote convent within the year."

My eyes fell on the rough sketch that showed a poised young woman with golden hair and freckles dusted across her nose. Yet, the quirk of her mouth suggested hidden mischief. Something about that faint arrogance made me pause. I trailed my fingertip across the outline of her face, then snapped myself out of it.

Sims shifted in his seat. "But . . . Solandris."

"The Dark Lord can manage it," Griffin whispered.

"But if . . ." Sims's voice lowered as the two of them furiously debated whether me going into Solandris was a good idea.

I let their voices wash over me for a moment before interrupting. "Enough. I'm well aware of Solandris's resistance to my magic. Besides, we'll be gone before the king's goons so much as brandish a magical crossbow. Her father apparently doesn't care much about her well-being, so his defenses won't be over the top."

Vex nodded, sliding a map forward. "She's traveling to her summer residence soon. If we want her, that's our window."

"Perfect," I said, leaning in to study the winding path. "The Whispering Woods. Good vantage points, easy terrain for an ambush." I paused. "What's her magical tolerance?"

Griffin flipped through the notes. "Above average. She inherited the First Hero's healing gifts, so proximity to your dark magic shouldn't incinerate her."

I chuckled darkly. "Always a bonus in a future wife." I drummed my fingers on the table. "We'd better avoid the Golden Rose Fields, though. My shadow warriors can't hold form there."

"Easy." Vex traced a slender nail along the route. "We catch her carriage in the Whispering Woods, knock out the guards, and whisk her away. Simple. Just be prepared for her unintentional disasters."

"At least it won't be boring," I murmured.

Sims cleared his throat again. "Kidnapping a noblewoman from Solandris could spark full-scale war."

"By the time King Auremar organizes his troops," I said, "I'll have the Heirloom activated. Let them come." My gaze drifted to the golden circlet resting on the pedestal.

"And if Lady Arabella . . . resists marriage?" Sims persisted.

I fought the urge to pull my shirt away from the burning scars on my forearm. "I've broken far stronger wills than that of a sheltered noble. All I need is her vow."

From her spot, Vex asked slyly, "Not planning on consummation?"

I glared. "The artifact doesn't require it. Words suffice." I turned to the mirror again, dropping the silence that cloaked it. "That's right, isn't it?"

The mirror rippled, beginning to speak, "In theory, the artifact might—"

Shadows snaked back over it with a snarl from me. "I only need vows," I said, ignoring the mirror's muffled squawking. "There's a difference between compelling someone to go through a ceremony and forcing my way into her bed."

Vex murmured, "How chivalrous."

I cast a pointed look at Vex, daring her to argue further. She merely lifted a brow.

"We're done here," I said, turning to the others. "Sims, prepare the Great Hall for a wedding. Vex, find me whatever legal documents we need and prepare invitations. This wedding must be official. Thorne, you handle the guards. Griffin, get my runes ready for the infiltration into Solandris."

They bustled into action, but Griffin hesitated. "Should we . . . prepare a welcome gift? Some, uh, token to soften the transition?"

I shot him a flat glare. "Griffin, I'm kidnapping a noblewoman. I doubt she'll appreciate a fruit basket."

He squirmed. "But first impressions . . ."

My eyes flicked again to her sketch. That ghost of a smirk still had me off-balance. "Fine. Send roses. Whatever number you deem appropriate for an abducted fiancée."

Thunder rolled outside the citadel, and lightning illuminated the war room's vaulted ceiling. I turned to the window, watching the sky crack open in a violent storm.

Sims spoke softly, pulling me back. "Your orders for the infiltration, my lord?"

I turned, feeling a rush of anticipation burn in my veins. "I'll do it myself. I refuse to risk one of you idiots confusing her with an interchangeable Violet." I leveled Griffin with a pointed glare. "Or Lord Sebastian and his scones."

Griffin shrugged helplessly. "To be fair, they are excellent sco—"

"Don't test me," I snarled, letting the shadows flicker menacingly. "You have your orders. And for the love of all that's dark, someone get me a cloak that says 'villain.' I want to look as dramatic as my reputation demands."

Griffin, trying too hard, added, "Do we also need a kidnapping net?"

My shadows clamped around his collar, lifting him an inch off the floor. "We are not using a *net*."

"Yes, my lord," he choked out.

"Get to work," I snapped, releasing him. They scattered, leaving me alone with the echoing thunder and that dreadful mirror. I walked toward the Heirloom, letting my fingertips glide across the cool metal. All that power was just waiting to be claimed, and ironically, it hinged on an absurdly traditional practice: a wedding with a woman who (if the rumors were true) might roast me alive by "accident" before I even said "I do."

Hm. I would need to ward Lady Evenfall's rooms against fire, just in case.

Lightning cracked outside. I strode from the war room with a grin that would have sent my enemies running for cover. I had a lady to kidnap, a wedding to prepare, and an artifact of unimaginable power to claim.

Just another day in the life of the Dark Lord.

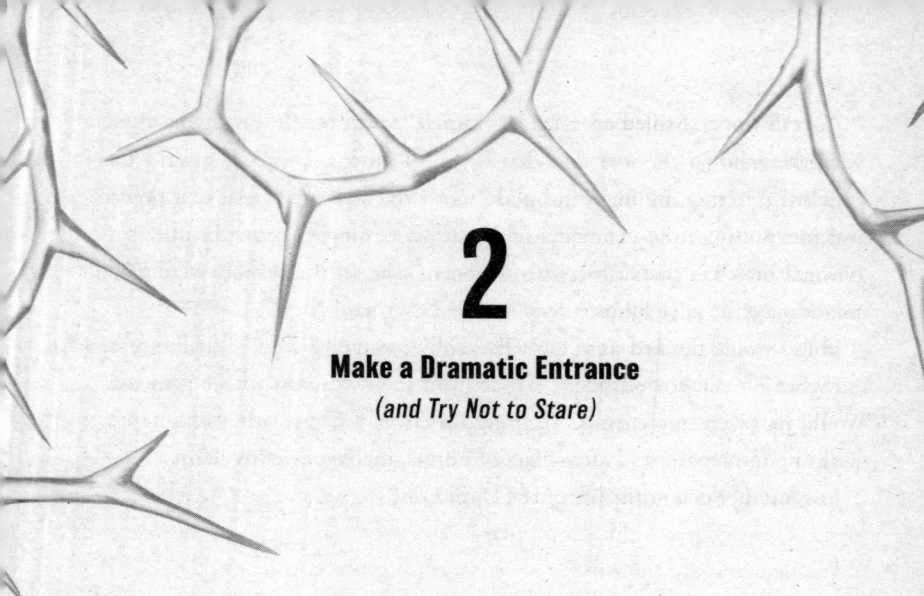

2

Make a Dramatic Entrance
(and Try Not to Stare)

Arabella

I clenched Father's letter until the parchment bit into my palm. Outside, the Golden Rose Fields of Solandris blazed in the sunlight, but I hardly saw them. Father's neat, imperious script held my attention:

> *Prepare for visitors, as I shall be arriving in three days' time with someone who has expressed a keen interest in securing an alliance with our house.*

Another suitor. Another performance for family honor. I crumpled the letter and let it fall onto the carriage seat.

"My lady?" Agnes, my lady-in-waiting, peered over her embroidery. "You look upset."

"I'm . . ." I swallowed my annoyance and pasted on a polite smile. "I was hoping for three months of peace. But apparently, Father's decided otherwise. I can practically hear his threats about locking me in the tower if I ruin another betrothal."

Agnes's fingers stilled around her needle. "I'm sorry. Another match, so soon after—"

"Lord Perris?" I cut in, grinning. "He deserved worse than a singed cravat."

Agnes snorted, then coughed to hide it. I gave a humorless laugh. "Just when I think I'm free of Father's meddling, he springs a fresh candidate on me. Maybe the next suitor will spontaneously combust."

The carriage lurched as we left the gilded shimmer of the Golden Rose Fields for the shadowed throat of the Whispering Woods. Branches knitted overhead, choking the light. We covered nearly two hours of muddy miles, long enough for Agnes to finish an entire spray of roses on her hoop, before the wood stopped whispering and simply . . . listened. No birdsong. No wind. Only a hush so thick it pressed on my ears.

I leaned closer to the window. "Agnes," I murmured, "do not panic."

"Wolves?" She went pale.

"I wish it were," I muttered. A prickle crept along my spine, magic wrong and heavy. "Driver!" I shouted. "Faster!"

The horses broke into a run just as thunder boomed overhead. One moment the canopy flickered with dappled sunlight, the next roiling clouds tore across the sky, turning day into instant twilight. Sleet-cold rain hammered the roof. The trees blurred in the downpour, but I caught a flicker of movement along the forest edge. Men, not beasts.

"Shit." The carriage fishtailed. The horses screamed, then stopped altogether.

"Stay down!" I shoved Agnes to the floor as the door tore open. Instinct kicked in, and I flipped healing magic inside out, slamming it into the intruder's chest. He staggered, gasping.

"Agnes, run!" I leapt into the deluge, my summer dress instantly plastering to my skin. She managed two steps before masked figures grabbed her.

They swarmed the road, clad in black and armed to the teeth. The air plunged past winter-cold, every raindrop flashing to needles around us. The pressure of pure, crackling sorcery rolled over the muddy track, making my bones hum. Shadows bled out of the tree line, coiling together until they sculpted a man-shaped storm. Runes of liquid silver crawled over the onyx fall of his cloak, and rain flowed over his broad shoulders, revealing lean, predatory lines built for ruin. He took one deliberate step forward, and the forest itself seemed to kneel, its branches bowing and the wind holding its breath, while his dark gaze locked on me.

Oh, I thought distantly. *Oh no.*

I knew that face. Everyone knew that face, though few had seen it up close and lived to tell the tale. Kazimir Blackrose, the Dark Lord himself. Sworn enemy of . . . well, everybody, but especially Solandris. Rumor claimed he could turn entire armies to ash before breakfast. His dark eyes slid over me, lingering on the soaked dress clinging to my curves. For a heartbeat he seemed so distracted he'd forgotten his own grand entrance.

"Shall I pose while you paint a picture?" I snapped.

He blinked, then offered a half bow. "Lady Evenfall." His voice was deep, rich with the kind of authority that expected instant obedience. "I've heard you make for lively company."

"Meaning I've failed to tremble appropriately in yours," I said, stepping away from the carriage as lightning split the sky. Behind him, masked goons pinned my driver. "Bold of you to attack in daylight, Blackrose. Were all the midnight hours booked?"

"You know who I am, then."

"Hard to miss the *Dark Lord,*" I said. "We can skip the pleasantries if you don't mind. I have exactly zero interest in your villainous monologue."

"Shame." His gaze lingered on me, just as dark and arrogant as every rumor described. "I prepared an excellent one."

Rain trickled down his angular cheekbones. Silver magic shimmered in his eyes. For one deranged second, I understood why half the realm whispered about his mesmerizing presence. Then I remembered he had Agnes cornered and was definitely not here for tea.

My mind ran through all the lurid tales whispered about the Dark Lord, stories of eaten souls and blood-filled baths. "You miscalculated if you think my father will pay any ransom for me."

"Your father," he said with a snort, "would sooner send a thank-you note for taking you off his hands."

I kept my tone bored despite the panic in my chest. "All right, Blackrose, what is it? Did my carriage splash mud on your favorite cloak?"

"I need a wife."

My brain stuttered. Water dripped into my lashes as I stared. "You're joking."

He flicked his cloak back with a theatrical swirl, revealing a dagger at his hip. Thunder rumbled behind him. "I conjured a storm to intercept your carriage. Does that strike you as a joke?"

"You conjured a storm . . . to propose?" I sputtered. "You're trying way too hard."

One corner of his mouth twitched. "I heard you like to set your suitors on fire. I wanted to make an impression."

"Congratulations," I said tightly. "You just made the worst first impression of all time. Now kindly burn in hell."

The Dark Lord inclined his head in mock courtesy. "I'm afraid I don't have the time, since I'm kidnapping you."

I jerked my chin toward Agnes. "Let her go."

"Release the maid," he said to his men, but his eyes never left me. "She's irrelevant."

Irrelevant. My jaw clenched, but I shot Agnes a swift look. "Go!" She fled while the thugs stepped back. Magic buzzed under my skin, begging for release. "You obviously don't know me. I can ruin that smug face with a flick of my wrist."

"I appreciate your confidence," he drawled, stepping into my space. Power seeped from him, raising the hairs on my arms.

My pulse hammered as I fought its pull. "Let me make something clear," I said. "I'm not a pawn in your game, and I'm certainly not marrying you just because you decided to make a dramatic entr—"

"*Come here*," he commanded, voice thrumming with compulsion.

The order slammed into my mind, nearly buckling my knees. Every shred of me wanted to obey, but I stayed upright, fists clenched as white-hot pressure filled my skull.

"*Surrender*," he added, and the compulsion intensified.

My vision narrowed further, and my foot twitched forward on its own. Gritting my teeth, I forced myself to hold. "Nice trick," I managed. "But I don't take orders well."

"Fascinating. You really do carry the First Hero's blood." Satisfaction colored his tone. He nodded to the trees. "Vex. Take care of the stragglers. Then meet us at the citadel."

A silver-haired woman appeared from the shadows and set to work.

"I'm not going anywhere with you," I spat.

Kazimir extended a polite hand. "This can be gentle or . . . not. Your choice."

I pretended to accept, then drove my knee at his groin. He blocked it with infuriating ease, spinning me until my back hit his chest and my arms were trapped. Heat rolled off him, unsettling in the storm's chill. Shadows beside us shaped themselves into a doorway of pure darkness, a portal.

"Stop squirming," he growled near my ear. "You'll tear yourself apart."

"Better than marrying a tyrant." I reached for one last burst of magic, meaning to blast him away. Power flared between us, then twisted and rebounded into me, flooding my sight with hard white sparks.

My knees buckled. Kazimir's grip tightened, keeping me upright. "I've got you," he murmured.

"Fuck . . . you . . . ," I hissed.

"Maybe later," he said with dark amusement, then launched us into the waiting portal.

3

Propose Before She Stabs You
(Timing Is Everything)

Arabella

The world went sideways in a dizzying rush. I gasped, and the taste of cold night and raw lightning coated my tongue. Kazimir's arms tightened around my waist, his chest hard and unyielding against my back as we hurtled through whatever nightmare realm existed between spaces.

Then reality snapped back with brutal force. We careened out of his portal and crashed onto a massive wooden desk, scattering papers and sending an inkwell tumbling. I twisted in his grip, reaching for the dagger at his hip. Our momentum carried us off the desk, sending us rolling across a plush carpet until we ground to a stop. I was crushed beneath him as he pinned my wrists to the floor.

He was even more devastating up close. His eyes weren't just gray—they were storm clouds, laced with slivers of bright silver that shimmered whenever the lightning flashed outside. A faint scar cut through his left eyebrow, and a single dark strand of hair fell over his face, making him look infuriatingly human for a man rumored to be the Terror of the Western Realms.

He was younger than I'd imagined, maybe a handful of years older than me. Either everyone exaggerated his reign of terror, or he'd found some cursed elixir to preserve his youth.

Rainwater dripped off the tip of his nose and landed on my cheek.

"Well," he said, voice still ragged from our struggle, "that was more dramatic than I'd planned. You really do enjoy making things difficult, Lady Evenfall."

"Get off me," I hissed, trying futilely to wriggle free. Every inch of me felt keyed up, thrumming with stubborn rage.

"Make me," he whispered, challenge humming in every syllable. "I have to admit, I'm curious to see what you'll try next."

I bucked my hips hard, and his eyes went wide for half a second. That tiny window of surprise was all I needed. Twisting sharply, I managed to flip us and snatch the dagger from his belt in one move. He hit the floor on his back, a grunt escaping him as I straddled his waist, pressing steel against his throat.

"Like that?" I asked.

He didn't struggle, just stared up at me with those enthralling eyes. "Impressive," he said, voice low. "And now, Lady Evenfall, what's your plan?"

Before I could snap a reply, a voice from the doorway quavered, "My Lord? Should we . . . give you a moment?"

I glanced up to find a gaunt man in formal attire hovering near the threshold. Behind him stood a handful of guards, servants, and an absurdly tall, robed man who appeared to be taking notes. They all regarded me with unnerving calm, as though their lord being threatened at knifepoint were a common occurrence.

My lip curled. "I'm going to kill him," I announced, pressing the blade until a thin line of blood welled at his neck, "and if any of you get in my way, I'll kill you too."

None of them seemed alarmed. One guard actually smirked. The robed man scribbled vigorously. Clearly, they'd seen wilder things in their service to Kazimir. My stomach twisted in a mixture of fury and dread as I realized the only reason we were in this position was because he allowed it.

The glimmer in his eyes was pure amusement. "Sims," he said without looking away from me, "Lady Evenfall and I need a moment to discuss the final details of our impending nuptials. Her negotiating style is . . . dangerously charming."

I pressed the blade closer, but he didn't so much as flinch. "I'm not marrying you."

He merely considered me. "Have you ever killed anyone, my lady?"

The question caught me off guard. I hadn't, no matter how many times I'd fantasized about it while locked in my father's tower. My answer must have shown on my face, because Kazimir's gaze softened, just a fraction.

"I thought not," he whispered. "Believe me, there's a difference between singeing a suitor's cravat and slitting a man's throat."

Some bitter voice in my head insisted I could close that gap in my experience right now, but the rational part of me realized I had no idea whether a simple dagger would be enough to kill a master of dark magic. Even if I managed, I would never fight my way past his retinue.

I tightened my hold anyway. "There's a first time for everything."

Before I could follow through on the threat, shadows curled around my wrist. The dagger slipped from my grasp. Kazimir shoved upward, reversing our positions so quickly my head spun. He settled between my thighs, his body pressing into mine. My breath caught, and I hated the little surge of heat that flickered all the way to my cheeks.

"Now," he said casually, "you've attempted to murder me, and I've attempted polite conversation. But make no mistake—I will have a bride, and that bride will be you." His voice dropped lower. "The only question is how difficult you intend to be about it."

I forced myself to stop thrashing, letting my body go limp. My eyes flickered up at him, drawing on a performance I'd polished over years of manipulating my father's guards. I let my lower lip tremble. I made my voice small, hesitant.

"I—I don't want to keep fighting," I whispered.

Suspicion crawled across his face, but he seemed eager to believe me. The victorious gleam in his eyes returned. Slowly the restraints around my wrists loosened. "Of course you don't," he purred. "You'll find I can be quite agreeable toward those who see reason."

I let out a single tear and blinked up at him. "Yes, my lord." As he eased his grip, I lunged to the side, aiming a knee at his groin. I missed my mark, but I caught him close enough that he hissed a curse, his control on me faltering.

I flung myself toward the dagger. My fingers just brushed the hilt before Kazimir's arm locked around my waist. He yanked me back, slamming me against the carpet. Pain ricocheted up my spine, driving all the air from my lungs.

"Enough," he bit out, his words rough with anger. Shadows thickened around me, binding my limbs to the floor. The potency of his magic thrummed in the air. A nearby bookcase rattled, sending a few heavy tomes crashing to the ground. His own servants retreated a step, wary of their master's mounting fury.

He got to his feet and stood over me, dripping rain and wrath, every angled feature sharpened by the flickering torches. I had no illusions now. This was the dark power that made kings lock their doors at the mere mention of his name. For the first time since our brawl began, real fear wrapped its claws around my heart, but I forced my mouth into a defiant smirk.

"That only works once," he warned, gaze raking over me.

I glared at him. "It was worth a try."

"Indeed. I'll be more careful about those doe eyes of yours in the future." A reluctant amusement flickered across his face. "But now that you've had your fun, we'll do things my way."

The fabled Dark Lord wasn't about to let me slip through his fingers. I tried to guess what came next. Chains, perhaps? Another locked tower? Other humiliations I didn't want to think about.

Despite my predicament, I refused to beg. I'd promised myself, after that dreadful year imprisoned by my own father, that I would never kneel before anyone again. Through the rush of my own heartbeat I could only manage a strangled laugh. "This is shaping up to be the best first date I've ever had."

Kazimir's answering smile held no warmth. "Good." The subtle menace in his tone rippled through me. "Because it will be your last."

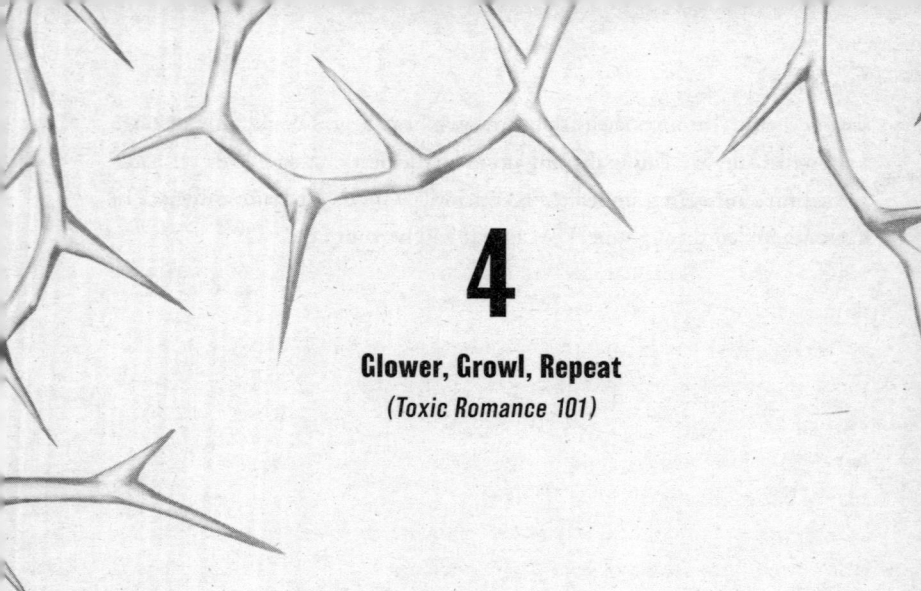

4

Glower, Growl, Repeat
(Toxic Romance 101)

Kazimir

For a long moment, I stayed exactly where I was—looming over my reluctant bride-to-be as she lay splayed on the floor of my study, her limbs bound by my shadows, eyes burning with defiance. It was an arresting sight.

"Why me?" she demanded. "Of all the nobles you could've stolen for this twisted plan, why choose the one with a crumbling estate and a tarnished name?"

I allowed a slow, humorless smile. "Because none of the others fit my needs quite as well as you do."

I finally turned my gaze to the crowd at the door. My staff who'd come to gawk. Sims had his hand half raised, as if he were pondering whether to comment on the bizarre scene. I felt a surge of impatience, tempered only by my fascination with the woman struggling beneath my magic.

"Out," I said, voice calm but layered with steel. I flicked my gaze over them, letting the runes carved into my bones hum with power.

They scattered instantly, leaving only Vex behind. She blended near the doorway with that infuriating knack for vanishing in plain sight. Meanwhile, I allowed Lady Evenfall to rise to her knees under my tight control, and then to stand. A lock of her golden hair fell loose from her braids, trailing across her flushed cheek.

"Now what?" she asked, glaring up at me. "Are we discussing the 'terms of my captivity'?"

"You're free to call it whatever makes you feel better." I circled her, letting the tension build. Create the feeling of being surrounded and even the bravest make mistakes. Yet this time, intrigue replaced triumph. Maybe it was her defiance. Maybe my usual intimidation routine was wearing thin. Or maybe part of me liked the challenge.

I stopped in front of her. "You'll stay in the fortress until the wedding. You won't attempt to escape or contact anyone outside. You *will* cooperate with the ceremony preparations. In return, I won't make your life exceptionally miserable."

She looked unimpressed. "Or you'll do what? Kill me? Torture me? Lock me in a dungeon? All of the above?"

I shrugged. "They've crossed my mind."

"How imaginative," she sneered. "I expected more from a fearsome warlord."

I took a step toward her. "Oh, I can be plenty imaginative, Lady Evenfall. Shall I demonstrate?"

"I've already been locked in a tower by my father," she shot back. "The lesson never sticks."

Her dismissal made something acidic twist in my stomach. I shoved the sentiment aside, focusing on her challenge.

"The wedding," I said icily, "is happening. Tomorrow night."

Her mouth fell open. "Tomorrow? Are you insane?" She sputtered, searching for words. "You can't expect me to—to actually go through with it. You can't force me to say vows."

I let my voice drop to a dangerous register. "I believe I made my intentions quite clear, and I hate repeating myself."

Anger flared in her bright eyes. "You failed to break me on the road. What makes you think you'll succeed tomorrow?"

I resisted the urge to prove my point with a tangible show of dominion magic. "Because I have all the power in this fortress, and you have none."

She lifted her chin in defiance, still unafraid. That brazen boldness sent a pulse of heat through my veins. I exhaled slowly, grappling for a calmer approach. "What's it going to be, Lady Evenfall?" I asked, letting shadows coil around her wrists to keep her still.

She said nothing, so I gently turned her palms up, feigning casual curiosity. "That trick on the road—turning your healing magic into a weapon. Where did you learn that?"

"Release my hands and I'll show you."

I grabbed her chin, forcing her to look at me. "You can fight every step, make this difficult for both of us, and still end up as my wife. Or you can accept the inevitable. I might be open to making your stay less . . . unpleasant, should you choose wisely."

"Nothing about this could be pleasant," she snapped.

I released her. "I'm beginning to see why your father wanted you contained." I summoned a guard, and one of the more thick-headed recruits ventured in. "Are Lady Evenfall's chambers ready?"

"Yes, my lord," the guard said, eyes nowhere near me. He stared at Arabella, blatantly taking in her damp silhouette.

Jealous fury roared up in me, so immediate and powerful that it surprised me. My dominion magic surged outward. The guard slammed against the wall. A mirror shattered, sending shards across the floor. I let the fool choke for a long beat, until his face purpled in panic.

Arabella's expression turned wary, though not quite terror-filled. If anything, it looked like confusion and something faintly reminiscent of twisted curiosity.

Without taking my eyes off her, I called for Vex, who was already emerging from the shadows. "Take Lady Evenfall to her chambers," I ordered. With a glance at the guard, I untied my cloak and tossed it around Arabella's shoulders. "Make sure she has everything she needs. I won't have my future bride drop dead of hypothermia before the vows."

Arabella gave me a long, measured look that might have bordered on pity. "You're going to regret choosing me," she said quietly, as though giving me a chance to back out.

My response was to pick up my discarded dagger and hold it tight by my side. "Let's clarify something," I snapped. "You can kick and scream, but you're mine until the ceremony is done."

She tilted her head. "And once it's over?"

I shoved down the odd flicker of unease. "That depends entirely on your cooperation."

Color rose in her cheeks, but she said nothing more. She only turned when Vex ushered her to the door, sparing one last look at the guard who still dangled in midair, gagging for breath.

When she was gone, I focused my attention on the unfortunate man. "You're new, aren't you?" I asked, letting him draw a ragged breath by relaxing the magic just a fraction. The smell of fear radiated off him.

He nodded frantically.

"Let me explain something very clearly." My runes throbbed in my bones, fueling my anger. "Lady Evenfall is dangerous. She is valuable. And she is mine. Understand?"

He nodded again, tears spilling down his face. I dropped him without ceremony, and he collapsed at my feet.

"Thorne!" I called. He appeared with unsettling promptness. "Take this idiot to the dungeons and teach him some manners. Start with Step Seventeen of the torture manual—the one with the spoons."

Thorne dragged the trembling guard away.

Alone at last, I turned to the tall windows. Storm clouds churned in the distance, black and roiling. I placed my hand against the glass, feeling the runes carved into my bones pulse in time with my heartbeat, leaving behind an ache that was half anger, half anticipation.

Threats hadn't cracked her. Perhaps torture would eventually work, but it would take more time than I cared to waste. If I wanted this wedding to go off without a catastrophic level of rebellion, I needed something beyond sheer intimidation . . . some leverage she couldn't shrug off. Except I hadn't the faintest clue what that leverage might be, and I hated that uncertainty even more than the stinging of my runes.

But some foolish, restless part of me felt more intrigued than I had in years.

Damn it all. If this was how matchmaking worked, no wonder people said love was more treacherous than war.

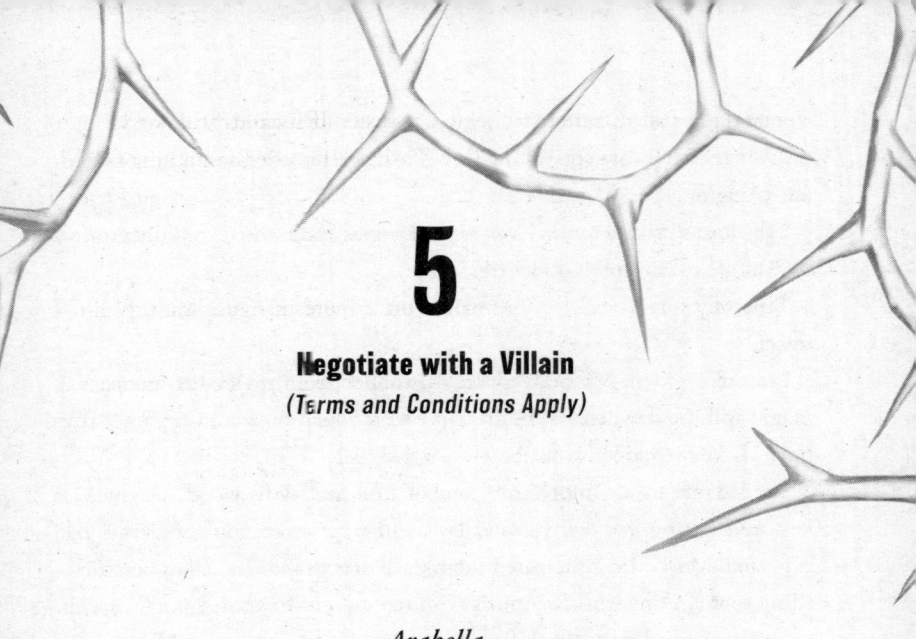

5

Negotiate with a Villain
(Terms and Conditions Apply)

Arabella

The shadow restraints vanished once we left Kazimir's study. Practical villains conserved magic when muscle would suffice. Vex held my arm firmly as we wound through the Dark Lord's fortress. Her grip suggested she could break bones as effortlessly as lighting a candle.

Cold now in my damp dress, I tugged the cloak closer around my shoulders, scowling at how it smelled so distinctly of him: winter storms and steel, undercut by the smoky tang of charred wood.

I felt a tiny spark of satisfaction remembering how Kazimir had flung that guard into the wall. My father had never once defended me from leering eyes, so I found it disturbingly pleasant to witness someone take actual offense on my behalf. Even if it was the Dark Lord. Even if I was still trying to figure out whether his anger had been about the guard's stare or something else entirely.

We reached a corridor lit by floating orbs of pale blue light. I glanced at a large mirror on the wall as we passed. My hair hung in half-fallen braids, and dust and smudges darkened my cheeks. I looked every bit the frazzled heroine from a tragic ballad, bartered away to a monster for a handful of goats.

"Where exactly are you taking me?" I asked after several minutes of wordless trudging.

"The lord's private tower," Vex replied impassively.

"And we're currently . . . where?"

"The Skyspire Citadel." She turned up a spiral staircase leading into a tower.

I bit off a groan. My body already throbbed from my earlier attempts at magic and the day's chaos. By the time we stopped on a landing, my calves burned. Vex remained stoic, barely winded.

She led me to an impressive door of iron and dark wood, produced a key, and swung it open. Beyond lay a suite far more opulent than I had expected. Maybe I'd anticipated a dank cell or a windowless chamber, something more in line with Kazimir's grim reputation. Instead, I stood in a circular room filled with lavish furniture, plush rugs, and a grand four-poster bed draped in burgundy silk.

My gaze snagged on the black roses. Vases brimming with them adorned nearly every surface. "Are those real?" I asked, stepping closer to one vivid cluster.

"Griffin's pride and joy," Vex answered with the faintest exasperation.

I reached out to brush a petal, only to jerk back at a sudden sting. A bead of blood welled up on my fingertip, and the flower's petals appeared to shiver in response.

"They bite," Vex warned me belatedly.

I sucked the drop of blood away and glowered at the malicious roses. "How . . . charming."

"Griffin has enthusiastic notions about decor," she remarked. "He thinks the future Dark Lady should be surrounded by intimidating symbols."

I nearly laughed at the absurdity. "Should I start practicing my villainous cackle, or is there an orientation handbook?"

Vex crossed the room to open a second door. "The bathing chamber is through here. You'll find fresh clothing waiting for you." She turned to leave.

"My people," I said, "what happened to them?"

Vex's posture stiffened before she answered. "Your maid is home. Your guards and driver are too. Safe or not—that's beyond my knowledge."

Relief mingled with a stab of guilt that I couldn't protect Agnes from whatever rumors would surely spread. At least she was free from this citadel.

Vex gestured at the main door. "I wouldn't try to leave before Lord Blackrose arrives to set the wards. The stairs have protections. If you try them without permission, you'll discover their defenses the hard way."

"Wait," I called as she made for the corridor. "Who are you?"

She paused, her expression unsettling in its perfect composure. "I'm the Steward of Skyspire." Then she slipped into the hall and turned the key in the lock behind her.

Steward of Skyspire, I mused drily, finding the title painfully inadequate for the woman who'd manhandled me up endless flights of stairs with the efficiency of a seasoned soldier. Definitely more than just Kazimir's glorified assistant.

I went to the nearest tall window, half expecting to see a courtyard or walls. Instead, I found whirling storm clouds *below* me. The fortress hovered in midair, tethered to nothing but jagged rocks floating in the same swirling darkness. Occasionally, streaks of violet lightning illuminated other shards suspended in the storm. At least one of the rumors about the Dark Lord was true.

"Well," I muttered, "that complicates things."

I tore my gaze away and wandered deeper into my gilded prison. The bathing chamber was pure indulgence: a huge sunken tub, brass fixtures, and an array of soaps that smelled of lavender and spice. The dressing chamber next to it brimmed with dresses in rich jewel tones, nightgowns trimmed in delicate lace, and even some riding attire. All in my size. All far more extravagant than anything I owned back home.

Exhaustion dragged at my limbs, so I stripped and sank into the tub. The hot water was an undeniable comfort, but as I scrubbed away the grime of the day, a deeper worry settled in my mind.

Why me?

Kazimir Blackrose had chosen the daughter of a financially ruined noble house. Our estate was nearly worthless. My father's favor was a joke among the gentry. But there was one thing in my family that still held value—

My mother's bloodline, traced back to the First Hero.

It was the only thing that made me valuable to someone like Kazimir Blackrose. But what could he want with heroic blood? I didn't like the answers my mind supplied. Dread pooled in my stomach as I imagined vile rites, forced heirs warped by dark magic, or arcane bargains where my veins would be drained to fuel some monstrosity.

I let myself shiver at the thought instead of trying to banish it. Information was power, after all. Now that I knew Kazimir needed more than just my compliance, I could attempt to negotiate. If I held any leverage at all, it was that special lineage he required.

When I finished bathing, I selected a simple forest green gown from the wardrobe. It slid over my skin as if tailored precisely to my measurements. I left my hair loose to dry in waves, then returned to the main room.

A timid knock drew me to the door. A young man—he couldn't have been older than sixteen—stood there balancing a tray piled with food.

"My lady," he mumbled. "I brought your meal."

I ushered him inside, watching as he set out roast chicken, bread, and vegetables on a low table near the fireplace.

"Thank you," I said. "What's your name?"

He stared at the floor. "Pip, my lady."

I thanked him for the meal, and he fled. Despite the knot of anxiety in my belly, I realized I was ravenous and devoured every bite. I'd just finished mopping up the last of the gravy with a piece of bread when the lock clicked and the door swung open without warning.

Firelight hissed lower, and shadows clawed across the rugs an instant before Kazimir strode through the doorway. He wore a fitted jacket of glossy black scales—dragonskin?—that shimmered darkly in the firelight.

His eyes, just as black, raked over me from head to toe. A thin red line on his throat marked where I'd cut him earlier.

He flicked a glance at the folded cloak on the chair, then at me. "The green suits you better than that."

"Your minions have interesting taste," I said, trying to sound nonchalant. "Though I'm grateful they didn't force me into a dress covered in black roses. I barely survived the ones in the vases."

His mouth tightened, but he prowled farther inside, one fingertip grazing the petals of a black rose. The bloom folded beneath his touch. "Griffin's been reminded of his . . . excesses. He tends to forget that not everyone appreciates carnivorous flora."

"Poor Griffin. He's probably sobbing into his man-eating roses."

Kazimir ignored the jab. "I came to set the wards. They'll keep you in this suite unless I grant you passage beyond."

"And here I thought you'd come to properly propose." The words slipped out before I could stop them. I trailed my finger over a velvet-covered chair. "But I suppose that would be too traditional for the Dark Lord."

He arched an eyebrow, clearly amused. His fingers flexed once at his side. "Traditional? You'd prefer I drop to one knee?"

"Well, you did kidnap me," I pointed out, crossing my arms. "I guess some semblance of courtesy wouldn't kill you."

For an instant, wariness flickered over his features. He stepped back, surveying me with those cold, beautiful eyes.

Then, to my utter astonishment, he dropped into a graceful kneel. But there was nothing submissive about the motion—if anything, he seemed more dangerous like this. Muscles tightened beneath the dragonskin as though measured violence might spring from that graceful crouch. His gaze lifted to mine, dark lashes framing a lethal smirk as he took my hand in his.

"Lady Arabella Evenfall, would you do me the honor of becoming my wife?" he asked in a low voice. "I promise to cherish your power and to make every submission worth the risk of wanting more."

His question rumbled through the room, bass notes vibrating in my spine even after the words faded. For one reckless heartbeat I wanted to lean into that velvet voice.

I swallowed the impulse. "That may be the worst proposal I've ever heard."

He stood in a swift motion, maintaining his grip on my hand. Leather and scale whispered as he rolled his shoulders. The air shifted, carrying that same scent of winter storms and charred wood across my skin. "List your previous offers, and I'll decide whether I should be insulted or amused."

I let the silence stretch, studying him as though I held the power. "How many proposals have you made? How do I know I'm not the latest in a long line of dead brides?"

"You, Lady Evenfall, are my first." His voice rumbled through me again.

"First . . . what?" It was important to pin these things down. Villains were notorious for creative interpretations of the truth.

A glint of humor lingered in his eyes. "First proposal."

"Then perhaps you're unaware that threats aren't usually part of courtship." His thumb traced a circle on my palm, and I pulled it from his grasp.

"Threats aside," he said, draping himself casually on the arm of a chair, "I suspect you need more than empty promises of devotion. You strike me as someone who values a certain edge."

That was more accurate than I cared to admit, so I just shrugged. "Speaking of edges . . . I'd like to negotiate the terms of this arrangement."

He watched me intently, giving away nothing. I took the lack of immediate refusal as permission to continue.

"You want me, specifically," I said, stepping around the bed to keep a barrier between us. "For my bloodline, presumably. And you need me to show up at the altar without kicking and screaming."

A faint smile tugged at his lips, though tension hardened his posture. "Go on."

"If you require my cooperation, then I have some conditions. First, I want freedom within the fortress. No guards on my heels, no locked doors. I won't be treated like a prisoner. Second, I want to develop my magic. All of it, not just the healing aspects my father permitted."

His eyes narrowed with interest. "Your father restricted your magical education?"

"My father saw my healing magic as profitable for potential suitors. He never let me learn anything else, especially if it hinted at a more lethal side."

Kazimir's eyes gleamed with genuine interest. "You want to explore your destructive talents."

I nodded. "That's part of it. If I'm destined to be some *Dark Lady*, I won't do it half blind."

He inclined his head. "Continue."

"Third, total honesty. I want to know exactly what you plan to do with my bloodline—and with me—after the wedding. My father treated me like a pawn. I don't fancy trading one master for another without clarity."

He gave a subtle, noncommittal shrug. "Is there more?"

I cleared my throat. "No sex."

That earned me a sharp look. "No sex," he repeated, sounding amused.

I ignored the twist of heat in my chest. "I refuse to be forced into anyone's bed. This is a marriage of convenience, not a love match."

He studied me for a heartbeat. Then a slow grin curved his lips. "Worried you'll end up enjoying it, Lady Evenfall?"

"Don't flatter yourself." I glared, color prickling my cheeks. "I'm worried about my autonomy. Frankly, you seem more than capable of ignoring boundaries."

Kazimir went utterly still. "Fine. I accept your terms, with two of my own. One: You walk to the altar proactively. No tantrums, no vanishing acts, no humiliating theatrics in front of my court."

I weighed that. "I can live with it. And two?"

"You'll get the details of my plans *after* the wedding, not before."

Of course. I should have expected him to hold back something. "How do I know you'll share them at all, or that you won't just kill me instead?"

He shrugged. "You don't. But if I intended to kill you outright, negotiations would be pointless. I have no interest in corpses."

I frowned, waiting for the pricking behind my eyes—my magical "truth-sense"—to indicate he was lying. But it never came. He was telling the truth, at least part of it. I crossed my arms. "All your villainous plans aside, what happens to me after you get what you want?"

"You remain my wife, with all the privileges and protections that entails." He rose and moved closer, transforming from casual to coiled in a single heartbeat. "Including protection from your father, should he attempt to reclaim you."

That . . . was not what I'd expected.

Kazimir studied my reaction. "He would never touch you again," he added darkly. "No one who harms what's mine lives long enough to attempt it twice."

The possessiveness in his tone sparked something warm and dangerous in my chest. I stepped back, needing distance, but my choice seemed clear. "I agree, then. I'll appear at the ceremony without incident, and I'll wait until after to hear whatever twisted scheme you've cooked up."

Satisfaction flickered in his eyes. "Good. As for the no-sex rule . . ."

I braced myself, certain he'd refuse.

He allowed a smirk. "No sex—until you ask for it."

Before I could level a scathing retort, he raised his arms and muttered words in a strange tongue. Sigils glowed around the walls and windows. A pulse of violet light rippled over my skin before sinking into the stone. The lingering tingle felt obscenely intimate, as if his magic had traced every nerve and decided to remember the shape of me.

"The wards," he announced, suddenly businesslike, "will let you freely roam the fortress interior. But any attempt to leave Skyspire Citadel will fail. Trust me, you don't want to learn how painful that failure would be."

He reclaimed his cloak then paused at the door, dark gaze lingering on me. "Rest well, Lady Evenfall."

A moment later, he was gone.

I stood there, my pulse still thrumming, and replayed every line of our bizarre negotiation. Had I truly gained a measure of freedom, or had he merely indulged me to secure my compliance?

Until you ask for it. The arrogance of the man was breathtaking.

My attention caught on the black roses by the fireplace. Their petals seemed to rustle like they were whispering, mocking my attempt at control.

"Shut up," I muttered at them, feeling more foolish than ever. "You're just flowers."

Somewhere in the back of my mind, I could have sworn they laughed.

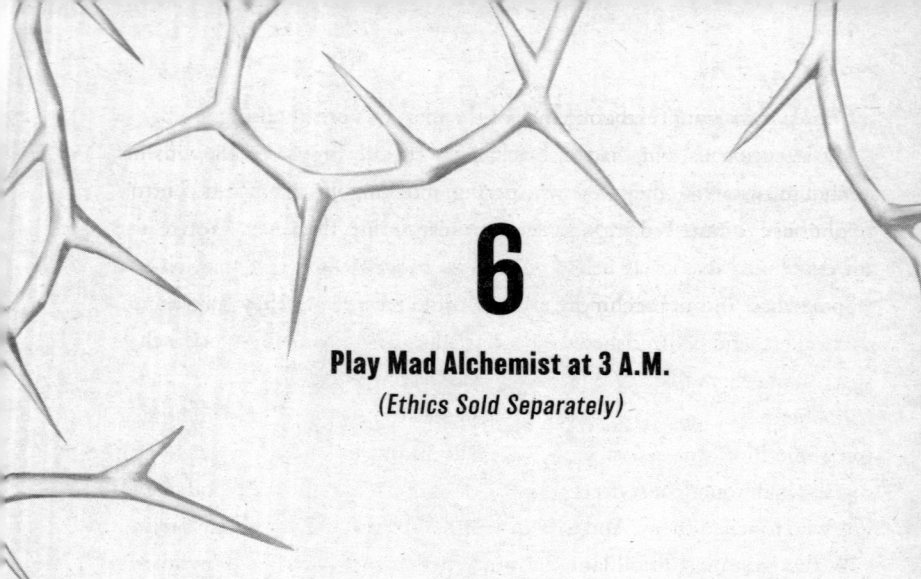

6

Play Mad Alchemist at 3 A.M.
(Ethics Sold Separately)

Kazimir

Dawn was still hours away, and I'd already accepted that sleep was a lost cause. My thoughts flitted between the ceremony tomorrow and the warded suite containing one furious Lady Evenfall.

I left my chambers, locking the door with both key and spell. Anyone with a shred of self-preservation would steer clear, but I couldn't be certain of my new fiancée. The fortress lay quiet except for the occasional hum of the floating orblights. Storm clouds billowed outside a high window, hurling lightning across the sky and sending thunder vibrating through the airborne stone.

I paused at Lady Evenfall's quarters, pressing my fingers to the still-warm sigils I'd etched hours before. The wards thrummed in response.

I huffed out a laugh. "I was going to toss her in the dungeon after the ceremony," I muttered. "Now she'll roam my halls, probably conjuring who-knows-what and setting my staff on fire. Brilliant, Kazimir. Truly."

I supposed it was my own fault. I'd planned to break her resistance, lock her away, complete the marriage ritual, claim the Heirloom's powers. Done.

Simple. Efficient. Textbook villainy.

Yet my glorious plan had devolved into negotiating freedoms with her as though we were equals. No, worse: I'd actively *conceded* points. Next, I might have to offer brunch privileges for her and the minions.

I descended five levels below my private rooms to my cramped, chaotic workroom. Racks of parchment, precarious stacks of ancient books, alchemical beakers, and half-finished mechanical contraptions littered every inch of space along the walls.

In the center, one broad workbench remained clear. I'd been itching to test something since discovering Lady Evenfall's blood on the enchanted roses, which weren't just decorative but designed to sample the blood of anyone who touched them. And I'd bottled that drop while she wasn't looking.

With a gesture, I lit oil lamps around the room and arranged my instruments. I retrieved the small vial from my pocket. Before I could go further, a knock sounded at the door.

"Enter," I called, not bothering to look up.

In crept Pip, carrying a cage with a nightingale inside. He set it on the bench, his hands trembling. "The bird you requested, my lord," he said softly.

I scrutinized the terrified little thing, tapping on the bars until it froze under my magic—no point chasing it around the workroom. On the periphery, I felt Pip shifting his weight from foot to foot.

"What?" I asked, letting annoyance creep into my voice. "I assume you have a reason to linger?"

His throat bobbed. "The kitchen staff asked about special requests for the wedding feast."

My fist slammed onto the table, rattling glass and sending flasks skidding to the edge. *Of all the trivialities . . .*

"This can't wait until daylight?"

He stammered, "S-Sims feared a repeat of—of the last feast, my lord—when Griffin animated the entrees—"

"Fine," I snapped, pointing toward the door. "Tell them to do whatever they like. Now get out before your sniveling anxiety ruins my concentration."

Pip bowed, turned too quickly, and smacked into a shelf. Several empty vials fell to the floor and shattered.

"I'm sorry, my lord!" he gasped, crouching to gather the shards and cutting his hand in the process.

I strode over in three strides and yanked him upright by the collar. The familiar dark swirl of my dominion magic crackled in the room.

"Get. Out," I snarled, letting the raw threat in my voice tighten the air.

He paled, eyes widening in terror, and fled without another word. As soon as the door slammed shut behind him, the shadows coiled back into my bones, leaving me scowling at my own momentary lapse.

I inhaled deeply, forcing calm, then lifted the nightingale from its cage. Its heart fluttered against my palm.

"Consider this your contribution to the greater villainous cause," I murmured, stroking its feathers. A flick of power, a whispered resonance through the runes carved in my ribs, and the bird's life force drained out in shining whorls of pale light. Setting aside the limp body, I poured the shimmering essence into a silver bowl.

I positioned two pristine crystal vessels on the workbench, priming one with a fresh prick of my blood, the other with Arabella's single drop. I connected them with delicate silver filaments. Chanting in the guttural, ancient tongue my mother had practically beaten into my skull, I felt each syllable vibrate through the runes beneath my skin. The bird's captured life force twined upward in blue tendrils, splitting into two streams that fused with both vessels. The filaments flared, bridging the gap between them.

In a flash, everything went incandescent. A shockwave of magic tossed me clear across the room, books and flasks crashing around me in a storm of shattered glass. I cursed, shielding my eyes from the surge of light.

The vessels sang, an otherworldly chord that reverberated through my bones. The runes carved on my ribs burned white-hot, a blaze of pure energy that should have hurt but instead felt dangerously euphoric.

What in the darkest hells?

I staggered to my feet, blinking through the radiance. Both crystal vessels shone bright as small suns, lines of power pulsing in perfect unison between them. My instruments—designed to read magical force—quivered off the charts.

"A fortyfold amplification," I muttered, disbelief hollowing out my voice. "That's . . . impossible. That's . . . Fuck."

The ancient texts hinted that my bride's heroic bloodline would amplify my dominion magic, maybe doubling or tripling it. *But this?* Forty times was an absurd fountain of potential.

The door flew open and Vex rushed in, dagger raised. "My lord, the entire fortress felt that. Are you—"

"I'm fine," I snapped, barely looking at her. My gaze clung to the dancing lights. "A minor experiment with unexpectedly large results."

She took in the wreckage, from the shattered glass to the still-humming power. "Should I fetch Griffin?"

"No," I said sharply. Then I reined myself in. "You can go. And don't speak of this to *anyone*. Understood?"

She gave a short bow, face tight with curiosity but she didn't give in to it.

As soon as I was alone again, I grabbed my journal and scribbled frantically, recording every measurement and observed effect. If Arabella's blood had done *this* with a few drops of bird essence, what might happen if we completed the entire Heirloom ritual?

I could reshape continents, I thought, pacing over glass. *Flatten kingdoms with a word. And with the Heirloom of Dominion fueling me, I could probably yank the moon down and wear it as a fucking hat.*

When I was done, I sealed the journal with a personal ward. Anyone who tried to peek would be vaporized on the spot.

The two vessels continued their eerie, harmonic glow. I rolled a broken crystal shard between my bloody fingers and mulled over how close I was to absolute might.

And how dangerously reliant I was on one obstinate bride who refused to kneel.

"The universe has a gruesome sense of humor," I muttered. "The potential for apocalyptic power . . . packaged neatly with the greatest vulnerability I've had in years. And it's all tied to one sharp-tongued, infuriatingly gorgeous noblewoman."

The vessels responded with a pulse of brightness, as if her blood resonated with my frustrated confession. Outside, thunder rumbled again, shaking the tower. I stood among the debris, adrenaline buzzing through the burned-out edges of my runes, alone with the realization that everything had just become a thousand times more complicated.

And dangerously more intriguing.

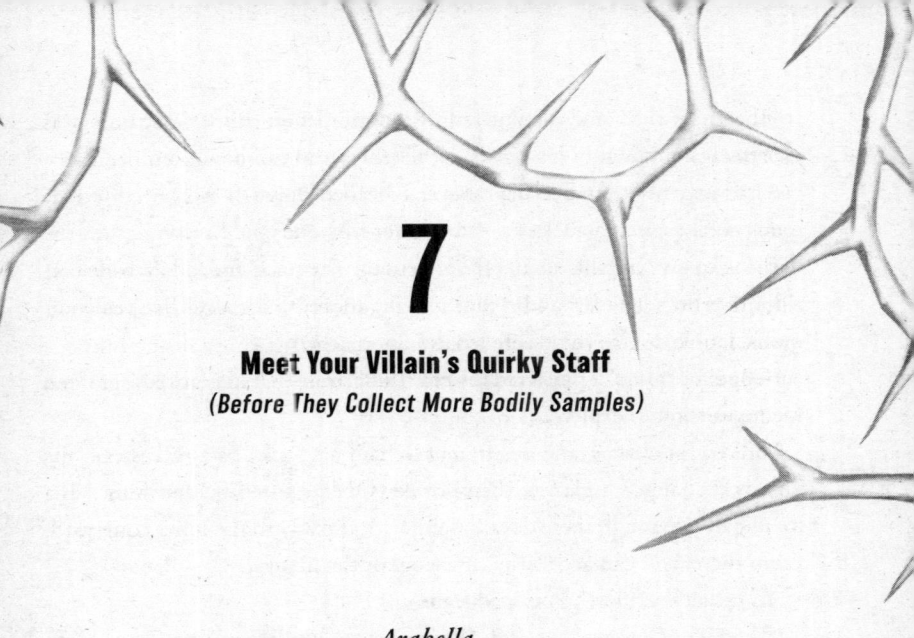

7

Meet Your Villain's Quirky Staff
(Before They Collect More Bodily Samples)

Arabella

I woke to silken sheets, a towering canopy overhead, and the sickening reminder that I was meant to marry the Dark Lord in a few hours. My stomach twisted.

"Fuck." I pressed both palms over my eyes. The word felt deliciously raw, so I repeated it loud enough to echo off the walls.

No one barged in to scold me for my language or lecture me on proper decorum. The emptiness felt alarmingly free.

I swung my legs over the side of the bed, bracing myself for the chill of a fortress perched among storm clouds. Even the plush carpeting under my feet couldn't hide how cold this place truly was. Only the hearth's crackling fire kept the room from icing over.

The wardrobe brimmed with choices—some practical, some absurdly lavish. Gone were the pastel frills my father favored. I chose a deep emerald tunic and black leather trousers, the sort of outfit a girl might wear if she planned to burn her captor's fortress.

Opening the door, I half expected a guard. Instead, a spiral staircase stretched upward and downward through silence. Either Kazimir was supremely confident in his wards, or he truly meant to honor our deal.

Assuming his chambers lay above, I headed down. I wanted to see as much of Skyspire Citadel as possible before anyone could second-guess the decision to give me this small bit of freedom. The stairs ended in a wide corridor that branched left and right. Straight ahead, two guards flanked enormous double doors. They stiffened as I approached.

"Good morning." I mustered my courtliest smile. "Lord Blackrose granted me permission to explore."

I braced for outrage and an attempt to haul me back upstairs. Instead, the guards exchanged a glance, then bowed. One gestured behind him. "The main hall is through these doors, along with the way to the inner courtyard. From there, you can access the east wing or the library."

"And that corridor?" I pointed right.

"The High Gardens," he said. "Beyond them, the observatory."

"Much appreciated." Their hands never strayed far from their weapons, but they didn't stop me.

The corridors formed a labyrinth of locked doors and meandering staircases. Eventually I discovered a narrow flight hidden behind an unmarked door. I climbed until my legs burned. A hatch above me leaked frigid air.

Stepping through, I found myself perched on an outer wall. Wind sliced across my cheeks as I leaned forward, clinging to the icy parapet. My heart gave a lurch at the sheer height. Dark, shimmering walls connected five towers spaced evenly apart, each one glinting with runes. In the courtyard below, an enormous pentagram was laid out in black stone. Every line and angle of the fortress seemed designed for magical synergy, an infernal masterpiece of architecture; Kazimir had built this domain to channel unimaginable power. A gust shoved me back and I decided I'd admired the view long enough.

Back inside, I roamed until I nearly collided with Pip, the timid servant from last night. Dishes rattled on his tray.

"Lady Evenfall!" he squeaked. A ragged bandage wrapped his palm, the gauze stained crimson.

"What happened to your hand?"

"Nothing, my lady. Just an accident in His Lordship's workroom."

"Let me see." I gently tugged his hand forward after helping him balance the tray. He seemed torn, but he obeyed. Beneath the sloppy bandage, I spotted shards of glass in a nasty gash.

"This is hardly 'nothing,'" I muttered. "You need this cleaned, or it'll never heal."

He shrank back. "I have other duties, my lady. Lord Blackrose is particular about timeliness—"

"Set the tray down," I said firmly, gesturing to a nearby alcove. "It won't kill him to have slightly cooler tea." Though, knowing Kazimir, I had my doubts.

Pip placed the tray on a stone bench, and I carefully unwrapped the bandage. The cut looked deep. Ignoring the faint quake of leftover exhaustion in my limbs, I covered his palm with both hands and summoned the familiar warmth.

For a moment, I remembered every forced demonstration of my "gift," when I was paraded before peasants to prove House Evenfall's heroic lineage. Back then, I'd played the part of the gracious benefactor, all while cursing my father under my breath. But now, with no audience and no pretense, the healing felt strangely honest.

Pip exhaled shakily. "It doesn't hurt anymore." He flexed his fingers in amazement. The gash was gone, leaving only a faint pink line. The small bits of glass had worked their way out as well. He wrapped them carefully in the old bandage.

"I suggest avoiding shattered glass next time." I anticipated the lightheadedness that followed using my magic. Strangely enough, it didn't manifest at all.

His gaze drifted to the tea tray. "I should go. If it's cold, he'll be furious."

"Tell him I waylaid you for directions or threatened to set the library ablaze. Whatever sounds plausible."

He offered a shy grin. "Thank you, my lady."

"Off you go. We can't have lukewarm tea starting the apocalypse."

Pip hurried away. I stood there a moment, inhaling the fortress's cold air and the faint tang of ozone. Kazimir's priorities were starkly clear: his tea delivered promptly, even if it meant his servant bled onto the tray. Arrogant bastard.

But if he thought this marriage guaranteed *my* obedience—the same kind of fearful deference he demanded over drinks—he was in for a shock.

I turned a corner and stepped into a circular chamber that stole my breath. This had to be the observatory.

An enormous crystal contraption hung from a domed ceiling, refracting the storm light pouring in from the floor-to-ceiling windows. Below, smaller crystals hovered over a ring of pedestals, each one displaying crackling pathways of light that linked towers to drifting islands. Bridges.

I edged closer to one pedestal, eyes fixed on the image of a bridge. As I watched, the structure flickered and changed positions, connecting to a new floating rock. The bridges weren't static; they could alter, fuse, or vanish at a moment's notice. No wonder Kazimir conquered kingdoms so easily. This place would be impossible to fully invade. One wrong turn, and you'd find yourself stranded on a floating chunk of rock with no way out. The man might be a brutal, domineering lunatic, but he was frighteningly clever.

I moved back to the pedestal where I'd started, trying to spot any runes or levers that controlled the mechanism. Almost without thinking, I touched the crystal.

Power slammed through me. The crystal flared to life, and I snatched my hand back—but not before I triggered some sort of magical meltdown. I heard shouts echo through the corridors. The bridge beneath my fingertips shimmered erratically, twisting in on itself. Nearby displays flickered and distorted.

"Shit," I hissed, scrambling backward. "Shit, shit, shit."

"Oh no, oh no, oh no!" A voice squawked from the doorway, so high and terrified it bordered on hysterical. "Not again! He'll murder me in a creatively awful way this time for sure! Possibly twice!"

A gangly figure lurched into the observatory with all the grace of a newborn colt. Impossibly tall, spindly arms and legs, hair sticking out like burnt straw, and a face that practically vibrated with panic—this had to be the strangest courtier I'd ever seen. He ducked beneath the arch despite the ample door height and made a beeline for the disrupted pedestal.

"Three guards on the eastern bridge," he muttered, "they'll plummet—"

He froze when he noticed me. His yellowish eyes went comically wide. "Wait, you're . . . oh, but you're not supposed to be here. No one's supposed to be in my observatory except Lord Blackrose and me, and definitely not messing with the crystals. I mean, clearly no one told you—"

"Who are you?"

"Griffin." He bobbed his head jerkily, practically a bow if you squinted. "I'm the citadel's enchanter. Among . . . other things." Then he waved at the pedestal. "If I might . . . ?"

I nodded, and he maneuvered those spidery hands around the crystal, murmuring some incantation under his breath. Gradually, the chaotic light calmed. The writhing illusions of the bridges slowed to a steady hum, and the distant shouting died down. My tension slipped away as everything flickered back to normal.

Griffin sagged, breath hissing out in relief. "Thank the gods. Maybe I won't be executed for letting the bride blow up the citadel on her first day here." He pushed a sweaty lock of singed hair off his forehead. "Lord Blackrose has enough on his plate, what with the wedding and the world domination and the perpetual brooding."

I folded my arms. "So this kind of crisis is a regular occurrence?"

His panicked expression twitched. "Oh, no. Well, there are . . . occasional issues. The system's temperamental. Usually it's my fault. But this—" He paused, eyeing me with a sort of nervous fascination. "How?"

I tried not to look guilty. "I accidentally touched the crystal. And it just . . . reacted."

Griffin's lips formed a silent *wow*. "The crystals should only respond to specific magical signatures—my own or His Lordship's. Anyone else would need at least a few rituals with goat's blood, plus nude chanting under a new moon for good measure. Yet you apparently skip all the fun steps and just . . . do it."

He looked me over again, and I felt my anger coil. "That might be because of your bloodline," he theorized, eyes brightening with scholarly excitement. "First Hero ancestry is potent. Lord Blackrose said—"

I seized the obvious lead. "So he's been discussing me with you?"

Griffin gulped. "Not in detail, just . . . that your lineage is important. That your presence matters. That I wasn't to bother you or do anything that might scare you away. Though I suppose me being here at all might count as bothering you, in which case I should probably go—"

"You created this?" I gestured to the crystal displays, deliberately changing the subject to put him at ease.

Pride momentarily replaced anxiety on Griffin's expressive face. "Yes! Well, with His Lordship's direction, of course. But the basic enchantment structure is mine." He gestured animatedly. "The bridges respond to the needs of the citadel, adapting to traffic patterns and security concerns."

"That's remarkable," I said, genuinely impressed. "What else have you created?"

Griffin's face lit up as if no one had ever bothered to ask about his work. "Oh, all sorts of things! The self-heating baths, the defensive wards that prevent assassins from approaching within ten feet of His Lordship . . ." He counted off on his long fingers. "Also a rather disastrous attempt at self-writing poetry quills that only produced erotic sonnets about tentacles, but we aren't supposed to talk about those anymore."

I raised an eyebrow. "The black roses?"

His amber eyes lit with pride. "Yes! Aren't they magnificent? Metallic petals, lore-binding properties . . . uh, I mean, that was just for aesthetic flair—"

"They're certainly unique," I said diplomatically. "Though one bit me last night."

"Oh!" He recoiled like I'd hit him. "Did it . . . draw blood?"

I stared him down, letting the silence speak for me.

He gave a nervous, wheezing laugh. "It's only meant to draw a tiny sample. They're, um, testing magical resonance. Completely routine if you follow the Northern Enchanters' Guild guidelines . . . after the last reform, anyway."

I stood straighter. "Lord Blackrose put sneaky bloodsucking roses in my chambers," I said flatly, "without my knowledge or consent."

"Not sucking," Griffin squeaked, "just sampling! Borrowing! Barely a drop. No harm done."

My hand curled into a fist before I forced it back down. "So the *Dark Lord* has my blood. What's he planning?"

Griffin's gaze skittered anywhere but my face. "I—I'm not sure. Could be part of the wedding rites, or maybe an ancient text about 'maiden blood' that—"

I cut him off. "Maiden blood, huh? Are you implying something about my virtue, Griffin?"

He spluttered as though choking on air. "No! Absolutely not! That's none of my business. I would never dare—"

I let him squirm for a moment, then decided to put him out of his misery, figuratively speaking. "All right, enough. Take me to him."

Griffin took a stumbling step back. "Lord Blackrose is busy in his workroom. He might be in the middle of . . . something, which is often hazardous. Occasionally humiliating for the poor soul who interrupts."

"I don't care if he's in the middle of raising the dead." I stepped closer. "You're going to take me to him right now, or I'll touch every single crystal in here and see what new chaos we can cause. Maybe all the bridges will collapse at once."

He blanched, eyes flicking around the room. "Y-yes, my lady. Right this way, please. Though if he incinerates me on sight, I'm blaming you."

"Deal." I gestured at the door. "Lead the way."

He led me through winding passages at a brisk pace, spouting apologies and nervous chatter, pointing out various features and occasionally apologizing for things I hadn't accused him of.

Eventually, we reached a familiar tower. Instead of going up toward my chambers, we proceeded down. At the base, we turned down a darker corridor and followed it until Griffin halted at a black door etched with silver runes. He hesitated. "Are you positive you won't consider drafting a polite note of complaint instead?"

I just stared him down until he sullenly knocked in a peculiar pattern—three quick taps, a pause, then two more. Without waiting for an answer, he pushed the door open and stepped aside.

"My lord," he croaked, voice jumping a full octave. "Lady Evenfall insisted on seeing you. Says it's urgent, definitely not my fault, I tried everything but she's scarily persistent—"

"Enough," came Kazimir's cool baritone from inside. "You may go."

Griffin shot me a half-hearted grimace of solidarity before scuttling off, leaving me alone to face the embodiment of my current fury.

Kazimir stood with his back to me, leaning over a table cluttered with arcane tools and glass vials. Magic glowed from an apparatus, casting flickers of eerie light over his tall form. He was dressed in plain black, the sleeves rolled up to reveal corded forearms crisscrossed with scars. Even my fury couldn't dull how unreasonably attractive he looked.

"Lady Evenfall," he said, not bothering to turn. "I was expecting you."

"Were you?" I stepped inside, letting the door swing shut behind me. "Perhaps you anticipated my visit when you stole my blood without my consent."

He muttered something that sounded suspiciously like "Griffin."

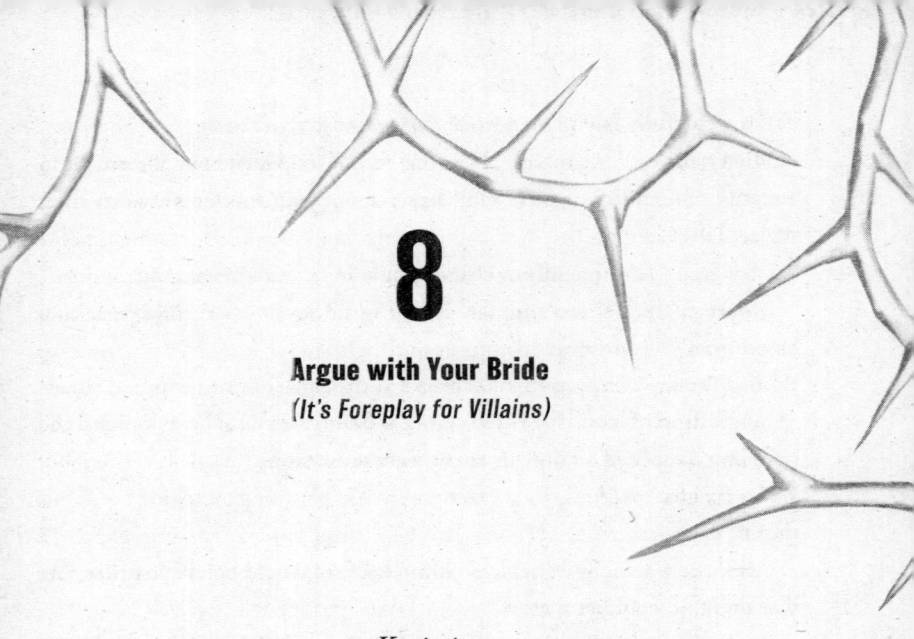

8

Argue with Your Bride
(It's Foreplay for Villains)

Kazimir

The moment Griffin fled, I felt the temperature in my workroom drop about ten degrees. Not from any spell, but from the sheer force of Arabella's glare razoring right through me. She hovered in the doorway, spine rigid, fury rolling off her in waves.

"Found out about the roses?" I set my face into a bored mask before finally turning around.

She stood firm, practically crackling with angry energy. She wore fitted trousers and a deep emerald tunic that brought out the green and gold in her eyes. Her hair was pulled back in a neat braid, baring the curve of her throat. Somehow, that tiny reveal of skin managed to spark heat in my gut, an annoyance I tried to ignore.

"You had enchanted roses collecting my blood," she said, voice dangerously calm, "without my knowledge or consent."

I set the arcane measuring device I'd been adjusting onto the workbench. "Clearly Griffin shouldn't have told you."

Inside my head, I cursed his loose tongue. He had a knack for unraveling half my carefully laid plans with a single panicked outburst.

"That's all you have to say?" Her tone rose. "You violate our agreement in a matter of hours, and you're more upset about your minion's honesty than the actual violation?"

I shrugged. "I don't recall any clause prohibiting routine magical precautions."

"Routine," she echoed through pursed lips. "So, in your world, sneaking blood from your prisoners counts as routine?"

"Yes," I said, sweeping a hand around at the clutter of reagents and runes. "A single drop of blood for ritual clarity is basic procedure here. Besides, the sampling happened before our terms were set in stone."

Her eyes flared. "And when exactly were you planning on telling me about this 'basic procedure'?"

"After the ceremony," I said, deciding honesty would needle her best. "At that point, it wouldn't matter."

She bridged the distance between us in a few quick strides—unafraid, which, strangely, I respected. "What are you using my blood for?"

An easy lie teased at the edge of my tongue, but I hesitated. She wasn't some next-kingdom princess I intended to hoodwink for a single day. She was set to be my wife, at least in name, and I needed her if I wanted the Heirloom of Dominion to bend to my will. Not to mention her recent . . . magical developments piqued my interest. Caution felt wise.

"Resonance testing," I said. "Determining the compatibility of your lineage with mine."

Her gaze hardened. "And?"

I paused, recalling the jolt of raw energy that had surged through my runes last night. Power magnified fortyfold. "The results were satisfactory."

"Satisfactory," she repeated, voice dripping with disdain. "You can do better than that, Lord Blackrose."

My patience thinned. "I don't owe you a complete breakdown of every magical test I conduct."

"You do when it involves my blood." She aimed a finger at me, and her voice rose several notches. "We had an agreement. After the wedding, you'd be honest about your plans. That doesn't grant you permission to treat me like some lab specimen in the meantime."

"Lab specimen?" I laughed, though it came out sharp. "It was a drop of blood, Lady Evenfall, not a vivisection."

"It's the principle," she hissed. "How am I supposed to trust you with anything else when you help yourself to my blood in secret?"

I found that genuinely amusing. "Trust? You're in the lair of the Dark Lord. Trust isn't a virtue here."

She held my gaze, undeterred. "Yes, trust. Without it, why shouldn't I escape the second I see an opening? Or sabotage the entire ceremony?"

She had a point. The Heirloom demanded a genuine wedding; and thanks to her stubborn resistance to my dominion magic, I required her compliance. Especially after my tests with her blood had shown just how dangerously powerful she might be.

"What do you propose I do, then?" I crossed my arms.

She pointed at me again. "I want you to keep our bargain. No more secrets, no more underhanded experimenting. If you need something—hair, blood, my signature on a demonic contract—ask."

I stared for a long moment. The typical hostage would be begging me to release them, not negotiating new terms with every breath. But this was Arabella Evenfall.

"Fine," I said, inclining my head. "From now on, I'll inform you of lab work that involves your precious bodily fluids. But don't forget where you stand. You're still my prisoner, agreement or not. Adapt, or you'll find yourself in a predicament you won't enjoy."

A flicker of . . . something crossed her face. Then she lifted her chin. "I've been adapting my entire life. But adapt doesn't mean surrender, Blackrose. You should learn the difference."

Her nerve was truly stunning. She stood in *my* workshop, in *my* fortress, yet she carried herself like *I* was the unwelcome intruder. It made me want to wrap my dominion around her throat just to see if she'd still speak so boldly.

"Careful," I said, letting a surge of half-tamed magic pulse along my spine. "I'm not known for my unlimited patience."

"And I'm not known for letting men—villains or otherwise—treat me as chattel," she shot back.

My control frayed. I strode forward, overshadowing her with the advantage of my height. "Maybe you need a reminder of your position."

She remained perfectly still. Not trembling, not cowering. Her eyes sparked with challenge.

"What'll it be?" She tilted her chin. "Another threat to do unspeakable things with my organs?"

"You won't break so easily," I allowed, letting my voice drop an octave. "Pain is just the most *direct* method. But there are other ways."

I reached out, grazing a fingertip along her jaw. She stiffened, but her expression blazed with refusal rather than disgust. "You're running short on creativity, Lord Blackrose," she said coldly, turning her head away.

I grabbed her arm before she could fully retreat. That faint, heated pulse skittered up my forearm again. It enraged me as much as it intrigued me. Was it simple adrenaline, or was there something about her that made me want to increase that closeness, test that defiance?

"Then tell me," I said quietly, "what else might convince you to show a little respect?"

"Respect," she said, glancing pointedly at my grip on her arm, "is earned, not taken."

The moment crackled, everything in me itching to test her *now*. Then I exhaled, releasing her, stepping back with effort. I refused to become a savage who couldn't control his own impulses. Possessive, yes. Reckless, never.

"Fine, Lady Evenfall," I said, deadpan. "We'll consider this an amendment to our agreement. You want honesty? You'll have it. In exchange, I'll personally oversee your magical training."

Her eyes narrowed. "You already granted me access to magical training."

"Reading dusty tomes and receiving actual instruction aren't the same." I gestured pointedly around the workroom. "I don't often offer hands-on lessons, even to my highest-ranking subordinates."

She hesitated, aware there had to be a catch. "You mean you want to control what I learn."

"Think of it more as guiding your potential." I allowed a thin, humorless smile. She was more critical to my ambitions than she realized . . . and more dangerous. "If you're going to be at my side, I need to know your capabilities."

"Because a powerful wife is an asset, no doubt," she said, voice thick with sarcasm.

"A very direct and pleasurable one, if done correctly," I murmured, letting my gaze flick over her. I took a stab of satisfaction when I saw something flare behind those eyes—resentment, attraction, both?

She exhaled. "And if I hate what you teach me?"

"Knowledge is power. You can wield it against me, if you dare." I shrugged. "At least you'd have an edge."

She weighed that carefully. Then she lifted her chin. "All right, Lord Blackrose. I accept. Honesty for honesty, power for power." She extended her hand. "But remember, whatever I become under your tutelage, you helped make me."

My fingers closed around hers. A faint spark of magic jumped between our palms—hers, not mine. Unintentional, but potent. It sent a whisper of heat along the runes carved in my bones.

"Excellent," I said, releasing her hand and noting how my skin still prickled where we'd touched. "The ceremony's at sunset. Vex will collect you beforehand. Then, you'll be mine . . . in every significant sense."

"And after the ceremony?" she asked, still standing stubbornly. "When do these lessons start?"

"Soon," I said. "If you wish."

She turned to go. I assumed she'd leave it at that, but she paused at the door.

"One last thing, Lord Blackrose."

I glanced her way, irritation simmering. "Yes?"

Her voice dropped to a quiet, lethal calm. "During these tests of yours, this 'resonance' business . . . If my blood hadn't provided the results you wanted, what would you have done?"

Her eyes bored into me, as though she expected comfort. I almost laughed.

"We wouldn't be having this conversation," I said truthfully. "There'd be no reason."

She inclined her head, as if confirming a private suspicion. "I see. Well, I appreciate that bit of honesty."

Then the door closed, leaving me alone with the echoes of our confrontation. I pressed a hand to my forehead, feeling the hum of raw dominion magic in my bones, stronger since last night's experiment. I exhaled and returned to my worktable. Still, I couldn't quite shake the memory of her unwavering gaze and the way my skin hummed in response to hers.

I told myself I could handle it. One woman wouldn't derail my carefully engineered plans. Even if she had the most glorious, unbreakable spine I'd ever seen.

9

Forge Rings with Bone and Hair
(Romance, Dark-Lord Style)

Arabella

The dress arrived late.

I stood in my chambers, arms crossed, watching Vex pace in front of the hearth. Her black coat slanted dramatically, and her newly dyed hair—black now instead of yesterday's silver—only made her impatient scowl more severe.

"If they've ruined the timing of the ceremony," she growled, "I'll personally remove their fingers, one knuckle at a—"

Before she could finish, the door burst open. Two servants hurried in, carrying a swath of fabric that looked like a dark waterfall. They were followed by a small, jittery man with measuring tape draped around his neck and pins bristling from his collar.

"Forgive the delay, Lady Evenfall," the tailor said, executing a deep bow. "The embroidery required additional attention."

Vex's sneer nearly made him drop the pins. "The ceremony begins in less than an hour."

"Then we'd better hurry," I said. I felt my heart hammering, no matter how hard I tried to steady myself. Reality was sinking in. Within the hour, I would marry the Dark Lord. Voluntarily, if one counted the string of negotiations and tenuous deals I'd squeezed him into.

The tailor and his assistants dressed me with swift, practiced motions. The moment the fabric settled over my shoulders, I drew a sharp breath. The midnight blue velvet appeared nearly black under the torchlight, the silver embroidery twisting into elegant vines of thorns as I moved. A high collar framed my neck, regal but not suffocating, and the fitted sleeves ended in points over my hands. From the waist down, the gown flared into rippling layers.

Vex gave me a slow once-over. "It will do," she pronounced, which might have been genuine praise from her. A servant stepped forward with a gleaming silver circlet set with sapphires—the bride's crown.

They began twisting my hair into an elaborate updo, weaving thin silver threads through the braids and nestling small black roses among them.

"Those don't draw blood, do they?"

"Not unless you ask nicely," Vex replied. She paused by my shoulder and lowered her voice. "A detail for the ceremony, my lady. I need a single hair from you."

I felt a twinge of irritation, but Vex merely stood waiting, not taking it by force.

"Fine," I said. I carefully plucked one strand free myself, handing it over. Boundaries, no matter how small, deserved to be maintained.

Once they finished with a subtle enchantment that made my skin glow from within and added smoky shadow around my eyes, I took in my reflection. The woman staring back had sharp lines and thorns embroidered along her bodice, as if to announce she was done being docile. I considered, for one wild moment, refusing to show up for the ceremony at all. But running would guarantee death, and if I died, whatever power lay dormant in my blood would remain untapped. I wanted to know what I was capable of.

"It's time," Vex announced. She pressed a small vial into my hand, the liquid inside clear as glass.

"Poison seems counterproductive at this stage," I said, but uncorked it anyway. A soft waft of lavender and mint drifted up.

She snorted. "A calming draft. If I wanted you dead, Lady Evenfall, you'd never have stepped out of that forest alive."

I tossed it back, feeling pleasant warmth spread through my veins.

Vex led me out of my chambers, along corridors teeming with swirling shadows, down multiple spiraling staircases, and past an airy courtyard. At last, we arrived at a tall tower doorway opening onto empty air. My heart lurched at the vast drop beneath the swirling clouds.

"The Great Hall is on a separate island," Vex explained. "We cross by lightning bridge."

Right on cue, sizzling arcs of electricity flared, weaving themselves into a narrow, pulsing walkway just like the one I'd accidentally rearranged in the observatory. The bridge hummed with power.

"Everyone except the Dark Lord—and now you—who enters the citadel must carry a magic token," she explained, "which allows them passage on the bridges that befit their rank and business."

I swallowed hard, grateful for the calming draft now warming my veins. Without it, I might have balked entirely at the prospect of crossing what appeared to be solidified lightning.

"First time is always the worst," Vex added, stepping onto the bridge. "Keep your eyes forward and don't look down."

My stomach tightened, but I forced myself forward. Each footfall sent tiny shocks through my boots. By the time we reached the far side, I'd gotten past the worst of the fear, but those bridges would take some getting used to.

Guards snapped to attention as we passed another archway. A short walk later, we reached towering black doors inlaid with silver. Griffin appeared, skidding to a halt in his too-short robes, the hem singed and his hair standing on end as though he'd just battled a thundercloud.

"Lady Evenfall!" he said breathlessly. "You look . . . remarkable. I—ah—wouldn't mention the dress delay to His Darkness. He nearly incinerated the tailor's first attempts. Mumbled something about 'my wife is not a showpiece for lesser men to ogle.'"

I blinked. "He personally oversaw the designs?"

Griffin bobbed his head. "Rejected three. The first was too revealing, the second too . . . traditional. The third one caught fire before we got his specific notes."

I gripped Griffin's scorched sleeve. "Does he always burn things when he's angry?"

"Only things he can replace," Griffin said, forcing a smile. "I'm . . . indispensable, or so I hope."

Vex cleared her throat pointedly. "We're late, Griffin."

He stepped aside, and at a nod from Vex, two guards pulled the doors open, revealing the Great Hall.

I stepped into a spectacle of roses, candles, and eerie light. Black roses crawled up columns and draped across the ceiling, their metallic petals reflecting the flicker of countless black candles with cold, otherworldly flames. Through the towering windows, a blood-gold sunset slashed across distant storm clouds.

The hall flickered with life. Some guests looked human, others . . . not. I saw a pair of unnervingly beautiful vampires who stood too still to pass for mortals; a cluster of fae nobles whose perfect features were offset by their chilling, hollow stares; and even a few delegates with horns and charcoal-gray skin.

Kazimir Blackrose waited on the dais. He wore a black velvet coat with silver embroidery mirroring the style of my gown, high-collared and refined. His hair was swept back, and his storm gray eyes locked onto mine the instant I stepped inside. Energy seemed to crackle in the space between us.

Vex leaned in to whisper, "Last chance to run."

I breathed out slowly. "And miss the chance to horrify all these fine people?"

She gave a curt nod and moved to stand among the other advisors. A low, throbbing music began. Not something melodic, but more like a vibration that sank into my bones. The crowd parted, leaving a wide aisle leading to the dais.

I strode forward, summoning every ounce of poise I'd once learned to impress highborn suitors. Chin up, steps steady, gaze forward. I wasn't doing this as a trembling bride. No, I was here on my own twisted terms.

Kazimir watched me approach, his expression taut. Behind him, shadows flickered at his feet, writhing for a split second before he quelled them. When I reached the dais, I could feel waves of controlled tension rolling off him.

He inclined his head. "Lady Evenfall," he murmured, his voice low enough that only I heard him. "You look . . . suitable."

I kept my own voice down. "High praise from the Dark Lord. You almost look civilized yourself."

A fleeting spark of amusement lit his eyes, then he turned to the officiant, a dark cleric whose eyes absorbed rather than reflected light, lending him a deeply unsettling look.

"Esteemed allies, honored guests, fearsome minions," the cleric intoned, his voice echoing oddly, "we gather to witness the binding of Lord Kazimir Blackrose, His Supreme Darkness, Scourge of Azroth, Terror of the Western Realms, to Lady Arabella Evenfall, Descendant of the First Hero and Mistress of the Healing Arts."

I shot Kazimir a sidelong glance at that last title. It was obviously a dramatic flourish he'd asked for.

The cleric continued. "We perform this ritual not by the insipid customs of lesser kingdoms, but by the ancient rites of conquest and alliance."

He cleared his throat and opened a heavy tome with pages that creaked with age. "From the Codex of Dominion, hear these words: 'When power seeks to multiply itself, let blood call to blood. When darkness seeks to expand its reach, let it find a worthy vessel. When conquest is achieved, let it be sealed in bonds that neither death nor betrayal may sever.'"

The cleric lifted a small blackwood reliquary. "Bone of the groom, strand of the bride. Let dominion bind what softer magics cannot."

He opened the lid, revealing a polished sliver of bone twined with the single hair I'd surrendered in my chamber. If Kazimir had truly contributed a piece of himself . . . I almost gaped, wondering when and how he'd harvested it.

Kazimir took the reliquary, and I heard the soft sizzling of his flesh meeting some potent magic. With a murmured incantation, both bone and hair melted into a thin ivory ribbon streaked with silver light. He wound the molten strip around my ring finger; it cooled instantly, fitting snugly. He forged a second band for himself, letting leftover sparks drift to the ceiling. We exchanged a glance in which I caught the faintest gleam of satisfaction in his eyes.

The cleric exhaled in awe. Then he produced a dark goblet of volcanic glass that shimmered crimson beneath the hall's blue-white torches. "The Cup of Dominion," he announced. "Forged in the Obsidian Mountain, tempered in the blood of a thousand warriors. Drink and let your essences mingle as your purposes align."

Kazimir took the cup first, eyes fixed on me. He sipped, then handed it my way, his fingertips lingering on mine. I braced myself for blood but tasted only a rich, smoky wine that somehow thrummed with raw power as it slid down my throat.

The cleric retrieved the cup and set it aside. "Lord Blackrose, do you take this woman as your consort, to share in your conquests, to amplify your power, and to stand as your equal in the eyes of your enemies?"

Kazimir's voice rang out confidently. "I do."

"Lady Evenfall," the cleric said, turning to me, "do you take this man as your consort, to share in his dominion, to embrace the darkness he offers, and to honor his authority in all matters of state and war?"

"I do," I replied firmly.

The cleric raised his arms, and Kazimir's shadows slithered across our wrists, binding us like ribbons before sinking into our skin in a cold, thrilling rush. It wasn't painful, but it left a tingling pressure near my heart that didn't fade right away.

"In accordance with ancient tradition," the cleric proclaimed, "if any here object to this union, speak now and be immediately executed for treason."

A startled laugh nearly escaped me—so refreshing, this blatant threat. The crowd remained tactfully silent.

"By the power vested in me by the ancient gods of chaos and order," the cleric said, "I declare this unholy union sealed. And now, seal this bond . . . with the traditional conquest of lips!"

Conquest of—

I froze. We hadn't negotiated this minor detail. My eyes flicked to Kazimir, whose posture was rigid. Neither of us made the first move. Emotions churned inside me—part indignation, part burning curiosity.

From the back, Griffin's voice rang out a bit too cheerfully, "Kiss her, my lord, or we'll think you've gone soft!"

Several guests snickered nervously. Kazimir's shadows darkened, and I heard Griffin yelp. Finally, Kazimir turned to face me, raising his hand to my jaw.

"My apologies," he murmured, lips so close I could feel his breath, "for what comes next."

He kissed me.

I expected a brief, formal peck. Instead, his mouth fit against mine with a devastating heat. Not bruising, not demanding, but thoroughly, unmistakably possessive. Warmth jolted through me from my lips to my toes, sparked by something more than just the physical contact. I tasted that same smoky intensity from the wine, mingled with his unmistakable magic. From Kazimir's slight hitch of breath, I knew he'd felt it too.

It was over in seconds, yet somehow it rearranged my breathing. He stepped back, eyes dark with something raw that jagged the edges of his composure. Then he schooled his features and turned to the crowd as though nothing seismic had just passed between us.

The cleric lifted his arms. "I present to you Lord and Lady Blackrose! May their enemies tremble and their alliance bring glorious destruction!"

The hall erupted in raucous cheers. I managed to keep my chin high, though my pulse was still skittering from that kiss.

At this point, Kazimir's enchanters and mages rapidly transformed the hall for the post-ceremony feast. Chairs scraped across the floor, and long banquet tables sprouted where there had been none, as if grown from the stone. Servants hurried in behind, bearing platters of steaming dishes, setting everything in place with flawless, magical coordination.

Kazimir offered me his arm as the room morphed around us. Reluctantly, I took it, aware of the watchful eyes from every corner.

"You played your role well," he said under his breath, guiding me into the new banquet space.

"And what role do I play next?" I murmured back, feigning a polite smile for the ever-curious onlookers.

"The devoted bride, of course."

The newly conjured feast sprawled before us, an uncanny mix of lavish dishes, some easily recognizable and others unsettlingly alive or glowing. Creatures, nobles, and more monstrous guests raised their glasses in salute. Kazimir held up our joined hands.

"To new beginnings," he announced.

They echoed his words, draining their goblets. As we weaved through the tables, he leaned closer, his grip tightening.

"Any one of these creatures might be a future ally," he murmured, "or a future enemy. Sometimes both. Keep your guard up, Lady Blackrose."

I kept my expression calm, even as the ring of molten bone on my finger seemed to pulse with a heartbeat of its own. "Yes," I murmured, "that seems wise."

10

Feast with Your Enemies
(and Call Them Friends)

Kazimir

Glasses clinked across the Great Hall. Magic buzzed in the air. My wedding feast simmered with false merriment, every courtier desperate to outshine the others with displays of power, so long as they didn't accidentally vaporize the person next to them.

I scowled into my goblet while Arabella sat beside me, the picture of a perfect bride. Courtiers showered her with hollow praise. Bored, I entertained myself with a mental count of how many I could kill before it became diplomatically awkward. Only the true monsters in my retinue—the shadow wraiths drifting by the rafters, the nightmare specters sipping from crystal flutes—seemed genuinely curious about my new wife.

Meanwhile, Arabella was *alarmingly* good at this.

She smiled. She nodded. She deflected probing questions with just enough information to satisfy without revealing a damn thing. She even managed to look fascinated by Griffin's droning explanations on the hall's enchanted architecture.

". . . and the chandelier crystals were harvested during a blood moon, which is why they pulse with that particular crimson undertone when—"

Over Griffin's shoulder, I caught sight of Viscountess Morana glaring at Arabella with open hostility. She wore the ornate dagger I'd given her during our brief and apparently misinterpreted winter fling. Nothing says "stabby ex-lover" like a woman who sleeps with sixteen daggers and names them all after previous conquests.

A feigned cough pulled me around to see Sims. He bowed so low his nose nearly grazed the polished floor. "My lord, the tribute from the Syndicate has arrived. Do you wish to inspect it now, or shall I let you continue your brooding?"

I shot him a look meant to blister his tongue. "Proceed."

He straightened his cuffs and signaled to servants near the main doors. They entered in a stately line, arms laden with chests, covered platters, and an unsettling sense of hush that crept across the hall.

"From the Syndicate of Seven Shadows," announced a well-dressed herald, "in honor of the union between Lord Blackrose and his bride, we present these tokens of respect and alliance . . . and definitely not bribes for any future favors."

I almost smirked. The Syndicate's packages always reeked of blood money. They unveiled exotic fruits that glowed with captive starlight, wine distilled from forbidden herbs, and beautiful jewelry carved from metals only found in the Obsidian Mountain.

Arabella leaned close, her voice lowered. "The Syndicate. Aren't they notorious for trafficking forbidden artifacts and occasionally misplacing the souls of their business partners?"

"Yes," I said, mildly surprised at her knowledge, "alongside a few other charming hobbies. They can be valuable allies, provided you enjoy living with a blade at your throat."

Her eyes followed the procession. "How generous of them to send such lavish gifts."

A flicker of humor nearly chased away my sour mood. "They're not truly gifts but down payments. They'll want a hefty return from me, with interest."

"Then why accept them?"

I glanced at her. "Because refusing a Syndicate gift is more dangerous than accepting one."

The herald came to our table and bowed deeply. He presented a pair of daggers on a velvet cushion, each hilt glittering with crystallized blood. "Forged in the darkness between worlds, bound so that what one feels, the other knows. A fitting symbol for this union—dangerous, alluring, and quite impossible to outrun."

I accepted the daggers, pulse kicking up as I felt the raw magic thrumming within the steel—and likely more than one embedded curse. "The Syndicate honors us," I said, dipping my head in a gesture that only barely feigned respect. "Our alliance remains strong . . . for now."

He stepped back with a slithering bow. The servants fanned out to deliver the remaining treasures before escaping the hall in practiced unison.

Arabella eyed the weapons. "Nothing quite says 'till death do us part' like matching implements of murder."

"The Syndicate's definition of romance is unique," I told her wryly.

"As is yours, Lord Blackrose."

I might have retorted but Vex appeared at my side. Her voice barely rose above a whisper. "My lord, may I have a word?"

I rose from my seat and gestured to Thorne. "Make certain Lady Blackrose remains unmurdered in my absence."

"Yes, my lord." Thorne moved behind Arabella's chair with the subtle menace of a mountain deciding where to avalanche.

Vex and I retreated to a small antechamber off the main hall. I closed the door behind us, dulling the clash of voices and music. Vex turned to me with a concerned look. Her composure rarely faltered unless the news was either dire or absurd.

"What is it?" I demanded.

"The staff," she said. "They're acting . . . strangely."

Instinctively, I reached for dominion magic, half expecting rebellion or demon summoning. "Strangely how? Are they plotting treason?"

Her lips twitched. "They're happy. Over the wedding."

That stopped me cold. "Happy," I repeated, as though the word belonged to another language. "You mean, in a rebellious sense, or—"

"In a festive sense," she clarified. "They're cooking celebratory meals, placing flowers in corridors you never visit, and the stablehands are allegedly planning a dance performance to honor you and Lady Blackrose."

My mind reeled at the utter nonsense. "Have they all been swapped with doppelgangers?"

Vex shook her head. "No enchantments are at play, at least none that I can detect. The only difference is that Sims announced a three-day holiday after the wedding."

"I didn't authorize that," I said sharply.

"No, but he used your name anyway, citing some 'traditional courtesy' extended by gracious lords," she said with a dry twist to her mouth. "They also believe Lady Blackrose negotiated improved conditions for them as part of your marriage contract."

I stared at her. "She did no such thing."

"Rumors can be stubborn. It's elevating her status in their eyes. They see her as a benevolent influence."

I huffed in annoyance. "Keep an eye on them. If anyone's overindulging in these warm, fuzzy feelings, remind them why they usually fear me." I gave her a searching look. "Anything else?"

Vex hesitated. That alone told me the next topic was both delicate and urgent. "It's about sleeping arrangements."

"What about them?"

"In preparation for tonight," Vex continued smoothly, "you had wine and other, er, amenities sent to your chambers. I assume that means Lady Blackrose will join you?"

My magic flared across my skin, shadows flickering in the corners of the room. "You overstep, Vex."

She seemed nonplussed. "I merely wish to arrange every detail according to your preferences. Rose petals? Warmed chains by the fireplace? A curated selection of—"

"Enough," I snapped, voice echoing with dominion. "Yes, she'll join me in my chambers. That's the plan."

She nodded, lips pressed into a careful line. "Does she know that's the plan, or is this one of your . . . surprises?"

I glared. "Our marriage arrangements are not your concern." The shadows responded to my anger, swirling thicker around my feet. "She's quite aware of her role."

"I see." Vex regarded me with unreadable calm. "So you've changed your mind about the 'no consummation' clause you mentioned before? Or is this just a power play?"

Her words ignited a spark of heat in my chest at the memory of that maddening kiss. "That's no concern of yours."

For a moment, I almost said more. But the blood resonance information was too valuable to share for now, even with Vex. And the no-sex agreement? My followers needed to believe I took what I wanted, when I wanted it. The reality—that I'd agreed to Arabella's terms because I needed her willing participation—would remain my private humiliation.

Vex saw right through me, but she held her tongue. I seized the opportunity to shift topics. "Make sure you have the eastern tower set and prepared for tomorrow's ritual. The Heirloom activation can't be delayed."

"Of course. We'll have cleanup crews on standby, just in case." Her gaze slid to the door. "The Syndicate's daggers—shall I have Griffin run spells to confirm there aren't any hidden curses?"

"Immediately," I said evenly. "The last 'gift' they sent tried to devour my soul during a full moon. I'd rather not repeat that."

She inclined her head but didn't leave yet. "Lady Blackrose is already adapting to life here. Remarkably so, for someone who was kidnapped a day ago and forced into marriage."

A hollow laugh escaped me. "She's resourceful. And cunning. Qualities worth noting."

Vex offered a mild smile. "I always analyze potential threats thoroughly, my lord."

"She's not a threat," I replied automatically, then felt a flicker of annoyance at my defensive tone. "She's an asset. A crucial piece in unleashing the Heirloom's full power."

Vex's smile deepened. "Of course. Just a piece of equipment. A particularly attractive cog in your grand machine."

I turned away, ending the conversation. "Return to the feast and make sure Viscountess Morana keeps her daggers where they belong."

Vex obeyed with an elegant bow and slipped out. Alone, I exhaled slowly as my mind drifted, unbidden, to that kiss . . . The magic had caught me off guard, sharp and unsettling in a way I couldn't explain.

I composed myself to rejoin my guests. Tomorrow, I would activate the Heirloom and secure dominion over entire realms.

So why wasn't I nearly as interested in world domination as I was in finding out how Arabella would respond to the rest of the evening—and the order to sleep in my bed?

Deep down, I knew this diversion was dangerous. Still, I was the Dark Lord. I didn't need to justify my decisions, even when they made me question my own motives. I forced the uneasy thought aside and stepped back into the clamor of the feast, determined to make this night unfold precisely as I commanded.

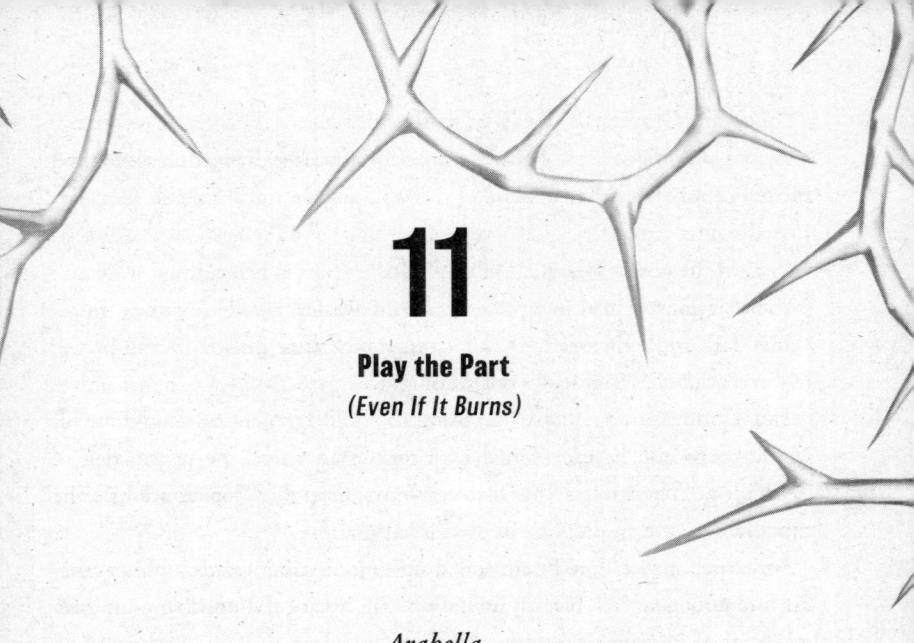

11

Play the Part
(Even If It Burns)

Arabella

My knuckles went white around the stem of my goblet. Two hours into this . . . *feast* . . . and Kazimir's court was descending into hedonism. Gasps and breathless laughter echoed through the banquet hall, punctuated by the clatter of dropped cutlery and the unmistakable sound of fabric tearing.

My cheeks burned, and I hated that I couldn't tell whether it was embarrassment or fascination. I forced my gaze away from a couple who seemed determined to set the tapestries alight with sheer friction, but everywhere I looked, limbs tangled, clothes disappeared, and bodies explored anatomical positions I'd never even contemplated.

I'd heard whispers of the Dark Lord's infamous celebrations, of course. Every kingdom had its gossips. But witnessing it firsthand was . . . educational.

Kazimir, ever the attentive captor, angled his chair toward mine. His dark eyes flicked down to my death grip on the goblet before meeting mine. I deliberately loosened my fingers.

"Your first bacchanal?" he asked softly.

Across the room, a red-haired woman disappeared beneath a table, and the man above her seized a fistful of the tablecloth in unmistakable pleasure. I tried not to stare.

I raised the goblet in a small salute. "I half expected beheadings or torture demonstrations," I said, my voice unexpectedly dry.

His dark smile flickered. "I can arrange that after dessert, if you prefer. My executioner is frightfully bored tonight."

I took a measured sip of wine, using the brief moment to steady myself. My father would have exploded with rage if he'd seen me in this den of revelry—no chaperones, no discreet bows or polite conversations. The thought gave me an illicit thrill of satisfaction.

An impeccably tailored man sidled up to a drifting wraith, unbuttoning his fine silk collar in a blatant invitation. The creature slipped through him in a curl of black mist, and he staggered, gasping, as if the darkness had caressed him somewhere very private indeed. Unfazed, he followed, tugging at the rest of his buttons with optimistic zeal.

Servants glided between tables, dousing a few of the floating lights to lend greater privacy (or maybe encouragement) to the unfolding scenes. Shadows revealed flashes of bare skin, plush silks pooled on the floor, and sweet music morphing into low hums of desire. I swallowed hard, determined to keep my composure and not let Kazimir see how rattled I was, or how curious.

"Your court is . . . energetic," I managed.

He gave a lazy shrug. "Wait until Midwinter. Then it gets truly depraved." His eyes danced with mischief. "Does it offend your delicate sensibilities, my lady?"

I shook my head, feigning a casual indifference I couldn't entirely feel. But I'd rather choke on my own tongue than let him see me flustered. My encounters had been furtive fumblings compared to this open indulgence. But it wasn't complete ignorance that made me uncomfortable—it was the sheer openness of it all. The unapologetic way these people took what they wanted, consequences be damned.

A small, rebellious part of me wondered what such freedom felt like.

Across the hall, a woman stared at me with open hostility, her fingers tracing the ornate dagger at her waist. There could only be one reason why I already had an enemy. "I suppose everyone at your court wants to sleep with you?"

"Not everyone." Kazimir's gaze slid pointedly to me before he followed my line of sight. "Ah. Viscountess Morana. She oversees Arvoryn Pass, between Solandris and my domain." His eyes shifted back to me, darkly amused.

I hid my unease behind another sip. The delicious burn of the wine spread through my chest and into my cheeks. "She appears territorial. You two have a history?"

He raised an eyebrow. "Are you asking if I've bedded her?"

My pulse gave an irritating little jump. "You're free to consort with whomever you like, Lord Blackrose," I said, my voice airy and false. "I'm merely wondering if she's going to hurl that dagger at my face."

Kazimir almost smirked. "She wouldn't dare. And no. We don't *consort*. Not anymore."

I took another sip of wine, abruptly aware that my gown felt unbearably hot.

He glanced at my goblet. "Careful. That vintage will sneak up on you."

I smiled my courtliest smile and swept my gaze over the revelers. "You're not telling anyone else to be careful."

The casual look of indifference he gave me was as fake as my smile. "True. The difference is that I won't have to carry any of them out of here when they overindulge."

I set down my goblet with a sharp click. Kazimir exuded smugness so thoroughly that it made my skin itch. I longed to hurl the wine in his face, though the sight of it trickling down his collar might have been more distracting than punishing.

He leaned in, lowering his voice. "Watching you pretend this doesn't affect you is rapidly becoming the highlight of my evening."

"It doesn't affect me," I lied.

He slid his chair closer to mine, the air between us growing thick. The soft glow of the remaining lights rendered his features dangerously captivating—long lashes, sharp cheekbones, that infuriatingly well-shaped mouth. My stomach executed a series of complex, unwanted flips.

"You don't have to pretend with me, Lady Blackrose," he murmured.

I forced a brittle smile in response, but any clever retort stuck in my throat. Strangely, my truth-sense hummed that he was being sincere. A slight exhale slipped past my lips.

Kazimir reached for his goblet, creating breathing space between us. He polished off his last swallow of wine. "We have a small problem."

My attention shifted to the chaotic knot of revelers in the center of the hall. "I'd say you have a few," I replied drily. "Your guests are fornicating on the dining tables."

He gestured, taking in the half-clothed courtiers, the indulgent moaning. "They expect a show. If we're not at least *seen* participating in their hedonism, they'll think I'm . . . distracted."

I stiffened. "Excuse me?"

He stood and offered me his hand. "Dance with me."

All my instincts shouted caution. He was playing a game. I'd agreed to appear cooperative, but "cooperative" now seemed like a trap. Then again, dancing was presumably safer than the alternative. And it gave me a chance to keep some control.

I placed my hand in his, ignoring the spark of warmth at his touch. "Fine," I said coolly. "I'm sure you're an adequate partner."

The corner of his mouth lifted, and he led me into a cleared space where a few couples had formed a slow, seductive dance. I caught glimpses of swirling fabric, parted lips, and wandering hands. Kazimir pulled me close, one hand settling at my waist, the other clasping my fingers against his chest. Pretense or not, every nerve I possessed seemed to buzz.

"Relax," he urged quietly. His hand slid up my back, a deceptively modest repositioning that sent a wave of tingling awareness through me.

I stared at my free palm, which hovered uncertainly near his shoulder. "I'm perfectly relaxed."

"I can feel your pulse from here," he said. "Now, look at me. Laugh as though I've just whispered something outrageous."

I tried one of my carefully rehearsed society giggles, but Kazimir frowned. "That's the polite, I'm-so-delighted-about-this-needlepoint laugh. I want the *other* one—the kind that suggests I've just whispered something wicked in your ear."

A retort formed on my tongue, but before I could speak, he bent his head, letting me feel the faint prickle of his stubble against my cheek. "They're all imagining how I'll take you tonight," he murmured. "You should give them a reason to envy you."

A breathy exhale escaped me, half laugh, half disbelief. The new wave of heat had nothing to do with the wine.

"There," he noted. "Much better."

We moved in slow, swaying steps, our bodies brushing in ways that felt *far* too intimate. My gown suddenly seemed both stifling and overly thin. I was aware of every inch of him—his fingers grazing my spine, the slight press of his thigh. My gaze flicked to his mouth before I could stop myself.

He spun me gently, guiding me until my back pressed against his chest. I now faced the full assembly of guests, many of whom looked on with eager curiosity. Some watched with hunger in their eyes, as though expecting us to morph into some public spectacle. Anxiety twisted through me, but Kazimir's warm presence at my back offered a strange, dissonant reassurance.

"Tell me to stop," he whispered against my ear, "and I will."

Instead of answering, I let my head tilt against his shoulder, my eyes slipping shut. My nerves crackled in time with the distant thunder that rolled outside. Power swirled through the black spires of his citadel, echoing the tension in my own body.

"You're trembling," he said softly.

"The wine," I lied, even as my pulse hammered.

His lips brushed the curve of my ear in a subtle grin. "Of course."

The shift of his thumb beneath my breast made my breath catch. He never truly crossed a boundary, but the promise of it hovered between us. Against my better judgment, I indulged the traitorous response of my body—heat, curiosity, a raw confusion about just how easily he unraveled me.

Everyone watched, enthralled. Kazimir's voice dropped lower. "They think I've devoured you. If only they knew how well you resist."

My defiance flared. I twisted enough to meet his gaze over my shoulder. "Who says I'm resisting anymore?"

His eyes darkened with something that might have been hunger, but we didn't have time to explore the moment further. A sudden crash split the air.

Viscountess Morana had drawn her dagger on one of the Syndicate's representatives. "How dare you!" she roared. Wine splashed. Chairs screeched back.

I tensed, expecting Kazimir to intervene. Instead, he released me, taking my hand in one smooth motion.

"Aren't you going to stop them?" I asked.

"They'll sort it out," he muttered, guiding me through the tightening crowd toward a side door. "And if they kill each other, it solves several problems at once."

I stole a final glance over my shoulder. The hall had plunged into chaos, courtiers scrambling, a few excited onlookers cheering. The viscountess lunged. Steel caught the candlelight, and blood spattered across a white tablecloth before the crowd closed around the fight.

Kazimir pulled me through the doorway, the heavy wood swinging shut behind us, instantly muffling the feast's roar.

And then we were alone.

12

Resist Temptation
(Even When It Sleeps Naked)

Arabella

I walked in silence alongside Kazimir, the sounds of revelry fading behind us. My pulse thundered. I fought to keep my breathing even, to hide how thoroughly the wine—and the press of his body against mine—had affected me.

As we approached, guards bowed deeply, their eyes averted. We passed them and climbed a narrow spiral staircase. To steady myself, I let my fingertips graze the cool stone wall. Kazimir's hand settled at the small of my back, light but impossible to ignore.

We emerged onto a small landing that opened to the night sky, and a blast of icy air sobered me more effectively than any potion could have. I drew a sharp breath, looking out over the dizzying drop.

It was the lightning bridge again.

During the day, it had been intimidating—now, in the darkness, the crackling radiance looked even wilder. The surge of light overwhelmed the distant spire, leaving only a stark, pulsing path.

Kazimir's arm encircled my waist, steady and warm. "Wouldn't want to lose you over the edge," he murmured in that smug tone.

Regardless, I clung to his support, furious at myself for needing it as I took the first step onto the bridge. The cold wind whipped at my face, lashing the last of the wine's fog from my mind. Hyperaware of his arm around me, I kept moving. By the time we reached the far side, the hum of tension in my body had only sharpened. He was so close. I hated how willingly I let him guide me, how the heat of his hand on my hip seared straight through my gown.

"You may call me Kazimir if you wish," he said abruptly as we descended another winding staircase.

I glanced at him. "And what makes you think I'd wish to do that?"

He gave me a knowing look. "Most people find 'Dark Lord' cumbersome in casual conversation. And 'my lord' seems . . . unlikely to escape your mouth without you spontaneously combusting."

I shot him a flat look. "I've found 'kidnapper' rolls off the tongue quite nicely."

We reached a landing and continued down another corridor. "We're married now," he pointed out. "Isn't it outdated to keep calling me your kidnapper?"

"I didn't realize abduction came with an expiration date."

His lips twitched. "Consider it a promotion, then. From victim to wife."

I studied him warily. "Since we're on the topic of our hasty nuptials, I noticed the vows were abbreviated. No promise to obey?"

He stepped closer, voice low. "That's rather archaic. And you can't obey anyone to save your life, can you?" His gaze flicked to my mouth. "Besides, I find your defiance far more stimulating than your obedience would be."

My stomach twisted at the subtle purr in his tone. "I'm not here to stimulate you."

"And yet," he murmured, tracing his fingers over my collarbone, "you do. Most efficiently."

Refusing to betray how his touch made my heart hammer, I forced myself to stand absolutely still under his caress. His fingers withdrew, and we walked on until we reached the staircase leading to Kazimir's tower. When I halted at my chamber entrance, his hand wrapped around my wrist before I could slip inside. He moved up the stairs instead, pulling me undeniably upward.

"Where are we going?" Suspicion crept into my voice, and I tried not to panic.

He kept climbing. "My chambers."

My throat tightened. For all my bravado, I recognized how precarious my power was here. He wanted me compliant—not physically forced, perhaps, but he was certainly capable of coercion. My pulse pounded in my ears.

"Our agreement," I managed, "specifically mentioned no sex. I sleep in my chambers. You sleep in yours."

He paused on the steps, so close that I nearly stumbled into him. "We agreed to no *sex*," he said in that infuriatingly patient tone. "You said nothing about sleeping arrangements."

"That was implied." I kept my voice even and my tone strong, but in a debate of technicalities I had the losing argument.

He pressed a hand to my hip, thumb digging lightly into the top of the bone, not hard enough to hurt but distracting enough to spike my pulse further. "I don't operate on implications, Lady Blackrose. You asked for no sexual contact, and I agreed. You *didn't* ask for separate quarters."

Heat gathered under my skin—anger tangled with something far more embarrassing. "Well, I'm stating it now." I placed a hand on his chest to push him back, only to realize I'd just made the mistake of touching him. He felt disturbingly solid beneath my palm. "I want my own bed, in my own room."

His expression hardened even as he leaned in. "That won't be possible."

A chill ran through me at the quiet menace in his voice. My hand remained where it was on his chest, torn between pushing him away and curling my fingers into the fabric of his coat. "Why not?"

"You're my wife." He said it with such finality, such ownership, that my thighs clenched traitorously.

I tried to cling to reason. "Yes, I am," I said. "And I played the part of the willing bride, as we agreed. But I won't be your plaything. Our terms are clear. If you want me to keep cooperating, you'll uphold them."

He exhaled, more an attempt at patience than frustration. "Fine. But the Dark Lady sleeps in the Dark Lord's chambers. All eyes here are keen. If you refuse my bed outright, the court will sense weakness. They'll question my control. Whispers become daggers at times like these."

I narrowed my eyes. "So this is about survival."

"Yes, mine, and by extension, yours. My position is maintained through a careful balance of fear and respect. Anything that undermines that balance puts us both at risk."

I wanted to argue further, but his explanation rang true. I'd grown up in a noble household; I understood how quickly whispers could corrode authority.

"Fine," I said at last, trying to ignore the tightening in my stomach. "No sex, though."

"As agreed." He inclined his head. "But perhaps we should clarify what *sex* entails."

My breath caught. "I think it's fairly self-explanatory."

"Oh? Does it include kissing? Touching?" His gaze dropped to my lips. "We've already broken that barrier, wouldn't you say?"

I swallowed. "That . . . was for show," I insisted, wincing at how uncertain I sounded.

"And yet," he said softly, leaning in, "you didn't seem to find it entirely unpleasant. Or was I misreading the way your body trembled against mine?"

"You were," I lied.

He didn't believe me, but he didn't push that point. "So, behind closed doors, I keep my distance." He outlined an imaginary boundary in the air between us. "But in public, I *will* touch you as needed."

"For what, exactly?"

"To keep up appearances," he said. His eyes traced the line of my throat. "A hand at your waist, a kiss to claim you. *All* for show."

"I don't belong to you." I retorted. Yet my pulse fluttered dangerously at the idea of that mouth on my skin.

"But in the eyes of my court, you do." He shrugged. "Unless you'd prefer a far more explicit display? They'd find that highly entertaining."

The scorn in his eyes told me exactly how far he'd go if pressed. My traitorous body flushed with unexpected heat at the thought of him possessively claiming me before his entire court. Gods, what was wrong with me? That I could find something so humiliating somehow . . . irresistibly arousing? I swallowed hard, blaming the wine for these unwanted fantasies. "Fine," I bit out. "In public, brief touches are allowed—for the act. But beyond that—"

"Let's be *very* clear," he interrupted quietly, stepping so close I had to tilt my head back to maintain eye contact. "No touching you between the legs, no mouth on your body, no removal of clothing?"

"All of it is off-limits," I managed, though part of me screamed in protest.

"And you on *me*?" he murmured, leaning in. "Do you likewise forbid yourself from ever putting those clever hands anywhere I might enjoy them?"

The question made my skin burn. "I have no intention of touching you more than necessary."

He lounged back, satisfaction flickering in his eyes. "We'll see."

Gods, his arrogance was maddening. I tried to refocus. "So you agree to these terms?"

"I do," he said, "but with one condition of my own." His gaze went dark.

My stomach knotted. "And that is?"

"A kiss."

I blinked. "A kiss? You just had one at the ceremony."

"That was for the crowd," he murmured, eyes roving over me with undisguised hunger. "I want one for *me*. To seal our new arrangement."

Heat flooded my face. "That's hardly necessary."

"All's fair in love and war, or whatnot."

"This is neither." I tried to ignore how my heart hammered against my ribs.

"How do you know?"

I weighed my options. I could refuse and potentially lose the other concessions I'd negotiated, or I could agree to one kiss—just one—and secure the rest of my demands. It was a simple calculation.

At least, that's what I told myself.

"Fine," I said, lifting my chin. "Then we're done negotiating."

His pupils dilated, amusement tugging at his mouth. "Agreed."

For a moment, nothing happened. The tension built until I thought my knees would give out. "Well?" I demanded. "Get it over with."

He slid a hand along my face with disarming gentleness, and a quick flutter in my chest robbed me of breath. The touch was so unlike the rough claiming I'd expected that I leaned into it before I could stop myself. Then he brushed his mouth against mine, once . . . twice. Teasing, testing. The tenderness disarmed me more than any aggression could have.

His hand slipped around my waist, pulling me against him. The kiss deepened, turning from a question into an undeniable demand. Where our wedding kiss had sparked, this one ignited. I gasped, letting him part my lips. His tongue teased mine, and I tasted wine and heat, my head swimming. I found myself responding before common sense could reassert itself, my hands fisting in his coat.

A soft noise rumbled in his chest when I returned his kiss, and his body pressed mine to the curving stairwell wall. I was too aware of my own heartbeat, throbbing everywhere we touched. This kiss felt . . . *devouring*, as if he was promising me he'd claim far more than my mouth one day.

An *I'm-going-to-fuck-you-one-day* kiss that left no room for misinterpretation.

At last, he pulled back. We were both breathing raggedly. His eyes were dark and fierce, and color tinted his sharp cheekbones. "There," he said, his voice hoarse. "That seals it."

I struggled to keep my face stoic, hating how my body hummed with unfulfilled desire. "Completely unnecessary," I managed.

"Maybe." His thumb brushed my lower lip, but I turned my head to the side, fighting the urge to pull him back to me. After a beat, he stepped back, though I still felt the hot press of his gaze. "You asked for distance. I'll respect it." He paused, letting the promise hang. "But if you ever *request* my touch again . . . I'll deliver it with interest."

My pulse pounded, and I cursed the traitorous wave of heat between my thighs. "I truly hate you," I whispered, voice still unsteady.

Kazimir smiled then—brief, brilliant, transforming his features in a way that stole my next breath. "Good. Hate is a potent form of passion, Lady Blackrose. I look forward to where it might lead."

We continued our ascent in oppressive silence, my stomach twisting with each step. I tried not to let even my sleeve brush him, unwilling to concede any more ground. At the top, we reached a heavy wooden door pressed into the stone. Kazimir laid his palm against it, and I felt a pulse of magic dissolve the wards. The door swung open into his chambers.

I half expected a throne of skulls or a bloodstained altar. Instead, it was all polished stone, dark drapes, an ornately carved bed, comfortable seating near a large fireplace, and musty books piled everywhere. One meager flourish of villainy caught my eye: a weight that looked suspiciously like finger bones holding down a scroll on his desk.

So the infamous Dark Lord was also a messy academic. With boundary issues. And flawless bone structure.

Kazimir leaned against the bed's tall post, arms folded over his chest. A lock of hair tumbled over his eyebrow from our earlier embrace, giving him a slightly disheveled look. "Not enough skulls for you?"

I shrugged. "I expected more. Maybe a throne of rib cages in the corner?"

"That's in the Chamber of Accords," he said lightly, crossing to a sideboard. He poured amber liquid from a crystal decanter into two glasses. "Drink?"

I hesitated, eyeing the strong spirits. But my nerves still competed with the lingering thrum of arousal, and I took the glass. The brandy was rich, warming me more thoroughly than I liked to admit.

Kazimir shrugged off his coat, draping it over a chair before starting on the buttons of his waistcoat. My heartbeat jumped. "What are you doing?"

I asked, unable to forget that hungry press of his body.

He lifted an eyebrow. "Undressing. These clothes are unbearable."

My hand clenched around the glass. Another button gave way, flashing the white linen below. "I'll . . . freshen up, then."

Kazimir paused, his fingers resting on the next button. "Before you do, there's something you should know." His voice dropped, turning velvet soft. "I sleep naked."

I nearly choked on my last sip of brandy. "You can't be serious."

"I can, and I am. My chambers, my rules."

"You're doing this on purpose," I accused.

"Without a doubt," he said unapologetically, "but also telling the truth." He fiddled with another button. "Now you're warned."

I stared, infuriated. His eyes glimmered with amusement, and I knew he expected me to run.

So I did.

I turned sharply on my heel and hurried into the bathing chamber, feeling his gaze burn on my back the entire way.

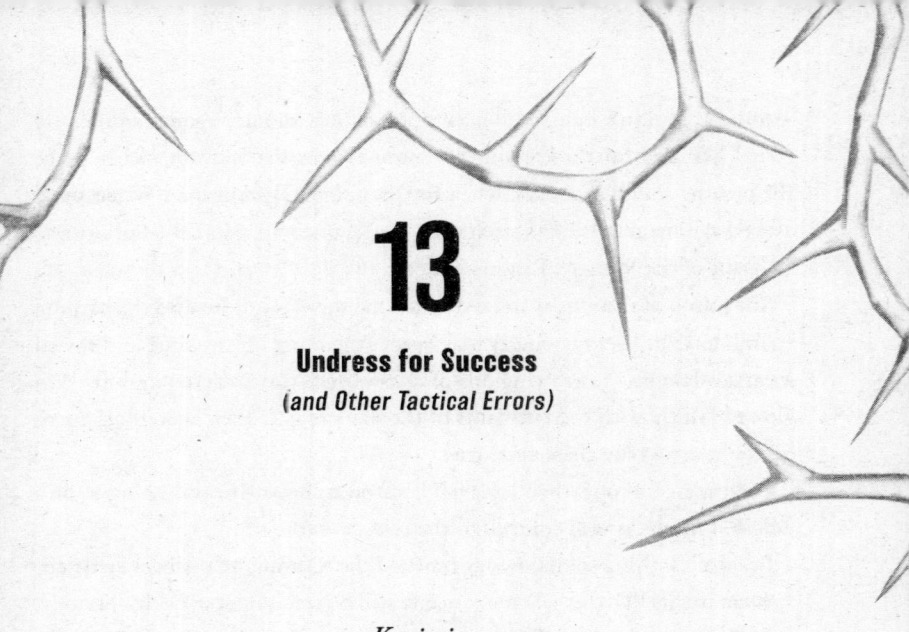

13

Undress for Success
(and Other Tactical Errors)

Kazimir

I flung my waistcoat across the study with unnecessary force, watching it land in a pathetic crumple by the desk.

One day. One fucking day since I'd stolen Arabella from her carriage, and already she was wreaking havoc on my well-honed self-control. The way she'd looked at me when we danced—regal, defiant, breathtaking—had made me want to claim her right in front of my court. And if Morana hadn't chosen that moment to create a scene of her own, I would have done something incredibly stupid.

And that last kiss on the stairwell? A disastrous mistake.

"Fortyfold amplification," I muttered, pouring myself another brandy with hands that were absolutely not trembling. "That's all it was. Magical resonance."

Snatching the glass off the table, I downed it in two long swallows. This was humiliating. I didn't get *flustered* over anyone, much less a woman who'd spent our entire acquaintance either stabbing me or plotting to do so.

Still, I couldn't banish the memory of her mouth against mine. I'd tasted her, and for those moments, been lost in the warmth of her body, the breathy sound she made when my tongue plunged deeper. When she'd arched against me, I'd forgotten every single one of my so-called priorities.

Terror of the Western Realms, indeed.

The sound of running water reminded me she was just behind the bathing chamber door. I set my empty glass aside, then tore off my shirt and tossed it carelessly onto the growing pile of clothes. The runes carved into my skin glowed faintly with the remnants of the day's magic, their scorching memory tight across my chest and arms.

I considered a robe, then let it fall back on its hook. If I was going to be a villain, I might as well commit to the role.

Besides, clothing sometimes aggravated the scarring on my back, particularly on nights like this when my magic still buzzed under my skin. Frankly, part of me wanted Arabella to see the monster in vivid detail. Maybe then I could scare her off or remind myself of the real reason I'd brought her here in the first place.

After discarding the rest of my clothes, I settled back onto the bed, deliberately sprawling atop the covers, one arm casually tucked behind my head and my erection proudly on display. My body, traitorous as it was, had stirred at the mere thought of her. She deserved to suffer a little, too.

When the faint click of the bathing chamber door finally came, I'd expected an outraged squeak or some show of shock. What I got was a momentary, breath-stealing pause where her gaze drifted down my chest and then lower, carefully cataloging every inch of exposed skin. My breath almost caught at the sight of her—hair damp in loose, golden waves, a robe clinging to her curves. She was almost too stunning, and it infuriated me that I reacted so strongly.

"You really weren't joking," she said, her tone admirably calm, though her cheeks turned pink.

"I rarely joke," I replied, hoping I sounded dismissive rather than unsettled. "Ruins the mystique."

She folded her arms over her chest. "You could at least cover yourself properly."

"I think you've confused me with someone who cares about modesty." I gestured to the empty half of the bed beside me. "Feel free to join me whenever you're ready. I promise I only bite by *request*."

Her lips pressed into a thin line, and she surveyed the empty space beside me, like she was calculating how far away she could lie without falling off the bed. "I need proper nightclothes."

I nodded toward the wardrobe. "You'll find some there, though I'm not sure how 'proper' they'll be."

She yanked the wardrobe door open, searched for a moment, and pulled out a slip of black silk. "This is practically see-through," she complained, holding it up in the moonlight.

I forced a lazy shrug even as my imagination helpfully supplied an image of that delicate fabric clinging to her curves. "It's what was available."

She made a sound of disbelief, then turned for the bathing chamber. Before she could vanish, I flicked my wrist, sealing the door with a pulse of magic. It closed with a neat click, leaving her standing halfway across the room, clutching that scandalous nightgown.

She spun to glare at me, eyes sparking with danger. "Are you serious?"

I smirked from my place on the bed. "Consider this a test of your resolve, Lady Blackrose."

For a moment, she stood frozen, her chest rising and falling with barely contained fury. I expected her to fling the garment in my face. Instead, her expression shifted. "Very well."

Without breaking eye contact, she let the robe slip to the floor, revealing every bare inch of herself as a deliberate counterattack. She was toned and soft in all the right ways, the interplay of moonlight and firelight coursing over her skin. My own breath stalled. I'd half counted on her modesty to keep things from getting out of hand, but she'd turned it back on me in an instant. Caught off guard, I stared. The memory of how her body had felt under my hands seared my mind, and for once, I had nothing clever to say.

She slid the nightgown over her head in one swift move. The silk was as sheer as I'd pictured, clinging to her body with an infuriating invitation. If she was out to prove she wasn't intimidated, she was succeeding. My palms literally itched to reach for her. And the rest of me wanted to . . . well, to do other things.

Lady Arabella was far more dangerous than advertised.

"So," she said, her gaze dropping to my almost painful erection, "is this how your marriages typically start?"

I leaned forward. "Most who talk back to me like you do don't live long enough to enjoy the show," I said, unable to keep a rasp from my voice.

She tossed her hair over her shoulder, ignoring the effect the movement had on her barely covered breasts. "I hate you," she announced, sliding under the blankets on her side of the bed.

"So you've said," I replied, "repeatedly. I might have it engraved on our wedding bands."

Rolling her eyes, she got back up to gather a spare stack of pillows from the couch. With brisk efficiency, she constructed a mountainous blockade right down the center of the mattress.

I raised an eyebrow. "A pillow wall?"

"Get used to it, Dark Lord," she shot back, slamming the last pillow down with emphasis. "Since you insist on trying to make me uncomfortable."

"I sleep naked because it's comfortable." I stuffed one arm under my head again and relaxed against the headboard. "Your discomfort is merely a bonus, like finding an extra cookie in the jar. Or an extra prisoner in the dungeon."

She glowered at me from behind her little pillow fortress, but something else flickered in her eyes before she schooled her expression. Then her gaze roamed over my runes, and I realized she'd spotted the scars covering my torso and limbs. "Do those hurt?" she asked quietly.

"Sometimes." My voice came out rougher than I intended. "If I channel too much or they're activated for specific spells."

She observed them with a directness that left me more exposed than if I'd simply stood naked before a crowd. "Some of these look like binding runes," she murmured, "but others . . . I've never seen anything like them."

I hesitated. Usually, I reveled in how people flinched from my scars, but Arabella's steady regard was unsettling in an entirely different way. "They're unique," I said at last. "Most deal with dominion spells . . . enhancements."

"Who carved them onto you?" She seemed surprised by her own question. "You can't have done it all by yourself?"

I met her eyes, resisted the urge to pull a blanket over my body, and kept my silence. The scars burned under her scrutiny, but some wounds were better left unexplained.

"Was it worth it?" she asked quietly.

A pulse of anger threatened to surge, but I forced a calm, measured tone. "Power is always worth the price."

Arabella's lips parted, but she didn't press. Whatever she saw in my face, it kept her from asking more. She exhaled, lying down again and turning away, as if to let the moment pass.

"You still haven't told me why you specifically needed a bride of heroic bloodline," she said.

I weighed my response. "I'll show you tomorrow," I promised, making sure my tone carried more command than warmth.

She was quiet so long I thought maybe she'd fallen asleep, but she spoke again, her voice drifting across the pillow barrier. "I still hate you."

I managed a crooked grin, letting my eyes roam over her form under the blanket. There was more than hatred there. "I know. But here you are, sharing my bed anyway."

She shifted, and I half expected her to lob a pillow at me. Instead, her voice unexpectedly dropped. "Why use your own bone for the rings? I recognized my hair, but . . . I didn't realize . . ."

Her question took me off guard. I let my gaze flick to the faint glow of my wedding band. "Because it needed both of us," I said at length. "Your hair, my bone. That's how the Cup of Dominion ritual works."

She let out a slow breath. "I'd ask if it hurt, but after seeing your runes, I imagine it was nothing."

"Nothing's ever truly nothing," I countered, surprised at my own honesty. "But if this arrangement is worth doing, it's worth doing properly."

A contemplative silence stretched out, and I felt her analyzing my words, or maybe me, in the darkness. It made me vulnerable in a way I didn't appreciate. I shifted, letting the covers drape strategically if only to ease the tension throbbing in my gut.

Finally, she scoffed softly. "I'm struggling to believe there's any sincerity in you."

"Then struggle," I said, letting my mask reassert itself. "I'd advise you to rest, wife. I've quite a morning planned for us both. Who knows what fresh horrors you'll discover about me tomorrow?"

She exhaled, and I heard the soft rustle of the sheets as she settled in, presumably not to sleep but to plot my demise in creative ways. Fine by me. *Plot away, my little hero. I'll be waiting.*

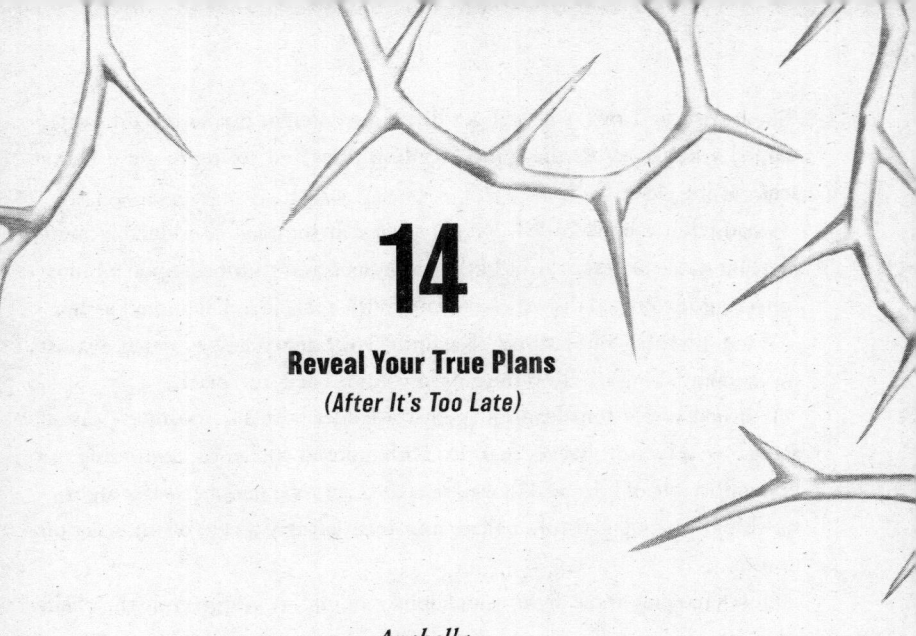

14

Reveal Your True Plans
(After It's Too Late)

Arabella

The next morning, I wandered through the fortress's library while waiting for Kazimir. The space felt exactly like stepping into a Dark Lord's gothic imagination—equal parts majestic and unsettling. Shadows loomed high under towering arches, swallowing the shelves in the gloom overhead. The shelves themselves were carved from a wood so dark I wondered if it sprouted from cursed soil. The smell was even stranger: old parchment, spilled ink, and something smoky that reminded me of raw magic.

Entire sections were devoted to topics that would give most sane people nightmares: *Proper Etiquette for Necromantic Summonings, 1001 Ways to Harvest Souls: A Beginner's Guide,* and basically everything you'd never think to keep next to a cozy reading chair. Rare manuscripts and gilded scrolls lined the shelves, painting a picture of Kazimir's wide-ranging (and occasionally horrifying) interests.

A tall, ancient-looking mage in long robes shuffled past the end of the aisle for the third time, glancing in my direction as though he expected me to start ripping pages out of his precious tomes. To be fair, that *did* sound like something I might do if I got desperate enough. But so far, I'd simply tapped a finger across the spines, reading titles and trying to get a better sense of the place.

I paused at a book called *The Joy of Hex*. It sounded considerably more pleasant than the rest... until I flipped it open and stumbled upon an illustrated guide to ritual disembowelment. With a shudder, I slammed it shut.

"Find anything interesting?" Kazimir's voice practically vibrated against my spine, making me drop the cursed volume back into place.

I turned to see him leaning against a ladder with far too much casual arrogance. His stormy eyes sparkled with amused challenge, reminding me uncomfortably of how he'd looked stretched across silken sheets last night—smirking, unapologetically naked, and infuriatingly aware of my reaction to him.

"Just enjoying some light scandalous reading." I gestured to the shelf, adopting my most unimpressed tone. "You have quite a collection. Where did all these come from?"

"I inherited many of them when I took over the citadel." He continued watching me with that mesmerizing gaze. "Stole some. Found others. Had some donated."

I swallowed a retort about the Dark Lord receiving "donations" and looked back at the spines. "*101 Creative Curses* caught my eye."

He nodded with mock gravity. "One of Griffin's favorites. Though in fairness, the author's brilliance was overshadowed by a teapot that gained sentience and exacted petty vengeance on him."

I raised a brow. "And that's why we don't mess with kitchenware."

"Precisely." He moved closer, and his magic-laced scent—steel and charred wood—caught me off guard. "Did you sleep well, Lady Blackrose?"

The formal address seemed strange between people who'd seen each other naked, but I welcomed it. Keeping him at arm's length was going to be the key to my sanity in this situation.

I forced a nonchalant shrug. "Like the dead," I lied. Truthfully, my heart had hammered all night, anticipating either an attack or an accident of the pillow wall toppling over and somehow landing me in his arms. "You?"

"Oh, much the same," he replied, far too pleased with himself.

I cleared my throat. "You mentioned you'd reveal more of your plans today?"

"I did," he agreed, eyes flicking to my mouth. "When I make promises, I always deliver."

"Your definitions of 'always' and 'deliver' might differ from mine." Still, I braced for him to give some cryptic nonanswer. Instead, he offered his arm in a parody of gallantry, leaning in just enough that I felt the heat of him.

"Walk with me," he said, managing to sound both charming and predatory at once. "I want to show you something that could reshape the entire realm."

He led me from the library, and I tried not to dwell on the feel of his arm under my hand or the spark that shot up my neck whenever I inhaled that smoky tang. Servants and guards cleared our path.

"The staff seems less likely to throw themselves out the windows at your approach," I observed, tapping my fingers against his arm.

Kazimir glanced down at my hand. "Apparently, there's a rumor circulating that you've negotiated better treatment for them. Something about actual meal breaks and not being fed to the void beasts for minor infractions."

"How tragic for your reputation." I failed to hide my smile.

"Indeed." He gestured me through a door ahead of him, making sure to close it after. "Next thing you know, they'll expect birthday celebrations and reasonable working hours."

"And to clarify, that's a joke because they don't already get those things."

Kazimir shot me a dark look, but I merely smiled sweetly in response. "So where are we going?"

"You insisted on honesty, so I'm taking you to see the Heirloom of Dominion. Think of this as me indulging your unwise curiosity."

"So what exactly is this Heirloom of Dominion? Besides something that apparently required you to kidnap and marry me."

We rounded a corner where two guards stood sentry, their postures stiffening as we approached. They looked as if they might faint if Kazimir so much as sneezed in their direction. He greeted them with a disinterested nod, then pressed his hand to the heavy iron doors behind them. Crimson runes flared under his palm, and the doors swung open with an eerie lack of sound.

"The Heirloom," he said as we climbed the spiraling staircase beyond, "is the keystone to harnessing the realm's ley lines. Your bloodline is crucial because the artifact requires a direct descendant of the First Hero."

I nearly froze on the steps. The runes shimmering along the walls pulsed with each footstep, reminding me of the power thrumming in the citadel. "Ley lines . . . you're talking about controlling the lifeblood of magic itself."

"And funneling it however I wish," Kazimir confirmed, his tone disturbingly eager. "You see the potential?"

"Potential for catastrophe," I said bluntly. "If you reroute the currents of magic, couldn't that destroy entire kingdoms?"

"Only for those who stand in my way." He shrugged, as though we were discussing mild property damage. "Solandris deserves a little inconvenience. The convergence of ley lines beneath it have allowed it to build its power for centuries."

Part of me was appalled. Another part remembered how Solandris had turned a blind eye to what my father did to me, and how much I'd resented that kingdom's indifference. "I'm . . . not wholly opposed to seeing certain people sweat," I admitted. "But there are innocents too."

Kazimir's face shifted, just a flicker of something that might have been respect. "Perhaps we'll refine the approach. Now keep going." He guided me up the last turn in the stairs, where a second set of doors stood. These glowed with an even deeper crimson light. He pressed his palm to the center, and the doors yielded to reveal a circular chamber dominated by a domed ceiling painted with rotating constellations.

At the center stood a pedestal of black marble supporting a golden circlet. A ring of arcane symbols in the floor pulsed faintly. My instincts screamed caution. This place practically sang with power, and every hair on my arms rose in response.

Kazimir's voice lowered. "The Heirloom of Dominion. Created by your ancestor—the First Hero. It's attuned to your bloodline, but it requires dominion magic to guide it."

"In other words," I said softly, "my blood plus your villainy."

He offered a crooked half smile. "More or less. Will you step into the circle?"

I hesitated at the threshold, considering all the lines we'd already crossed. He could force me, but he was extending his hand like it was a dance invitation. I glanced at the circlet, a deceptively simple design with an undercurrent of raw, pulsing potential that I felt in my bones.

"What happens if I do?" I asked.

"Then we learn if all my years of plotting and your heroic lineage are enough to shape the realms." His tone vibrated with eagerness, a boy with a shiny new toy. Except that toy could probably end civilization if we got it wrong.

I told myself to refuse. I told myself that after everything he'd done, I shouldn't help him. But my father's face rose in my mind, the memory of that tower, the hypocrisy I'd witnessed in Solandris. Maybe if I could shape how Kazimir used this artifact, I could spare a lot of people. Or maybe I was just as power-hungry as he was, albeit less honest about it.

Drawing a steadying breath, I took Kazimir's hand. I felt the faint shock of his touch—electric, dangerous—and walked with him into that chamber.

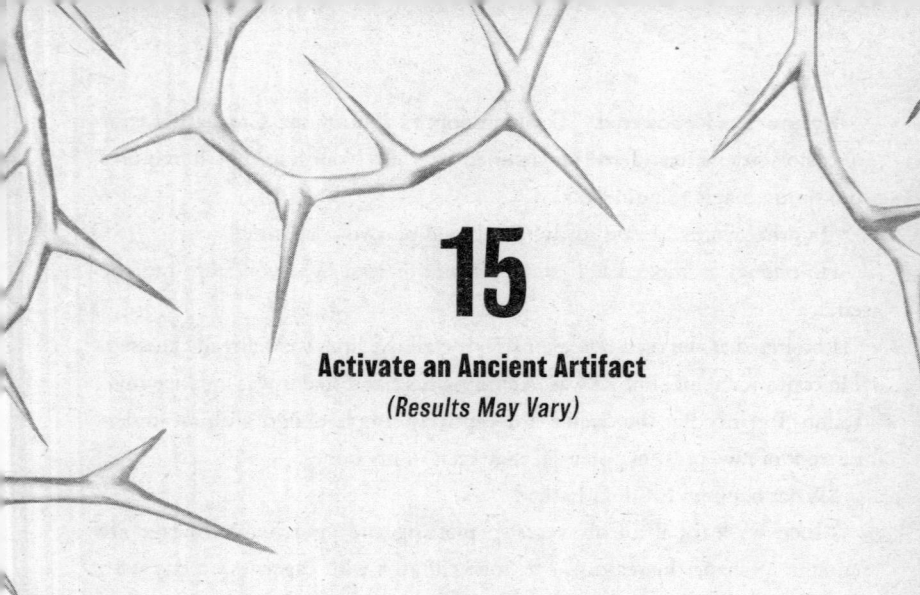

15

Activate an Ancient Artifact
(Results May Vary)

Kazimir

Arabella swept into the chamber like she owned it, her deep blue gown hugging curves that nearly had me flinging compliments right and left. I hadn't decided yet whether my tailor deserved a medal or a beheading for crafting something so distractingly perfect. Her gaze traveled over the rotating constellations on the ceiling, then dropped to the concentric crimson runes carved into the stone floor. Three nights' worth of blood, sweat, and magic had gone into those etchings, and I felt an odd satisfaction at seeing her pause in admiration.

Her hand was still in mine when a sharp rap on the door broke through my concentration. I cleared my throat and forced myself to let her go.

"Enter," I called.

Vex slipped through first, her hood pulled low. Griffin followed, lanky limbs folding in on themselves as he squinted at the sudden brightness. Sims stepped in behind them, wearing his traditional "we might all die today" expression, and Thorne lumbered last, practically forcing the doorframe to widen in self-defense.

"Ah, the morning-after committee," I said, leaning against the windowsill. "How was the rest of the feast?"

"Only three people died, my lord," Sims reported with his usual calm efficiency, as if that were good news.

"Who?"

"Lord Vico's second cousin choked on a chicken bone, one of the kitchen staff fell into the main hearth, and Viscountess Morana's personal guard was found with a dagger in his throat."

I muttered a curse under my breath. "So not Morana or the Syndicate representative, then. Figures."

Griffin, looking as though he wanted to expel the night's mistakes along with his next breath, groaned and massaged his temples. "I don't even remember how I ended up naked on one of the outer isles. Last thing I recall is challenging someone to a duel over . . ." He squinted at me. "Was it pudding?"

"You enchanted the dessert spoons to chase people around the room," Vex informed him drily, tugging at her hood. Beneath it, her now-silver hair was a frazzled mess. "While hiding under the table giggling and declaring yourself a genius."

Griffin's frown carved a deep line between his brows.

Vex kept going. "Then you thought the lightning bridge needed 'improvements.' You vanished soon after."

"Ah," Griffin muttered, vaguely horrified. "That explains the scorch marks."

Thorne's booming laugh filled the chamber and rattled the windows. "Doesn't explain why both diplomats from the Ashen Wastes followed you across that lightning bridge."

Griffin's pallor turned nearly translucent. "I'm . . . rather concerned about what I might have promised them." He put his face in his hands. "Those horns aren't just for show."

Sighing, I made a mental note to double his supervision. Last time he tinkered with the bridges, we lost an entire platform of tax collectors. Not that

I missed them, but the paperwork had been dreadful.

Meanwhile, Sims smoothed his jacket. Once again, he was the only one unruffled by the night's debauchery. "The court was quite taken with our new Dark Lady," he said, inclining his head toward Arabella.

"Why wouldn't they be?" I replied, stepping away from the windowsill to check the Heirloom. "She was enchanting." That was an understatement; she'd been half the reason guests hadn't torn the place apart—and the main reason I'd spent most of the night struggling to maintain my usual icy composure.

I felt Arabella's stare against my back, but I refused to glance her way. After last night's . . . tactical errors, I needed distance, even if it felt like having splinters hammered under my fingernails.

"There was never any doubt," Thorne rumbled, crossing his massive arms.

"And the guests loved Lady Blackrose's spirit," Vex echoed, shooting a mischievous look at Arabella.

As one, we all turned to my bride, who stood there openly observing us, not a flicker of hesitation on her face. Even when a room full of professional villains discussed her like a prized asset, she didn't bat an eyelid. My entire staff could learn something from that spine of steel. Well, except for Thorne, who had a literal spine of steel courtesy of a blacksmith's curse. But that was another matter.

I left the Heirloom and joined the others. "Now that we're all here, we should begin."

At once, the mood in the chamber shifted. Vex, Griffin, Sims, and Thorne moved to their assigned positions. It was almost refreshing to see them snap into professional focus, like a severely dysfunctional family that only bonded over hardcore villainy.

"My lord, everything is prepared as you requested," Sims announced with a clipped bow.

I guided Arabella toward the dais. The Heirloom glowed faintly, answering our combined magic. Her lineage, my rune-carved bones . . . together we had enough raw power to blow up Skyspire just by arguing too intensely.

The thought thrilled me more than it should have.

"The ritual is straightforward," I explained, trying to keep my voice steady. "We stand in the innermost circle. I recite the activation phrase, you place the Heirloom on my head, and the marriage bond should satisfy the bloodline requirement."

"Should," she repeated, arching one of her perfect brows.

"Will," I corrected, holding her gaze. "The blood tests confirmed it."

She shot me a pointed look at the mention of those tests—still a thorn in her side, apparently—but said nothing. Instead, she focused on the Heirloom with a generous measure of doubt etched across her face. "It doesn't look like much."

"The most powerful artifacts rarely do." I extended my hand. She only paused for a heartbeat before slipping her fingers into mine. Together, we stepped into that innermost circle of runes.

The instant our feet crossed the boundary, scarlet light pulsed outward, flooding the stones in concentric circles. The air thickened, pressing in on every inch of my skin. Arabella took a sharp breath beside me, her grip on my hand turning ironclad.

Steeling myself, I positioned her on the opposite side of the pedestal. The Heirloom, a simple golden circlet, seemed to drink in the crimson glow. This was it. Years of planning, searching, and killing . . . all culminating here.

I recited the incantation, the harsh words grinding out of my throat. Dark power crackled through every rune carved into my bones, and I nearly winced at the familiar, searing pain. Internally, I cursed my mother for the thousandth time. Externally, I maintained my usual "I have everything under control" sneer.

When I finished, I nodded to Arabella. She delicately picked up the circlet. Her eyes widened as golden ripples danced across the surface, answering her presence. Then those same eyes flicked to me, gauging me, revealing a spark of—doubt? Resolve? Something that made my heartbeat stumble. She inhaled long and deep, then stood on tiptoes to place the circlet on my brow.

For one endless second, I felt nothing but the chill of metal against my hairline. Then the lines along the circlet flared. Magic surged through me, raw and heady. I sensed worldwide ley lines flickering at the edge of my consciousness, trillions of threads of energy just waiting to be molded.

Yes, I thought hungrily. This is what it would feel like to command entire realms.

I reached for that power, extending my will along the nearest ley line—

And then . . . nothing.

The magic winked out as though I had imagined it. The air lost its electric charge, and the circlet dimmed, leaving me wearing an unimposing bit of metal. My heart plummeted from my chest.

"W-what's happening?" Arabella asked in a hushed voice.

My muscles locked as I yanked the circlet off my head, scanning it with furious intensity. The lines on the surface had gone completely dark. I slammed it onto the pedestal, my hands shaking. "It didn't work," I snarled through gritted teeth, letting my shadows writhe at my feet.

Griffin approached, swallowing nervously. "Maybe a mispronounced—"

"There was. No. Error." I bit off each word. "I've studied this ritual for years."

"Then maybe the problem isn't the ritual," Vex suggested, her sharp gaze falling on Arabella. "Might be the bloodline?"

Arabella's entire body bristled.

"Her bloodline is not the issue," I snapped, my dominion magic crackling through the floor. "She carries the First Hero's blood, strong and true."

"Then what went wrong?" Vex demanded, crossing her arms.

"I don't know," I said, and I hated admitting that. The air itself felt too thin. I reeled in my shadows, noticing one of them had nearly strangled Griffin where he stood. With a sigh, I waved it back. "But I intend to find out."

I steadied myself with a deep breath. "Griffin, analyze the artifact. Check for tampering. Sims, review each step of the ritual text for any hidden disclaimers. Vex, see if we've had unwelcome interference. Thorne, lock down the tower. No one enters or leaves without my direct permission."

They hurried off to their assignments, though Thorne paused by the door. "And the lady?" he asked carefully.

I turned to Arabella. Despite everything, she'd done as requested. I couldn't even muster the rationalization to blame her for this. "Lady Blackrose stays with me," I said, letting my words resound off the walls.

Her brows lifted, but she said nothing as the others filed out. Once the door shut, I circled the now-empty pedestal. Griffin was examining the artifact. The runes glowed faintly with each step, mocking my frustration. We had the real Heirloom. We had the correct incantation. We had the right bloodline. Why the hell had it failed?

"You're certain it's not me?" she asked, voice quiet but steady.

I halted, facing her. "Yes."

"How can you be so sure?"

Memories of the test results pricked the back of my mind, reminding me how dangerously strong her magical synchronicity was with mine. I wasn't sure if telling her would be wise, or if it'd simply give her more leverage. "Let's say the resonance was . . . unusually high," I allowed. "Stronger than expected. You're not the issue."

She narrowed her eyes. "You're still withholding something."

I glanced toward the artifact again. "I am. But I don't have time for that now." I needed to gather my thoughts before throwing more revelations at her. I'd forced her into this marriage to begin with, and now I might need more from her than originally planned.

Before she could press me, Griffin cleared his throat near the workbench. "Lord Blackrose, I did a quick inspection. The artifact isn't damaged. All core enchantments are intact. It's just . . ." He grimaced. "Dormant."

"Meaning?" I demanded, coming up behind him.

"It's waiting for something," he said hesitantly. "I—I can't say what. But it's not broken."

"That's all you've got?" I slammed a fist onto the bench. Griffin and the Heirloom both jumped.

"Lord Blackrose," Arabella said softly.

I whipped around, ready to snap, but her expression wasn't mocking. I saw no pity either, just a detached understanding, as if she recognized what it felt like to have an entire future dangle just out of reach. My frustration hissed in my bloodstream, but I forced myself not to lash out at her.

I closed my eyes for a moment, exhaling. "Fuck," I muttered, which was not the eloquent statement I'd planned, but it summed things up nicely.

Griffin sagged with relief as I unclenched my fists. I fixed him with a cold look. "Stay here and study this worthless hunk of metal. Thorne will guard Lady Blackrose. No accidents, no explosions. I might still need her if we ever figure this out."

My voice came out sharper than intended, but I had no restraint left to soften it. Arabella bristled, her eyes flicking to Griffin and then back to me with the beginnings of a glare.

I turned on my heel and stalked out of the chamber. My mind churned with half-formed curses at every ancient scholar who'd written about the ritual. I was already strategizing how I'd resurrect each of them, only to kill them again for writing incomplete directions. Whatever was missing, I had to find it—and fast.

After all, I'd already married her. I refused to accept that it was all for nothing.

16

Tell Fairy Tales to Villains
(They're Surprisingly Good Listeners)

Arabella

The echo of Kazimir's rage mingled with the residual magic in the air. His parting words still rattled around my head: *I might still need her.* Every syllable dug sharp edges under my skin. In that moment, it was hard not to picture myself as a half-failed experiment lying on his workroom table.

Griffin and Thorne watched me as if I might shatter. I tried to look bored, and not as if my existence in the citadel had just been called into question.

"He really didn't mean it quite like that," Griffin said gently, hunched over his workbench. "The Dark Lord gets . . . intense when plans fail."

I couldn't help a dry laugh. "I noticed. How many people has he executed for disappointments like this?"

When Griffin and Thorne exchanged uneasy glances, I sighed. "Filling me with confidence here."

"He rarely kills useful . . . assets," Griffin offered, wincing at his own words.

Ignoring the unpleasant knot in my stomach, I moved closer to his table. On the cushion sat the object that supposedly caused all this trouble. The

Heirloom of Dominion. Latent magic still clung to it.

"May I?" I asked, gesturing toward it.

Griffin hesitated only a second before nodding. I lifted the circlet, already half convinced it would jolt me with eldritch lightning just to prove its worth. But it only felt cold and ordinary.

I turned it in my hands. A faint rose motif—thorns chasing thorns—twined around the inside. Worn with age, barely visible unless you held it up to the light. "It's . . . underwhelming," I said at last.

"Ironic, I know," Griffin said, rubbing the bridge of his nose. "But it should work. The ritual was correct, the incantations tested, the newlyweds both present . . ."

"And yet it failed," I finished, setting the Heirloom back on its cushion. "He mentioned spending a decade on this plan?"

"At least that," Griffin said, looking relieved I'd changed the subject. "He hunted it before anyone started calling him 'Dark Lord.' Legend said it didn't exist. But here it is."

"And he found it where?"

Griffin's eyes lit up with that storyteller's glimmer. "He fought a chimera guardian with three heads. They battled for three days and nights—"

"Is that true?" I interrupted. "Or just the story he tells?"

Griffin deflated. "Well, I wasn't there personally. But Thorne was."

At that, I glanced at Thorne, who inclined his enormous head in confirmation.

"So, a real three-headed beast," I murmured. "And now we have a worthless circlet that refuses to cooperate."

"It's supposed to be powerful," Griffin said, glancing anxiously at the door. "The texts were explicit about your bloodline and his dominion magic."

My gaze drifted back to those tiny roses etched in the metal. Memories surfaced of petals, vines, and a fireside story I hadn't thought about in years.

"Did it ever occur to him," I asked, crossing my arms, "that there might be more to my bloodline than a single drop of heroic ancestry?"

Griffin stilled. "What do you mean?"

I brushed a fingertip over the engraved thorns. "Roses were always central to the First Hero's power. And they weren't just decorative. Have you ever heard of 'The Hero's Garden'?"

He shook his head, and Thorne gave the barest tilt of curiosity.

Even though I was young, the story remained as sharp as the day my mother whispered the tale to me. I felt a tiny pang in my chest. My father had always mocked those tales, but they were a link to her I'd held on to.

"Will you tell it, my lady?" Griffin asked.

"All right," I said, sitting on the table like a bard about to earn her supper. "Once upon a time, when darkness shrouded the kingdom, there was a young man named Soriven who tended a garden at the edge of a village. Everyone feared the beasts skulking among the shadows, but Soriven kept growing his flowers. The villagers called him foolish."

Griffin watched me with wide eyes. Thorne, too, shifted closer, like he didn't want to miss a word.

"One day, the Shadow King's army arrived. The villagers had no warriors, so Soriven offered them seven magical roses, telling everyone to plant one by their door before sunset. They scoffed, but desperation outweighed their doubts. When night fell and the Shadow King's soldiers marched in, each rose grew into massive thorny vines that burned any foe who approached. House after house glowed with golden light. The army couldn't break through."

I picked up a few metal components from Griffin's table, arranging them into a neat circle. "Incensed, the Shadow King demanded that Soriven face him. Soriven offered one last rose as a token of peace. The King wanted to crush it, but the instant he touched the petals, something changed in him. His rage subsided—some say the rose let him see truth instead of darkness. From that day forward, the Shadow King was changed and helped heal the land."

I slid off the table, suppressing a wistful smile. "That's how Soriven defeated him, not by sword but by transformation."

Griffin set down the tool he'd been clutching. "I've never heard that version. Everything we have says the First Hero vanquished the Shadow King with raw power."

"It's easier to pitch a story about a glorious battle than one about compassion," I remarked drily. "You think Lord Blackrose researched that angle?" I lightly touched the circlet again. This time, a flicker of energy sparked under my fingertips. I jerked my hand away. "Did you see that?"

Griffin sprang forward with a muttered incantation. After a moment, he shook his head. "I don't see any change. But . . . maybe the nature of the hero's power is different than we assumed."

"Or maybe the Dark Lord's approach is all wrong. The original hero used empathy and roses, not bare-knuckled conquest." Even as the idea spilled from my mouth, it felt treasonous in this stronghold of villainy. Yet it also felt strangely satisfying to say it aloud.

Or perhaps, I thought but didn't say, the Heirloom required something more complex than just my bloodline. As the story went, the Golden Rose Fields of Solandris were originally planted from those first seven. And it was those, not a convergence of ley lines, which were responsible for Solandris's prosperity.

Griffin blew out an anxious breath while scribbling in a notebook. "He'll figure it out soon. He may be . . . intense, but he's brilliant."

I heard genuine respect in his voice. And in that moment, I realized my curiosity about these people was a lot bigger than mere survival. "Why serve him?" I asked quietly. "Why stay in a place like this?"

He chuckled. "He lets me build things others deemed 'too dangerous.' In the kingdoms, I was an outcast. Here, my eccentricities help fortify a fortress. I've made wonders no highborn lord would ever dream of allowing."

I thought of the roving lightning bridges, the biting black roses. Strange marvels, but marvels all the same. "I do understand what it's like to be dismissed," I admitted, surprising even myself.

Griffin's gaze grew wary. "Your mother . . . ? You mentioned her telling this story?"

My mood darkened at the memory. "She died when I was eight."

"I'm sorry," he said softly.

It stung less than I expected to hear his sympathy. I ran my finger along the circlet's smooth edge, the ghost of a spark tingling under my skin.

After she died, Father decided my only worth lay in how my bloodline could save our house from ruin, and he'd never allowed any of her stories to be told in his presence. Perhaps he never realized they might matter one day.

The circlet warmed against my skin before turning cool once more. Or perhaps, it was simply a story, and it'd felt good to tell it to people who seemed to appreciate it. Nothing more.

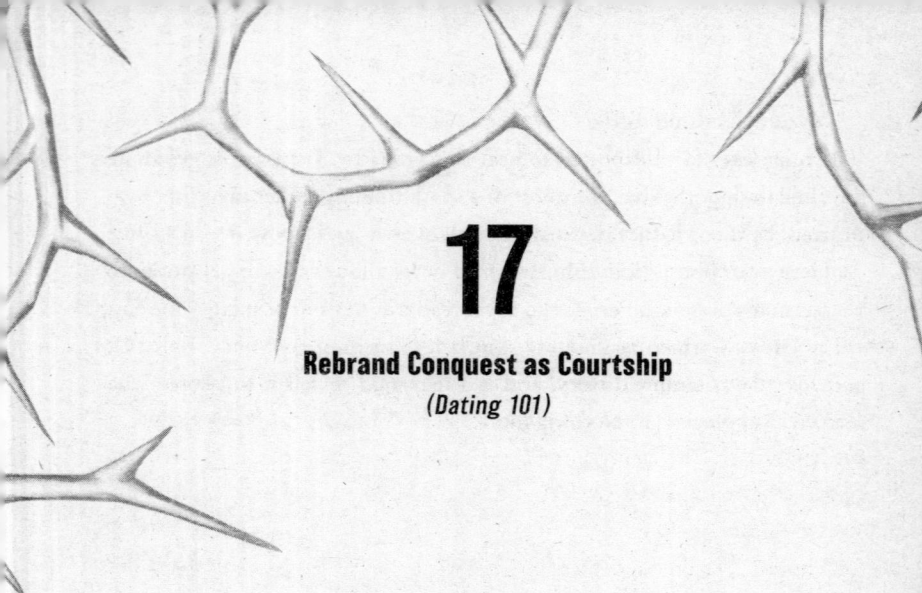

17

Rebrand Conquest as Courtship
(Dating 101)

Kazimir

I hurled a priceless artifact against the wall of my war room and watched with grim satisfaction as it exploded into dust. Ten years of my life, spilled out in one violent rush of frustration.

"Ten. Fucking. Years."

I punctuated each word by smashing another item within reach. A crystal paperweight, an enchanted compass, even a skull I'd been saving for a special occasion. All were sacrificed to the altar of my rage.

Ten years of trudging through ruins and crypts for clues. Ten years of poring over tomes older than dirt—texts that dissolved if I so much as breathed on them too forcefully. Ten years of wringing knowledge out of cowardly priests and stuffy scholars who'd rather die dramatically than share their library cards.

And now, the Heirloom of Dominion refused to bend to my will.

I stalked across the war room's wreckage and stopped in front of the ornate mirror. "Explain yourself," I growled, slamming my palm on the carved frame. Blue runes flared beneath my fingers, and the surface of the glass rippled as though it were a pool of water.

"My lord is displeased," the mirror observed in a voice as flat as stale liquor. "How may this humble repository assist?"

"The Heirloom failed to activate." I gritted my teeth and felt a fresh wave of heat ripple up my spine. "I need to know why."

"Have you tried asking it nicely?" the mirror inquired, just a little too sly for my taste.

I stood back, scowling. "You're a magical artifact, not a second-rate jester."

"One adapts to one's master," it replied archly. The surface swam with fleeting images—dog-eared grimoire pages, diagrams of ley lines, bits of ancient script. "The Heirloom of Dominion, forged by the First Hero to harness the power of the earth's veins. It requires a bearer of heroic blood and a user of dominion mag—"

"I know," I snapped, continuing to pace. Broken shards crunched underfoot. I'd destroyed half the items in the room, and I still felt no relief. "I confirmed Lady Evenfall's lineage. The ritual components were flawless. And still . . . nothing."

The mirror's reflection stilled, darkening around the edges so it nearly swallowed my image. "Perhaps not everything was correct, my lord."

I practically vibrated with the need to fling yet another priceless relic across the room. "Explain."

"You performed the binding ritual and recited the words of power. You placed the Heirloom on your brow," it said, thick with condescension. "Yet the marriage remains . . . incomplete."

I paused in the act of reaching for another potential projectile. My hand twitched. "We spoke the vows. We drank from the Cup of Dominion. I sliced off a piece of my own bone for the rings. The officiant pronounced us wed."

"Words and ceremony," the mirror replied, tone smug. "Such primal magic requires more. Especially the kind used by the First Hero."

I pressed my fists onto the desk, ignoring the stray bits of broken compass dragging against my knuckles. "The marriage must be consummated."

"Indeed," the mirror agreed, sounding far too pleased.

With a curse, I swept the maps and scrolls off the desk in a single swipe.

"That's out of the question. We have an arrangement." My thoughts leapt to Arabella and the steel in her gaze when she insisted on no forced intimacy. "I promised her I wouldn't push that boundary."

"How inconvenient for your world domination plans," it said with a mock sigh.

I whirled to face it. "Show me proof. Ancient texts. Runic footnotes. Divine graffiti scratched into a crypt wall—anything."

The surface of the mirror swirled, settling on an image of battered parchment streaked with nearly unreadable script.

"This source is obscure," it admitted, "found in the ruins of the First Hero's sanctuary. However, it states quite clearly that the union must be fully realized."

I leaned in to examine it. "One source? This entire fiasco hinges on one fragment of an ancient text?"

"Nevertheless," the mirror purred, "the Heirloom has done exactly nothing, despite everything else aligning perfectly. Perhaps you should reconsider your promise."

I hissed through my teeth. My vow to Arabella might seem trivial to everyone else, but I knew the second I broke my word, any chance of her cooperation would vanish forever.

"Damn it," I muttered, at a loss for anything else to say.

"Since when does the Dark Lord's word outshine his lust for power?" the mirror prodded.

I stayed silent. Without her genuine involvement, the entire plan might collapse faster than I could carve another rune.

Eventually, I made myself step back from the wall, squaring my shoulders as though I could literally pull my dignity back into place. "This complicates matters."

"Indeed," came the mirror's smug reply. "How will you proceed?"

My gaze shifted from the mirror to the shattered remains of my tantrum. "Carefully," I said, turning from the broken relics. "Very carefully."

...

I entered my private study about an hour after my little outburst, pretending my loss of control had never happened. Vex, Sims, Griffin, and Thorne were already inside.

Thorne quietly shut the door behind me. "I've doubled the guards around the tower, my lord," he said. "In case we're dealing with sabotage."

I leaned against the desk with a tired sigh. "We're not," I said flatly. "That would be far too easy. This is something worse."

"Shall I fetch someone from the dungeons for a sacrifice?" Sims asked, smoothing his robes as if human sacrifice were no more dramatic than a trip to the bakery.

"Tempting, but no."

Griffin opened his mouth—likely to seek further clarification—but froze when I shot him a sharp look. He made a faint squeaking sound instead, which was marginally entertaining.

The runes under my skin prickled with annoyance. "Where's Lady Blackrose?"

"She left the eastern tower a while ago," Vex said, "then wandered the halls until I escorted her back to her chambers. She's still trying to find her way around the citadel, though she won't admit it."

Sims cleared his throat. "My lord, have you determined what went wrong with last night's ritual?"

I hesitated. My staff had witnessed me do monstrous things—summon shadows to tear men limb from limb, fill entire villages with unstoppable illusions, warp reality until it sang my name. Yet somehow, telling them I had promised my wife I wouldn't force her into bed felt embarrassing.

Finally, I pushed aside my pride and said, "The Heirloom isn't a simple relic. It demands . . . a more complete bond. According to the more archaic volumes, the marriage must be fully realized."

Vex's eyes narrowed a fraction, keying into my meaning. Sims took longer to catch on, but then he nearly toppled over before muttering, "So the union requires consummation."

I gave him a thin smile. "Gold star for you."

Thorne grunted in a practical, warrior-like way. "Then you know what to do, my lord. Take her to bed. Problem solved."

Griffin's face went taut with alarm. "But forgive me, my lord, didn't Lady Blackrose try to kill you? She might not be . . . receptive."

I directed a hard stare at him, the one I typically reserved for kings right before they signed over their kingdoms to me. Griffin swallowed visibly.

"She's my wife," I said. "And the details of how I handle that are none of your concern."

Griffin, apparently wanting to dig his own grave, squared his shoulders. "Yes, my lord. It's just . . . perhaps you should consider *dating* her."

A hush descended on the room. My shadow magic stirred at the edges. "Dating," I repeated, as though the concept offended me to my very bones. "As in . . . courting my own wife."

Griffin, suicidal fool that he was, nodded. "Yes, precisely. Marriage requires continued affection—"

Vex cut in, concealing a wince. "He's been reading some truly terrible romance scrolls from the Enchanted Isles. They may not be . . . entirely scientific."

Griffin turned beet red. "I was researching relationship bonds for magical amplification purposes—"

"Enough." I lifted a hand. My runes were searing beneath my skin, an itch I couldn't scratch without incinerating someone. I drew a deep breath until I felt the worst of my anger recede.

"What matters," I said, going to the window, "is I'm dealing with it. The Heirloom will activate. We proceed with our plans."

I pointed a finger at Griffin, who almost jumped out of his boots. "You'll prepare my training room for Lady Blackrose. Bring in all relevant texts and equipment. We begin tomorrow."

His eyes lit up. "What kind of magical training, exactly—?"

"Everything," I said, remembering the way she'd tried to wield magic against me on the road. "I want to see what she can do firsthand."

I glanced at Vex and jerked my head, dismissing the others. "Stay," I ordered her. "We have further matters to discuss."

Sims, Griffin, and Thorne exited, exchanging sidelong looks that begged for any crumb of gossip. Once alone, Vex perched on the edge of the desk, crossing her ankles in a deceptively casual pose.

"You never told them about your arrangement with Lady Blackrose," she said matter-of-factly.

I gave her a hard look. "I didn't tell *you* about it, either."

Briefly, I thought her eyes shifted to my exact storm cloud hue—an unnerving trick she sometimes did—before she let out a wry grin. "I've simply observed how tense you've been since the kidnapping. Given the circumstances, I guessed you promised her something unusual."

"It's none of your concern," I repeated, though my tone lacked conviction.

Vex swung her feet against the desk, fidgeting. "Just tell her the truth about the Heirloom's requirement. Negotiate new terms."

The jeweled dagger on my desk caught my eye, and I picked it up, rolling it between my fingers. "And give her more leverage?" I scoffed. "I'd rather juggle searing coals."

"So what's your plan, then?" Vex stilled. "Force her?"

My magic flared with genuine offense, shadows creeping along the floor. "No," I snapped. "I'm not *that* kind of monster."

I tested the dagger's weight, flipping it by the hilt and catching it by the blade. A shallow cut formed across my palm, and blood welled up. The faint sting of pain kept me present, reminding me I was still in control. "I'll seduce her," I said. "She wants me. She might hate it, but I've seen the way she looks when I corner her. She's not made of ice."

Vex tilted her head thoughtfully. "That's . . . a new approach for you."

I glared. "I've seduced people before."

She shrugged. "Yes. To extract secrets or distract them before slitting their throats. This is different."

Her words stung more than I cared to admit. For a beat, I said nothing. Then I shot back, "By the time she discovers the truth, the Heirloom will be active and she'll realize I'm still her best option. She's too pragmatic to sabotage herself in retaliation."

Vex shook her head. "You really believe she'll forgive that level of manipulation? If I were her, I'd cut your throat in your sleep."

I forced a smirk, ignoring the uneasy clench in my stomach. "She can try. Not sure how successful she'd be, but I do admire her spirit."

Something flickered across Vex's face—an emotion gone before I could identify it. "All right. But you might do better with a more conventional tactic. Court her properly. Show her the person behind your fancy titles and brooding scowls."

I bristled. "And what do you know of courting?"

She held my gaze a moment longer than felt comfortable. "Enough," she said quietly, then set off toward the door. "Just remember, my lord, conquering a kingdom is nothing compared to winning over the right person."

And then she slipped away, leaving me alone in my study with the sting of her words echoing off the stone walls. I tossed the dagger aside, letting it clatter across the desk. Outside, a tempest boiled on the horizon, matching the storm in my head.

I—the Dark Lord who had toppled three kingdoms by the time I was twenty-five—now had a new, far more daunting challenge than war.

I had to woo my own wife.

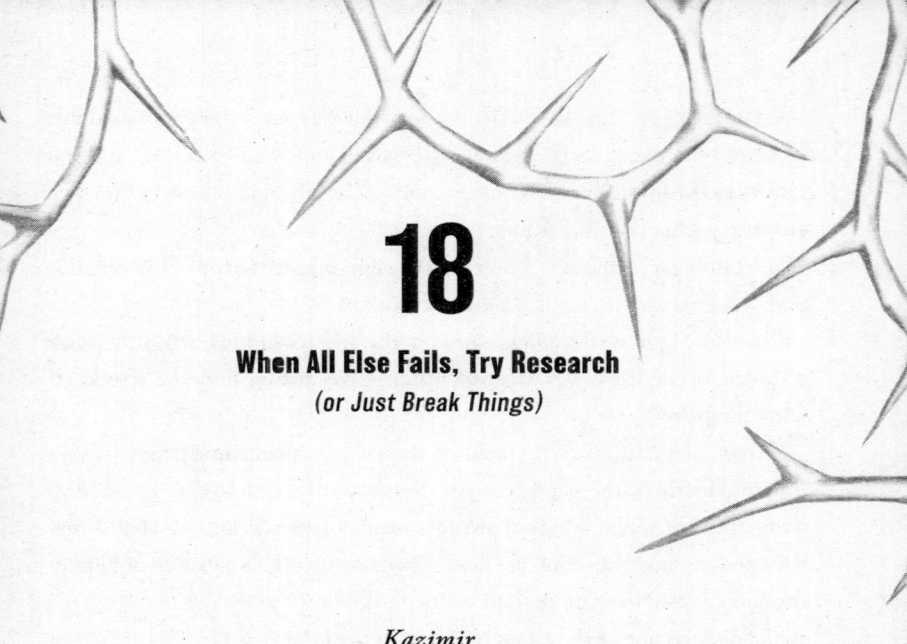

18

When All Else Fails, Try Research
(or Just Break Things)

Kazimir

"Useless." I dropped the book to the floor with a thud. Dust and brittle parchment fragments swirled around me, adding to the mess I'd been creating in my study for the better part of the night. The runes under my skin pulsed with mounting impatience. Every text I consulted repeated the same lifeless tales of the First Hero, none of them offering a single clue about the garden or transformation Arabella had mentioned to Griffin.

I'd left her in our bed hours ago. Not that she cared. The pillow wall had been in place when I arrived and was there when I left after an hour of sleep. Before I'd gone, I made a point of leaving a vase of black roses by her side. More of a taunt than an apology—after all, I'd all but told her I still needed her assistance. For power, yes, but also . . . other needs my traitorous mind refused to ignore. I flipped open another dusty text. The faded green leather cover squeaked, revealing gilded illustrations.

"The Triumph of Soriven," I read out loud, voice flat. "How the First Hero vanquished the Shadow King and claimed dominion over the Western Realms . . ."

I slammed the cover shut when I realized it was yet another glorified tale of heroic conquest. Forty-seven worthless accounts and counting, and not one included anything about compassion, roses, or forging alliances through empathy rather than brute force.

"Damn it all," I muttered, tossing the eight-hundred-year-old book aside with a bit more care than I'd shown the others.

Predawn light was seeping through the high windows when a knock sounded at the door. Vex stepped inside, gaze flitting over the wreckage. "Any progress?"

"None." I gestured at the field of ripped parchment underfoot. "Every source tells the same tedious myth. Soriven arrives, destroys the Shadow King, and triumphs. Magical swords, spells, or cursed lutes—what difference does it make?" I shook my head. "Not one mentions a garden or blooming roses as anything more than poetic fluff."

She nudged one of the fallen scrolls with her boot.

I raked my fingers through my hair. "I've combed through everything in my personal collection." Unless the answer was hidden in *Advanced Pickling Techniques of the Northern Isles*, which I hadn't gotten to yet, it'd all been a waste of time. "Magister Vellum's attempts were equally useless. Sims is in the eastern tower archives, rummaging through any half-legible scrap that might hold an alternate version of events."

Vex picked up a random manuscript from the rubble, skimming its calligraphed title. "You've enlisted the Syndicate, then?"

I nodded sharply. "I want every obscure legend, no matter how ridiculous, found and delivered here before lunchtime. Maybe one of them will tell me how to properly activate that blasted Heirloom."

"Or," she said mildly, "maybe one of them will confirm Lady Blackrose is right about needing a different approach altogether."

I dug my coat out from under a toppled atlas. My mood worsened every minute I didn't have the artifact's power under my control. "If the Heirloom demands another path like empathy or some such nonsense, then I need to know how to replicate it without giving up my entire identity. Do you see me handing out daisies and hugs?"

She tucked the manuscript under her arm. "And if you do have to . . . adapt?" she asked carefully. "Do you think Lady Blackrose might help, or will it still just be a seduction attempt?"

My mouth tightened. Vex always had a way of reading my intentions, sifting through my arrogance to find the embarrassing truth. "Let me worry about my wife." Flicking an invisible speck of dust from my coat's shoulder, I straightened. "Are the preparations for Lady Blackrose's training in order?"

Vex nodded. "All set, my lord. Griffin added additional protective wards, just in case."

"Excellent," I said curtly. "Thorne's security sweep is done?"

"He found a nest of venomous spiders in the southern passages. Nothing else."

I grunted. Ordinarily, I'd have made a dark joke about unleashing the spiders on unwanted guests, but I couldn't summon the humor. A faint ache throbbed at the base of my skull. "I'll be in the Grand Archive after Lady Blackrose's session."

Vex raised an eyebrow. "Yes, my lord. But might I ask—"

"Make her late," I cut in evenly. "I want her to show up to the training room uncertain, still catching her breath."

The exasperation on Vex's face was priceless. "You know, dominating the schedule might not be the best way to—"

"Thank you for the input," I said, turning toward the door.

She exhaled with long-suffering patience. "And who's going to deal with all these books you flung around?"

I shot her a parting smirk. "Cleanup duty suits know-it-alls, don't you think?"

She didn't dignify my remark with a response.

As I stepped into the corridor, my mind buzzed with half-formed plans—an unstoppable swirl of strategies for coaxing, cornering, and captivating Arabella Evenfall without admitting I needed anything more from her.

That, at least, was the plan. It was going to be a very interesting morning.

19

Assess Your Wife's Magic
(with Ulterior Motives)

Arabella

I woke to the mournful howl of wind circling the tower. After blinking away the haze of sleep, I peered over my pillow barricade, only to find rumpled sheets where Kazimir should have been.

A cluster of black roses waited on the bedside table—a sign that I was still a valuable prisoner-bride after the fiasco with the Heirloom? Or a prelude to ritual sacrifice? When I poked one, it snapped at my fingertip.

"Charming," I grumbled. "Even your apology flowers have teeth."

I splashed my face with cold water until I was awake enough to attempt the stairs. Then, I wrapped a silk robe around my shoulders and left Kazimir's chamber. He'd allowed me to keep my personal rooms for daytime use, and I had no intention of lingering in his domain one second longer than necessary.

My bare feet froze on the stone steps, but I didn't dare bring up more clothes. It would only encourage him.

By the time I reached my chambers, Pip was arranging breakfast on a side table. He jumped at my entrance. "My lady! I didn't expect you so early."

I raised an eyebrow. "Relax, Pip, you're not going to the dungeons for seeing me in my nightclothes . . . not today, anyway."

His face turned ghostly pale, suggesting my attempt at dark humor might need refinement. "I—I brought extra pastries. The kitchen staff said you barely ate anything yesterday."

"The kitchen is keeping tabs on my appetite?" I asked, picking up a pastry that oozed sweet fruit filling.

"They're worried you'll weaken," Pip said in a hushed rush, "especially with your magical training starting today."

A flicker of anticipation ran through me. I was about to unlock my power under the tutelage of the most nightmarishly talented sorcerer in the realm. It was *almost* worth being kidnapped for.

Pip's hands shook as he poured tea. "Thorne says it's the first time he's seen the Dark Lord so focused since the Midnight Drought incident."

"The what incident?" I slipped behind the dressing screen, where I'd already laid out clothes.

"Years ago, he redirected an entire kingdom's river system overnight—dried up lakes, left thousands starving. Fantastic, right?" Pip fidgeted with a napkin. "But people who swore fealty got their water back, so there's that."

I poked my head around the screen. "How magnanimous. So geographical rearrangement is just another weekday for him?"

"The Dark Lord rarely sleeps," Pip replied. "Cook swears he's part demon. Thorne threatened to gag her if she kept spreading rumors. Of course, no one truly knows what happened during the so-called Incident That Shall Not Be Named."

I tugged my tunic into place and stepped out from behind the screen. "Oh, a forbidden event. I like a little mystery before breakfast."

He shrugged, clearly uncomfortable. "It's just servant gossip, my lady."

I bit into another pastry and perched on a chair's edge, giving Pip a pointed look. "How long have you worked for him?"

"Almost two years," he said. "I was apprenticed to a carpenter before that, until my master was killed when Lord Blackrose's forces arrived."

I set down my pastry. "I'm sorry."

He quickly shook his head. "It wasn't Lord Blackrose. It was a guardsman who accused my master of hiding weapons when he only had tools. After that, the Dark Lord had orphaned apprentices brought here to fill positions. Said skilled labor shouldn't be wasted."

My chewing slowed. "He did?" I couldn't quite picture him as a savior of orphans, but apparently even wicked overlords had layers.

Pip forced a weak smile. "He's terrifying but fair, in his own twisted way. If you do your job well, you eat. If you fail . . . Well, you don't."

I finished my eggs, then sipped my tea thoughtfully. "And what about people outside the citadel? How are they faring under his rule?"

Pip's eyes flicked to the still-open door. "Better than most believe. At least they have protection from raiders or mercenaries. The king's guard doesn't bother much with remote villages."

"Protection, or extortion?" I challenged softly.

His gaze dropped. "My cousin's village got raided last winter and the king's men arrived too late—only to demand taxes from what little was left. People under Lord Blackrose are heavily taxed but safe, so . . . they don't mind so much."

It sounded suspiciously practical, especially for the realm's biggest villain. "You're surprisingly open with me, Pip," I observed.

"Lord Blackrose told us to answer your questions honestly. Said it'd be worse if you caught us lying." He swallowed. "He also said if we upset you, we'd get reassigned to scrubbing blood off dungeon walls."

I must have looked alarmed, because he hurried on, "But you healed my hand, so I'd have told you anyway."

A knock at the door interrupted us, and Vex swept in, her silver eyes skimming my attire and breakfast remnants in one motion.

"Good, you're dressed." She set down a pair of leather boots. "You'll need these. The Dark Lord wants you in the training chamber in ten minutes."

I scooped them up and gave them a cautious once-over before dropping into a seat to pull them on.

Vex turned to Pip. "Out." He nearly flew out the door. "We can't be late. The Dark Lord hates tardiness."

I tied the laces, rolling my eyes. "I wouldn't want to upset the schedule of the man who *kidnapped* me. Heaven forbid I disrupt his sense of order."

Standing, I tested my balance. The boots molded to my feet as if I'd worn them for years. I took a few experimental steps, admiring how they supported without restricting movement. Damn him for getting even this right. Was there anything more infuriating than a competent villain?

"Let's go," Vex said from the doorway.

I hurried to follow her out. After all, being taught magic by a possessive Dark Lord might be the strangest opportunity of my life. And if it gave me even a shred of power back, I was more than ready to seize it.

20

Trust a Villain with Your Magic
(What Could Possibly Go Wrong?)

Arabella

Vex led me through stark, utilitarian corridors I hadn't explored before, and the chill in the air intensified with every step. When we reached a twisting spiral staircase, thin veins of frost clung to the stone walls, making the descent feel more ominous than I would have liked.

"Where exactly are we going?" I asked, trying to keep any quiver of nerves from my voice.

She didn't bother looking back. "The lower levels. Lord Blackrose prefers to conduct magical training in a remote location. Less collateral damage that way."

That struck me as darkly reassuring. I quickened my pace until I walked beside her. "Has there been much 'collateral damage' in the past?"

"The north tower needed rebuilding two years ago because Griffin's experimental amplification spell collided with the Dark Lord's dominion magic."

"Collided?" I prompted.

"It exploded," Vex said, as if discussing an ill-timed rainstorm. "No one died. A few singed eyebrows and bruised egos, but that was all."

It almost humanized Kazimir to imagine him messing up so spectacularly. Of course, he'd probably done it with that signature sneer in place.

We reached a landing where the stairs broadened into a corridor streaked with silvery veins in the stone. The floor hummed beneath my boots, a faint vibration like some slumbering beast breathing beneath us.

"What is this place?" I whispered.

"It's the old foundation," she explained. "Lord Blackrose kept this part intact when he redesigned the fortress. The natural magic in the stone makes it ideal for serious spellwork."

Eventually, we stopped in front of a colossal door made of dark, iron-banded wood. Crimson runes—similar to the ones I'd seen etched into Kazimir's skin—glowed along the surface.

Vex gestured toward the door. "This is where I leave you. Only Lord Blackrose and you are keyed to these wards. Anyone else is considered an intruder."

I quirked an eyebrow. "Not even his trusted advisor gets an exception?"

She gave a half shrug. "If I tried to pass now, the wards would disintegrate me. Or worse." She nodded toward the door. "Place your palm on the center. The runes should recognize you as Lady Blackrose."

"And if they don't?" I asked.

"I'll have the unpleasant duty of telling Lord Blackrose that his brand-new bride got reduced to cinders." Her tone was drier than desert bones. When my eyes widened, she sighed. "I'm joking. The wards will probably just reject you. Now hurry."

"Your sense of humor fits this fortress." I pressed my palm gently to the door. The runes flared, bathing my skin in that same ruddy glow. A tingling sensation buzzed across my hand, and then with an almost polite shift, the door swung inward on silent hinges.

Vex stepped back. "Good luck," she offered, then turned on her heel and vanished back into the corridor.

I entered a spacious chamber with a vaulted ceiling at least thirty feet high. Braziers lined the walls, filling the area with a warm light that somehow didn't chase away the deep shadows clinging to every corner.

The floor was marked with a large circle of runes that pulsed with a soft, blue-white glow. Kazimir Blackrose himself stood at the center of that circle. He guided a sword through a series of fluid, precise motions while strands of darkness curled around his free hand like serpents waiting to strike. I nearly stopped breathing. He moved with lethal grace, a choreographed blend of physical prowess and magical menace. And—because of course the universe hated me—he was shirtless. Sweat gleamed along each etched muscle and every rune carved into his chest.

For a moment, I just stared. The swirl of shadows around him made an almost hypnotic display of threat and power. Suddenly, he spun and launched a bolt of raw shadow right at my face. I instinctively raised my arms, but the darkness broke apart inches from my skin, dissolving into faint wisps of cold air.

"You're late," he said, lowering his arm. The sword vanished into nothingness, as though it had never existed.

I worked to steady my breathing. "Vex brought me at the agreed time."

"That time was half an hour ago." He retrieved a simple black tunic from a wooden bench. I tried not to watch his every lean muscle disappear beneath the fabric. "I expected more enthusiasm."

"It was ten minutes at most," I argued, stepping forward while the door to the chamber clicked shut behind me. "I bet you told Vex to wait on purpose. You do love asserting dominance."

He made a neutral sound, not quite a denial.

"Was the sword part of your dramatic 'greeting' too?" I asked, nodding at the spot where it had vanished.

"It was my morning training," he said. "Physical exertion pairs well with spellwork. One informs the other, keeps me sharp."

I approached the circle's edge. "So you're all about synergy, then? Mind and body united, presumably for maximum destruction."

He shrugged, that predatory glimmer never leaving his gaze. "Most definitely." He extended a hand, inviting me deeper. "Step into the circle, Arabella."

My nerves lit up in a flustered combination of annoyance and something hotter. So far, he'd mostly stuck to "Lady Blackrose" or "wife." Hearing my name in that melodic baritone stirred memories of his lips crushing mine.

I tried not to shiver as I asked, "What exactly is on the agenda today? Summoning an army of the damned, turning your enemies to frogs?"

"That all sounds fun, but first, I intend to discover what you're truly capable of." Kazimir's gaze held a raw, waiting hunger that unsettled me.

I breathed in slowly and stepped inside the circle. The runes flared bright azure, humming with a contained crackle of energy. The air tasted charged, like the moment right before lightning forks across the sky.

"What exactly is this space?" I asked, trying to keep my voice even.

"A focus chamber," he said, standing so close I felt warmth radiating from his body. "If something misfires, the damage stays inside these boundaries, protecting the rest of the citadel."

"Because you'd rather not blow up your whole fortress?"

"Correct." He allowed a small, wry smile. "Though Griffin tries his best to circumvent every safeguard I create."

I glanced around, taking in the vaulted ceiling. "Why exactly do you keep him employed?"

"I value brilliance more than caution, and Griffin's results—when they succeed—are impressive." He let his gaze drift over me in a way that sizzled more than the runes. "Speaking of brilliance, what magical education did you have in Solandris?"

My heart hammered, though I kept my tone casual. "My father didn't want me studying anything beyond healing. I learned bits and pieces in secret, from stolen books."

Kazimir slowly circled behind me. I fought the urge to pivot with him. "Why did your father object?" he murmured.

My pulse fluttered. "He believed destructive magic was beneath a lady's dignity. That I was meant to nurture, not harm. He wanted a sweet, docile daughter."

Kazimir appeared in front of me again, eyes flashing with curiosity. "Yet you developed a reputation for clumsiness and chaos. Surely that wasn't all by accident."

"Sometimes I tested my boundaries," I admitted, remembering illusions I'd cast on unsuspecting guards or jewelry I'd enchanted to flicker. "But mostly, I was locked in a tower. A girl's got to keep herself occupied, right? Healing's useful, but it doesn't stitch up the part of me that wants . . . more."

He paused, letting me see the faint shift in his expression—a flicker of understanding, or maybe anger on my behalf. Then he stepped closer, so close our breath mingled. "What if you could control both healing and destruction?"

A jolt of longing tugged at me. "I suppose I'd find out who I really am."

He inclined his head. "You can't grow if you're too afraid to confront the potential darkness as well as your light."

Something tugged in my chest at his words. No one had ever embraced my magic the way he did, even if he dangled it like bait to keep me under his thumb. It was heady and far too thrilling.

"So." I forced a teasing note. "Do we start by tossing around shadow-bolts? Or maybe reanimating an undead horde to do your tedious chores?"

He allowed a small chuckle. "We'll begin with fundamentals. Then we'll see how bold you and your power truly are."

I exhaled. He wanted me to peel off my father's limiting expectations and embrace something new and dangerous? Fine. I could handle a little moral dubiousness.

I squared my shoulders. "All right, Lord Blackrose, let's see what I'm made of."

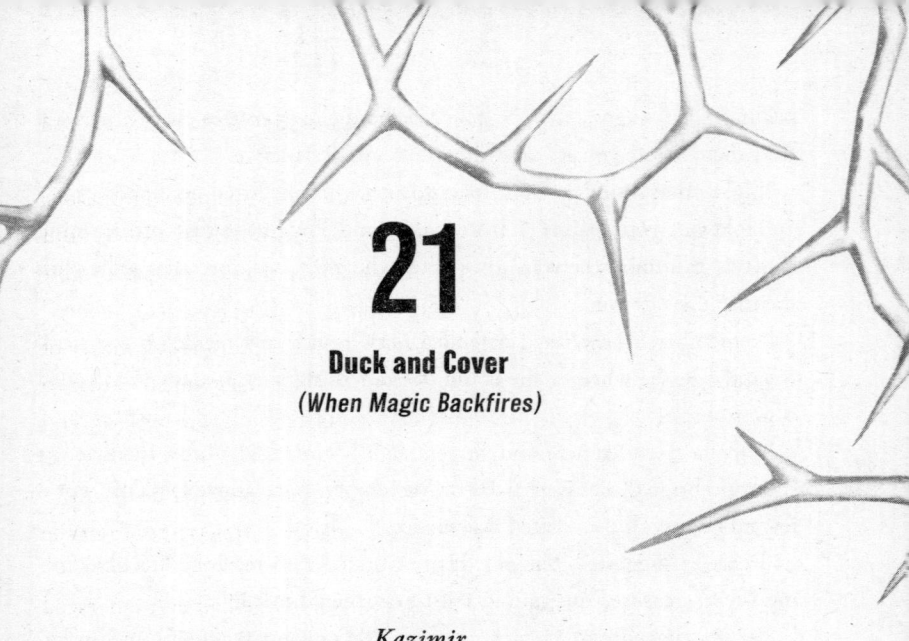

21

Duck and Cover
(When Magic Backfires)

Kazimir

Arabella stepped into the focus circle, her shoulders squared like a soldier preparing for battle. Even untrained, her magic rippled across the chamber, scattering the energies I'd spent the morning methodically calibrating.

I moved closer, forcing my frustration into a measured tone. "Let's begin with something simple."

"Define 'simple.'"

"Simpler than healing a shredded hand," I replied, giving her a pointed look. "According to Pip, you managed that without breaking a sweat."

A faint blush tinted her cheeks. "That was different. Healing comes naturally."

"All magic should come naturally," I said, conjuring a small orb of shadow that hovered over my palm. "It's about intent and will. Visualize what you want, then channel your energy to make it real. Simple."

She eyed the dark orb as though it might sprout teeth and lunge at her. "What exactly am I supposed to visualize?"

"Light." I closed my fist around the shadows, snuffing them out. "Your healing talent suggests you're good at channeling positive energy, so we'll start there before you try anything more . . . destructive."

"Light. That sounds straightforward enough." She lifted her hand.

"Hold out your palm," I instructed, "and imagine a tiny sun forming above it. Summon the warmth, picture the glow, and feed that glow with the magic inside you."

I remembered how she'd defended herself with raw magic on the road. I wanted to see whether she could do something similar under controlled conditions.

Arabella extended her hand, fingers slightly curled. Her brow furrowed as she concentrated, her gaze fixed on the empty space above her skin. For a few moments, all she created was silence.

"Relax," I suggested. She practically vibrated with tension. "It's like taming a wild creature. You gain its trust first, then direct it."

Her lips tugged into a reluctant smirk. "So now my magic is some unpredictable beast?"

"Think of it that way if it helps," I said, pleased by her humor. "Close your eyes, if that makes it easier."

Arabella exhaled and did as I suggested. She took a long breath that drew my reluctant attention to her figure, and the air above her hand began to shimmer.

"So far, so good," I murmured. "Concentrate and give it purpose."

A spark of light appeared. It trembled on the verge of extinction.

"It's . . . slippery," Arabella whispered.

"That's a typical first attempt. Nurture it. Let it feed on your will."

The spark brightened until it was about the size of a coin. Arabella's eyelids fluttered open, her face lighting in triumph. But the second her attention shifted from quiet focus to celebration, the spark swelled and flared.

A blinding flash scorched the air. I cursed as fierce light burst outward, knocking me back a step. The warded runes in the floor sizzled blue, containing most of the energy, but a wave of heat still pummeled my chest.

When my vision cleared, I realized Arabella was gaping. I also realized my tunic was on fire.

She sounded horrified. "Your shirt!"

I patted the flaming fabric, but the fire danced along the cloth faster than I could snuff it out. "Yes. I noticed."

She shifted uselessly on her feet. "Can't you, I don't know, command it to stop?"

"That's not how—" A lick of flame nearly singed my eyebrow. I let out a sharp oath and yanked the tunic off entirely, tossing it to the floor. Flare after flare ate at the remains until I smothered them with a single, vicious twist of dominion magic.

Arabella's cheeks flamed almost as brightly as those damned sparks. "I—I'm sorry. I have no idea what happened."

I silenced her with a terse motion, kneading the soreness in my chest where the flames had caused my protective runic markings to throb. Then I focused on the *still sizzling* ruins of my shirt, muttering another spell to extinguish the last flickers. Only the charred scraps remained.

"Well," I said after a beat of silence, "that was unexpected."

She bit her lip, as though trying to hold back a laugh. "I did warn you about my track record."

I glanced down at the soot marking my chest. "If you wanted to see me shirtless again, you could've asked."

"If this had been deliberate, I'd have aimed for your pants, too." The moment she said it, she choked in horror, her face turning scarlet. "I mean—I didn't—I'm just—" She covered her eyes with her hand and muttered a curse.

It was adorable watching her flail, though I refused to let it show on my face. "We can save the pants-on-fire scenario for advanced lessons," I said drily. I knelt to brush my hand over what had been my favorite tunic. "This wasn't just a mild slip in control. The power you channeled was substantial."

She folded her arms but the mortification still burned on her cheeks, making her freckles stand out. "Is that criticism or praise?"

"An observation." I rose, dusting ash from my hands. "Most novices struggle to conjure more than a flicker on their first day. You created a full-blown magical inferno."

"Lucky me," she muttered. "I have a gift for accidental destruction."

I shrugged. "No real harm done." Apart from the throbbing ache in my vaguely singed chest.

"Any chance you'd like to find another shirt before we continue?" She tried to keep her gaze up, and mostly succeeded. The faint upward twitch of her lips suggested she noticed far more than she let on.

I chuckled, impressed by her resilience. "We'll carry on. I have a few more shirts . . . if I feel the need."

But instead of finding one, I rummaged in a nearby cabinet for a crystal sphere. "Here," I said, returning to the circle. "A focus stone. It's meant to absorb and regulate raw magic. It should spare my clothes, at least for now."

Arabella accepted the crystal, cupping it between her palms and letting out a soft gasp. "It's warm."

"It responds to your energy," I told her, standing near enough to guide her without crowding her. "Try again, slowly. Pour your magic in but imagine it filling a vessel. If you visualize it as water, control how fast you let it flow."

She nodded, a resolute set to her jaw. Arms trembling slightly, she closed her eyes. The crystal's faint inner light flared from pale blue to a richer gold as she channeled her power.

"That's it," I coached softly. "Keep a steady flow."

Her breathing turned ragged, and I saw perspiration beading at her temple. The sphere glowed brighter and brighter.

"Lord Blackrose," she managed through clenched teeth, "it's—"

I reacted instinctively, knocking the crystal from her hand as I lunged forward to shield her body with mine. We both fell. The crystal shattered with a glassy pop, spraying shards in every direction. Once again, the runes on the floor blazed in response, but I still felt stinging cuts rake across my back as the fragments pelted us.

When the noise subsided, I found myself sprawled over her, chest pressed tight against her softer frame. Arabella's eyes were wide as she stared up at me. Her breath puffed against my lips, close enough to remind me of precisely how quickly our dynamic could slide from lethal to . . . less polite territory. I knew exactly how she looked in that thin nightgown, and my traitorous body flared hot with the memory.

"Are you hurt?" I asked gruffly.

Arabella managed a shake of her head, still struggling to piece together words.

I was not, nor had I ever pretended to be, a gentleman. So I stayed there a beat longer than any decent person would have, forcibly telling myself it was only for dramatic effect. Then I rolled to one side and got to my feet, ignoring the faint sting of the cuts. I extended a hand to help her up.

When she was on her feet, I dropped her hand. Every nerve in my body felt hyper-alert. "That was . . ."

"A disaster?" she blurted, brushing debris from her tunic.

"Educational," I countered. I inspected the rune work on the floor. It'd soaked up most of the blast, but scorch marks had marred the stone's smooth surface. "You have enough power to be dangerous as hell. Now we just have to manage it."

She looked at me uncertainly. "I don't understand. I controlled my healing spells so easily at home, and I used magic against your men on the road. Why is it suddenly blowing up in my face?"

"It takes practice to harness different forms of magic." I crossed my arms, conscious of the way it drew her gaze to my bare torso. "We can keep going—unless you plan to destroy the rest of my wardrobe."

She huffed out a breath, not quite a laugh. "I refuse to fail at this. If I can mend wounds, I can conjure a simple light without starting a bonfire."

I gave a curt nod. "Very well. Let's continue."

For hours, we drilled through basic exercises. Arabella practiced lighting a candle's wick without melting the wax, conjuring a gentle breeze to push a feather across the floor, warming water in a cup without boiling it. Each success came after several explosive failures, and by afternoon, we were both drenched in sweat and battered by her near-disasters.

Finally, I noticed the tremor in her arms and the deep circles under her eyes. "Enough," I said. "We've made progress. You're far more in control than you were this morning, even if I'm still worried for my clothes."

Arabella exhaled in frustration. "It's still not enough. I can't keep my grip on the magic for more than a few seconds."

"No one masters this overnight," I said. "You have raw power. Controlling it just takes time you never got under your father."

She sagged with fatigue, brushing damp hair from her face. "I'd kill for a bath right now. Possibly with scalding water."

Images I had no business entertaining flitted through my mind—her in a steaming tub, water shining on her skin. I cleared my throat and turned away to reorganize the scattered training elements. "Would you like Vex to escort you back to your chambers?"

She shook her head. "I'll manage."

"Try not to set the halls ablaze, will you?"

She started for the door, then paused. "Lord Blackrose?"

I lifted a brow, waiting.

Her gaze shamelessly dragged over my chest, lingering on the faint soot smudges. "Next time," she said, a flicker of wicked humor lighting her eyes, "maybe wear something less flammable."

With that, she walked out, leaving me alone in the circle. A chuckle rumbled in my chest. Seducing her might be easier than expected, if I could avoid being cremated in the process.

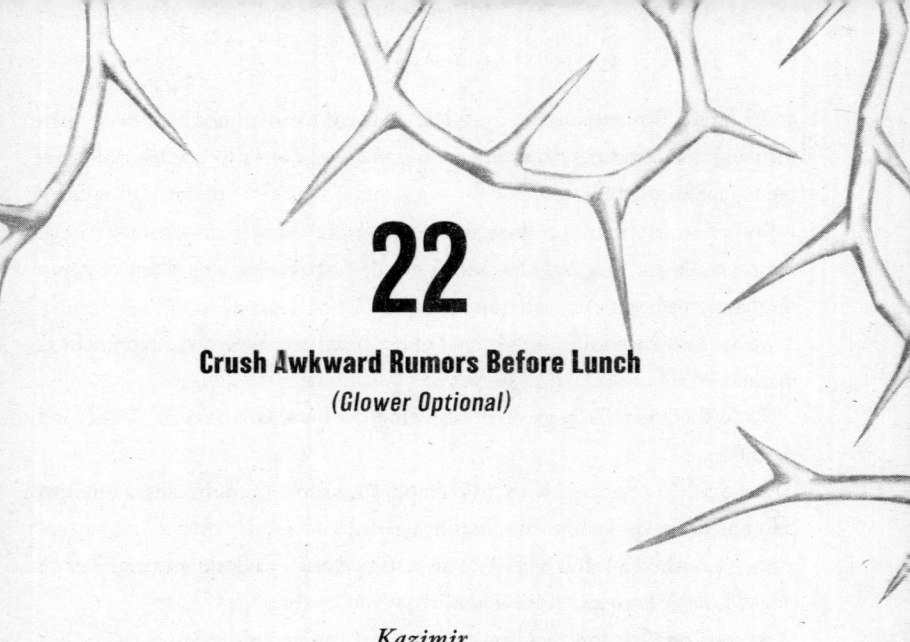

22

Crush Awkward Rumors Before Lunch
(Glower Optional)

Kazimir

I stood at the base of my tower like some overeager suitor, a sharp breeze tugging at my cloak. Several days had passed since Arabella had set me on fire. Since then, I'd commissioned a new tunic made from fire-retardant fabric (the tailor's barely restrained eye roll when I requested that modification still annoyed me). In the interim, my wife and I managed two more sessions, lighter on flames but heavier on the tension that lingered between us.

Outside those training hours, though, I barely saw her. My sources—Vex, with her wry reports, and Pip, who babbled anxiously—kept me informed that Lady Blackrose roamed the citadel with what appeared to be genuine curiosity.

I knew full well she wasn't attempting an escape. If she were, I'd have caught a whiff of half-baked schemes or sudden inquiries about the wards. Besides, she had no father's estate worth returning to, no friends I knew who would—or could—hide her, and she showed too much genuine excitement during training.

Now, however, the practical side of me saw the potential for mishaps, and a guided tour seemed . . . prudent. I'd sent word an hour ago with firm instructions: *Dress as a dark lady, wear a cloak, and meet me outside my tower.* No explanation.

But when Arabella appeared at the bottom of the winding stair, I had to force myself not to stare. She wore a hooded cloak over a dark velvet gown that clung to her in ways that made me regret our agreement all over again. Aside from the wedding ring forged of my bone, she wore no jewelry, which made it all the more striking.

"Lord Blackrose," she greeted, adjusting the hood so it pooled against her shoulders.

"Kazimir," I corrected with mild emphasis, watching for her inevitable eye roll. She obliged, if somewhat half-heartedly.

She smoothed a velvet sleeve. "You said to dress as a dark lady and wear a cloak. Don't blame me if it's darker than you intended."

"It suits you," I said, holding out my arm. "Come along, then. Time for a tour."

She took my arm but shot me a suspicious look. "A tour of the citadel? How unexpectedly considerate."

"Would you like to inspect our dungeons first?" I asked. "We could start with the darkest cell, if that feels more traditionally villainous."

She almost smiled. "Lead on, my lord."

I guided her onto the broad stone walkway leading from the tower. Beneath us, clouds drifted in and out of view. If she felt uneasy about the dizzying drop, she concealed it well, though her fingers tightened slightly on my arm.

"You promised me more freedom," she said as the wind whipped a lock of hair out of her braid. "So I've been familiarizing myself with your fortress."

"Yes, I know."

She shot me a mild glare. "No one is *supposed* to be spying on me."

"They're not," I said confidently. "But this is my citadel, and I hear about anything notable that happens within it."

She sighed, conceding the point. "I'm not trying to escape, if that's what worries you."

I dipped my head in acknowledgment, remembering all the ways I'd verified that truth. "I believe you. Though there are certain places you should avoid unless you'd like a face full of serpents or illusions. The North Tower is one of those places. Several minions lost fingers in the aftermath of Griffin's last incident."

She paused to brush the hair out of her face. "You do realize forbidding something only makes it more tempting?"

I shrugged. "Go ahead, then. When you're screaming from a barrel of snakes, I won't come rescue you."

She scoffed, then flashed me a wicked grin. "Perhaps the snakes are the ones who'd need rescuing."

I resisted the urge to laugh. "Fair enough."

We reached a place that overlooked the central courtyard. "Welcome to the Inner Sanctum proper," I announced. Five spired towers stood equidistant from each other in a vast star formation, connected to one another by a strong outer wall. I pointed them out in turn: "Our tower in the west, the Observatory in the southwest, where you've already caused mischief—"

"I wasn't going to tell you about that."

"Griffin always caves. He can never keep a secret from me. And now you, apparently."

Arabella sniffed, only half repentant, before I continued pointing out the remaining towers. "Gate Tower in the southeast, the Heirloom's tower in the east, and the Northern Labs you should steer clear of. The courtyard here anchors the wards."

She eyed the massive pentagram carved into the black stone. "A giant pentagram inside a villain's fortress—subtle."

"The fortress predates me," I said with a shrug. "Though I've taken creative liberties to fit my purposes. Functionally, the structure is almost impossible to breach, and that's before all sorts of nasty ward work I've planted into the foundation."

She turned her gaze to the distant isles suspended in clouds. "And this is only the main fortress, right?"

I nodded. "We call them the Outer Court. The Great Hall is out on a separate isle, as you know, and it also houses the guest quarters. There are other isles for staff and kitchens, stables, and so on. Each platform is linked by those lightning bridges."

"The entire fortress is incredible. But aren't you worried it'll one day just . . ." She fluttered her fingers in a downward gesture. "Fall out of the sky?"

"I have contingencies in place. I'll share them when it suits me, or if we start plummeting."

She faced the watery sunlight cutting through the clouds. "How many people stay here?"

"About five hundred on average," I said. "Soldiers, staff, a few insane inventors . . . The number fluctuates whenever Griffin's contraptions backfire."

She glanced at me sharply. "People aren't numbers."

"That's precisely what Vex keeps arguing," I said drily. "We track them by name now, so I suppose that's progress."

She let out a short laugh but didn't press. We continued along the walkway, heading for the High Gardens—a glass-enclosed conservatory nestled between the western and southwestern towers. Sunlight, filtered through rolling clouds, cast the greenhouse in ethereal light. Within, raised stone beds brimmed with bizarre flora, and thick vines curled along the pathway, swaying toward us as we passed.

"Don't wander here alone at night," I noted. "Some of these plants like to grab."

Arabella took a pointed step back. "Let me guess—a team of terrified gardeners maintains all this?"

"Terrified or exasperated, depending on your perspective," I replied. "They insist my very presence makes the plants anxious."

She looked amused. "Plants don't have emotions."

"Try explaining that to the trembling ferns," I retorted.

We exited at the far end, crossing a stone walkway that circled toward the Gate Tower. "Just like the bridges, the entire fortress can appear and disappear at will," I explained. "At least that's what the rumors say. In truth, we can move the citadel slowly and with great effort. It's still enough to terrify superstitious villagers who think it hovers overhead waiting to devour them."

She nodded thoughtfully. "My father tried to ban the servants from telling me stories about the Dark Lord, which guaranteed I heard every lurid detail."

That sparked my interest. "And what delirious rumors were you fed?"

Arabella leaned against the stone battlement, wind tugging more hair loose from her braid. She'd already given up trying to contain it. "That you had every inch of skin covered in unholy tattoos." She glanced at my chest. "But thanks to your extreme lack of modesty, I can confirm it's scars instead of ink."

That spark of wicked amusement in her eye was becoming dangerously addictive.

"Disappointed?" I asked, voice dropping suggestively.

She colored slightly but managed a wry smile. "Still withholding judgment."

I chuckled. "What else have they said?"

She pursed her lips. "That you collect virgins from border villages."

I blinked. "Collect them? To do what, exactly?"

"Sacrifice them during the full moon," she answered, trying to keep a straight face.

I let out a genuine laugh. "If I needed blood, I wouldn't go searching for the rarest subset of the population."

She flashed a grin and pressed on. "Then there's the rumor you can read minds."

"That one I encourage," I admitted. "It keeps people honest. But reading minds is simplistic. Reading *people*—their fears, their ambitions, their tells—that's a far more useful skill."

Arabella tilted her head. "Can you read me, then?"

The question was loaded with challenge. I made a show of studying her, though I'd been forming an answer since the day I captured her. "You're a survivor who's learned to turn society's assumptions into tactics. You are far cleverer than you let on, and you know how to weaponize being underestimated. You'll do anything—*anything*—when cornered. Including accidentally wielding volatile magic," I added, unable to resist the dig.

A brief flicker in her eyes told me I'd struck close to truths she wasn't used to exposing. She breathed out slowly. "I hate that I can't deny it."

The wind turned cold, and Arabella shivered despite the wards that kept the worst of the high-altitude temperatures at bay. I paused in a small archway while she pulled her hood up.

"Any other scandalous rumors?" I asked as we resumed walking.

"Many." She pulled a face. "There seems to be a preoccupation with virgins in general, though. Like the one that claims you can shift into a great black wolf and . . . well, I better not tell you in case it offends your villainous sensibilities."

"How considerate of you," I said, whirling to face her. Caught off guard, she stopped just short of running into me. "Though if you're curious about just how depraved my sensibilities can be . . ." I let my voice trail off, watching her reaction.

Arabella's eyes widened slightly, but then she sidestepped me and continued on her way. "*I* thought taking their virginities as a wolf seemed counterproductive," she called over her shoulder, "if you also planned to sacrifice them."

Amused, I hurried to catch up. "So you admit you've been thinking about me, Lady Blackrose. That *is* scandalous."

She shot me a practiced glare, which did nothing to hide the delightful flush staining her cheeks. "They also say 'Blackrose' is just another lie," she continued. "That you changed your name along the way."

"Names can be chosen," I allowed, "and they can be changed if one's past is worth discarding."

Curiosity flickered across her face, but I offered no more, and the wind made further conversation difficult without shouting.

At the Gate Tower, the guards snapped to attention, almost as deferential to Arabella as to me. I'd thrown one of them in the dungeons for leering, yet gossip had fixated on how she'd pressed a blade to my throat.

She'd earned their approval without uttering a single syllable in their direction—an economy even I had to admire.

We continued over the lightning bridge to the Great Hall's imposing black doors. I paused before entering. "You'll need to come here with me sometimes, to project a united front. That's part of your role as Lady Blackrose."

She exhaled in a resigned sort of way. "Aren't you afraid I'll set someone on fire?"

"I like your thinking," I said in a low voice, "but incinerating minions tends to make people too terrified to function. Besides, if I'd wanted to keep you hidden away like a guilty secret, I wouldn't have thrown that ostentatious wedding."

Without waiting for her retort, I pushed open the doors.

"Do I have to do anything?" she asked, smoothing her windswept hair self-consciously.

A handful of staff and soldiers milled about, but quieted when they saw us.

"Sit there and be astonishing," I said quietly. "And let me terrify anyone who looks at you the wrong way."

"You're a truly gracious host," she murmured.

The guard at the dais announced, "Lord Blackrose and Lady Blackrose!" A hush swept the hall. Eyes flicked to Arabella.

I guided her up the steps, savoring the moment. As she hesitated at her new seat next to mine, I bent near her ear. Letting my breath fan across her skin, I pressed a none-too-innocent kiss to the curve of her neck. "You look every inch a dark lady," I whispered, voice pitched so only she could hear. "It suits you better than you think."

The faint hitch in her breath was reward enough. I took my seat, noting the curious stares with mild satisfaction. For the next half hour, I uttered sentences of doom and issued verdicts, fielding petitions from farmers, merchants, and those incompetent enough to suspect magical vermin among their livestock. Anyone looking at my wife too intently felt my dominion magic hum in the air. Not a single soul dared question her presence or her status as my bride.

Throughout it, I kept glancing at Arabella. She sat with queenly calm, not speaking unless necessary. And whenever my gaze caught hers, a tiny spark flashed—a trace of amusement or rebellious fury. I couldn't quite decide which.

When the last complaint ended, I rose and offered her my hand. Once we were free from prying eyes, she pulled her hand away.

"All that posturing," she said. "Was it truly necessary?"

"Completely," I said, adjusting my cloak. "It makes you less of a target. If they realize I'm protective, they won't dare test you."

She regarded me with a faint frown, then huffed. "And that kiss? Another public show?"

I let just a little bit of heat into my gaze for her benefit. "A tactical display of possession," I answered. "As per our agreement."

Arabella gave a small shake of her head. But as she turned toward the lightning bridge, I sensed the subtle satisfaction in her posture, like she'd claimed some power in that hall. I nearly called after her, intending to suggest we explore the deeper parts of the citadel. But a guard jogged up with a quick salute.

"My lord," he said. "Urgent message from patrols in Arvoryn—bandits are raiding the border villages. We suspect Solandris's interference."

Anger coiled up my spine. *Solandris again.* "Very well. I'll handle it immediately."

He bowed, casting a wary glance at Arabella before hurrying off. She stared after him, then turned to me, eyes filled with curiosity. "Bandits?"

"Nothing too dire," I lied. "But I need to see them crushed."

Her posture shifted. "You'll go personally?"

"I usually do, when warranted," I said, letting steel bleed into my voice. "I doubt it'll take long."

She hesitated a beat before saying, "Don't get yourself killed, kidnapper. You owe me the rest of that 'grand tour.'"

I let out a quiet laugh. "Death doesn't suit me. I'll be back soon . . . with new horrors to show you." I brushed my fingertips lightly against her hand, feeling that stubborn spark again, before pivoting away.

The citadel demanded my unwavering attention. So did Arabella, in a way that unsettled me more than any bandit threat. But for now, I'd handle the day's crisis and hope no brand-new disasters awaited me upon returning.

No rest for the wicked—or for a villain hopelessly intrigued by his troublesome bride.

23

Save Villages, Steal Loyalty
(and Other Acts of Accidental Heroism)

Kazimir

I sank my blade into the bandit's chest, savoring the resistance of muscle and bone before the inevitable give. His eyes went wide, as though death was an unexpected plot twist in his chosen career path. Blood bubbled at his lips before he slid free of my sword, collapsing into the mud alongside his unfortunate companions.

"Mercy," rasped the last survivor. A burly brute with a battered face and a broken arm, he squinted through a gash that nearly took out his right eye. "Please, m'lord."

I crouched to press my blade against his throat. In the hush that followed, I heard only the ragged sobs of villagers hidden in their homes. The air stank of fear, smoke, and fresh blood.

"Mercy," I repeated thoughtfully. *Did we cover that in Villainy 101? I think I was absent that day.*

"We were just . . . ," the bandit babbled. "Following rumors. Trying to make a living."

I pressed the steel deeper, cutting a shallow line. "On whose orders?"

"N-no one specifically . . . Just h-heard these villages were easy targets. No soldiers, no protection."

"Where did you hear that?"

He hesitated, pupil flickering with the impulse to lie. I angled the sword. His breath caught. "The truth buys you a quick death," I said softly. "Lies end in a far messier one."

"A man—fancy Solandrian accent, paid us in gold. He claimed these settlements had no guard. I swear that's all I know!"

I believed him. Standing, I regarded the bandit with deliberate calm.

"You promised m-mercy," he stammered.

"I promised nothing," I corrected. "But I am efficient."

With a single fluid motion, I separated his head from his shoulders. Quick, clean, final. I felt a stirring of triumph, the runes carved into my bones heating beneath my skin. This sort of fieldwork always brought a rush—raw proof that my dominion magic and steel did more than feed nightmares.

It was also excellent exercise. I wondered, fleetingly, if Arabella might appreciate how I looked after a bloody scuffle—sweat clinging to my skin, the metallic tang of violence in the air. Or would she be repulsed by the sight, that flash of disgust snuffing out any spark of attraction? Hard to say with her.

Thorne strode up, his broad shoulders spattered in gore. "That's the last of them. Twenty-three total."

"Any casualties on our side?"

"Minor wounds. Nothing to fret over."

I nodded in satisfaction, surveying the carnage. My three shadow warriors—summoned from the dark corners of my own runes—drifted among the bodies, silent and lethal as ever. With a flick of my hand, I dismissed them. They twisted into wisps of shadow and seeped under my scarred flesh, leaving me with a jolt of power that crackled cold across my nerves.

"String them along the road outside the village," I said evenly. "To send a message."

Thorne gave a curt nod. "And the villagers?"

I cast my gaze over the ramshackle huts. Every door and window remained barricaded, the people too afraid to see what fate awaited them. "What do people think of the Dark Lord these days?"

"Probably that you roast people alive and bathe in the blood of virgins," he replied solemnly. "Same old story."

I almost chuckled at the memory of Arabella telling me something similar only a couple days ago. Still, I quite liked rewarding terror with a firm dose of reality.

"Out!" I barked at the huts. "Now!"

Slowly, doors opened, revealing pale, hollow faces. A few men carried makeshift weapons, more posture than threat. Women shielded children behind them, trembling. An elder in a worn robe shuffled forward, determined despite the stoop of his shoulders.

"You're the Dark Lord," he said calmly.

I inclined my head. A ripple of tension went through the crowd.

"Why help us?" the old man asked. "The viscountess—"

"Is spread thin," I interrupted. "Now, how long have these raids gone on?"

"Three weeks," he answered. "They started small—stealing livestock, pilfering storehouses. Last week, they torched the mill in Oakhollow and murdered the miller's family."

I frowned. "And Viscountess Morana sent no soldiers?"

"She recalled most of them north," someone else muttered darkly.

"And what of King Auremar?" I pressed. "Solandris is only a breath away."

A bitter laugh escaped a tired-faced villager. "He's busy polishing his towers. We've sent messengers—none returned."

I took another step, letting them all see the gore staining my sword. "And yet I stand here, not Auremar or Morana. Ironic, wouldn't you say?"

No one dared laugh. They just stared, fearful and half hopeful.

"What do you want of us?" the elder ventured.

I liked his directness. "Simple. Trade with my territories. Pay me tribute—crops, livestock, resources. I'll ensure no more bandits trouble you."

"You want us to abandon the viscountess."

"If you prefer being ransacked to aligning with me, go right ahead." I swept a glance over the ragged villagers, letting silence underscore how close they'd come to annihilation.

The hush stretched before the elder drew a trembling breath. "She won't like it," he whispered.

My expression turned cold. "Leave her to me."

At that precise moment, hoofbeats cut across the tension. Soldiers galloped in from the eastern road, bearing the silver serpent crest of Arvoryn. The villagers parted, uncertain whether to hide or watch. I remained where I stood, sword still in hand, as Viscountess Morana dismounted.

A tall woman with braided dark hair and calculating eyes, Morana radiated an aloof elegance. No fewer than five expertly crafted daggers were displayed on her belt, with more likely hidden within her clothing. When her gaze alighted on the dismembered corpses, shock slid over her features before she masked it with chilly composure.

"Lord Blackrose," she greeted with forced cordiality. "You've been busy."

"Cleaning up your bandit infestation," I replied. "They were having a grand time terrorizing your villages."

Her jaw tightened, but her voice remained even. "My forces have been engaged elsewhere. And you took the liberty to handle it without informing me?"

"It didn't require your permission," I said, voice dangerously smooth. "Unless you'd rather the bandits continue making a hobby of murdering villagers."

Morana's attention flicked to the townsfolk behind me, then back. "We can discuss this privately."

I cast a final glance at the elder. "Gather your people. Distribute the bandits' stolen supplies. My men will see to a portion of your needs." The older man bowed gratefully.

Morana and I headed to the battered village tavern, a creaking building that smelled of stale beer and old grease. Inside, the innkeeper anxiously handed us two mugs of watery swill. I took one sip, nearly gagging on the sour tang.

"It's been a while since I tasted a brew that makes me appreciate stale swamp water," I said, pushing the mug away.

Morana glowered. "You're overstepping, Kazimir. These are *my* lands."

"You're welcome," I returned evenly, leaning forward. "For saving your people while you were . . . otherwise occupied."

Her eyes flashed, but she kept her tone level. "My scouts reported trouble in the north. I had no choice but to pull forces—"

"Allowing these bandits through your territory, unchallenged, possibly aided by Solandris. Either your intelligence is lacking, or there's a more sinister game at play." I shrugged. "Either way, I provided the solution."

She folded her arms, gaze tight. "And what do you want in return?"

"An addendum to our existing treaty," I said, unfazed by her scowl. "I've just promised these villages my protection. And certain trade."

Realization flickered across her face, followed by bitter resignation. Agreeing would deepen my hold over Arvoryn. Refusing would expose her as heartless in front of her own subjects. Morana was too cunning not to see the trap snaring tight around her.

"Fine," she said, voice clipped. "We can discuss the details at my estate. Soon." Her eyes lingered on mine. "Bring your new wife. Or . . . come alone, whichever you prefer most."

Ah. There it was—the real source of her tension. Not just my incursion into her territory, but my recent marital status.

"Lady Blackrose has been occupied," I replied casually. "But I'll be sure to pass along the invitation."

"If I'd known you were in the market for a bride when your men came through last week, I might have negotiated better terms," she said, bitterness creeping into her tone. "A royal wedding is quite the event to spring on one's allies without warning."

I regarded her coolly. "Our arrangement was never meant to be long-term, Morana. You knew that from the start. We had fun testing which of your daggers were properly balanced for throwing at moving targets, but that was never going to end with me down on one knee."

Her lips pressed into a thin line, but she tried for one last volley. "We had fun. We could again."

I let out a low laugh. "We both know you're more interested in power than pleasure. I have a new bride. You have a husband whose best talent is staying out of your way. Let's not pretend there's anything more here than political convenience."

Her gaze hardened. "I see. Well, remember that loyalty can shift. Quickly."

"So can my mood," I said softly, letting a sliver of dominion magic snap through the air. The tavern's rafters groaned ominously.

She relented, turning her attention to the swirling dregs of her mug. "You suspect these raids weren't random?"

"Someone told those bandits exactly where to strike," I confirmed. "Gave them gold, knowledge of your troops' movements."

Morana's anger simmered. "If you're implying—"

"I'm implying someone—maybe not you—wants you destabilized. Perhaps they thought you'd be too distracted by your own intrigues to notice."

Her hand shifted involuntarily to her bandaged arm, still healing from the brawl at my wedding feast. "Your concern is . . . touching."

I snorted. "You keep Arvoryn peacefully buffering my domain from Solandris. If you decide to sabotage yourself with foolishness, that's your choice, but you're more useful alive than dead. I'm sure you'd like to keep it that way."

She rose, tension vibrating under her skin. "I should return to my men."

I stood as well, ignoring the watery ale. "I'll be leaving a small garrison in each village. Consider it me making sure the roads stay safe."

Her jaw clenched, but she offered no argument. She only paused at the door, leaning in low enough that no one else would overhear. "I've heard Solandris troops were spotted near the pass. Not the usual patrols. Something more secretive."

I kept my expression cold. "Does that warning come freely?"

"Call it a gesture of our continued friendship." She slipped on her riding gloves. "Despite recent changes."

I inclined my head, not bothering to hide a smirk. "Your goodwill is noted."

She walked back outside. The villagers watched with an odd mix of awe and suspicion, their loyalties drifting inexorably toward me. Morana felt it too, that subtle shift in the crowd. She mounted her horse and forced a smile for their sake.

"Thornwick!" she called out. "Know that Lord Blackrose and I will ensure your protection."

They nodded, but it was clear who had already saved them. Morana and her retinue galloped off, and that was the end of their half-hearted performance.

I exhaled a quiet breath, half irritated, half amused. Morana was growing more resentful. Or jealous. She'd never been one for genuine attachment, but apparently the idea of me standing beside someone else—claiming real power through a marriage bond—gnawed at her. She'd be trouble in the future. I'd need to decide precisely how to handle her soon.

"Orders, my lord?" Thorne asked.

"Leave six men to guard the village. Make sure the locals know they're under my protection."

In the late afternoon, we traveled to a hidden clearing where my enchanters activated a portal. A translucent shimmer expanded, turning into a swirling gateway.

On the other side, I emerged atop Portal Isle—my citadel's primary nexus to different corners of my domain. Guards straightened at attention and Vex appeared from the gloom, silver hair reflecting the portal's glow.

"Back in one piece, I see," she observed. "The bandits?"

"Neutralized," I said flatly.

"And Viscountess Morana?" Her voice held just enough curiosity to imply she suspected our reunion could have sparked more than conversation.

"Alive," I said drily. "For now."

We crossed into the inner courtyard, moving away from the scattered courtiers trying to catch my attention. Rumors of my marriage and the potential power shift had them all scrambling.

"And how's my wife?" I asked, trying to sound indifferent.

"She trained alone this morning," Vex answered. "Then kept to her chambers. Also, your commission for her is complete."

"Good," I said, stripping off my bloodstained cloak and handing it to a startled attendant. "Send word for dinner in the private hall. Inform Lady Blackrose she'll be joining us this evening."

With that, I marched onward, half focused on Arabella's inevitable scowl when I presented her with what I'd had made. Not that I *cared* about winning her approval, of course. It was strictly professional curiosity about whether she'd appreciate my gift or try to strangle me with it.

Marriage, it turned out, was an annoyingly complicated arrangement.

24

Seduce Her with Gifts
(and Broken Machinery)

Kazimir

An hour later, I paused outside Arabella's chambers with the midnight blue leather training gear—supple, enchanted, and ruinously expensive—draped over my arm. I was a man of many hobbies, but surprising my reluctant bride had rapidly become an unexpected favorite.

I was, however, still the Dark Lord, not some shy errand boy. Knocking was for peasants and heroes. So I opened the door and stepped inside without the courtesy of a warning.

Arabella's room had changed since her arrival. Once stark and impersonal, it now felt almost cozy: a book lay open on its spine atop a chaise, wildflowers tussled gently in a porcelain vase, and the ever-present black roses infused the air with their alluring, dangerous scent. Standing by the tall window, Arabella turned at the soft click of the latch, her hair catching the twilight in shimmering waves.

"Lady Blackrose," I greeted, moving closer than necessary. "I trust your solo training went well, since the fortress is still intact."

She gave me a quick once-over, like she was checking if I was still in one piece. Then her face returned to its usual combative set. "What do you want, Lord Blackrose?"

I lifted the folded leather gear. "I come bearing a gift. Before I escort you to dinner."

Her eyebrows shot upward. "A gift?"

I let the silence spool out for a moment, enjoying her faint hint of curiosity. "Training leathers," I clarified, extending the bundle. "It occurred to me that since you keep turning my shirts into ashes, you might want something durable—and flame-resistant—for yourself."

She hesitated, then reached out. The moment her fingertips brushed the supple leather, I spotted the tiniest flicker of delight in her eyes. Strange how that small flash made my chest tighten . . . though I needed to keep that tidbit under lockdown.

I cleared my throat. "They're enchanted to resist fire and lessen impact."

She swallowed, expression growing thoughtful. "I . . . Well, I've never worn anything like this before."

I waited, giving her space to elaborate if she wished.

"My father always insisted on dresses," she said finally. "Even when riding, he'd demand I sit sidesaddle."

"Your father sounds like a world-class prick," I said with perfect sincerity.

A short laugh escaped her, too abrupt to be entirely forced. "Yes," she agreed. "He is."

I tapped the leather. "Tonight's dinner is private—just my advisors. Informal enough. You can wear these if you want."

She gave me a little smirk. "Right . . . while you plot the realm's downfall between one course and the next?"

"Don't forget the part where we debate infrastructure," I said. "Now, try them on."

She narrowed her eyes, searching for a trap. I did love that look on her. But for once, I just stepped back, crossing my arms as if bored. "I'll step out if you prefer."

Arabella blinked, probably not expecting me to give her an ounce of privacy. That was precisely why I offered it. If Vex's talk of "courtship" had taught me anything, it was to keep her guessing.

After slipping outside the door, I propped a shoulder against the cold stone wall and tried not to dwell on how surprising it felt to be . . . considerate. It wasn't that I was turning into a hero. I simply enjoyed messing with my wife's expectations. That was it. Definitely no stirring, inconvenient warmth in my chest at the idea that I might actually please her with this. No, absolutely not.

Finally, she emerged. My pulse stuttered. The midnight blue leather hugged her curves, making her look more feminine and more dangerous all at once. My personal black rose crest—stitched in dark thread—adorned the collar and the subtle detailing along her back. Coupled with her boots, she looked every inch the formidable Lady Blackrose I'd envisioned. Actually, she looked better than anything I'd dared to picture, and I felt an uncoiling heat in my gut that I refused to let show in my expression.

"Well?" she asked, rotating just a fraction, as though both proud and self-conscious. The interplay of her golden hair against the dark leather sent a satisfying jolt through me.

I nodded. "They fit perfectly," I managed. "The enchantments will align with your magic when you need them."

She ran her hands down the jacket, almost . . . shy? A faint smile tugged at her mouth. "They feel strong."

"They suit you," I said lower, meeting her gaze. The corridor felt charged with the tension that had become familiar—and maddening—between us. I found myself picturing her in that gear, hurling spells at me, grinning wickedly.

Arabella glanced away first, forcing a half laugh. "I suppose it's strange to wear these at dinner."

I lifted a brow. "You are Lady Blackrose. If anyone disagrees, you can set them on fire."

A flicker of relief crossed her eyes so quickly, I almost missed it. She likely expected criticism if she strayed from standard noble dinner attire. She'd yet to realize I didn't care for anyone else's standards. I was the standard.

With that, we walked side by side down the stairs, the stone echoing with our footsteps. I couldn't decide which was more intoxicating: the flicker of gratitude she tried to hide or the subtle way her presence made my blood hum.

It made me wonder if she found this pull between us equally addictive.

I smothered that particular curiosity before it could grow legs. After all, analyzing feelings was dangerously close to having them. The Dark Lord didn't *wonder* if his bride found him attractive; he made damn sure of it, preferably while keeping his own inconvenient reactions to himself.

"I suppose I should thank you," Arabella said finally, her voice softer than usual. Then, as if catching herself, she added, "Though I'm sure you had some nefarious purpose behind it."

I paused to let my gaze sweep pointedly over her curves. "I assure you," I said in a low murmur, "every purpose I have is nefarious. But I'll let you unravel the rest of my intentions at your leisure, Lady Blackrose."

I gestured to the dining room doors and gave her a mock bow. "After you."

The private dining chamber lacked the ostentatious trappings people usually expected from a Dark Lord. There were no gilded chandeliers dripping with crystallized tears, no tapestries depicting the exact moment hope left my enemies' eyes. Instead, it was simply a comfortable room with a roaring fire and a round table that could seat six.

When Arabella and I entered, my odd little court had already assembled. Vex stood by the fireplace, her dark hood drawn low enough to reveal only a quick silver glint from her eyes. Sims sat hunched over a stack of documents, wearing the perpetually constipated expression that defined him. Thorne polished his blade with the kind of tender care most men reserved for lovers. And Griffin—

"Careful!" I called as a metal contraption clattered to the floor.

"It's fine, perfectly fine," he insisted, chasing the scattered gears across the floor. "Just a minor hitch, but I nearly had it worked out."

Arabella stepped between the debris without disturbing so much as a single gear. "What are you trying to build?" she asked, her tone politely curious.

Griffin beamed as he snatched up the gears with his long fingers. "It's a self-adjusting cartography apparatus that maps ley lines beneath any territory. Brilliant in theory . . . provided it doesn't explode first."

Vex shook her head. "No instructions, I take it?"

"Instructions stifle creativity," Griffin said, waving a dismissive hand.

"And prevent explosions," Sims muttered in that melodramatically dour voice of his.

I guided Arabella to the seat on my right. My advisors all noticed her transformation. Vex offered the ghost of a knowing smile, while the others reacted more like they'd seen a house cat transform into a panther.

"This feels . . . cozy," Arabella noted, eyeing the round table and the warm flames.

"Were you picturing skull goblets and bone furniture?" I asked, feigning hurt.

She tilted her head. "At a minimum. Although, those might be somewhat unwieldy for daily use."

I nodded solemnly. "We reserve the bones for special events. State visits, birthdays, the odd execution here or there."

A servant entered with the first course, an aromatic soup steaming in carved bowls. I'd ordered the meal prepared in a style reminiscent of Solandris. A subtle manipulation, yes, but one I presumed would remain inconspicuous. There was no hiding it from Vex, of course, but she would keep her observations to herself unless it proved relevant.

"I heard you started magical training with Lord Blackrose," Griffin said, still fiddling with gears. "How are you finding it, Lady Arabella?"

She cast me a brief, sidelong glance before answering. "I set him on fire." Her tone was almost casual, but she wasn't quite hiding a hint of mischief. "Apparently, I've got more raw power than expected."

"Magnificent!" Griffin glowed like a kid given unlimited sweets. "Oh, the complexities of spontaneous magic! Did you notice focal color shifts, temperature anomalies—?"

I cut him off with a warning look. "Griffin, hold off on the in-depth magical inquiries until after dinner? We have brewing border disputes that take precedence over my wife's fireworks."

Griffin let out a long-suffering sigh and turned to Arabella with an apologetic grin. "Of course. But if you ever want to see how your magical surges might integrate with mechanical systems—"

Thorne cleared his throat impatiently. "We've got three new raid reports from the border," he said, sparing Griffin nothing but a curt glance. "Villages hit in the last week alone."

"The bandits again?" Arabella asked, her spoon pausing halfway to her lips.

"So it seems," I answered, watching her intently. "Though they're better organized than most common thugs."

Vex's tone brightened, and she turned toward Arabella as if she were giving cheerful news. "Lord Blackrose personally dispatched the latest groups."

Arabella's expression flickered—something that looked more like deep thought than horror. She set her spoon down.

"And the troublesome part," I went on, "is the location of these raids. The villages fall into a muddled no-man's-land between Arvoryn and Solandris."

Griffin fumbled with his contraption again, producing a high-pitched squeal that set my teeth on edge. He twisted a gear, silencing the device with an apologetic grin.

"You mentioned Viscountess Morana," Arabella said quietly. "Doesn't she watch over Arvoryn?"

"Yes, but these villages traditionally belong to Solandris," I clarified. "But there's enough dispute that Morana lays claim as well and has pledged protection."

A spasm of motion from Griffin's contraption promptly died when he jostled the apparatus too hard. He cursed under his breath, turned a little valve, and then returned his attention to dinner, muttering about calibrations.

Arabella drew a slow breath. "Who's actually responsible for defending these villages, then?"

"Exactly the question," Sims said, sliding a fresh map across the table. "These red zones show territory historically claimed by both Arvoryn and Solandris. King Auremar pulled back his patrols from that region three months ago."

Arabella's brow furrowed as she studied the map. "And Morana doesn't have enough soldiers stationed there?"

"She claims she does," I told her, slicing a piece of roasted meat. "But the raids keep happening. If she's truly protecting them, she's doing a piss-poor job."

My wife looked unconvinced. "That doesn't sound like Auremar. He's always portrayed as the Peacemaker King, champion of his people."

"Propaganda," I said, my voice flat.

Dinner continued, and I took advantage of the lull to watch Arabella's reaction: the crease in her brow, the set of her shoulders. It suggested she cared more than she let on.

"All right," she said finally. "What proof do you have that these raids are more planned than random?"

That was the opening I'd been waiting for. "I arrived at Thornwick village this morning and found it burning. The bandits were in the midst of slaughtering farmers who couldn't escape. A survivor claimed they'd sent messengers to Auremar, pleading for help, yet no reply came."

Griffin's contraption clattered again. This time, a small spring shot across the table and landed in Thorne's wine. He fished it out with a long-suffering sigh.

"Sorry, sorry," Griffin murmured, accepting the dripping component.

"I questioned one of the bandits before executing him," I continued. "He confessed that a well-dressed man from Solandris had been feeding them information—patrol timings, best targets, even paying in Solandrian gold."

Arabella's gaze darted over to me, her face grave. "You think King Auremar ordered it?"

"Maybe not directly," I said, "but he didn't stop it. Failing to protect his subjects while funneling resources elsewhere is almost the same thing."

Vex added in a soft voice, "The Golden Roses. It always comes back to them."

A collective hush spread across the table. Griffin even paused in his tinkering.

"What do the Golden Rose Fields have to do with border villages?" Arabella asked.

I put my knife down and measured my words carefully. "Have you witnessed the rose harvest ceremonies?"

She shook her head. "They're restricted to those close to the crown."

"I'm surprised your mother never took you, since she was of heroic blood herself," I probed.

A flicker of hurt crossed Arabella's face so quickly, I almost missed it. "She died when I was eight. If she participated in any royal ceremonies, I was too young to remember."

Quiet settled over us. The fire's crackle sounded too loud, as if breaking some unspoken taboo.

"My condolences," I said, surprising myself with the sincerity behind it.

She seemed just as surprised. "Thank you," she replied softly.

Clearing my throat, I steered us back on track. "The Golden Roses aren't just ornamental, as you know. They hold ancient power that Solandris harvests, but in a flawed way."

Arabella's eyes narrowed. "Flawed?"

Griffin jumped at the chance to elaborate. "If done properly, the roses can heal mortal wounds and bolster wards. But for years, their potency's been on the decline. And King Auremar, being the shrewd merchant he is, keeps raising prices."

"Years ago," I explained, "rose essence could save a man half-dead. Now it's hardly enough to soothe a mild fever. Meanwhile, Auremar diverts protection from remote villages to the Golden Rose Fields, leaving many outlying areas vulnerable to bandit raids."

Arabella pressed her lips into a thin line. "That still contradicts the stories I've heard about Auremar."

I suppressed a chuckle. "Stories, indeed. They're worth less than the paper they're inked on."

Griffin's contraption suddenly whined again, and he twisted a gear to silence it. A faint beam of light shot directly into Sims's eye, provoking a stream of curses from him.

"Minor calibration problem," Griffin offered lamely. Then, to everyone's surprise, the machine whirred softly and projected a three-dimensional map of glowing lines above the table.

Arabella's eyes widened. "What is that?"

"The ley lines," I said. "Specifically, those running beneath Solandris. This power is what sustains Auremar's precious roses and what currently makes it difficult for me to infiltrate his lands."

Her gaze turned from the projected light back to me. "So that's why you can't just storm in. The combination of rose essence and the ley lines resists your dominion magic."

"Indeed." My voice felt tight. I was rarely so transparent with anyone, but she deserved this small glimpse if I wanted her fully on my side.

The contraption sputtered, then sparked. Griffin groaned in frustration and snatched a goblet of water, dousing it with minimal ceremony. A hiss of steam rolled into the air.

Dessert arrived—Solandrian pastries stuffed with a sweet berry compote. While we ate, Arabella stayed uncharacteristically quiet.

"I'm trying to reconcile King Auremar as you describe him with the man I saw years ago," she said eventually. "He always seemed the epitome of goodness."

I studied her carefully. "Have you met him, personally?"

"A few times, though I had only one real audience." Something in her voice hardened. "My father tried to get me placed in the royal court as a healing prodigy. The king politely declined."

That bitterness in her eyes was fleeting but potent. It told me more about

Auremar's supposed benevolence than any rumor could.

Griffin's contraption sparked again, drawing all eyes as a puff of black smoke wafted up. He scrambled to salvage the pieces, muttering frantic apologies.

Arabella turned to me. "One thing still bothers me. Why do you protect these outlying villages at all? You don't rule them."

I allowed a slow, dark smile. "Many reasons. One is ensuring their gratitude, which often proves more durable than forced tribute and makes them happy to have my garrisons nearby. Another is sabotaging Auremar's reputation. And, well, I like to irritate him."

She took that in, then muttered, "Practical villainy at its finest."

"I try." I set down my utensils and signaled the servant to clear the plates. "Which brings us to our next matter: Viscountess Morana invited us to Arvoryn Pass."

Arabella's eyes narrowed. "Us?"

"She specifically requested you," I said, relishing the slight annoyance that flashed across her face. "And if you go, it flaunts our marriage in her courtyard and undermines her expectations that this union is a temporary arrangement."

"She did nothing but glower at me during our wedding," Arabella pointed out.

Thorne snorted. "She looked like she wanted to carve you up with a butter knife."

Vex let out a sardonic laugh. "Her brawl with the Syndicate that night also left her guard dead, which complicates things. Three letters from the Syndicate in one week, each more threatening than the last."

Sims shuffled his documents. "The Syndicate demands compensation for the injuries to their representative. Meanwhile, Morana claims her guard was murdered under mysterious circumstances."

"Convenient that nobody can pin it on any single party," Thorne added. "Might've been the Syndicate or Morana herself."

I dismissed it all with a wave. "We'll handle that in Arvoryn. And remind her that attacking Syndicate affiliates leads to problems I'd rather not address."

Arabella observed me for a moment. "So I'm basically an accessory to piss her off and demonstrate solidarity."

"An accessory with insight," I corrected, letting my shadows flicker playfully. "And you'll see for yourself what Solandris has turned into. Arvoryn sits exactly on the border—close enough to glean plenty of revelations."

"I doubt the viscountess requested me for my charming company."

"You needn't worry," I assured her. "The viscountess knows better than to harm what belongs to me."

Arabella's eyes flashed. "I don't *belong* to anyone."

My shadows flared in response, and a candle guttered in protest. The table fell silent as my advisors suddenly found their plates fascinating. I allowed her rebuke to slide, however, since I needed her cooperation.

Arabella held my gaze for a measured moment, aware of every advisor watching their Dark Lord yield ground.

She took a deliberate sip of wine.

Just then, Griffin's apparatus coughed back to life. A bright band of light projected onto the ceiling: the glowing rivers of magic twisted and turned, forming a pattern that resembled some ancient script when viewed from below.

"There!" Griffin crowed, triumphant for half a second before the machine popped in a shower of sparks, but the image remained. "I'll recalibrate it tomorrow," he promised, looking crestfallen.

The moment of magic lingered as we gazed at the swirling lines. Then Arabella turned to me, and I recognized the intent in her eyes—curiosity, determination, a wariness that hadn't yet resolved into trust.

"All right," she said at last. "I'll go. I need to see the truth myself."

Griffin's apparatus gave a final, pitiful sputter and died for good. Sims looked far too satisfied as he set his papers aside.

With the tension broken, conversation meandered into smaller topics. Arabella asked about Griffin's latest failed experiments. She traded sly barbs with Sims and laughed at Thorne's gruff jabs about incompetent raiders. I leaned back in my chair, letting her interact with my advisors on her own terms.

While she laughed with Vex about some lesser demon fiasco, I found myself studying the lines of her face, how her mouth curved when amused, how her hair glinted softly in the firelight. Another unwelcome ache settled in my chest at the sight of her so at ease.

I reminded myself that I was a warlord with plans to topple a kingdom; she was the key to harnessing power I'd dreamed of for years. Still, that logical reasoning wobbled dangerously every time I imagined her laughter turning softer, intimate, as if shared only for me.

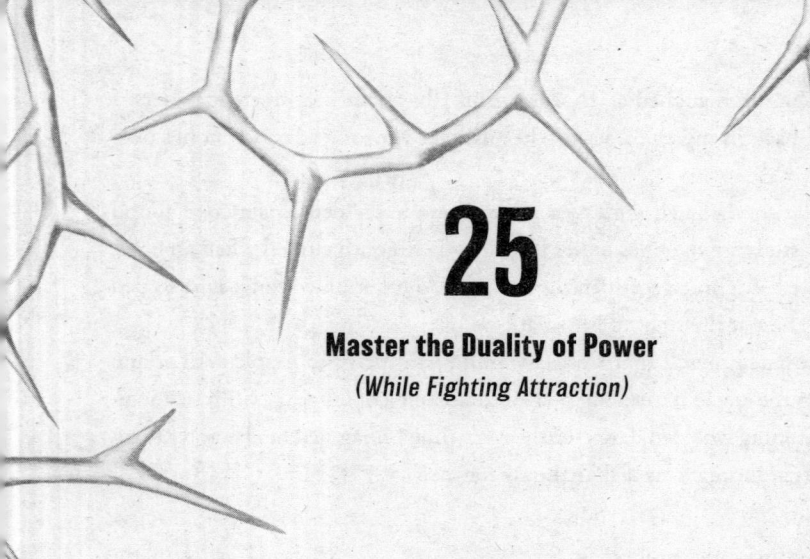

25

Master the Duality of Power
(While Fighting Attraction)

Arabella

"Again."

I gritted my teeth, sweat running down my face. The lily on the table trembled under my stare, as vibrant and alive as when I'd started. After a week of escalating magical exercises, my fingertips buzzed with a power I barely understood.

Kazimir's voice came from somewhere behind me, smooth and maddeningly calm. "You're still hesitating. The magic's there, Arabella, but you refuse to channel it correctly."

"I'm *trying*," I snapped, flicking a damp strand of hair from my face.

"You're not."

He stepped around the table, leaning against its edge. He looked so infuriatingly composed in his black tunic, while I felt like I'd been dragged backward through a thornbush.

"You're scared of your own potential," he pressed. "You've spent your life healing and creating. You think tapping that same source to destroy is unnatural."

I clenched my fists. "I'm not afraid."

His mouth slid into a half smile. "Then prove it."

There sat the lily, mocking me. Healing was effortless—mending injuries, soothing fevers—simple. But I couldn't bring myself to crush something that had done me no harm, even if it was just a flower. Every fiber of my being screamed no.

Kazimir leaned forward, hands splayed on the table. "Stop acting like destruction is a violation. It's transformation. The same energy, just reversed."

I let out a harsh breath. "Easier said than done."

"You're overthinking." He circled until he stood beside me. "May I?" He lifted his hand as though asking permission to guide my own.

A reluctant curiosity bloomed inside me. "Fine." I tried to sound dismissive, but my pulse throbbed in my throat. Part of me craved to learn exactly how far I could push my magic.

He positioned his hands just above mine, and a charge sparked between our palms.

"Close your eyes," he instructed, his voice dropping, a little too intimate for my liking.

I complied with a sharp exhale, half suspicious, half eager.

"Now, tell me what happens when you heal."

"I reach out," I said slowly, "find the injured parts, and give them what they need to mend."

"Excellent." A hint of approval colored his tone. "But you're forgetting that you're a conduit, not the source. The energy isn't strictly yours. It's drawn from the life force around you."

I felt his fingertips shift closer; the air between our hands crackled.

"When you heal, you channel energy toward the target. This time, I want you to do the opposite—pull it *out*."

I stiffened. It sounded so simple, but it went against everything I'd ever associated with magic. Still, I remembered dark moments: guards doubling over after touching my bedroom door, or one of Kazimir's henchmen collapsing the day he kidnapped me. My power had lashed out reflexively, draining them.

"That's it," Kazimir encouraged, his voice quiet. "You've done this before."

His lingering presence sent my heart hammering, but I focused on the lily. I pictured reclaiming its life instead of gifting it. A tug, an inversion, the same gentle push I used for healing, but in reverse. Warmth buzzed up my arms. Then, the lily shriveled before me, its petals blackening, stem drooping. Within seconds, it was dust.

I jerked away from Kazimir, my breath stuttering. "I didn't— I—"

"Yes, you *did*," he said flatly, but I detected satisfaction in his voice. "And beautifully."

Staring at the scorched remnants, I felt a swirl of horror and exhilaration. That surge of power coiled inside me, potent as good wine.

"How does it feel?" he asked, his gaze boring into me.

I swallowed. "Terrible," I lied, before admitting, "and . . . amazing."

He actually chuckled, and the sound held no mocking edge, just genuine pride. "The duality of power. Creation and destruction."

I wanted to argue that simply because it was easy didn't make it right. But my pulse, still high from the taste of that stolen vitality, contradicted me.

Kazimir moved away and rummaged through a shelf, returning with a small cage that held a white mouse. My stomach sank.

"No," I hissed. "Absolutely not."

"It's a logical next step," he said. "Same principle, more complexity."

I stepped back, crossing my arms. "I'm not killing an innocent creature just to show off."

He raised an eyebrow. "You eat meat, don't you? This mouse was bred for magical use and destined to be fed to Griffin's familiars."

I pressed my lips into a tight line. "I'm not doing it," I repeated.

"Fine." With a shrug, he replaced the cage. "We can revisit that lesson another day."

Relief flooded me as he set the mouse aside. Even with my newfound destructive power thrumming, I was grateful I wouldn't be forced to kill it.

"Let's try something else." He gestured to the arcane circle. "Join me."

I followed him slowly, still tingling with leftover adrenaline.

"You saw what that inverted healing did to a flower," he said once we stood inside. "Now watch what dominion magic can achieve."

Shadows gathered around his boots, swirling upward like living smoke. He lifted his hands. Black tendrils wove themselves into the shapes of wolves, their eyes shining that stormy gray that matched Kazimir's own. They prowled the perimeter of the circle, appearing unnervingly real.

I'd seen him use dominion magic in patches before, but never like this. My chest tightened. He truly looked like a villain from a fever-dream story, except I was uncomfortably aware of how enticing I found the command in his posture, the way raw power seemed to vibrate around him.

"Dominion is about control," he said, voice taut. "Bending the world to your purpose. It demands certainty and the boldness to shape reality as you see fit."

The wolves solidified until I swore I heard their breathing. A chill prickled over my skin.

"Impressive," I said, letting some awe slip into my voice. "But beyond terrifying people, what's the practical use?"

A chilling grin spread across his face, and his eyes glowed faintly silver. My stomach flipped over in a traitorous swirl of attraction. I hated that I was drawn to the darkness in him, but denying it felt pointless.

"They can scout, defend, fight. And this"—he flicked his wrist, dissolving the wolves into a vortex that spun around us—"is just the visible side." Energy thrummed in the air, causing small objects around the room to vibrate. The vortex pulled into a tight sphere between his palms, flickering with tiny pinpricks of stars. A universe in miniature.

"The real power," he said evenly, "is how dominion can reshape entire landscapes."

The darkness expanded, enveloping us. Suddenly, I wasn't in the training chamber, but standing on a vast plain lit by twin moons. Crystalline structures as tall as trees rose around us. Everything looked surreal, dreamlike.

"Is this real?" I murmured, reaching for the nearest crystal tree. My hand passed straight through.

"It's a vision," Kazimir answered, his voice echoing over walls that weren't there. "A possible reality I could make tangible with the right power."

The scene blurred and became an altered vision of Solandris's capital. The palace was dark stone, the gardens glowed with strange luminescent blooms, and overhead hovered Kazimir's own citadel like a shadowy sun.

"You want to remake Solandris into *this*?" I asked, turning to him.

"When I conquer it," he corrected, "I intend to tear out the corruption and build something better."

The illusions wavered, then vanished. We stood once more in the training room, the wards and dusty floors reappearing around us. Kazimir lowered his hands, the glow dimming in his eyes.

"That was . . . eye-opening," I conceded. I wasn't about to stroke his ego further, no matter how mesmerizing the display had been.

A laugh escaped him. "High praise indeed." He took one step back into the center of the circle, arms crossed. "Your turn. Show me what your magic can do, unhindered."

My heart pounded. I'd spent so long masking whatever unorthodox talents I had. Even healing was only acceptable because it seemed benign—my father's attempt to make me useful while maintaining a veneer of virtue.

"You saw the lily," I started, "and you know I won't drain a live mouse—"

"Then pick a different focus."

I bit my lip, scanning the training chamber. "I need something that's already dead."

Kazimir raised a brow, then left briefly. He returned carrying a small, cloth-wrapped bundle. When he set it on the table, I saw it was a dead robin.

"Flew into a tower window," Kazimir said. "Griffin found it earlier. It must have gotten swept up in the storms below the citadel."

I swallowed, lifting the little bird's limp body. "I'm not sure what'll happen," I warned him.

"Just be careful," he said softly. "And don't injure yourself."

Ignoring the uneasy flutter in my gut, I closed my eyes. The room teemed with leftover magic from Kazimir's displays, an environment saturated with potential. Slowly, I tapped into that energy, letting it flow through me the way healing magic always had—except this time, I aimed it into a vessel past saving.

The bird twitched. My eyes flew open. The robin's wings flapped once, then again. Its clouded eyes opened, fixating on me in a way that felt both eerie and enthralling.

Behind me, Kazimir inhaled sharply. I realized his posture had gone rigid with surprise.

Maintaining the connection felt like juggling streams of lightning. My veins crackled as I fed the bird an imitation of life, not true resurrection but an echo.

I opened my palms, and the robin fluttered upward, circling the training room with uneven sweeps. Each small course correction was a thread tugging on my soul.

"Necromancy," Kazimir breathed, wonder creeping into his tone.

"I wouldn't call it that," I muttered, though the lines were definitely blurred. "It's more like replicating function rather than actual life."

"Semantics," he countered, but his eyes gleamed with respect.

The bird flitted back to my arm, perching with unsettling precision. Stopping it was as simple as letting the borrowed magic slip away. The moment I severed the connection, the robin slumped back into death.

A wave of exhaustion slammed into me. My vision flickered for a moment, and cold sweat dampened my neck.

Kazimir calmly rewrapped the tiny corpse, but I sensed the wheels turning behind his storm gray eyes.

"How long have you done this?" he asked.

I shrugged, refusing to sound too impressed with myself. "Stumbled upon it when I was younger. My estate was half rotten, so it wasn't rare to find dead mice or birds in corners."

"And you hid it from everyone," he said, gentleness creeping into his voice. "Death magic, or anything like it, could have gotten you branded a heretic."

I nodded, trying not to sway from fatigue. "My father didn't need more excuses to punish me."

Kazimir set down the bundle and took a step closer. "You did well. Possibly better than I expected."

I met his gaze, acutely aware of how close he was. The silver flecks in his eyes still shimmered, sending a twist of heat through my stomach. "I told you, I'm not just some helpless noble."

His gaze flicked to my lips, then back up again. "And I'm starting to believe it."

The thickening tension in the air made me wonder what his next step would be—kiss me? Mock me? Demand I raise an army of undead nightingales? The more we pressed each other, the less certain I was of anything.

To save face—and possibly my sanity—I stepped back. "That's enough for one day. I'm tired."

Kazimir studied me for a moment, disappointment overshadowed by acceptance. "Tomorrow, then. We'll see how far you can push that power."

I rolled my eyes. "What is it with you and testing people to their limits?"

He didn't answer, just offered an arm in that mocking show of courtesy he loved. "I'll walk you back to our tower."

"I can manage fine," I started to say, but then a wave of dizziness rolled through me. I staggered, and Kazimir caught my elbow.

"Clearly," he said wryly, "you're brimming with stamina."

My scowl was half-hearted; I genuinely needed the support to stay upright. "Fine," I relented, "but I'm not collapsing just to amuse you."

He smiled—a real smile, not his usual smirk. "Heavens forbid I find any amusement in my wife."

We made it to the corridor just as frantic footsteps echoed from around the corner. A disheveled messenger skidded into view, panting. The second he spotted Kazimir, he dropped into a half bow.

"My lord," he wheezed. "Urgent correspondence from Solandris."

Kazimir's eyes narrowed. "From the king?"

"No, my lord. From Lord Evenfall."

My father. Of all the names that could rip me out of my haze, that one did the job. My spine prickled with dread. Was he demanding my return? Threatening petty vengeance? Or informing Kazimir that I was disowned, no longer his concern?

That last idea had merit.

I stepped forward, hoping the letter was somehow meant for me. But the messenger held the silver tray toward Kazimir alone. My father had written directly *to him,* not even acknowledging my role in this twisted marriage. The sight made me want to shred the parchment.

Kazimir broke the seal and read. His expression darkened to something harder.

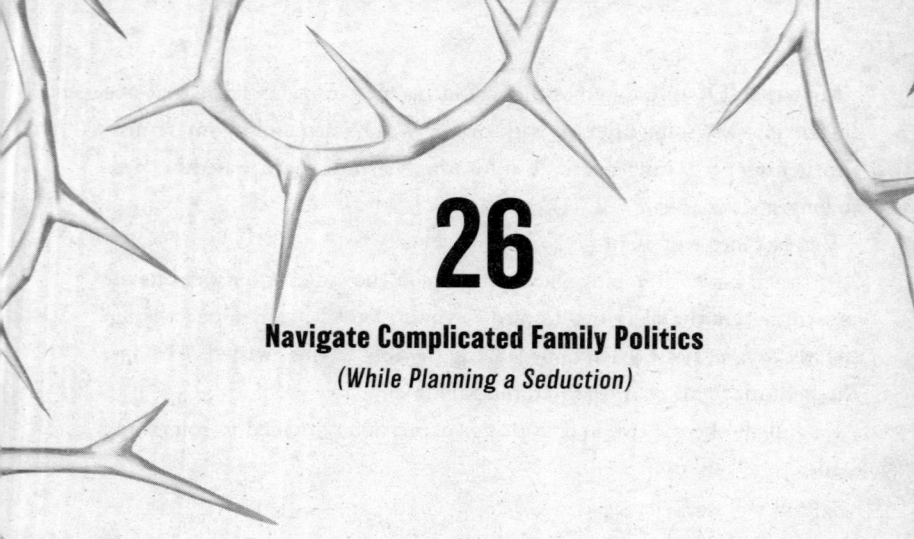

26

Navigate Complicated Family Politics
(While Planning a Seduction)

Kazimir

Lord Evenfall's elegant script stared back at me from the parchment, all pretentious flourishes with none of the substance.

> *Lord Blackrose,*
>
> *While I understand that the whims of villains are beyond the comprehension of civilized men, I must insist upon appropriate compensation for the theft of my daughter. Lady Arabella's value to our household extends beyond mere sentiment. Her bloodline and magical aptitude represent significant political currency in the current climate.*
>
> *I demand reparations of no less than fifty thousand gold crowns, to be delivered within a fortnight. Additionally, I expect the return of Lady Arabella by month's end, as her absence has created inconvenient complications with previously arranged negotiations.*

Should these reasonable terms prove unacceptable, I shall be forced to pursue more aggressive avenues of resolution.

With all due consideration,
Lord Atticus Evenfall

I crushed the edge of the parchment. Not a single question about Arabella's well-being. Just a neat price tag and a threat. The veins in my temple throbbed with the urge to destroy something. I'd known her father was a callous bastard, but seeing it spelled out so blatantly made it all the more infuriating.

Behind me, Arabella spoke up in a quiet but sharp voice. "Well?"

I turned, noticing how she leaned against the corridor wall, breathing heavier than usual after our training session. Her face was pale but defiant, a combination that tested my composure in ways I didn't appreciate.

I handed her the letter.

Arabella's gaze flickered across the page, her face hardening into a mask so practiced I almost missed the slight tightening around her eyes.

"Fifty thousand gold crowns," she said distantly. "That's what I'm worth to him. That and whatever 'previously arranged negotiations' he's worried about."

The messenger beside us coughed nervously, sensing the gathering storm. My first instinct was to send him back with a severed head as my formal response. But a disconcerting thought about whether Arabella might actually know Evenfall's courier—like him or, gods forbid, care about him—stopped me. Apparently, I'd developed a streak of sentimentality.

I jerked my head in silent dismissal. The messenger boy bolted.

I turned back to Arabella, who was still staring at the letter. "No mention of my safety, or whether I've been tortured or killed. Just the money."

"He didn't even pretend to be concerned. Only demands and deadlines."

"I'm not surprised. This is exactly who he is." She pushed off the wall, forcing her chin high as she handed the letter back to me. Pride radiated from her, even when she looked about ready to collapse.

I offered a tight nod. "He's a man who'd trade his own daughter for a handful of coins and call it diplomacy."

Her lips twitched in a mirthless smile. "If you think this is insulting, you've never faced him in person. This is mild by his standards."

The way her voice quavered at the edges told me that behind those barbed words lay a deep, old hurt. Despite myself, I felt a surge of anger so fierce it made the torchlight dance along the walls. Perhaps it was because I, too, had been used as a bargaining chip in my parents' twisted schemes. Or maybe I simply hated the idea of someone else—anyone else—treating Arabella the way *I* did. Disrespecting her was my territory.

She sagged a little against the wall. I stepped forward instinctively, but she waved me off. "I'm fine."

I recognized stubbornness well. I lived by it. "You need rest," I said, not bothering to mask it as a suggestion.

"What I *need*," she retorted, "is to not be treated like a commodity to be bartered between powerful men."

I gave a pointed shrug. "For once, we agree." I suspected my next words might sound contradictory, given I'd forced her into marriage for my own ends, but I said them anyway. "I have no intention of returning you."

She looked up, eyes narrowing. "Because I'm more valuable to you here, right?"

"Yes. But I also gave you my word when I said your father would never touch you again, and I intend to keep it."

I had no illusions about my own hypocrisy. Yes, she was critical to the Heirloom's activation, but there was something else that made me bristle at the thought of giving her away.

Arabella drew in a sharp breath. "My father's always playing a deeper game. I wonder who these 'previously arranged negotiations' involve."

"He said he'd resort to 'aggressive avenues' if I refuse," I said, the words coated in derision. "My fortress is more than a match for his meager resources."

I let my gaze wander over her a moment too long. She was stripped raw, physically and emotionally. Seducing her right now might be easier than ever because her defenses were down. Yet some spark of conscience (how irritating) told me to show restraint. Still, I'd made plans, and we had to eat.

I cleared my throat. "I've asked the kitchens to prepare something special for dinner. You've progressed remarkably with your magic, and I'd like to . . . talk."

Her eyes narrowed. "Why do I doubt that's the entire reason?"

An involuntary smirk crossed my face. "Must you always suspect an ulterior motive?"

"Yes," she snapped, "because you always have one."

She had me there. "Let's call it a chance to discuss your father's letter after you've had time to rest."

Arabella studied me. Finally, she exhaled. "Fine. But don't expect me to be pleasant company."

I gave her a slight bow. "I'd be disappointed if you were."

There might have been the faintest twitch of amusement at the corner of her mouth. I motioned for her to walk with me, and we headed down the corridor. She steadied her shoulders with every step, refusing to show weakness no matter how tired she was. At her chamber door, she paused, hand resting on the handle.

"Lord Blackrose," she said, still not meeting my eyes. "You could have just hidden the letter, but you didn't. So . . . thank you."

The genuine note in her voice wrenched at something in my chest. "Our agreement includes honesty," I managed. "Even when it's unpleasant."

A flicker passed over her face, maybe gratitude or relief, before she opened the door and stepped inside. I found myself staring at the carved wood, as if I could see past it to the woman who'd become the biggest chaos factor in my carefully ordered life.

With a muttered oath, I turned and strode toward the war room. My father-in-law wanted a ransom. My Heirloom demanded a "true" consummation I'd so far delayed. And I had a wife whose loyalty—or at least partnership—I needed to secure.

If I played my cards right tonight, I might start unraveling all these knots. Then again, if I failed, I'd have one more reason to curse Lord Evenfall to the bitter end. Either way, dinner promised to be interesting.

I cracked my knuckles, letting my mind swirl with the details. First things first: a letter to respond to, a seduction to refine, and a father-in-law to put in his place.

I couldn't help a dark smile. Villainy was never dull.

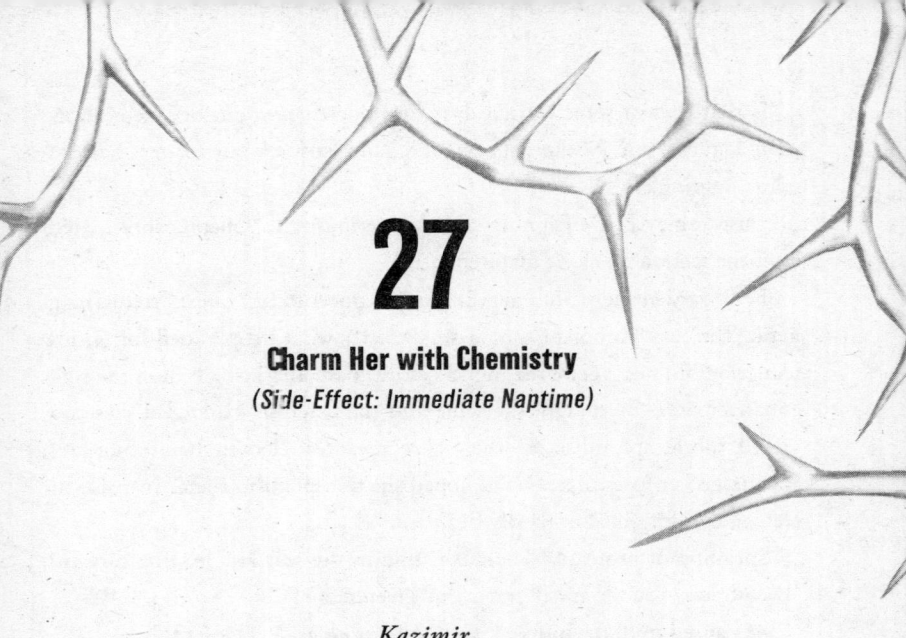

27

Charm Her with Chemistry
(Side-Effect: Immediate Naptime)

Kazimir

I lifted the crystal decanter with a flourish. "More wine?"

Arabella considered it briefly, then held out her glass. "Why not?" she said. "It's excellent."

I filled her goblet slowly, letting my fingertips barely graze hers in the process. It was a small gesture, the kind that skirted our rules but didn't break them outright. To my surprise, she didn't wrench her hand away. A promising sign.

We were alone in my private dining room, illuminated by candles and a roaring fire. I'd dismissed the servants after the main course, preferring the intimacy of pouring wine myself.

She took another bite of venison, closing her eyes for a moment as she savored the flavor. "I never expected such refined cuisine in a villain's lair," she remarked. The glow from the candles highlighted the gold in her hair, setting them ablaze against her deep green gown.

"We villains have standards," I replied, swirling my own wine. "Good food keeps everyone happy."

"Is that part of some official dark lord doctrine—right between 'always monologue before killing your enemies' and 'ensure your fortress has dramatic lighting'?"

I raised an eyebrow, feigning complete seriousness. "Chapter three. Right after the section on cloak maintenance."

She rewarded me with a genuine smile, one I found unexpectedly magnetic. The easy humor in the air was exactly what I'd planned for: a slow seduction built on gentle teasing, excellent food, and just a hint of the right enhancements. By design, the wine and the carefully curated dishes contained subtle aphrodisiacs. They were meant to loosen her inhibitions, encourage her to escalate. I had hoped she'd respond to them. Instead, she seemed comfortable but hardly beguiled.

"Speaking of protocol," I said, shifting in my seat and leaning forward, "I've noticed you never call me by my given name."

She paused midbite, blinked, and set her fork aside. "Don't I?"

"No," I said. "It's 'Lord Blackrose' this, 'Lord Blackrose' that." I placed my glass on the table with deliberate care. "And I'm curious why."

A slight flush rose up her neck before she bit into another piece of venison. "Force of habit, maybe."

"You're on a first-name basis with Vex and Griffin." I drummed my fingers on the cloth. "But you persist in calling me Lord Blackrose."

She set her silverware down, tilting her chin up with a quiet challenge. "Would you rather I call you something else? I've got a few ideas—"

"Kazimir works," I said, noticing how her eyes narrowed. "As I've suggested more than once."

She hesitated, gaze locked on mine. "Names imply a certain closeness," she said finally. "It would suggest . . . something else."

"That we're more than just captor and captive, perhaps?"

She inclined her head, eyes serious. "I'm not ready to admit that. Not yet."

Her honesty caught me unaware. I leaned back, sizing her up by the light of the fire. After a moment, I nodded. "Point taken," I said. "Though I hope someday you'll change your mind."

She studied me with that same thoughtful intensity. "Why does it matter to you so much?"

I turned my wine goblet between my fingers. I hadn't planned on being this candid, but the answer slipped out. "As you said, names imply different things. When you call me Lord Blackrose, you're acknowledging the villain, the warlord. But if you said Kazimir . . . it might be directed at the man, not just the darkness."

I rolled my shoulders to shake off the strange twist in my chest. My strategy tonight involved carefully orchestrated chemistry, not confessions.

"At least I don't address you as Your Darkness, or something equally ridiculous," she teased, a sly spark lighting her eyes. "I assume that would roll right off you, anyway."

"Your Darkness?" I repeated. "Not a bad ring to it. Maybe I'll add that to the ever-growing list of my exalted titles."

She snorted softly. "Given your minions' flair for drama, I figured it was only a matter of time."

I topped up my wine. "My staff calls me everything from 'sir' to the more extravagant 'Scourge of Azroth.' Hardly essential, but I let it slide."

"Quite the brand you're building," she quipped. "Supreme Darkness, Terror of the Western Realms . . . I'm surprised they haven't tried Supreme Overlord of Doom yet."

I couldn't resist a smile. "That's a good one. I'll have Vex send a memo."

We continued to chat over the remnants of our meal, drifting from flirtatious banter to the political webs woven around Solandris and Evenfall. I found myself surprisingly drawn to how her mind worked. She possessed a cunning that belied her father's attempts to stifle her.

Eventually, Arabella tilted her head, studying me intently. "You're distracted tonight. Is my father's letter that worrisome?"

I grimaced slightly. "There are details I can't reconcile."

Arabella sighed, pushing her plate away. "He's always got layers. If he's involved in negotiations while pressing you for ransom, something bigger is in motion."

"What do you suspect?"

Her lips pursed, and she tapped the table as though she wanted to stab it. "The Royal Envoy to the Eastern Kingdoms is up for appointment soon. My father's coveted it forever. He's likely bartering me away—or was, before you abducted me—to seal that deal."

It made perfect sense. "He'd have used your marriage to secure that post. No wonder you became so adept at driving suitors away."

She shrugged, a wry bitterness flashing in her gaze. "I discovered if I humiliated them thoroughly enough, they'd run."

I allowed a hint of admiration into my tone. "I'm shocked."

She laughed, bright and genuinely amused. I liked that I could pry laughter from her. The moment flickered by, then Arabella sighed again. "My father's last letter threatened 'severe consequences' if I refused to play his perfect daughter. I guess you saved me from that, in a twisted sense."

Hearing that subtle quiver in her normally fierce voice made my fingers tighten around my wine glass. I felt a sudden urge to track down her father and ensure he never had the chance to manipulate her again. "Would you like me to kill him? I'd even make it look like an accident."

Her eyes widened, but then her look turned suspicious. "You've been . . . different tonight. The wine, the candlelight, the compliments . . . Are you trying to seduce me, Lord Blackrose?"

I was preparing an answer, something reasonable to disguise the aphrodisiacs. But before I could spin my denial, she yawned, broad and unladylike.

She clamped a hand over her mouth, blinking with surprise. "Sorry. Now that I think about it, I'm incredibly sleepy."

A second yawn overtook her, impossible to hide. She looked more annoyed than anything else. "So that's what you laced the food with, hm? Something to coax me into enthusiasm?"

I blinked. An uncomfortable prickle of embarrassment worked its way up my spine. "It wasn't meant to knock you out," I said, clearing my throat. "It was an aphrodisiac, technically. A mild one. I planned on—"

"I grew up at *court*," she informed me wearily, "and I discovered years ago that those potions have an unintended effect on me. Instead of making me . . . overly affectionate, they just make me tired. Sorry to disappoint."

I nearly choked on my own wine. Her triumphant, sleepy grin let me know I'd just blundered spectacularly. My entire plan, ruined by her bizarre constitution.

"They were just supposed to, you know, set the mood," I muttered.

"Naturally," she said, obviously amused at my expense. "Like watering a plant or something?"

I winced. "Don't put it like that."

She stifled another yawn, arms folding. "I'm too tired to be furious right now, but we'll talk about your manipulative approach tomorrow."

I inhaled slowly through my nose, forcing composure. "Fine. But at least let me help you to bed? For sleeping it off, I mean."

She eyed me suspiciously, but her exhaustion seemed to win out. "All right. But only because the alternative is an undignified face-plant on your carpet."

I rose and offered an arm, which she accepted with minimal protest. We ascended the winding stairs toward our tower suites. Each step she took felt heavier, and by the time we reached the top, her eyes drooped so badly that she was practically asleep on her feet. With a resigned sigh, I scooped her into my arms. Her soft murmur of protest faded as she collapsed against my shoulder. I felt the gentle rise and fall of her breath and tried not to dwell on how perfectly she fit against me.

In the bedchamber, I laid her down with the utmost care. She curled onto her side, hugging a pillow, while I removed her shoes. One hand brushed against my sleeve in her half sleep, and something uncomfortably warm bloomed under my ribs. A pang of unexpected longing tugged at me—how different this evening might have been if my plan had succeeded. She cracked one eye open, words slurring with fatigue.

"You're not undressing me in my sleep, are you?" she mumbled.

"I wouldn't dare," I said. "Though that dress will be awful in the morning."

She made a lazy gesture of dismissal. "Don't care . . . pillow wall . . ." Then she drifted off, eyes sliding shut completely.

Sighing, I stacked pillows around her the way she insisted. Tonight, it was certainly unnecessary—she was too far gone to be lured into anything. I felt a laugh bubbling in my chest at the sheer irony. *Kazimir Blackrose, undone by the wrong tincture.* How humiliating.

I brushed a loose strand of hair off her face. Her only response was a soft, contented sound. The sight of her dozing so peacefully sent a pulse of protectiveness down my spine. It startled me enough that I quickly backed toward the door, determined to escape that strange pull.

I headed for my study, intending to work until I collapsed as well. Lord Evenfall's demands. The Heirloom's locked power. My own half-baked attempts at seduction. None of it had gone as I intended.

And at every turn, Arabella had a way of confounding me. I suspected I'd be thinking about it long into the night.

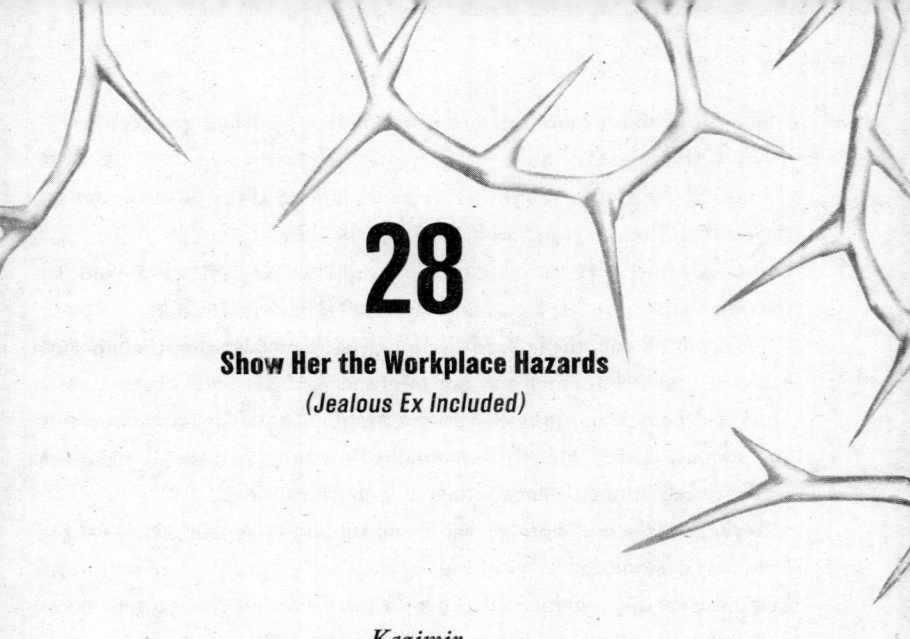

28

Show Her the Workplace Hazards
(Jealous Ex Included)

Kazimir

"Is this entirely necessary?" Arabella asked as we approached the narrow lightning bridge to the Portal Isle. "You have personal portals. We could simply—"

"The personal portals are for emergencies," I explained, stepping toward the bridge's edge. In the predawn gloom, the glow of the lightning bridge blotted out everything else. "They drain too much power to use casually."

She ignored my offered hand—of course she did—and walked onto the bridge herself, cloak billowing behind her to reveal her training leathers. They hugged her in all the right places, a fact I continued to note with no small amount of satisfaction. I'd known the moment she chose them that she meant to irritate Morana. I appreciated that level of calculated spite.

"Besides," I continued, catching up to her in a few strides, "Portal Isle has permanent gates that require minimal maintenance."

She glanced over her shoulder. "How disappointingly sensible."

I shrugged. "I save the extravagant displays for special occasions."

"Like kidnapping?" she shot back, a mischievous edge to her voice.

The corner of my mouth tugged upward. "You were being . . . spirited."

"I was trying to kill you."

I tapped the spot on my throat where she'd pressed that blade in our initial scuffle. "I've developed a nice scar. I rather like it."

She rolled her eyes but couldn't quite suppress her smile. The wind battered her hair across her face, and she shoved it back with a huff.

We'd moved past the aphrodisiac incident a few days ago, though she'd made it absolutely clear I was not forgiven. Arabella had cornered me at breakfast the next morning to deliver a comprehensive dissertation on trust and respect, during which I'd maintained my most remorseful expression while secretly admiring her command of creative insults.

At the far edge of the bridge, the Portal Isle shimmered into view—a perfect circle of stone dotted with seven ancient arches, each carved with runes that pulsed at different intervals. I felt the platform's hum beneath my boots; it was always surreal, the way magic vibrated here.

I moved to the eastern arch, letting my fingertips trail across its cool carvings. "Each portal is keyed to a fixed destination. Some are public knowledge—the route to the markets, for instance." I indicated the archway in front of us. "Others remain exclusive. With all of them, only those who have the necessary tokens can pass, just like the lightning bridges."

Arabella folded her arms over her chest. "But you and I don't use tokens for the bridges."

"And *I* don't need them for the portals," I replied, injecting just a hint of smugness into my voice.

She tilted her head, incredulous. "You think if I had access, I'd jump through one at random just to escape?"

"No," I said, fighting off a smile. "You're far too cunning for that, and if you were going to flee, you wouldn't announce it beforehand."

No denial came from her, only a pensive silence. Triumph flickered through me. I activated the portal with a spark of dominion magic, the archway filling with a rippling veil of shadow laced with silver.

"After you, Lady Blackrose." I gestured with an exaggerated bow.

She eyed me warily, then squared her shoulders. "If I end up in a dungeon somewhere, I'll make you regret it."

A low laugh escaped me, darker than I intended. "Is that a promise? Because I can imagine some very entertaining ways for you to seek vengeance."

She flushed at that but didn't look away. Her defiance made my pulse quicken. With a final glare, she stepped through the black-and-silver veil, and I followed instantly, feeling the portal's icy pressure crush me before releasing me on the other side.

Blinking away the frost clinging to my eyelashes, I saw a clearing of ancient pines. Dawn touched the horizon, bathing everything in a pale glow. I drew a breath, my chest stinging from the abrupt change in air pressure.

Arabella stood a short distance away, clutching at a tree trunk and blinking as though the ground had wobbled under her feet. "Breathe, it helps," I said, dusting a little frost from my sleeve. "The disorientation passes."

She glared at me pointedly but followed my advice. Her cheeks were tinged with cold. "You could've warned me about that," she said.

"And miss a chance to see you off-kilter?" I countered with mock innocence. "Never."

I waved toward a distant ridge. "We're at the northern edge of Arvoryn Pass. Morana's territory lies just beyond those hills."

Branches snapped behind me, and I turned to see Thorne stepping forward with a string of horses. "Lord Blackrose, Lady Blackrose," he said, handing over the reins. "Compliments of Viscountess Morana."

I almost snorted at that. Morana's hospitality was typically laced with daggers. But as I turned to Arabella, I found her entire demeanor brightening. She reached for the reins of a sturdy bay mare, her hand gliding over the saddle's seat.

"I insisted on no sidesaddles."

She glanced at me while she stroked the mare's neck. "You remembered."

I forced a casual shrug. "I prefer efficiency, that's all. Can't have you breaking your neck on the way there." I stepped in to help Arabella mount, though she hardly needed the assistance. My fingers lingered on her calf, pressing lightly into the supple leather. She gasped, just barely audible, and a spark of satisfaction crackled through me in response.

"I half expected you to insist I ride with you," she said, reins in hand.

A lazy smile spread across my face. "Is that something you'd prefer?"

"No," she said a little too quickly. "Not at all."

I sighed in mock regret. "Pity."

I mounted my own horse, and we set out along a winding path through the pines. Thorne and two guards rode ahead, another pair behind, giving us a measure of privacy.

"You ride well," I noted after a while.

Arabella stayed quiet for a breath or two. "It's something I've always enjoyed." She shot a glance at our enclosed guard detail. "Why bother with an escort? You could annihilate a militia with your magic, all by yourself."

"The escort isn't for me," I said, ducking under an overhanging branch. "It's a courtesy to Morana. She enjoys the illusion that I respect her territory enough to observe her protocols."

Arabella snorted. "Or that you don't overshadow her by flaunting just how powerful you really are."

"Precisely. All power structures rest on fragile egos. Hers, mine, everyone's." I caught her gaze. "I'm managing them, just as I manage you."

She gave me a sidelong look. "And who's managing *you*?"

"You've been doing a fine job," I said truthfully. "My ego has never been so bruised and inflated at the same time."

Arabella murmured a low, noncommittal sound, but a ghost of a smile crossed her face.

Soon enough, the forest gave way to open highlands. The morning sun crept higher, lighting up the rolling hills dotted with standing stones. Jagged mountains guarded the horizon. Arabella's face turned toward the sunlight, her posture relaxing—no doubt enjoying her first taste of freedom from the citadel.

"You're staring," she said without turning.

I didn't bother to deny it. "Just making sure you're not foolishly planning to run."

She finally glanced my way, an amused gleam in her eye. "You already pointed out I wouldn't risk it. So, obviously, you're enjoying the view."

I let the moment stretch, savoring her self-assured challenge. "Maybe I am."

We rode for a while in comfortable silence, with Arabella still drinking in the view. Finally, she looked at me. "I know Skyspire isn't the extent of your domain, but how much of this is yours?"

"My territories extend from the eastern sea to these highlands, north to the mountains, and south to the desert."

"All conquered?"

"Some conquered. Some negotiated." I adjusted my reins. "Some inherited."

Her eyebrows rose in surprise. "Inherited from your family?"

The mention of my family sent a familiar surge of cold rage through my veins. "In a manner of speaking. My father didn't part with his lands willingly."

Understanding dawned in her eyes. "You killed him."

"At seventeen," I confirmed. "He was reaching for his wine glass when I severed his head from his shoulders. The rest of the table sat in stunned silence for three full seconds before the screaming started."

Her horse shifted beneath her as she studied me. "There's more to that story."

"There always is." I nudged my horse forward, ending that particular line of conversation.

We crested a hill that overlooked the blackened ruin of what had once been a village. Charred beams jutted from the rubble, and only a sad, half-collapsed well stood in the center. I reined in my horse, feeling Arabella stiffen beside me.

"A week ago, it held forty-seven people," I said quietly. "Farmers, mostly."

She dismounted and walked through the remains of the village. When she returned, her expression was colder and more resolute than I had ever seen it. "And Solandris did nothing?"

"From what I hear, their patrols retreated months ago."

She swallowed hard, then climbed back onto her mare.

We arrived at Arvoryn Manor about an hour later. Unlike my citadel, it was all sharp angles and fortress walls rooted in the mountainside—functional and intimidating. Arabella pulled her shoulders back.

"Nervous?" I couldn't resist asking.

She squared her jaw. "I'm not afraid of Morana."

"Good." I nodded toward the gates. "Because here she comes, and she's wearing her stabbing corset."

Morana marched out to greet us, clad in practical black leathers that showed zero interest in subtlety. Two gleaming daggers hung at her hips. Her husband, Edmund, scurried in her wake, wide-eyed as usual.

"Kazimir," Morana greeted me. "How kind of you to grace us with your presence."

"Morana," I replied, dismounting. Then I turned to help Arabella, only to find her already sliding neatly from the saddle. Morana's sharp gaze landed on Arabella, and I didn't miss the way her mouth tightened at the sight of my wife in those leathers, which made her look distinctly more forbidding than she had at the wedding.

"Lady Blackrose," Morana said, voice measured. "Welcome to Arvoryn Manor."

Arabella gave a curtsy that managed to appear both graceful and defiant, which was quite a feat. "Viscountess. Thank you for hosting us."

Morana narrowed her eyes but forced a smile. "Lunch awaits. Follow me, and we'll see about getting you settled first."

I leaned in toward Arabella, dropping my voice so no one else would hear. "Don't eat or drink anything until I say it's safe." Then we trailed after Morana and her entourage. It would be a very interesting day indeed.

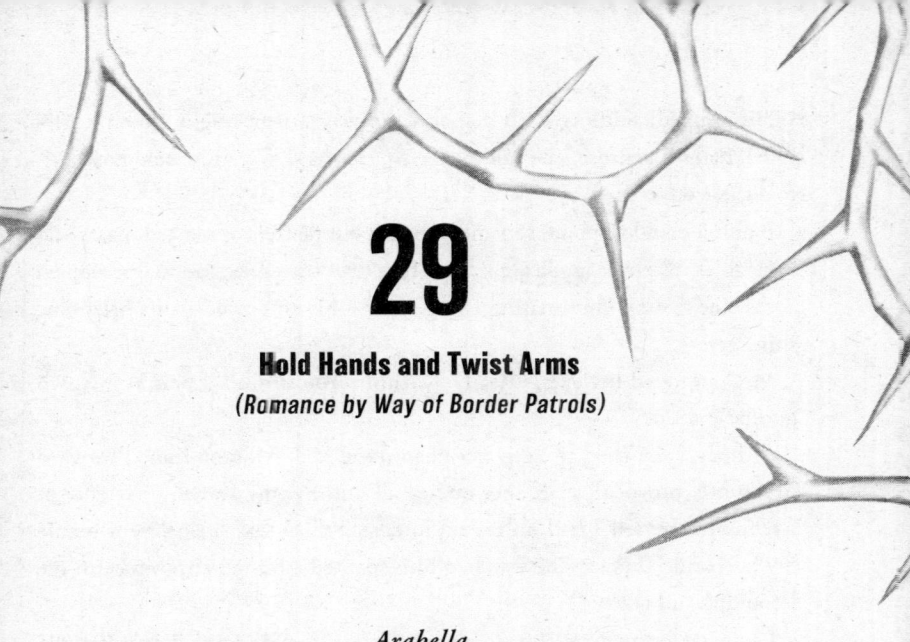

29

Hold Hands and Twist Arms
(Romance by Way of Border Patrols)

Arabella

I tried not to stare at the mounted heads glaring down at me from every inch of the manor's dining room. A three-headed serpent loomed above Morana's seat, its unblinking glass eyes seeming to track my every move. I swallowed back a shiver and channeled my best impression of polite curiosity.

"An interesting collection," I said, inclining my head toward the walls. "Did you hunt all of these yourself?"

Viscountess Morana returned a thin, chilly smile. "Most of them. Edmund managed the chimera—though, of course, he needed help." She flicked a dismissive glance toward her husband, who looked like he wanted the floor to swallow him whole.

Lord Edmund was the soft polar opposite to his wife's lethal elegance. Where Morana seemed carved from knives, Edmund appeared to be a bundle of nerves stuffed into noble attire. He hadn't once met my eyes since we arrived. A pang of something—empathy, perhaps—stirred beneath my frustration.

"Lord Edmund," I greeted. "A pleasure to make your acquaintance."

He jumped, fiddling with a spoon the way others might clutch a lifeline. "Lady Blackrose," he said, voice squeaking. "We, ah, rarely host visitors these days."

Before I could respond, servants brought out platters of roasted meats and vegetables. Kazimir made a quick gesture over the table, and magic rippled across the dishes, illuminating two goblets—his and mine—in a brief blue shimmer.

Morana rolled her eyes. "Really, Kazimir? You think I'd poison my own guests?"

Although she tried to keep her posture relaxed, Morana leaned forward in a subtly provocative arc, her bodice all but inviting Kazimir's attention. I reminded myself I had no reason to care. Still, I was sitting right beside my husband. The way she watched him sparked a heated annoyance in me I couldn't fully bury.

I reached for my wine. It was apparently safe now, but that didn't dampen my caution when I took a small sip. "The vintage is superb," I offered, cutting through the quiet. "Your vineyards, Viscountess?"

Morana collected herself, her focus snapping away from Kazimir. "Yes. The southern slopes produce a particularly robust red."

Edmund perked up a little. "You know wines, Lady Blackrose?"

I gave him a polite smile. "Father insisted. He believed a proper lady must select the right wine for any occasion."

"And what sort of occasion is this?" Morana asked, tone barbed.

I let my gaze sweep around the table. "Hopefully the sort where everyone leaves alive."

Kazimir's knee bumped mine under the table, a silent tap of approval that I allowed. "My wife has a refreshing directness, doesn't she?" he drawled.

Morana's lips tightened fractionally. "Indeed. Though I wonder if directness helps in a marriage such as yours."

"Such as ours?" I repeated, raising an eyebrow.

She carved into her meat with a pointed savagery. "A political arrangement. What else?"

At that moment, I surprised even myself by deciding I'd had enough of Morana's insinuations. Without overthinking, I reached over and took Kazimir's hand. His fingers stiffened briefly before softening around mine. I shot him a practiced smile, the one I'd honed in countless forced court appearances back home.

Morana's expression froze, and I glimpsed raw fury in her pale eyes. Apparently, Kazimir had never indulged her in such a simple public display. Interesting.

Edmund broke the tension with an awkward cough. "The, er, weather has been mild . . ."

No one answered him. I released Kazimir's hand, and he took his wine glass. "I was surprised to learn your garrison is still to the north, Morana," he said, letting that cool, ominous edge leak into his voice.

Her expression turned stony. "Intelligence suggested the mountain clans might attack. I shifted my forces to show strength."

I felt the faint pricking of my truth-sense behind my eyes. What she was saying wasn't a lie, but something in her voice hinted at missing details.

Kazimir gave a small nod. "And how accurate was that intelligence?"

She measured her words carefully. "The clans retreated to the high passes for now."

I could practically taste her reluctance to share more. I'd been so focused on reading her, I almost missed the subtle flicker of frustration crossing Kazimir's face.

"Convenient," he said, "for the bandits who swept through the villages down south."

She bristled. "If you're accusing me of abandoning my own subjects—"

"I'm noting a coincidence," Kazimir cut in. "One that serves no one's interest. A decimated settlement can't pay taxes."

Morana's knuckles whitened around her knife. "I'm managing my territories just fine without your magical shortcuts."

The chandelier's flame shuddered, and the room darkened an extra shade around Kazimir. "Those 'shortcuts' have served Arvoryn well, Morana.

Don't forget that, especially when you deal with the Syndicate."

She paled at the mention of the Syndicate but quickly fired back. "I'm merely seeking reimbursement for my lost guard, and someone has to hold this pass."

Kazimir's jaw tensed. "Meaning I should recall how precariously balanced your status is. Let's not dance around it."

Morana glared. Edmund looked like he wanted to crawl under his chair.

I leaned forward, deciding to step in before those tense undercurrents exploded into outright threats. "Perhaps we can discuss the shared border patrols. They seem reasonable if we want to avoid further 'coincidences.'"

Morana's gaze flicked to me, eyes calculating. "You've picked up much, Lady Blackrose, especially for someone who was recently confined in her father's house."

"You seem very captivated by my marriage, viscountess," I replied coolly, ignoring the flicker of memory. "Perhaps you're jealous?"

Shock flared in her expression before she masked it beneath contempt. "You mistake scorn for envy."

I studied her for a long beat, letting a small smirk touch my lips. "I don't think so."

She blanched, fury turning her cheeks a brighter shade. She looked about ready to vault across the table.

Kazimir ended the staredown by speaking in that low, authoritative tone that reminded me exactly who he was. "Enough."

The entire room seemed to hold its breath at the command. My pulse quickened. Gone was the almost playful partner who'd teased me earlier. This was the Dark Lord who had leveled entire strongholds. Morana recognized it, too. She squared her shoulders, her earlier bravado reined in.

"The treaty," Kazimir continued as though the confrontation hadn't just spiked. "You'll patrol the border of Arvoryn in rotation with my forces. No village remains uncovered for more than a day."

Morana gave a short, brittle nod. "And what will I get in this exchange?"

Kazimir swirled his wine leisurely. "I'll provide enchanted tokens for up to twenty of your people to trade with Skyspire and a trade portal for your goods, if you choose to be cooperative."

I wasn't surprised at the concession. He'd mentioned that with Arvoryn wedged between a pair of hostile realms, they'd been struggling for provisions. It was simply another element of the Dark Lord's strategy to make her reliant on his support.

"The tokens would be . . . useful," Edmund ventured, looking nervously between his wife and Kazimir.

Morana shot him a look that could have frozen fire, but he didn't flinch. Perhaps there was more to Edmund than I'd initially thought.

She folded her arms, trying to appear less unsettled. "I want at least thirty tokens."

"Twenty-five," Kazimir countered. "And I'll give you the diagrams for a receiving portal platform. Your enchanters can build it themselves—though they can't access my network without my permission."

A tense silence took root, finally broken by Morana's clipped acceptance. "Fine. Thorne has the documents, I assume?"

Right on cue, Thorne strode in carrying a worn leather folder, placing it before her. She scanned the pages with an unreadable frown, then signed with a flourish that resembled a dagger slash.

"Done." Morana shoved the parchments back, standing so rigidly that it looked like she was physically holding herself together.

Kazimir rose. "We have pressing business elsewhere. Thank you for your hospitality."

Her gaze slid to me, that cold, seething challenge in her posture. "Lady Blackrose. Enjoy your accelerated education at your husband's citadel."

I matched her stare with practiced grace. "You've been most enlightening, Viscountess Morana."

Edmund, somehow remembering his manners, escorted us to the courtyard with jittery small talk about the harvest and the stable's new horses. Watching him left me torn between pity and contempt; he deserved better, yet he seemed locked in his own quiet hell.

Kazimir paused in the courtyard, peering at his horse's foreleg. "It seems my horse is lame," he stated.

I glanced at the animal, which appeared perfectly fine. Kazimir shot me a devilish grin. "No time to saddle a spare. We'll have to ride double," he announced with a casual shrug.

My annoyance flared. "Our agreement—"

He didn't wait. In one swift motion, he hoisted me onto my mare's back before sliding in behind me. The warm press of his chest caught me off guard. As he took the reins, I felt the air shift with a crackle of energy.

"Surely," he whispered in my ear, "you wouldn't have me walk all the way back?"

I recognized the game—no doubt Morana had a perfect view from some high window. "You're impossible," I muttered, cheeks heating.

Kazimir's only response was a low chuckle as we set off, Thorne and the guards forming a protective circle around us. A brisk wind whipped down from the mountains.

When we were a safe distance from the manor, I muttered, "You could have told me ahead of time you wanted a dramatic exit."

"Would you have agreed?"

"Probably not," I admitted.

He lowered his face closer to mine. "Exactly."

Despite my frustration, I settled into his hold, genuinely relieved for the added warmth. "We're out of Morana's sight now," I pointed out. "You can stop clutching me."

He didn't loosen the arm around my waist. "I've grown quite fond of this arrangement."

I snorted, refusing to feed his smugness with a direct retort. But after a while, the rhythm of the horse's gait relaxed the tension in my limbs. I caught myself leaning back against him and quickly straightened, ignoring the sudden flutter in my chest.

Kazimir's voice dropped, the teasing note returning. "You better be careful. If you get too comfortable, you might start to like me."

"Doubtful," I replied primly.

"Keep telling yourself that." Amusement laced his tone, but I sensed a thread of genuine yearning beneath it. For all his lethal bravado, he sought acceptance from me. It made me uneasy because, in some twisted corner of my mind, I wanted to give it to him.

Silence fell as we rode, broken only by the chatter of birds and the distant bleating of goats. My thoughts drifted to the destroyed villages.

Kazimir's breath ghosted over my ear as he murmured, "A gold coin for your thoughts, Lady Blackrose."

"Auremar and his negligence," I said. "He used to be fair, I thought. Respectable. Now . . ."

Kazimir shrugged, the motion pressing me against him. "Or you only saw the image he projected. Power often makes it easy for people to conceal their true natures."

I couldn't argue, but the idea left a bitter taste in my mouth.

A moment later, I blurted, "You could have married Morana, you know. She clearly has . . . interest in you."

His grip on the reins tightened. "That was never an option."

"Why not? She adores power, obviously. And seems to share your *methods*."

He paused so long that I wondered if I'd hit a nerve. When he finally spoke, his voice struck flint against the mountain air. "Because slipping into her bed cost fewer soldiers than storming her walls, and Edmund makes excellent insurance if I decide she's outlived her usefulness. I kneel to no one—least of all Morana."

The words thudded between us. I twisted, studying the hard set of his jaw. "So . . ."

"Yes, Morana was already married. Yes, Edmund knew. Shocking revelations all around."

"Still," I muttered, turning forward again, "Morana isn't some moon-eyed courtier. Slice her pride and she'll slice back."

Kazimir laughed, low and edged. "She can try."

That wasn't bravado. I felt the chill certainty in his magic coiling around us. Suddenly the pass seemed too small for Morana's ambition and his foresight to coexist.

I swallowed hard. "So . . . Lord Edmund . . . ?"

"Has watched his wife collect 'conquests' for years," Kazimir murmured wryly into my ear. "And no, I didn't particularly care about his feelings. I'm the Dark Lord, after all."

His casual acceptance of that cruelty unsettled me more than I wanted to admit. We lapsed into silence again, the tang of pine and distant woodsmoke drifting on the air. I reminded myself he was, indeed, a villain.

My patience frayed enough for me to poke at him. "I suppose our marriage is just another pragmatic arrangement, then. If I wanted to indulge in lovers the way Morana does—"

Kazimir's arm crushed me to his chest in a single, decisive motion. My heart hammered as his voice dropped to a dangerous whisper. "You won't."

A strangled promise of violence laced each syllable. My breath caught. He kept me pressed to him, as if reminding me he could extinguish my enemies—and possibly me—without blinking. When he released his punishing hold to something more measured, I still felt his heartbeat thrumming behind me.

I swallowed the thrill of adrenaline. I'd only meant to taunt him, but the response left me rattled . . . and oddly flattered. I squared my shoulders, forcing casualness. "So you'd kill any hypothetical lover that came near me?"

"Hypothetically," he agreed, the corner of his mouth brushing my ear again, "yes."

A nervous laugh escaped me. I didn't doubt him. Not entirely. And I had no idea what unsettled me more: the threat itself or the flicker of twisted, possessive attraction that sparked dangerously between us.

We rode on in silence, while I tried not to think about how I might actually enjoy being property the Dark Lord wouldn't share.

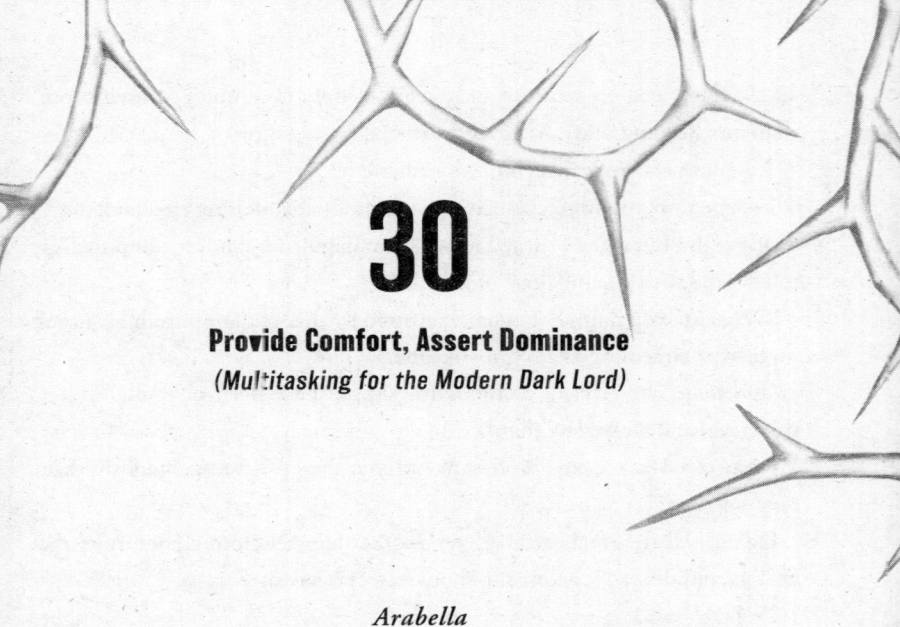

30

Provide Comfort, Assert Dominance
(Multitasking for the Modern Dark Lord)

Arabella

I couldn't seem to get warm.

Despite the scalding bath I'd taken after our return to the citadel, despite the roaring fire in Kazimir's chambers, and despite the four blankets I'd cocooned myself in, a stubborn chill clung to my bones. I blamed the last crossing over the lightning bridge. The icy wind had sliced right through my cloak, and hours later I was still shivering.

"Are you still cold?" Kazimir asked from the bed. He lay there with maddening ease, naked except for the book resting on his chest.

I shot him my fiercest glare from within my mountain of blankets. "What gave it away? The chattering teeth or the fortress worth of bedding?"

He turned a page without looking up. "You're huddled there like a half-drowned kitten."

"I'm fine." I lied, tucking my frozen feet beneath me. The fire snapped and sent sparks dancing toward the chimney, but its warmth fizzled out before it reached my couch.

Kazimir's noncommittal hum said he didn't believe me. I tried to focus on the dusty text on gemstone magic I'd brought over, but it worked better than any sleeping draft. My eyelids drooped.

"I know a way to warm you," he said at last.

I opened my mouth to launch a snark about abandoning innuendo for a single night, but when I turned he was rummaging for clothes, not prowling toward me with a scandalous proposal.

"What are you doing?" I asked, confused by this deviation from his usual nightly pastime of trying to provoke me.

"Dressing," he replied, as though it should have been obvious. "You're shivering, and we can fix that."

I narrowed my eyes. "And how do you propose to accomplish that, exactly?"

He crossed the room, fetched yet another blanket from a chest near the hearth, and draped it across my shoulders. "Follow me."

"Where?"

"Must you question everything?" He sighed, but his voice lacked true irritation. "Just come along, unless you plan to freeze solid."

I mulled over my options: stay alone in his lair where the dangers were well-charted, or follow the Dark Lord into unknown territory. Predictably, curiosity won.

"Fine." I clutched the blankets and rose. "Lead on, Lord Blackrose."

He opened the door and gestured for me to go first. The corridor was hushed, the orblights dimmed for the late hour. We descended the spiral stair, then wound through a slanted passage that burrowed beneath the citadel. Gradually, the air grew warmer, laced with a comforting, spiced aroma.

We emerged into a snug kitchen—smaller than the grand one I'd glimpsed before. This looked older, part of the fortress's original design. A generous hearth dominated one wall; copper pots glimmered overhead; bundles of dried herbs perfumed the air.

"The main kitchens are always busy," Kazimir explained as he headed toward a cabinet. "Plus, they're across another lightning bridge. This little corner of the Inner Sanctum is quieter."

"I didn't know this existed," I admitted, drifting toward the hearth's glorious heat.

"There's much about the citadel you still don't know." Without warning, he caught me by the waist and set me on the counter like I weighed nothing. My stomach swooped at his casual strength.

"What are you doing?" I demanded, clutching my blankets.

"Preparing mulled wine," he said, pulling spices and a jug of deep red wine from the cupboard. "Maybe something to eat. Hungry?"

Only when he asked did I notice the hollow ache. "A little."

He moved with confident ease—wine into a copper pot, cinnamon sticks, cloves, citrus peel—decidedly domestic for the Terror of the Western Realms.

"I had no idea you could cook," I said while he stirred.

"Heating wine isn't cooking." He shot me an amused glance. "You're too easily impressed, Lady Blackrose. Though perhaps I should have tried this tactic first instead of kidnapping you."

I snorted. "Nothing says 'marry me' like mulled wine at midnight."

The scene felt surreal: me barefoot on a kitchen counter while Kazimir Blackrose fussed over a pot of spiced wine. He poured the steaming wine into two earthenware cups and handed one to me.

I wrapped both hands around it, greedily absorbing the heat. One sip and an involuntary moan slipped out. "This is amazing."

"I know." A faint, smug smile crossed his face.

He sliced bread, layered it with cheese and cured meat, and passed me a plate. The first bite was bliss. Silence settled, but it was a comfortable hush, fragile and precious.

"So," I ventured warily, "why the sudden kindness? Slipping aphrodisiacs into my wine again?"

"No." One eyebrow arched. "Would you rather I let you turn into an ice statue?"

"I just wasn't expecting . . . this."

"I told you from the beginning I had no interest in harming you."

"Harming me is one thing," I said, picking at a stray crumb, "but mulled wine in the dead of night is another."

"Maybe I prefer you warm and coherent." He took a drink.

My body certainly approved; the tremors had stopped. "Thank you," I muttered, setting the empty plate aside. "It helped."

Kazimir lifted one shoulder in a careless shrug, as if to dismiss my gratitude. "Shall we stick to safer topics, or do you want to keep analyzing my every move?"

"Oh, I intend to keep analyzing."

He chuckled. "I'd expect nothing less."

Summoning my nerve, I chose to address the issue that had bothered me since our journey from Arvoryn Manor. "Earlier, when I teased about taking lovers, you were . . . upset."

Kazimir's gaze fixed on his wine, swirling the last of it. "Are you planning to take a lover, Arabella?"

"That's not the point."

He set down his mug. "It is to me."

I refused to flinch under his intense gaze. "You and Morana were lovers, and it didn't bother you one bit that she had others, or even a husband. Yet at the mere hint I might do the same, you snapped like an enraged wolf. Why?"

His eyes darkened with possessiveness. "Morana and you are not the same."

"Our agreement doesn't prevent me from seeking another bed," I reminded him.

He stalked forward and braced his hands on either side of me, leaning into my space. "You seem to think I was joking." He lowered his voice. "What's mine stays mine."

A forbidden spark lit beneath my ribs. I should have been outraged. I *was* outraged—but also disturbingly heated by it. "I'm not a trinket in your hoard."

"No." His gaze dipped to my mouth. "You're a force in your own right. Being mine doesn't diminish that—it amplifies it. My resources, my protection, devoted to preserving exactly who you are."

My heart hammered. "And you? Planning to collect another lover?"

His posture stiffened, as though the notion offended him. "I have no interest in trifles," he said roughly. "I find myself sufficiently occupied with one infuriating woman."

The blunt honesty stole my retort. He looked so intense in that moment—dark eyes locked on mine, a stray piece of hair falling across his forehead. But he also seemed vulnerable, the fearsome Dark Lord letting slip a confession he might not even realize was a confession.

"Oh," I managed, feeling ridiculously breathless.

His mouth curved slightly. "Yes. *Oh.*"

He stepped back, restoring a sliver of distance. The earlier chill was long gone; I was warm from head to toe, and the mulled wine wasn't solely to blame.

Grateful for the reprieve, I cleared my throat. "Fine. New subject?"

"Gladly." He leaned against the opposite counter, arms folded. "That tale you told Griffin, 'The Hero's Garden.' My library holds no record of it. Where did your mother learn it?"

I shrugged. "She never said. But she believed the roses represented transformation, not conquest."

Kazimir looked skeptical. "The Golden Roses are powered by ley lines—no moral lesson involved."

"Then explain the heroic bloodline's role in activating the Heirloom and the roses inside the crown. Coincidence?"

"Long exposure to high magic can shape bloodlines. It's not necessarily divine or mythical."

My truth-sense told me he wasn't being fully honest. "Have you discovered why the Heirloom failed?"

Kazimir shook his head. "No. We're still investigating."

Lie. I felt it but swallowed the retort. If I forced the issue he'd retreat behind his walls, and I wanted to know what he was hiding before confrontation became inevitable.

He exhaled slowly, as if relieved I hadn't pressed, then nodded at the dishes. "If you're finished, let's go back to bed."

I slid from the counter—the wine left me pleasantly lightheaded. He extinguished the lamps with a wave, leaving only the embers in the hearth.

When we arrived back in his chambers, I paused near the threshold, suddenly uncertain. The bed loomed, a familiar battleground of tension and carefully negotiated boundaries. But the memory of the wine, warmth, and Kazimir's low confessions lingered around me.

He rested a hand on the doorframe near my shoulder, leaning close enough that I caught the scent of winter storms and steel. "Feeling better?"

The almost tender note in his voice tightened my throat. "Yes," I murmured. "Warmer."

"Good." His gaze traced the line of my mouth.

I took a deep breath and looked away from his intensity. But my eyes only landed on the buttons of his loose shirt, and my mind helpfully supplied the image of what lay beneath. I couldn't blame it on the wine; I hadn't drunk enough.

His hand lifted—slow, almost hesitant—fingers brushing a stray curl near my temple. He paused, and I looked up to see the question plain in his eyes.

Something in my chest cracked. If he touched me, I might forget every reason to resist. I caught his wrist gently, moving his hand before stepping out of reach. A flicker of disappointment crossed his features, but he dipped his chin in acceptance and let his hand fall.

I retreated to the bed, where the pillow wall already waited. Still wrapped in my blankets, I crawled in on my side, pulse still thrumming with the phantom of his almost-touch.

Instead of joining me, Kazimir remained at the doorway, watching as I attempted to get comfortable under his gaze. The quiet stretched, thick with things unsaid. Finally, he straightened. "Good night, Arabella." His voice was rough with unsated want.

Before I could respond, he left, closing the door behind him.

His side of the bed stayed empty all night, and I couldn't decide which was more surprising—that he possessed enough restraint to keep his distance, or that I'd spent half the night wishing he hadn't.

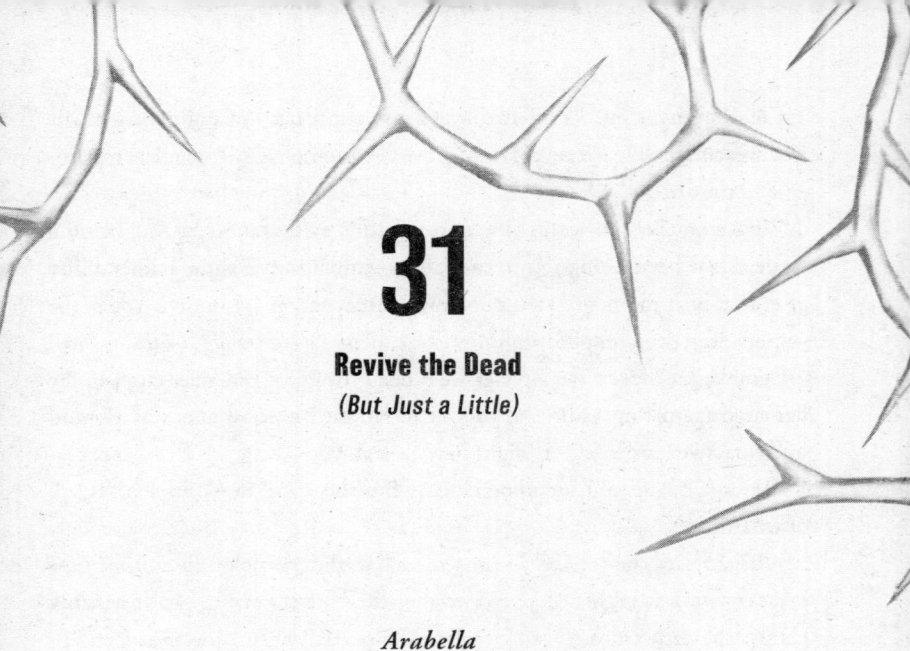

31

Revive the Dead
(But Just a Little)

Arabella

"We've been over this," I said, sending a pulse of my magic through the withered rose. "I can make it move, but I can't make it truly live again. There's a difference."

The shriveled petals twitched in a macabre little dance before they slumped back into stillness. After weeks of intensive magical training, we'd established a routine: Kazimir's impossibly demanding instruction, my skepticism, and the explosive moments when I surprised us both.

Kazimir paced behind me, so quiet he might've been a ghost. "You're still seeing life and death as fixed points," he said. "They're a continuum. Everything carries both."

I pivoted, leveling him with an exasperated glare. "That's a charming philosophical take, but this flower is very clearly dead."

He exhaled like I was missing the obvious. Moving to the table, he held a hand over the desiccated rose. "You've already shown you can animate it. You can make it unfurl, bend, move—none of that is imaginary. You're pouring your energy into it."

Crossing my arms, I huffed. "That's just puppetry. I'm not giving it life, just wearing it like a necromantic glove." For emphasis, I wiggled my fingers in the air.

"That's one way to see it." He narrowed his eyes even as he fought off a smile. He'd been doing that more lately—unwilling to show vulnerability after that near-moment in the doorway. "Life is energy in motion. You're the source. Stop overcomplicating it."

I grabbed a silver letter opener we'd been using for practice, tapping the flat edge against my palm. "If you try to sell me on necromancy as a brand of 'aggressive gardening,' I might have to stab you."

"Try again," he said, stepping closer. "But this time, don't force it. Think of what it was."

With an over-the-top sigh, I turned back to the crumpled rose. *Remember what it was,* I thought. I focused on the rose's former energy—the weighty petals, the lush color. A trickle of magic stirred within me, gentler than usual. I let it slip through my fingertips, coaxing a memory back to life, reminding rather than demanding.

A sudden surge shot from my hand, far more than I intended. I gasped, stunned by the force. I felt the rose reaching for me in return, as if a distant echo had finally answered.

"That's it," Kazimir murmured, his voice unexpectedly calm. I glanced up and realized he was standing at my side, close enough that my breath hitched. "You're not dominating it. You're inviting it."

For the first time, the rose twitched on its own. As though breathing, faded color seeped into the petals—not quite living crimson, but a ghost of it. The stem straightened and leaves unfurled.

A grin broke across my face before I could contain it, and I thought I'd drop from sheer excitement. The rose wasn't alive, not exactly, but it was more than dead. "I did it."

"You did." His voice was low with approval, but when I glanced at him, I found his heated gaze pinned on me. "Though you don't realize how much that took out of you."

The second he spoke the words, a wave of exhaustion crashed in. My knees buckled. It took all my stubborn pride not to collapse entirely.

Kazimir's arm darted around my waist. "Sit before you faint," he said, steering me to a wooden bench nearby.

As soon as he helped me down, the rose quivered once more, then crumbled into its original, withered husk. My hold on it snapped, and I felt a pang of disappointment at the finality of the motion.

"That was . . . different," I admitted, rubbing my forehead. My skin felt clammy with exertion.

Kazimir took a seat next to me, close enough that my arm brushed his. His body heat was uncomfortably distracting. "Your control is growing faster than I imagined."

He rarely handed out compliments, so I was momentarily speechless. Which only made him look smug.

I huffed. "I'd hate for someone to find out you're capable of being an actual decent human being."

"I'm sure my reputation would never recover." He glanced over my face with a scrutiny that made me hyperaware of how messy I must seem—sweat on my forehead, hair loose from its braid. Meanwhile he looked like he just stepped out of a portrait: composed, immaculate, and infuriating.

I rolled my eyes, then had to fight off another wave of dizziness. "I should clean up before dinner." I pushed off the bench, but my legs wobbled and I had to clutch the edge of the table for support.

He hovered a hand near my elbow. "Before you rush off, I had a different plan in mind, if you think you can manage."

I narrowed my eyes suspiciously. "Another aphrodisiac feast? I'd hate to see you embarrass yourself again."

Humiliation flickered across his face so fast I almost thought I imagined it. "I'm never hearing the end of that, am I?" he asked.

"Absolutely not," I said brightly, giving his shoulder an exaggerated pat. "Never, Dark Lord."

Kazimir shot a pointed look at my hand until I moved it. "I was going to suggest something else," he said. "Unless you truly are too wiped out."

He slipped that challenge in so smoothly I spoke before I could stop myself. "I can handle anything you're planning." *Damn him.*

His smile was all predatory triumph. "Excellent. Meet me in the east courtyard in an hour."

"Why not now?"

"Some things require preparation," he said in that smug, cryptic tone, "and you definitely need a wash. Let's not pretend otherwise."

I touched my cheek and felt the gritty tackiness of dried sweat. Wonderful. "Has anyone told you you're excruciatingly arrogant?"

"Often," he replied, not at all insulted. "Usually right before they beg for mercy."

Brute. I scowled at him. "Charming."

He offered me a mocking bow. "In one hour, Lady Blackrose. Don't keep me waiting."

Then he spun and strode off, black coat sweeping behind him with absurd drama. Such a show-off. I let out a snort.

Alone, I turned back to the rose, now utterly lifeless. Whatever surprise Kazimir planned, I doubted it involved flowers and gentle lullabies.

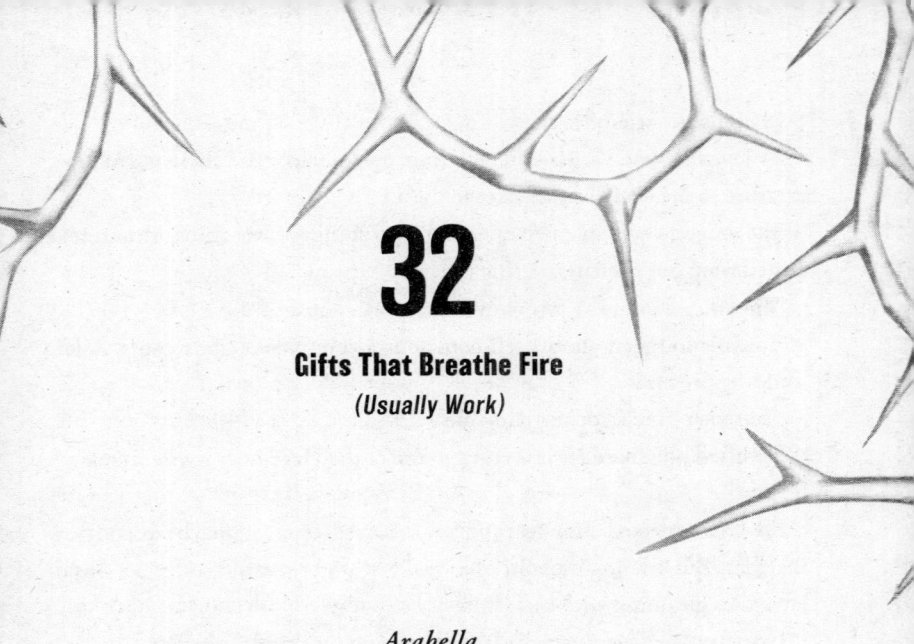

32

Gifts That Breathe Fire
(Usually Work)

Arabella

I wrapped my cloak tighter around my shoulders just as the sun slid behind the walls. The east courtyard wasn't much more than an alcove tucked against the fortress, a smaller offshoot of the main courtyard with the obscene pentagram. But I supposed the staff had to label each portal-to-possible-doom somehow, so "east courtyard" it was.

At first, I figured I was alone, but then I spotted Kazimir, his back turned toward me. He stood near the far wall, posture unusually rigid, almost as if he were . . . nervous? I almost laughed. The famed Dark Lord, nervous? Unthinkable. Yet something about the set of his shoulders gave him away.

He glanced over when he heard my footsteps and summoned me closer. "Try not to startle anything."

Naturally, I froze. "Should I expect something toothy?"

He angled his chin toward the corner. "Potentially. Best not to agitate it."

Definitely toothy, then. I approached carefully. Against the stone wall crouched a large shape. At first, it reminded me of a coiled shadow. Except shadows didn't typically have ridged spines and leathery wings.

My pulse knotted. "Is that—?"

"A juvenile shadow dragon," Kazimir murmured, gaze flicking from the creature to me. "My beastmaster found her."

The dragon's eyes snapped open to reveal shining silver irises. Thin smoke curled from her nostrils, stirring the crisp evening air.

"She's . . ." I couldn't form any other word. "Beautiful."

Kazimir sounded almost self-conscious as he spoke. "She's yours. A late wedding present."

I stared at him. "You're giving me a dragon?"

He lifted one shoulder in a shrug. "You're the Dark Lord's wife. It felt . . . fitting."

I'd half expected him to produce a cursed tiara or maybe brand-new shackles. But a living dragon? She was downright mesmerizing, her obsidian scales gleaming with each shift of her body.

I cautiously edged forward. "I'm clueless about dragon care."

"Fortunately, my beastmaster isn't." His voice found that usual note of haughtiness. "She's young enough to bond. Especially since you've got unusual magic."

I hardly heard him. "Can I get closer?"

"Carefully. Hand out, palm up. Let her decide."

He also mentioned the creature's name—Nyx—and told me I could rename her if I wanted. I didn't think I would. "Nyx," I murmured. "Hello there, magnificent girl."

Her nostrils flared, sampling the breeze around me. Then, with a sleek, serpentine movement, she slithered across the flagstones. My entire body braced in terror, but my heart pounded with something like wild, irrepressible joy.

Nyx paused inches from my hand, her breath hot against my skin. The shadow dragon's black scales rippled, creating an illusion of constant movement across her sleek form. Her nostrils flared, sampling my scent with interest, while those unsettling silver eyes—intelligent, ancient despite her youth—locked onto mine with unnerving focus. She smelled of lightning storms and charred sugar.

I swallowed nervously, waiting. Finally, after a few moments of steady puffing against my hand, she pressed her snout into my palm. A shock fired through my bones. In a sudden rush, I saw fleeting memories: webs of midnight clouds, the thrill of plunging through darkness, the thunderous echo of wings. The sensation stole my breath. When it passed, I realized I'd sunk to my knees, hand still cupped around Nyx's muzzle.

Kazimir cleared his throat. "Looks like she's taken to you."

My vision blurred. I shook off the haze, blinking up at him. "I—I don't have words for this."

His expression flickered, something vulnerable there, gone in an instant. "Consider her yours. Regardless."

Nyx rumbled deep in her throat, practically purring. I stroked her warm scales, a little awed she wasn't just a coiled shadow that could vanish any second. "Is it right?" I asked softly. "Binding a wild creature like her?"

He crossed his arms, black coat catching the breeze. "She chooses, actually. From what I heard, she nearly perched on my beastmaster's back to come here. And possibly tried to eat him. That bit is somewhat unclear."

"Thank you," I managed, looking him in the eye. "I never thought . . ."

He shifted his weight. "It's only natural you have an impressive mount. Part of the villainess starter kit, if you will."

"Is that covered in your personal handbook?" I teased.

"A whole chapter," he deadpanned.

Nyx snuffled at my shoulder, her impatience booming through our tenuous new bond. "She's starving," I said.

Kazimir nodded. "They've prepared a meal for her in the stables on Menagerie Island. Let me show you."

We started across the courtyard, stepping over cracks in the stones that the fortress's wards had fused long ago. I glanced at him. "Shadow dragons can slip through realms, right? If she grows big enough, she could carry me away. Past your wards. Past you."

He held my gaze. "She won't be large enough to carry you for a year at least. And then yes, you could leave."

I studied his expression. "That's a hell of a gamble."

He tried for a cocky grin. "I imagine you'd appreciate some freedom eventually, if you wanted it."

Something inside me twisted. The simplest possibility for bringing me such a gift was that he needed me to remain compliant. And yet, the look on his face said there might be more to it than a tactical bribe.

Nyx butted my side, projecting a hungry whine that fluttered in my mind with pictures of raw meat. "All right," I said, offering her a scratch. "Dinner's coming."

Kazimir gestured toward the walkway, and we crossed over toward the stable area. But I paused before we reached the volatile lightning bridge. "You know, it's strange—someone like you, giving a gift that literally hands me a way out. Almost like . . . trust."

"Don't read too deeply into it," he said, but the façade of arrogance wavered.

I curled my fingers lightly around his forearm for just a moment. "She's the most incredible present I've ever received," I said. "Truly."

He dipped his gaze, then gave a playful grin. "All right, don't get sappy. We villains prefer ominous declarations and chaos."

We crossed the bridge to the stables, where an attendant was already gaping at Nyx. Kazimir launched into a lecture about keeping the dragon from demolishing the walls, directed mostly at the attendant and maybe a little at me. I feigned attention while trying to figure out the contradictions of a man who would force me to marry him, then present me with an escape plan.

Nyx stretched and flexed her claws impatiently like a cat. Kazimir sighed at the fresh gouges in the stone, while I stifled a laugh. "Yes," I said, "feeding time. Let's get to it."

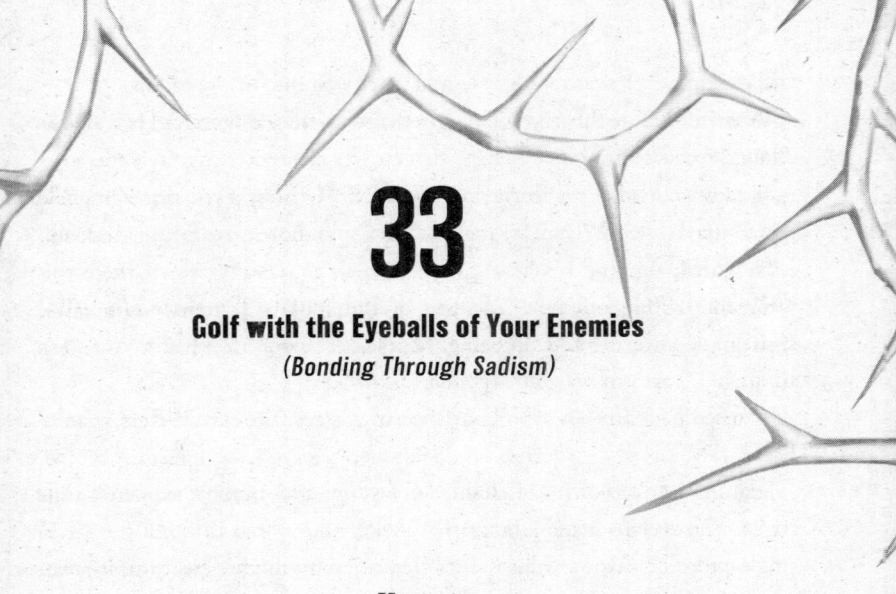

33

Golf with the Eyeballs of Your Enemies
(Bonding Through Sadism)

Kazimir

The wind whipped around me as I stood at the edge of the western parapet, my grip so tight on the club that the leather handle creaked.

Six weeks. Six fucking weeks of lying beside Arabella every night with nothing but fabric and feathers between us. Six weeks of waking hard and aching, forced to slip away before she noticed the effect she had on me. I wanted her beneath me, above me, against every surface of my fortress. Yet every night, I honored our agreement like some honorable knight from a fairy tale.

The restraint was costing me—nights spent pacing the study rather than returning to our chambers, cold baths at ungodly hours, and the maddening awareness that she wanted me as well, but was too stubborn to give in.

Behind me, Sims cleared his throat with practiced politeness. "Your turn, my lord," he said, and I detected the faintest thread of impatience in his tone.

I didn't bother looking at him. Instead, I swung my club a few times with slow deliberation, measuring the angle. In front of me, perched on a little wooden tee, was a fresh eyeball from yesterday's would-be assassin. Viscera still clung to it. It was repulsive—and utterly fitting for my mood.

"Anytime before the next solstice, perhaps," Griffin muttered. He was loud enough to be heard, quiet enough that he was clearly testing my patience.

Shadows curled at my fingertips. I whirled. "Griffin, if you'd prefer a field trip to the dungeons, I can arrange that. I'm told the rats are feeling peckish."

He paled, dipping his head. We'd sent three servants down there this week for trifling offenses. The rest of the staff had smartly adopted a strategy of cowering and tiptoeing. "Apologies, my lord," Griffin said. "I'm simply . . . eager to see your legendary skill."

I turned back to the eyeball, satisfied by his contrite tone. "Then watch," I said.

Leaning into the swing, I channeled a surge of dominion magic into the strike. The eyeball made a fantastic squelch and soared through the air. A single pulse of shadow adjusted its trajectory midflight, ensuring it splattered graphically against a distant rock formation on a floating island—visible proof of my skill, even from here.

Vex, leaning against the parapet, offered a wry nod. "Well done, my lord. Though I doubt we can reuse that one."

I flicked off a bit of gore from the club. "Sacrifices must be made. Speaking of which, has Lady Blackrose finally emerged from the stables, or is she still doting on that overgrown lizard I was fool enough to give her?"

Vex and Griffin exchanged a look that made me want to fling them both from the parapet. "Well?" I prompted irritably.

"Lady Blackrose spent her morning in the library," Vex said, "researching dragon husbandry."

"How riveting," I replied. My jaw tightened without my permission. "I'm thrilled she's occupied while the fate of this fortress hangs in the balance."

Sims stepped up to take his shot, eyeball in place. He swung so poorly that it tumbled straight into the swirling clouds. "To the abyss with that one," he muttered.

Griffin clasped his hands behind his back. "That's four eye casualties today, Sims."

Vex straightened, posture all business. "Continuing where we left off: No word yet from our agents in Solandris about Lord Evenfall's plans. He's keeping his dealings very quiet."

My grip on the club tightened, the mere mention of Arabella's father curdling my mood further. "What about the mercenary recruitment, then?"

"No solid leads. He's approached at least three companies this past week, but we can't track them all," Vex admitted.

Griffin picked up the next eyeball, rolling it in his palm with forced casualness. "He's not actually trying to mount a direct assault on a floating fortress, is he? That'd be suicidal."

"Indeed," I said, thinking how the Heirloom's stasis complicated everything. "But Evenfall is desperate, and desperation can drive a fool to unimaginable risks."

Sims consulted a small notebook. "His coffers have been empty for years. His only decent asset was—"

"His daughter," I finished flatly, a stark fury worming into my mind. "Who's now of no use to him because she belongs to me."

Griffin set his eyeball on the tee, lined up, and—*thump*. The organ soared, dropping neatly onto a midrange island. He crowed with triumph. "That puts me ahead by two!"

"Temporarily," I warned him, though my mind was elsewhere. "It's curious, isn't it? Evenfall acts as though he expects me to simply hand over both his daughter and a fortune, despite knowing full well who I am."

"Perhaps he's counting on your well-known mercy and generosity," Vex suggested, her tone so dry it could have parched the Ashen Wastes.

I snorted. "That must be it—my reputation for compassion precedes me." I stepped up to the tee. "Perhaps I should send him a gift basket full of severed fingers."

"*Did* you send a response?" Griffin asked, handing me another eyeball.

"I debated removing his courier's head as a token," I said, "but that seemed too polite. So I offered a different message."

Sims hesitated as he jotted it all down. "Which was?"

"That if Evenfall persists in demanding his daughter's return, I'll consider it an open war with Skyspire. And then I recommended he partake in certain . . . anatomically elaborate activities while waiting for the nonexistent ransom."

Griffin grimaced. "Very diplomatic, my lord."

"Some traditions must be maintained," I said, channeling my irritation into a second shot. I examined the eyeball, which had an unusual golden fleck in the iris. "This one looks familiar."

"It should," Vex said with a grim smile. "That's all that remains of the guard who couldn't keep his eyes to himself when Lady Blackrose first arrived."

The eye squished slightly as my anger flared, hot and possessive. I forced myself to relax before I ruined a perfectly good projectile.

Sims sniffed. "He should have known better than to ogle the boss's wife."

"He made his choice," I said, placing the eyeball on the peg. My swing was vicious. I watched with satisfaction as it arced through the air, then gave it a subtle magical nudge so it landed precisely in the courtyard below. It was followed by a spectacular chorus of cursing.

"That's Thorne," Griffin announced, peering over. "You've got superb aim, my lord."

"If he'd only joined us instead of inspecting the new recruits, he might have avoided such misfortune."

The sound of rapid footsteps drew our attention to the stairway. A moment later, Arabella emerged, looking irritated. Nyx bounded after her, emitting little chirps.

"Lady Blackrose," I said, all smooth courtesy. "We're in the midst of a . . . recreational session."

Her gaze moved from my face to the gore-smeared club in my hand, then to the table of eyeballs. "You're playing some horrific version of golf?"

Griffin offered a bright grin. "Indeed! Care to join?"

She stiffened, flicking a nervous glance at Griffin. Something in her expression warned me she'd prefer not to speak freely in front of him. "I need to speak with you," she insisted. "Privately."

I raised the club as if I might continue. "Surely it can wait until I've trounced Griffin."

"It can't," she pressed, stepping forward to snare my full attention. Her voice dropped. "Please."

Her "please" disarmed me. Arabella rarely begged, which meant it was serious. Before I could respond, Nyx lurched into a wheezing hack. We all turned, and with a final gag, the dragon retched up . . . something small, bloody, and disturbingly furry onto the parapet stones.

Griffin's face whitened. "Whisper?" he croaked. "My new familiar?"

Arabella looked guilt-stricken. "I tried to stop her, but Nyx—she just—"

"Is a dragon," I supplied, amused by the scene. "And I suspect your precious new fox offended her palate."

Griffin knelt, mouth slack in mingled grief and fascination. "The enchantment is gone. Months of binding effort, undone." He sighed like a man who'd lost not just a pet, but a fraction of his soul.

Arabella knelt too, remorse twisting her features. "I'm so sorry, Griffin. I'll replace it or make it right somehow."

An unwelcome jolt of jealousy sparked under my ribs. "No, you won't," I said, the words coming out sharper than I intended. "I'll see to Griffin's compensation. I had the dragon brought here. Which means it's my responsibility in the end."

Arabella slid me a startled but grateful look. Something in my chest warmed.

Griffin stood, eyeing the soggy remains. "I . . . appreciate that, my lord."

"Now," I said briskly, "resume your turn, if you please."

He picked out another eyeball but did so with less enthusiasm.

Arabella stared at me incredulously. "That's it? You're just going to continue with . . ."

"A team-building exercise," Sims supplied helpfully.

A spark of curiosity flickered in Arabella's eyes, though she tried to hide it. "It's barbaric."

I shrugged. "These particular eyeballs belonged to people who would have happily seen both of us dead. Consider it recycling."

"Very sustainable villainy," Vex added with a straight face.

Griffin made his shot, and the eyeball landed perfectly, drawing a somewhat half-hearted whoop from him. Normally, that would have infuriated me. At present, I was too focused on how Arabella's cloak shifted to reveal the hollow at the base of her throat.

"Want to try?" I asked, offering her my club.

Arabella exhaled. "Maybe I should get Nyx back downstairs."

I arched a brow. "Afraid you can't match my skill? I realize not everyone has the aptitude for this game. It requires a certain finesse."

She stiffened, hazel eyes sparking. "Give me that club."

I passed it to her. "The secret to a perfect shot is in the follow-through"—I leaned in—"and a bit of control."

She set the eyeball on the tee, eyes flicking across the fortress before gesturing at the far eastern spire. "That gazebo."

Griffin let out an incredulous laugh. "That's a bit bold for a first attempt."

"Go big or go home," she said, glancing at me over her shoulder. "Isn't that the villain way?"

I huffed. "Something like that. But don't be offended if you miss. It takes pract—"

She swung with lethal precision, and my jaw dropped when the eyeball sailed in a neat arc and landed dead-center on the gazebo's rooftop. Griffin sputtered. Sims nearly swallowed his tongue. Vex just grinned.

"Impossible," Griffin breathed.

Arabella handed me the club with a smug grin. "Apparently not."

"You've done this before." I scowled. "Did you use magic?"

Arabella shook her head. "At court, I was good at a version of this game. But they used little wooden balls, not . . . body parts." A flicker of old resentment shadowed her face. "People thought I cheated then, too. But I just have good aim."

"There you have it," Vex said brightly. "The new champion, humiliating you on her first try, my lord."

Ignoring Vex's glee, I tilted my head in grudging respect. "Well played, Lady Blackrose. I'd invite you to join our gruesome little tournaments more often, unless you're too busy with that dragon."

Arabella's expression softened. "I might take you up on that. Although I should probably keep Nyx from devouring more unsuspecting creatures." She glanced over her shoulder at the broodling, who was sniffing our eyeball supply.

Sims ruined the moment by clearing his throat. "About Lord Evenfall . . . We were in the middle of strategy?"

Arabella's smile faded. "What about my father?"

Her gaze locked on me, as if we were the only two there. Now, after six weeks of dancing around each other, I was starting to realize how satisfying it was that she sought answers from me, not from anyone else.

"We have reason to believe," I began, beckoning her over to the small table where Sims's map was spread, "that your father's meeting with mercenary companies, to mount some 'rescue.' If so, it could lead to open conflict."

She crossed her arms. "My father is unscrupulous and manipulative, but he's not a tactician. If he's planning something, he's allied with someone who is." She traced a finger over the Solandris capital, scowling. "Like King Auremar. If he believes I'm an unwilling captive . . . my father might persuade him to intervene."

Griffin exhaled. "That'd pit us against the might of Solandris."

For an instant, my frustration flared. Arabella was supposed to be the key to bridging my vulnerability there, but our marriage remained unconsummated while my enemies circled like vultures. "We must keep one step ahead, then, and send in more spies. I want to know if Auremar is mobilizing."

Griffin set aside the map. "Now, if that's settled . . . I do believe it's my turn again?"

I waved him forward, letting him amuse himself. My focus snagged on Arabella, who stood mere inches away.

She murmured, half to herself, "This is going to be bad. If my father's threatened, he'll lash out in some cunning, despicable way."

"We'll be prepared." A prickle of protectiveness thrummed in my chest.

Nyx was drooling over the eyeballs. Arabella attempted to corral her. "You, stop. Please. We'll find you something else to chew."

She was about to slip away, presumably to drag the dragon downstairs, but I caught her wrist. "Stay." I wasn't sure whether it was an order or a plea. Arabella met my gaze—surprised, uncertain. I seized on the first reason that sprang to mind. "You bested me at my own game. Surely you'd enjoy seeing Griffin flounder as well?"

Her features softened by a fraction. "One more round," she allowed. "But then I really do have to take Nyx before—"

I interrupted with a half smile. "One more round," I echoed, pressing an eyeball into her hand. My eyes dropped to her lips against my will, and I crushed the flicker of desire that stirred. She'd be mine in earnest eventually. I just hadn't found the perfect strategy yet.

For now, I'd relish what little victory I could take: Arabella's presence at my side, even if we were lobbing bloody eyeballs at random landmasses.

All I knew was that I wasn't letting her go, even if I had to go to war to keep her.

34

Detect Half-Truths
(While Training Your Dragon)

Arabella

I wiped soot from my face and let out a ragged breath.

"Nyx!" I shouted, voice cracking. "Control the flame. Don't just—"

Too late. The dummy erupted into a bright column that singed my eyebrows and filled the courtyard with thick smoke. My skin prickled from the heat, sweat trickling between my shoulder blades. I coughed, waving my arms to clear the air.

"Dammit," I muttered, dropping what remained of the charred pole. "That's the third one today."

Nyx perched on her haunches, swishing her tail in smug satisfaction. If dragons could smirk, she was definitely smirking at me.

"Don't give me that look," I warned, wiping my hands on my grimy leathers. "We agreed on controlled bursts, remember? Small. Precise." I held my thumb and forefinger barely an inch apart. "Not incinerate-everything-within-reach."

An amused snort escaped Nyx's nostrils, accompanied by a puff of smoke. In the short time since Kazimir had given her to me, she'd nearly doubled in size and now stood as tall as my shoulder, wings sturdy and broad enough to force the beastmaster to reinforce the stable doors. Her attitude had grown right along with her wingspan.

"At least you hit the target this time," I added drily, "sort of."

Nyx let out a low rumble, her version of a laugh. Through our connection, I felt bubbles of glee. Chaos was her playground, and she clearly believed I should stop complaining and join her.

"You know Griffin will have my head if we torch all his training dummies before sunset," I grumbled. "And then where would we be?" She instantly sent me a flashing mental image of us flying far away, leaving the citadel behind—all freedom and scorching carnage. "Yes, very funny," I said, rolling my eyes. "But we still need to learn control, especially after you ate Griffin's familiar. He's not forgiven you for that . . . or me, by extension."

She rumbled in lazy contentment, as if my scolding was funny. I grabbed another dummy from the nearly depleted stack, half dreading the next misfire. "Okay," I coached her gently, "small and precise, like we practiced yesterday. One more shot, and—"

The dragon inhaled, chest expanding. For a moment, hope flickered in my chest—maybe she'd actually do it right. Then mischief lit her eyes.

"Nyx," I warned, "if you incinerate this one too, I'm telling Griffin it was your idea to practice flame control near his experimental menagerie."

That gave her pause. With a grudging huff, she exhaled a stream of violet fire that scorched only the dummy's midsection. I grinned and clapped.

"So you could do it after all!" A burst of pride warmed me. She was a relentless trickster, but she was mine and I loved her for it.

"Impressive discipline," a deep voice drawled from the courtyard entrance. "Though I suspect your threat was more effective than your instructions."

My heart skipped a beat as I turned. Kazimir leaned casually against the archway, arms folded over his chest. Even in the twilight, his presence managed to dominate the space. My traitorous pulse kicked up several notches.

"Sometimes fear works better than reason," I tossed back, meeting his gaze. "I believe that's the first rule of being a villain?"

His mouth curved into one of those dark half smiles that made me want to either punch him or pounce on him. "Would you like to find out what else I know about motivation, Arabella?"

Heat flared across my cheeks. Nyx snorted, tail thumping the cobblestones like she found us both ridiculous. I busied myself brushing ash off my leathers to hide any traitorous flush.

"Not tonight," I said with a breezy tone. "Unless you came to donate your wardrobe for target practice. Nyx would enjoy torching your shirts."

"Tempting," he said, pushing away from the wall and walking toward me with that predator's grace he wore so well. My gaze settled on the breadth of his shoulders, how the tailored coat hugged his frame. "But I'm here on business."

My collar suddenly felt too tight. "What business?"

Nyx stepped over, pressing her head into his hip. He scratched her eye ridges, and the dragon nearly melted from delight. She wasn't the only one purring on the inside.

Kazimir's expression turned serious. "We've had more attacks on our border villages, as well as those that trade with my territories. All within days of each other."

"More bandits?" I found myself stepping closer, even though my better instincts told me to keep my distance.

He nodded. "They aren't successful, but the pass offers ideal cover. Morana's been sending messages for extra men and supplies."

"You think she's involved?"

His tone chilled. "I think Morana does whatever's best for Morana. She's allied with me right now because I've given her no other choice. The instant something better comes along, she'll take it."

"Or," I ventured, "my father's behind these raids, using King Auremar to stir up trouble."

Kazimir nodded, taking a seat on a stone bench and gesturing for me to join him. I hesitated then sat, leaving a deliberate sliver of space between us. He was way too tempting at close range.

"I've sent more patrols along the trade routes, though that might not please Morana."

"She can cope," I said, letting some of my frustration mellow my voice. "Isn't that what you do—force others to cope with your decisions?"

Kazimir ignored my barb. "Tell me, Arabella," he said, looking at the burned remains of the dummies, "if your father did succeed, if Auremar sent his forces to 'save' you, would that make you happy?"

The question rattled me. I stared at the courtyard stones before answering. "No. It wouldn't." The words sounded raw, even to my own ears. But I had no illusions about what life would be like if I returned to Solandris.

I looked up to find Kazimir studying me. "What?" I inhaled the faint stench of burnt straw still clinging to the humid night air. Nyx snorted beside me, her smoky breath huffing across my leg. I drew my shoulders back, reminding myself to hold steady. "What?" I repeated under my breath, as if Kazimir's gaze were an interrogation.

A flicker of something stirred in his expression. "You answered quickly, that's all."

"Well, I'm not about to pretend escaping back to my father would be a dream come true." My voice felt smaller than I intended, but I kept talking anyway. "I know exactly how that story goes. I'll always be just another pawn in his scramble for power."

I brushed an ember off my sleeve. Part of me wanted Kazimir to stop looking at me that way, to stop dissecting my every word. Another part found it comforting, being truly seen, even by a villain.

"Besides," I added self-consciously, "I'm married to you, aren't I? It's not like I'm available."

Kazimir's gaze was unrelenting, full of a hunger that made my stomach flutter. He reached out, fingers brushing my chin, forcing me to look him straight in the eye. "What's mine," he said softly, "stays mine."

That quiet promise—I should hate it, right? But instead, something in me loosened, like I could exhale after holding my breath for too long. I tried for a scoff, or at least a clever retort, but all I managed was a shallow breath.

"Arrogant warlord," I murmured at last, voice rasping.

"Always."

An uneasy silence settled. Eventually, he stood, glancing up at the emerging stars. "I'll leave you to your training. I have some research to do on our situation at the borders."

The subtle tingle behind my eyes alerted me to a part truth, part omission. "Right," I said softly. "I'll see you later, then."

Without another word, he turned and strode back into the fortress, coattails swaying. My gaze tracked him until he disappeared. Nyx nudged me, a knowing look in her silver gaze.

"Yes, he's hiding something," I told her, sighing. She blew a faint bit of smoke. Smug creature. I forced my attention back to the new dummy. "All right, one more attempt before we call it quits."

I braced the dummy upright, and Nyx eyed me with that cheeky glint. "You're on my side," I reminded her. "Aren't you?" Any illusions I had of being in complete control vanished under her playful stare.

"It's the principle of the thing," I muttered, mostly to myself. "He kidnapped me, put a macabre ring on my finger, and then acted surprised when I didn't immediately jump into bed. As if I'd fall all over him just because he's the mighty Dark Lord." I planted the dummy with unnecessary force. "Yes, he's attractive, but that's—" I blew out a breath. "It's just biology."

Nyx issued a disdainful snort that almost sounded like laughter. "You hush," I snapped, rubbing a spot of soot off my leathers. "Sometimes, for three seconds, I almost forget how much I hate him."

The dragon swished her tail skeptically. She wasn't fooled by my deflections any more than I was. I still couldn't figure out Kazimir's real game—he wanted me for my bloodline, but sometimes he looked at me like he actually wanted . . . me.

What's mine stays mine.

I sighed. "All right. Small and controlled, remember?"

Nyx inhaled, then promptly unleashed a massive jet of flame. The force knocked me flat on my back. When the flames died, the dummy had been reduced to a smoldering mound of char.

The dragon ambled over and peered down at me with veil-thin amusement. Her expression practically said *Oops*.

"Yeah, yeah," I grumbled, picking myself off the flagstones. "Perhaps we'll save what's left of Griffin's dummies for another day."

35

Stalk Your In-Laws
(for Research Purposes)

Kazimir

I hadn't planned on skulking like a common thief in Evenfall's overgrown gardens. When I'd sought out Arabella in that smoky courtyard earlier, my only intention had been to discuss the bandit situation. But as often happened whenever we found ourselves in close proximity, I blurted out something else entirely—something that prompted her to lower her guard just enough for me to glimpse the raw hurt she carried. That single moment revealed how little I truly understood regarding what her father had done to her.

She had chosen to stay. When I'd given her the chance to leave—like a complete fucking idiot—Arabella had chosen me.

So there I was, risking magical backlash in enemy territory to see the bastard for myself. I needed to understand what kind of monster locked his own daughter in a tower and broke her so completely that even a villain like me felt like the preferable option in her eyes.

When I told her, "What's mine stays mine," I meant it with every scarred inch of my body. I needed her for the Heirloom, certainly, but there was more to it now. Evenfall had damaged her, and I wanted proof of how deep that damage ran.

I crept along a vine-choked wall, letting shadows swirl around me while I pushed aside briars overgrowing the old manor boundary. Each breath tasted of Solandris's smug defenses, reminding me I had only a narrow window before they began to sap my dominion. I slipped over the wall, dropping onto the grounds in a crouch among what must once have been meticulously trimmed topiaries. They had become a wretched forest of tangled limbs. Behind them, the main house rose like a malignant growth. Unsteady lamplight glimmered against mismatched windows—some expensive, modern glass, others warped and riddled with age.

I inched closer, hugging the house's stone façade until I found an unobstructed view through a tall window. Lord Atticus Evenfall was there, perched behind an oversized desk as though he fancied himself a king. He was smaller than I'd expected, with thinning hair and a pinched mouth. His fragile hands cradled a crystal decanter, and he refilled his glass so often that I needed no further proof of his lack of discipline.

My dagger slipped into my grip unbidden. A single shadow-step would have taken me inside, let me slash his throat, and watch his blood soak through that pretentious parchment. Problem solved.

My fingers tensed around the hilt.

Then Arabella's face filled my mind. Eliminating her father without her permission would hardly earn me her gratitude. She deserved her confrontation, deserved to see him answer for his deeds in person. If I ended him now, I'd be denying her something vital.

My magic flared, hungry for violence, but I shoved the blade back into its sheath with a low curse. Since when did I hesitate over a kill? Only a year earlier, I'd have opened his throat for sport, yet now I stood there pausing like some indecisive fool, all because of Arabella's possible reaction.

I slipped along the manor's perimeter, near the kitchens, and discovered a servant's door. It opened under the faintest nudge of my dominion magic. Hilariously simple. A dingy corridor lay beyond, haphazardly furnished with both brand-new pieces and tattered rags. Imported rugs had been slapped over cracked marble, the entire layout chaotic despite the attempt at wealth.

I pressed onward, brushing my fingertips over the ornate wainscoting. Intricate carvings caught my attention—runes embedded in the wood. A subtle magical field lay across the manor like a sour film on the air. I tested one with a faint thread of shadow magic, but the persistent burn in my bones was due to Solandris itself. These runes didn't target every mage who might wander through.

Just one.

My lips curled into a silent snarl. So that was how Atticus contained Arabella. He'd turned the entire estate into a magical cage.

The further I prowled, the more runes I found, etched into frames, woven into rugs, hammered into ceiling beams. Layers upon layers, some new, others older and more elaborate. Eventually, they led me to a heavy door reinforced with iron bands. Dread prickled along my spine. A hush lingered behind that threshold—a faint wrongness, as though the manor itself wanted me to stay away.

One whisper of command opened the door, revealing a spiraling staircase up into a tower. I followed it up, each step steeped in magic that felt like cold nails raking my lungs. At the top, I emerged into a cramped circular room. A barred window let in a sliver of moonlight. A narrow bed, a tiny desk, a battered stack of books, and a single floral blanket tried desperately to mask the fact that this was a prison cell.

Arabella had lived here. Atticus had locked her up in this tiny chamber, drowning her abilities under ancient wards. The fury that simmered in my chest burned hotter than I expected. My mother had carved runes into my bones to make me strong—sadistic, yes, but she'd shaped me into something unstoppable. This bastard had done the opposite to Arabella: strangle her magic so she'd remain docile and powerless.

I studied the older wards, noticing where new ones had been layered over them. The net must have tightened over time as Arabella's magic grew, ensuring she never managed to break free. It reminded me of the resonance

I'd observed in her blood. She possessed raw, volatile power. If she'd developed any magical skill here at all, the strength she might achieve beyond these walls was unimaginable.

A creaking sound behind me made me turn in time to see a guard climbing the stairs with a lantern. I could have vanished into the shadows, but my rage demanded an outlet. His eyes widened the instant he spotted me.

"You—" he tried to shout.

Shadows lashed out, wrapping around his throat before he could finish. The lantern slipped from his hand, smashing on the stones. Flames flickered, but my magic smothered them instantly.

"Tell me," I growled, stepping over the broken glass. "Were you the one who guarded her cell? Did you stand here and pretend not to hear her screams?"

"I—I've only been here six months," he choked, clawing at the shadowy noose. "I don't know anything, I swear!"

He fell to his knees, gasping for air. I released a fraction of my hold. "So you're too new to be directly guilty?" I said coldly, half to myself. "That's just bad luck, then."

"Please," he begged, voice rasping, "I have a family—"

"I am not known for my mercy." I tightened the shadows.

I had killed countless men with little more than a passing shrug. But this time, each savage heartbeat carried fresh anger. He was only one guard, practically insignificant, but he worked for the man who'd locked Arabella away. That was enough to invoke my wrath.

It was a messy kill—bloody, vicious. When I finally let the darkness recede, he lay in a twisted heap, blood staining the runes embedded in the floor. I stood there, breath coming heavy. "Wonderful," I muttered bitterly, removing my gloves. Stealth no longer served me now that I'd left a corpse in my wake.

I drew a sigil in a smear of blood and spun a quiet incantation. The lines shimmered, and space itself began to dissolve around me. Blood-based teleportation was nauseating, but it was my quickest route out without draining enormous energy on a fully opened portal.

An instant later, the manor flickered and vanished. I reappeared in my private workroom at Skyspire Citadel, the dead guard sprawled at my feet. The metallic tang of blood clung to the air, and my head reeled from the recoil.

I might have summoned Vex or Sims or Thorne to deal with the remains. It was standard procedure. But an even stronger impulse tugged me out of the workroom, through the winding corridors, up toward my private chambers. My clothes were stiffening with gore, my pulse still hammering from the kill. Servants scattered at the sight of me, eyes wide and fearful. Usually, I welcomed that terror. Tonight, I barely registered it.

I halted in front of my chamber door. Arabella slept inside, presumably safe and oblivious—far from that cursed tower, far from her father's manipulations. A feral protective anger still coiled behind my ribs. I wanted to burst in and proclaim I would defend her freedom by any means.

She didn't know I'd sneaked off to Evenfall or that I'd left behind one fewer guard for her father. Part of me wanted to keep it hidden, yet another part wanted her to see the blood and realize I was prepared to fight for her no matter how vicious it became. I might not be anyone's hero, but I would make damn sure no one bound her in a cage again.

Steeling myself, I reached for the handle. Whatever reaction she might have to the blood, I'd face it. Because, apparently, I was the kind of villain who cared what his wife thought. The irony left my heart pounding for all the wrong reasons.

With a growl and a push, I opened the door.

36

Share Your Magic
(Not Your Feelings)

Kazimir

I found Arabella perched on the sofa's edge, rubbing her neck with a pained expression. Firelight touched her loose hair, creating an unfairly golden halo that only intensified the tug I felt toward her.

Her head snapped up at my entrance, eyes widening as she took in my blood-soaked appearance. A flicker of genuine worry crossed her face before she smoothed it over with deliberate neutrality.

"You look like you've had an interesting evening," she said, voice steady.

I held her gaze, taking in every detail, from the way her fingers stayed curled near her throat to the subtle tremor in her posture. She was here, perfectly safe. And here I'd just burst through the door like a madman. A slew of confessions skittered across my mind before I snapped my usual mask back in place. I began unbuttoning my ruined shirt.

"What are you doing?" Her voice hitched slightly.

"I have entrails all over me," I said curtly. "I'd rather not stew in them."

"Why do you have— Never mind. I don't want to know."

I attempted a smirk, determined to bury those confusing impulses under my usual taunts. "If you're curious, you could watch me undress. Otherwise, I'm taking a bath."

She shot me a pointed look. "You could strip off in the bathing chamber instead of giving me a show."

"Why?" I let my shirt drop with a wet plop on the floor. "This is my room, too."

I stepped close enough for her to see the streaks of crimson drying across my scars. Her fists tightened on her lap, but she didn't flinch.

"Are you injured?" she ventured.

I shook my head, then braced my hands on either side of her, leaning in just enough to crowd her space without touching her. She stayed planted, spine straight, gaze flickering from my chest to my face. "Good."

Only one word, but it unclenched a knot in my chest I hadn't realized was there. "You could join me," I suggested.

She raised an eyebrow. "In your bath with the entrails? No thanks."

"I'll wash them off first. Problem solved."

A flicker of amusement crossed her features. The more I stared at her, the more the rest of the world receded. Rage still simmered in my veins from the things I'd done tonight, but just looking at her alive and unbound steadied me in a way that felt treacherous. My usually detached attitude cracked, and genuine concern poured out in my next question.

"Are *you* injured?"

"Nothing I can't handle." But her face betrayed a flash of discomfort.

"You've been avoiding me," I said, circling behind the sofa. "Wearing yourself out with that dragon so you'd be too tired to think about our . . . situation."

"That's not—" she began but stopped herself.

"May I?" My hands hovered above her shoulders. "After what I'd discovered tonight, I found myself uncharacteristically reluctant to touch her without permission. "No ulterior motives. Just relief."

"I'm surprised," she said, "that you're not just looking for another excuse to touch me."

I recognized the deflection as the same defensive mechanism I used when feeling vulnerable. "Is that a yes?"

Arabella gave me a long, measuring look. Then she sighed, dropping her gaze. "Fine. But no funny business."

"You have my word," I said, trying to sound serious and absolutely failing to kill the dark amusement in my tone.

My hands settled on her shoulders. Her muscles were knotted tight, practically twisted around her spine. When I began kneading carefully, she made a noise that sent a shiver across my arms. The sound was almost lost in the crackle of the fire, but it carried a soft hint of pleasure that, quite frankly, I found distracting.

"Relax," I murmured, continuing the slow, careful pressure of my thumbs.

"Your commands don't work on me," she retorted, but she leaned into my palms anyway, tension loosening under my touch.

"It wasn't a command." I leaned down, my lips almost brushing her neck. "It was an invitation."

I dug my thumbs into a particularly stubborn knot and felt her body stiffen, then ease with a soft, involuntary groan. Had I been capable of pure altruism, maybe I'd find it comforting to release her tension. But I tasted a darker spark of satisfaction in giving her relief. My motivations were a tangled mess, and I hardly cared to sort them out at that moment.

Once her muscles loosened, I lifted my hands and stepped back. I needed to rid myself of the blood crusting over my skin. "Better?"

"Yes," she admitted. "Where'd you learn that?"

"Villainy requires attention to anatomy," I said with a smirk. "With all sorts of applications . . . Massaging is just one of the nicer ones."

She shot me her customary exasperated glare. "Should I be concerned?"

"Only if you find competence threatening." I moved toward the bathroom, shedding the rest of my bloody clothes as I went.

In the bath, I scrubbed off gore and tried to wrestle my thoughts into submission. The swirling red water reminded me of my anger when I saw that guard. As if a switch had flipped in my head, urging me to eradicate every threat to Arabella. It was a weakness I wasn't sure I could afford.

I stepped out of the water and wrapped a towel around my waist. At least she was safe. And we had an arrangement.

When I finally emerged, Arabella was staring at the fireplace with a focus that looked forced. Her gaze flicked to my bare chest and the water droplets trickling down my torso. A faint pink color tinted her cheeks. I suppressed my smile.

"What's making you so smug?" she asked.

Instead of answering, I opened the wardrobe to find a pair of sleeping pants. "You seemed worried," I said, "when I walked in covered in blood."

Her expression flickered. "I was thinking of Nyx," she said too quickly, turning her back to the fire.

"Ah yes, the fire-breathing dragon who can eat a whole cow in a day. She looked fine when I saw her with you a few hours ago."

"Jealous?" Arabella asked quietly, as if testing that word on her tongue.

"Yes," I said over my shoulder. "I dislike sharing you with anything that might tear you away from me."

I dropped my towel, catching the subtle sound of her breath hitching. Even now, some twisted part of me relished that reaction.

Arabella retreated to the window. "A little warning next time," she muttered.

"Does my nakedness offend you so deeply?" I asked, unable to hide the teasing in my voice. "Or is the problem that it doesn't offend you enough?"

Her cheeks colored, and she turned to face the stars. I finished toweling my hair, crossing to stand beside her. We both stared at the night sky, lightning arcs occasionally flickering along the fortress walls outside.

"What has you awake at this hour, anyway?" I asked. "I expected you to be asleep after today's training."

She flicked a glance at me. "Couldn't sleep." She bit her lip.

I snorted softly. "Maybe I should've slipped you another aphrodisiac-laced dinner. That worked wonders for knocking you out last time."

She rolled her eyes. "That's not remotely funny."

"It's a little funny," I muttered, tossing the towel aside.

She exhaled. "You look pensive."

"I've had a long, bloody night."

"I'm glad you're not hurt," she said softly.

Something in my chest tightened at that. Vague, unexpected gratitude. I turned to her. "Why are you really awake?"

Arabella hesitated. "I was just thinking about a reversal spell from our last training session. How I can't grasp the exact feeling."

I studied her face. "Most novices struggle with the concept, not the sensation. You're sure that's it?"

She gave a quick, tight smile. "I'm not most novices."

"No," I said, softening my voice, "you're not."

We stood there for a few heartbeats. Whatever she concealed behind that deflection, I let it be. "Do you want me to show you?" I asked. "It's easier than explaining it."

Her cautious reply came after a brief pause. "All right."

I extended my hand, palm up. "Give me your hand."

She placed her hand in mine, and for the slightest moment I savored the warmth of her skin. "Close your eyes," I murmured.

She complied, her lashes dark against her cheeks. Vulnerable. Trusting.

"Magic normally bleeds outward from the caster, but reversal changes the direction." I let a gentle thread of magic slip along the connection between our hands.

She inhaled, lips parting in surprise. "That feels . . ."

"I know." I kept my voice low. "Now send it back."

The air hummed around us as she tried to redirect it. After a moment, the faint golden threads of her power mingled with my shadow, swirling around our clasped hands. Even her hair responded, drifting on the magical current.

"Good," I murmured. "Now, we add complexity."

I introduced more structured patterns, letting her sense how each current layered over the previous. She not only replicated them but added her own flourish, twisting the magic in a way that sent a jolt of exhilaration through me. The energy connecting us flared with shifting lights and swirling darkness. The temperature dipped and then rose again as the wards in the chamber reacted.

Stepping closer, I let more of my power flow into her. She gasped and grabbed my chest with her free hand to steady herself. Sparks crackled, tiny arcs of gold dancing among the black haze that enveloped us.

"Too much?" I asked, unable to hide my grin.

She shook her head, voice unsteady. "No . . . I— This is . . . educational."

I traced a slow circle on her palm, feeling the ripple in our magical bond. Shadows pooled around our feet, thickening and thinning with every shared breath. "Open your eyes, Arabella."

When she did, our gazes locked. My pulse pounded. Her power felt more attuned to me than I'd expected—less a forced exchange and more a collaboration. It wasn't just about harnessing her to activate the Heirloom. I wanted to see her unleash every ounce of her potential.

"It's not only about redirecting magic," I said quietly. "It's about transforming it. Taking something meant for one purpose and shifting it."

I brushed a loose strand of hair away from her forehead. "Destruction becomes creation. Pain becomes pleasure. Hatred becomes . . ."

I trailed off, suddenly unwilling to finish the thought.

Her soft whisper reached me. "Becomes what?"

Instead of answering, I pushed the energy deeper, intensifying the surge between us. She leaned into me, eyes closed again, expression caught between shock and excitement. We both felt it when her power melded with mine, altering its dark current and reshaping it with that subtle, life-infused signature that was so undeniably hers. The result poured into me with an electric jolt. The shadows spiraled out, shattering a nearby vase. Neither of us cared.

"Perfect," I said, my voice strained. I traced another circle on her palm, savoring the lingering connection between us. "You made it your own before returning it. That's advanced work, Arabella."

For an instant, pride lit her features. Then caution slipped back in, and she tore her hand away. The connection severed with the sound of a thunderclap, leaving the two of us panting in a dark, ordinary room.

Annoyed at the loss of that moment, I watched how she tried to steady her breathing. I wasn't any calmer myself.

Wordlessly, we performed the usual bedtime dance. She set up her pillow barrier on the bed, an oddly quaint defense after we'd just shared raw, unfiltered power. But I was too wrung out to fight it. I dropped my pants and slipped under the covers on my side, turned on my elbow to watch her silhouette. The hearth's last embers cast ruddy highlights across her hair.

A thousand impulses crawled along my skin. I wanted to tell her about the warded tower, how my fury scorched my reason the moment I saw those runes. But the words jammed in my throat.

Instead, I asked, "What are you thinking?"

She turned to face me, propping herself on an elbow in a mirror of my position. "That reversal exercise . . . I've never felt magic that . . . intrusive. Like it was changing me."

I moved one of the pillows so I could see her properly. "Reversal demands a high level of trust. That alone feels personal. You're not just shaping external magic—you're letting it shape you a little, too."

She frowned. "That sounds dangerous."

"With the wrong partner, it is," I said, letting the admission hang between us. "Dark magic doesn't lie. It forces us to face the cost of power. Some people can't handle that."

"And what price have you paid?" she asked quietly.

The question struck closer to home than she could know. The runes on my skin. The isolation. The years of believing power was the only thing that mattered. "More than I anticipated," I admitted. "Less than I feared."

She seemed to understand it wasn't a full answer, but also that it was all I could offer. "We should sleep," she said.

I replaced the pillow between us. "Sleep well, Arabella."

"Good night, Lord Blackrose."

I shut my eyes and willed myself to sink into oblivion. Instead, thoughts of that tower, of Lord Evenfall's wretched runes, and of how I'd felt compelled to kill in her name roiled through my mind. The moment I realized I cared less about strategy and more about ensuring she never suffered that prison again . . . that shook me thoroughly.

Her voice drifted in the darkness. "Still awake?"

"Yes."

I tried not to let the silence linger too long. "I was thinking about your training," I said. "We might need to expand on your offensive capabilities."

She turned, moving the pillow again. "I thought we were focusing on controlling my existing powers."

"We were. You proved you can handle it. But I think you should learn shadow manipulation. If you can heal, you know how life works. That same knowledge can be used to hurt."

I heard her sharp inhalation. "I'm not sure I want to turn healing into a weapon."

I let out a low laugh. "Don't you? Darkness suits you more than you admit."

"I'll think about it," she promised.

Satisfied, I settled back. "Good. Now get some sleep."

Arabella reached for the pillow but paused, her hand hovering in midair. After a moment, she withdrew it, deliberately leaving the gap between us.

As the last ember winked out and her breathing grew steady with sleep, I felt something crack inside me. Arabella had no idea how wild my anger ran whenever I imagined her father's cruelty. The Dark Lord wasn't supposed to feel protective or tender, yet here I was, wanting to shield her from nightmares she didn't even know I was fighting.

I shut my eyes and tried to drift off, but the image of her parted lips, trembling in shared magic, scorched itself behind my eyelids. It occurred to me I was in far deeper trouble than I'd ever been.

And, disturbingly enough, I didn't regret it.

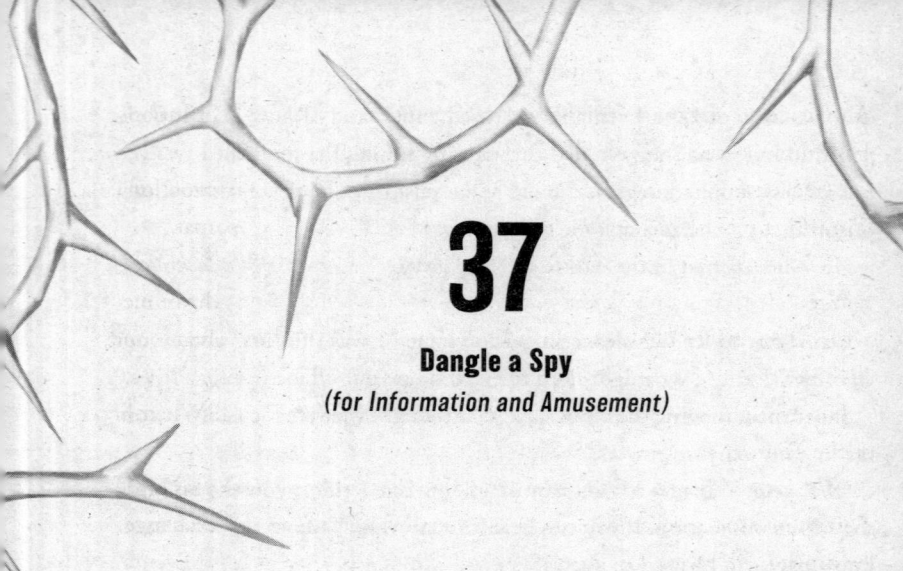

37

Dangle a Spy
(for Information and Amusement)

Kazimir

"Please! I'll tell you anything else you want to know!"

I dangled the spy upside down over the lightning bridge, his body swaying in the bitter wind that whipped around Skyspire. My shadows were wrapped tightly around his ankles as he hung suspended over certain death. Below, energy crackled across the magical bridge with enough voltage to reduce a man to ash in seconds. His face had turned an interesting shade of purple, possibly from the blood rushing to his head or from sheer terror. Perhaps both.

I loosened my shadowy grip just enough to drop him a few inches closer to that crackling death. His eyes bulged, and a pitiful whimper tore from his throat.

"I understand the king sent you to assess our defenses," I said, leaning against the stone parapet while feigning interest in my fingernails. "What else do you know?"

The spy hiccupped out a sob. "Nothing! I swear on my mother's grave!"

I tapped my fingers against the cold stone. "You expect me to believe King

Auremar sent you on a suicide mission without explaining his motivations? How disappointingly predictable."

I cracked my neck and let out a small sigh. This was taking far too long. Time for a more direct approach. I activated the rune over my throat.

"*Tell me what you know about King Auremar's plans for Lady Blackrose,*" I commanded, lacing my voice with dominion magic. The words thrummed with power, clamping down on the spy's mind just like the shadows around his ankles.

His eyes glazed over, pupils dilating as my magic took hold. When he spoke again, his voice was flat, compelled by my will.

"The king arranged with Lord Evenfall to take Lady Arabella as his bride. Forty thousand gold crowns and a seat on the royal council in exchange," he droned. "We were sent to assess if extraction was possible. Lord Evenfall claims she was taken against her will."

The king? And Evenfall had demanded *fifty* thousand from me, so the greedy bastard was negotiating from both ends.

I tightened my grip on the parapet. "And when was this arrangement made?"

"Before her abduction. Lord Evenfall was finalizing terms when you took her."

"Was Lady Evenfall aware of these plans?"

"No. She was to be informed only after everything was arranged. No option for refusal."

The shadows around his ankles pulsed with my anger, turning black and violet in time with my heartbeat. Evenfall had been mere days away from selling his daughter off to Auremar, without even giving her the courtesy of a choice.

As my dominion magic receded, clarity returned to the spy's eyes. He blinked and then scowled when he realized what had happened. "If you could just force me to speak, why go through this dramatic display?"

I flashed him a cold smile. "Because dangling spies over energy bridges is one of the few pleasures in a Dark Lord's day."

Movement in my periphery caught my attention. Vex appeared at the doorway, arms crossed, one eyebrow raised. Her slight tilt of the head indicated mild interest in the spectacle.

"Interrogation going well?" she asked drily.

"Splendidly," I replied, sweeping a hand toward our guest. "Our friend was just explaining how King Auremar and Lord Evenfall arranged Arabella's marriage before I kidnapped her."

Vex stepped closer and peered down at the spy with open disgust. "The king is three times her age."

"Yes." My hands balled into fists. "The only thing more pathetic than an old man buying a bride is a father willing to sell her."

The spy immediately started babbling. "I have a family . . . children—"

"You should've thought about them before working for men who trade women like livestock." I released the shadow bonds.

His scream lasted three seconds at most before the lightning bridge's energy consumed him in a flash. Not even ash remained.

"Was that strictly necessary?" Vex asked, though she didn't look particularly upset.

I brushed imaginary dust from my sleeves. "I was feeling dramatic."

"You're always feeling dramatic." She kicked a loose stone over the edge, watching it vanish into the clouds below.

My shoulders tensed as the runes under my skin flared with leftover aggression. "So the king wants his bride back."

"And Lord Evenfall wants his gold," Vex added, coming to stand beside me. "You inadvertently rescued Lady Blackrose from a fate that makes your abduction appear downright chivalrous."

I snorted. "I doubt she'd agree." I dragged a hand through my hair. "Queen Arabella of Solandris," I muttered, the words tasting sour. I pictured Auremar's withered hands anywhere near her, and my shadows flickered furiously across the stones. Would she have preferred a crown and kingdom over this fortress and a Dark Lord? The question lit a fresh surge of rage in my veins.

"She'd have had power," I said to Vex. "Resources. Royal guards instead of my shadows. An adoring court instead of terrified servants."

"And a husband who bought her," Vex said softly.

"As opposed to one who simply took her." A humorless laugh escaped me. "No wonder she despises us all."

"Maybe she wouldn't, if you told her the truth." Vex eyed me. "No leveraging, no threats. Just honesty. Stop treating her like a prize and treat her like a partner."

I glared at her. "You make it sound so simple."

"It is simple," she corrected, undaunted by my scowl. "Just not easy."

I turned back toward the parapet, staring down at the crackling bridge. Arabella was far from a simple captive. She'd fought, argued, defied me at every turn. After a lifetime of having her choices ripped from her by her father, she now clung to whatever autonomy she could grasp. And I'd approached her as just another conquest. How arrogant that now seemed.

I'd realized my error the night I returned from Evenfall's estate, blood-soaked and raw with anger. I hadn't told her what I'd seen yet, though I'd planned to soon.

"You're overthinking this, Kazimir."

I turned. Vex had only used my given name once before. "I'll consider it," I said at last.

She nodded, then melted into the shadows, leaving me with the wind and the echo of thunder below. I remained at the parapet long after she was gone, watching storm clouds churn until the sky fused with the abyss. I supposed I should feel guilty for depriving Arabella of her chance to be a queen. But I didn't. Not even a little bit.

The wind dragged at my coat. I forced myself to turn for the stairwell, intending to return to my chambers, where she waited, still unaware of what I'd learned or what I had done.

Tomorrow, I might take Vex's advice and try honesty for once. What was the worst that could happen?

Well, besides Arabella trying to kill me again.

38

Teach Deadly Magic
(and Win a Prize)

Kazimir

The mouse skittered across the table, its whiskers twitching frantically. Arabella's shoulders were rigid, her jaw set with clear reluctance. Her moral compass was so godsdamn inconvenient sometimes.

"Focus," I commanded evenly. "Feel the life force within it. Then pull."

"This is wrong," she whispered, her fingers trembling slightly above the table.

"It's necessary," I insisted, despite my growing impatience. After learning about the king's plans yesterday, I could no longer allow Arabella to be selective about what she learned. "You need to understand the full spectrum of your abilities."

The mouse darted for the table's edge, so I flicked a tendril of shadow to herd it back to the center. It squeaked in helpless protest.

"I can't," she muttered, her voice tight.

"You can," I countered, more harshly than I intended. Memories of her father's twisted schemes still clung to my mind. "You already proved that with the flowers. This is just the next step."

She turned to face me, hazel eyes sparking with defiance. "Flowers don't have heartbeats. They don't feel fear."

I studied her face, the stubborn set of her jaw. That conviction was wrapped in a deceptively delicate package. "The world won't always give you flowers to practice on," I pointed out, trying to soften my tone. "Enemies come with teeth and claws."

Her arms folded over her chest. "So this is about preparing me to face enemies?"

"Among other things," I said.

She narrowed her eyes. "What aren't you telling me?"

"Many things," I admitted, noticing the mouse making another bid for freedom. A flick of my hand dragged it squeaking back toward Arabella. "But right now, we're focusing on your training. Try again. Don't hesitate."

I'd been driving her hard since returning from the Evenfall estate. Three hours in this chamber today alone, but she hadn't complained. She exhaled a shaky breath and closed her eyes. A faint shimmer of golden light illuminated her skin, signaling the stir of her magic. My own power answered, reaching for hers in a way I still couldn't fully control.

The mouse gave a final squeak, then went limp. A warm orb of pure, throbbing energy hovered above Arabella's palm, pulsing with stolen life force.

"Good," I murmured, stepping closer. "Now mold the energy."

A crease formed on her forehead as she concentrated. Gradually, the shimmering ball took shape. Wings, a beak, tiny feet. Until it coalesced into a small bird of light. It fluttered around the chamber in a trail of radiant sparks.

"Beautiful," she whispered.

"And deadly," I reminded her, tracking the bird's path. "That construct could blind an opponent, poison them, or explode on impact."

She shot me a glare. "That's not why I created it."

"You've made something extraordinary. What you do with it is your choice," I said briskly. "I'm only giving you options."

Arabella's concentration wavered, and the bird dissolved into a shower of sparks. She wobbled on her feet, and I lunged to catch her shoulders before she fell. Her skin burned hot beneath the enchanted leathers.

"You've done enough for now," I managed, my voice rough.

She pulled away, bracing her hand on the table. "I'm fine. What's next?"

I almost told her all of it. Her father's betrayal, the Heirloom's requirement, everything I truly needed. Instead, I swallowed the truth. "We'll start something different. A test of your defense."

Without warning, I pulled a bolt of shadow magic from the rune carved along my forearm and hurled it at her chest. She reacted instantly, forming a glowing, golden barrier that absorbed the hit.

"Not bad," I said, allowing approval into my tone. "But that was a warning shot."

I struck again, multiple tendrils arcing around her from every angle. She spun with impressive agility, extending the shield until it enclosed her in a radiant dome. My shadows hammered at it, searching for weaknesses and finding none.

"You're still thinking like a healer," I called, circling her as black power battered the edges of her barrier. "Defense isn't merely blocking. It's redirecting."

She adjusted, letting the shadow energy flow along her shield instead of resisting the impact head-on.

"Better," I noted. "Now send it back."

She drew on my own dark force and hurled it at me. I deflected with practiced ease.

"You're a quick study, Lady Blackrose."

She gave me a brief, amused glance. "I have a good teacher."

Our eyes locked and tension flared between us again, bright and undeniable. My next breath caught in my throat, so I turned and snatched a small vial from a nearby shelf. Thick, black liquid swirled inside.

"This is alchemically stabilized shadow essence," I explained. "Think of it as a smaller, manageable sliver of pure shadow magic. I want you to manipulate it without touching the vial."

She eyed the container warily. "And if I fail?"

"The essence will explode and consume everything within several yards," I said lightly, though it wasn't an exaggeration.

Her gaze flicked from me to the vial. "You'd risk that here?"

"I have faith in your potential," I replied.

Cautiously, she extended a golden tendril of magic toward the vial. I watched every twitch of her face, her wary curiosity, the tension in her parted lips.

"It's alive," she breathed, sounding startled.

"To an extent," I said. "Shadow essence is semisentient. It responds to will and intent."

She reached out again, allowing the darkness to curl toward her magic. I saw the moment she nearly withdrew, but she held firm.

"Don't retreat," I urged, my voice dropping. "Control it."

She maintained the eerie connection, drawing some of the shadow essence into herself. The vial trembled ominously, the black fluid straining against the glass.

"Careful," I started. "Too much, too—"

A crack, and the vial shattered in a razor hiss. The freed essence exploded, expanding into an inky cloud that swirled toward her. Arabella let out a frightened gasp as she tried to form a barrier. But instead of blocking the blackness, her magic pulled it in. My eyes widened in raw fascination as she absorbed it into her very skin, an otherworldly glow rippling across her body.

It was too much. I moved on reflex, grabbing her hands. My energy surged over hers, helping stabilize the flood of swirling darkness. Our connection flared hot and intimate, more personal than I'd ever intended.

"Breathe," I rasped, forcing my voice steady. "Use my energy to balance out the shadows."

Arabella drew on me just as she'd drawn on the shadow essence, forging a conduit I felt in every cell. Gradually, the swirling darkness settled inside her instead of splintering her from within.

When the danger finally passed, sound rushed back into the room—the ragged cadence of our shared breathing, the faint crackle of errant magic fizzling across the floor. Shadows and golden motes drifted around us. I was holding her protectively against me, and she was holding me back. Her fingers clutched my shoulders, the molten heat of her body flush against mine.

I didn't let go. Couldn't. The raw power still throbbed between us, a thread tugging me closer with each heartbeat.

"That," I said, breathing hard, "was not what I expected."

Arabella remained within the circle of my arms, her eyes dark with a mixture of shock and desire. "What did you expect?" she asked softly, her gaze flicking to my mouth.

"I assumed you'd repel it," I said, forcing my focus to her eyes even as my gaze kept drifting lower. "Not absorb and integrate it."

"Is that . . . bad?"

"No," I admitted, my thumb brushing a slow circle along her hip, feeling the shiver that chased my touch. "It's astonishing. You continue to surprise me, Arabella."

A smudge of shadow clung to her cheek. I lifted my hand, intending only to wipe it away, but the moment my thumb grazed her, the world narrowed to that single point of contact. She leaned in ever so slightly. When my thumb moved to the corner of her mouth, she parted her lips.

I don't know who moved first. Maybe we both did. One moment we hovered on a knife's edge. The next, my mouth crashed onto hers.

Her lips yielded, soft heat melting into mine before pressing back with a desperate, answering hunger. I ran my tongue along her bottom lip, and she opened her mouth in a breathy moan that went straight to my groin. She arched against me, and every rune carved into my bones sparked alive, singing at the feel of her. My hand slid from her cheek to her neck, then lower, tracing the curve of her waist through the training leathers, memorizing the shape I'd already dreamed about.

Arabella's fingers threaded into my hair, a fierce tug that sent lightning down my spine and ripped a low growl from my throat. I backed her into the table and lifted her onto it. She seized my collar, dragging me closer until her thighs wrapped around my hips and the last sliver of distance died between us.

I ran my hand along her leg, savoring the impossible contrast of hard muscle beneath supple leather. The damned material was in the way now, and I wanted to rip it off her. I palmed her breast, relishing her sharp inhale, then dipped to taste the faint salt at her collarbone, branding the spot with my tongue. She tugged me up again, devouring my smirk in a kiss so scorching it threatened to unravel every scrap of control I had.

My hand slipped beneath the loose edge of her jacket, tracing the seam where leather met hot skin. She gasped into my mouth. This was the prize I had sought through every lesson, every taunt, every sleepless night.

Tell her the truth, a traitorous voice hissed.

I answered with a deeper kiss, plunging my tongue savagely into her mouth. Truth could wait. Her hands found the edge of my shirt and ran under it to caress my abdomen. I cupped her ass and ground my arousal into her, letting her feel me through our clothing. She arched into me. Desire roared, yet even as it devoured me, I slowed. My hands moved to her waist, and I tore my mouth from hers long enough to find air.

"Wait," I forced out, my voice ragged.

She let out a husky noise of protest. "What?"

I caught one of her wrists and pressed a kiss to her racing pulse. "You don't know what you're agreeing to."

"I'm not agreeing to anything but this," she said, fierce and breathless, leaning in as though proximity alone could restart the kiss. "Right now."

Her jacket hung off one shoulder, her lips swollen, eyes bright with need. It was everything I craved. Still, I somehow mustered the will to step back, my body screaming in frustration.

"This isn't . . ." I raked a hand through my hair, trying to tamp down my own desire. "There are things you don't know about me—about us—before we—"

A sharp chime rang through the training chamber, a magical alarm announcing someone's urgent request. The door flew open and slammed against the wall. Sims stood on the threshold, wide-eyed.

"My lord, there's an incident at the—" He froze, noticing Arabella's disheveled state and my half-undone shirt. "I apologize for interrupting."

My teeth ground together. "What incident?"

Sims was either brave or foolish enough to meet my gaze. "A breach in our defenses near Arvoryn. Immediate attention required."

"Understood," I muttered, barely disguising my fury. "I'll be there shortly."

Sims bowed so fast he nearly toppled over, then backed out of the room. I slammed the door shut behind him with a wave of shadow. The echo died away, leaving a silence heavy with everything left unsaid.

Arabella slid off the table, straightening her clothes with almost regal composure, though her cheeks still burned.

"Arabell—"

"Don't," she snapped. "Just don't."

I reached for her but let my hand fall uselessly to my side. "We should talk about what just happened."

"What's to say?" She avoided my eyes. "You got carried away. It happens."

"That's not—"

"It doesn't matter," she said icily. "Deal with your breach, Dark Lord."

She pivoted and walked out, not once looking back. The door slammed behind her, leaving me standing alone in a swirl of frustration and unslaked desire. My breathing was still ragged, and my mind buzzed with the memory of her taste, the way she felt in my arms. She deserved the truth. Soon, I told myself.

But first, I needed to murder whoever caused that damn breach. And possibly Sims, for his supremely shitty timing.

39

Retreat and Regroup
(and Hate Him More)

Arabella

I reached our chambers at a near run and slammed the door behind me, pressing my back against the heavy wood while I tried to steady my breathing.

"That arrogant, insufferable—" I swore, then kicked my boot against the door. A dull thud echoed across the room. My heart pounded so hard it felt like it might crack my ribs. My skin still tingled from where his hands had been. Where they almost had been. By the gods, what had I been thinking?

I hadn't been thinking at all. That was the problem. One moment, we'd been training. The next, his mouth was on mine, his hands braced around my waist, and I was ready to let him have me right there on the table.

Then he stopped.

And now, I was left alone with this . . . this *need* clawing beneath my skin.

"Damn him," I whispered, tugging at the collar of my training leathers. Everything felt too warm and tight. My hands shook, whether from the lingering shadow essence I'd absorbed or from the memory of his touch. I could no longer tell. Magic, hunger, and confusion all blurred together.

I finally managed to unfasten my jacket and fling it across the room. It knocked into a vase of black roses, sending water and petals scattering.

"Perfect," I muttered. I stomped over to the mess and kneeled to gather the fallen flowers. Their bitey petals nipped my fingers, drawing tiny beads of blood. The sting was sharp and bracing, but it was something tangible I could hold on to, given how badly everything else swirled in my head.

"'Things you don't know, Arabella,'" I said in a mocking imitation of Kazimir's measured tone. "Yes, of course. Are you planning to sacrifice me to an ancient god, or—"

A knock on the door cut through my rant.

"Go away!" I shouted.

The knock came again, more urgent this time.

Fuming, I ripped open the door, prepared to slice someone to ribbons with my words. A young servant girl stood there, trembling violently enough that she nearly dropped the silver tray in her hands.

"S-sorry, my lady," she stammered. "Lord Blackrose said to bring you refreshments."

The tray held a decanter of wine and a steaming dish that smelled infuriatingly appealing. Kazimir, the meddling bastard, was always one step ahead.

"Fine," I said briskly, taking the tray. "Thank you."

I shut the door with another satisfying slam, set the silver tray on a table, and poured myself a large glass of wine. I downed half of it in a single gulp.

"You will not think of him," I warned myself, pacing the length of the room. "You will not remember how his hands felt on your waist, or how his—"

When Kazimir got angry, he just broke things. I glared at my wine glass, thinking about hurling it at the wall. But that would be messy.

So I turned and flung the glass into the fireplace instead. It shattered in a glorious spray of crystal and red. The flames hissed as they swallowed the remains. A little tension seeped out of my body. I considered throwing the decanter next but decided not to waste the rest of the wine. Instead, I stripped off the rest of my training clothes and stormed into the bathing chamber. I cranked the faucet so hot water gushed into the tub and slipped into its rising steam, hissing at how the heat stung my sore, shadow-kissed skin. The traces of dark magic still curled beneath my flesh, as if they had nowhere else to go.

The warmth eased my muscles, but it did nothing to calm my racing thoughts. "'Things you don't know,'" I repeated, anger dripping from every syllable. "Yes, please, keep whatever it is from me, Kazimir. I'm sure there's no possible way that can backfire."

I scrubbed myself with almost violent determination, as if I could scour away the memory of his hands and my own traitorous response. My elbow knocked over a jar of bath salts, sending shimmering blue crystals into the water. They stained the water with a vivid azure that clung to my skin.

"Shit," I muttered.

A scratching sound at the window made me pause. Through the rippled glass, I glimpsed Nyx pressing her muzzle against the pane.

Sighing, I stood and wrapped myself in a towel. When I unlatched the window, Nyx seemed to melt through the impossibly small opening. She reminded me of a mouse squirming through a crack in the wall—if the mouse had no bones.

So that was how she'd been getting into Griffin's lab.

Once inside, she shook droplets of rain off her inky scales, and I backed into the door to get out of the way. "I hope you haven't eaten anything unfortunate."

Nyx tilted her head, blinking at me as if to say she'd never do such a thing. That smug look in her eyes betrayed otherwise, but I didn't have the energy to press her.

I threw on a robe, and we trailed back to the bedroom. The mess lay in wait: broken glass, scattered petals, puddles of water, and my clothes left in a careless swirl.

"It needed a woman's touch," I said.

Nyx hopped onto the bed and promptly began shredding a pillow, filling the air with drifting feathers.

"Glad you approve," I muttered. Grabbing the decanter of wine, I took a solid drink from the neck, then flopped onto the bed. Nyx abandoned her growing pile of feathers and curled up beside me with keen amusement. Thunder rumbled in the distance, echoing the storm still raging in my chest.

Kazimir was off dealing with that so-called crisis and had left me to stew here, alone. Would he come back to finish what we started? Or would he ice me out again, the way he had when I'd practically been ready to rip his clothes off?

My lips still throbbed with the memory of his kiss. The sheets smelled faintly like him—winter storms and charred wood, a scent that struck me as both forbidding and safe in a twisted way. Like a bonfire blazing in the coldest night.

"I really do hate him," I announced to Nyx, who rested her head on my stomach. "His damn secrets, his maddening hands, his ridiculously perfect cheekbones."

Nyx let out a soft rumble that sounded too close to laughter. Rolling my eyes, I stroked her muzzle.

He had no right to tease me like this, and I intended to make that perfectly clear the moment he returned. The reminder sparked fresh anger in my chest. I took another deep swig of wine, then set the decanter aside.

The wind and rain battered the windows. Part of me hoped Kazimir would stay away until dawn. Another part of me wanted him to walk through that door right this second.

I hated that part of me most of all.

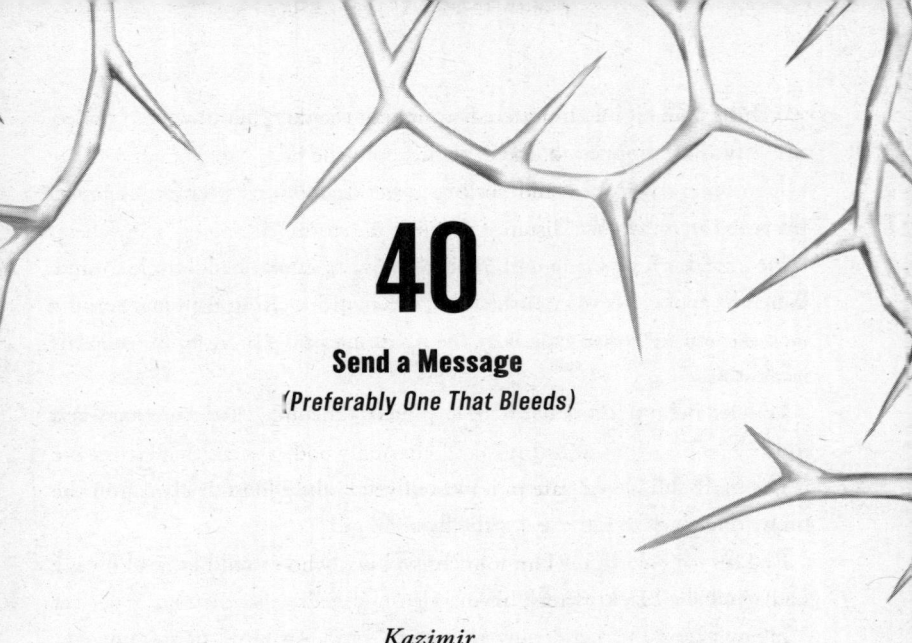

40

Send a Message
(Preferably One That Bleeds)

Kazimir

Moonlight filtered through the ancient pines while I circled the spy, mud squelching beneath my boots. The forest stank of damp leaves and rot. Behind me, Thorne waited, his measured breaths hinting at the violence on his mind.

High above us, my Skyspire Citadel hovered against a backdrop of churning clouds. I pictured Arabella up there, halfway furious and maybe halfway something else. I vaguely wondered if she sensed the uproar below, or if she even cared right now, given how I'd left things between us. I shoved the thought aside—she had enough reasons to hate me. No point adding this one.

I halted in front of the spy, who was on his knees in the mud, blood oozing from a jagged cut at his temple. My soldiers had delivered his introduction with a mace. An unrefined but effective approach.

"I'm on a tight schedule," I told him, rolling my shoulders to ease the ache in my runes. "So let's skip the part where I pretend you won't suffer."

I tapped into the dominion rune carved along my throat. A wave of scorching pain bit into my neck. Familiar, unpleasant, but undeniably effective. My voice dropped to a dark pitch.

"Tell me everything," I said, letting power flood every syllable. *"Who sent you to spy on my citadel?"*

He jerked, eyes glazing over as the dominion hooks sank into his mind. When he spoke, his voice turned flat, mechanical. "King Auremar wants a map of your defenses, especially the lightning bridges. So he can identify weaknesses."

I circled behind him, each step slurping in the mud. "And Auremar's next move?"

His body shuddered. Dark rivulets of sweat and blood dripped from his brow. "He plans to retrieve . . . the Evenfall girl."

Red fury spiked in my chest. I clamped my hand around his jaw. "She is Lady Arabella Blackrose. My wife."

He managed a pathetic, quivering nod. "Y-yes, my lord," he stammered.

Thunder growled overhead, a throaty rumble that matched my mood. I shoved him away, and he flopped forward. So far, he'd told me nothing that changed the game, but a warning needed to be delivered.

I activated another rune along my ribs, letting the fiery burn wash through my old scars. Dark magic sparked under my skin, coiling, ready to be unleashed.

"Open your mouth," I commanded.

He obeyed, displaying rotted teeth and a tongue that trembled. I pressed my thumb to his forehead, channeling a trickle of shadow. Where my flesh touched his, darkness spread beneath his skin, a slow, creeping stain. Tendrils of it curled down and wrapped themselves inside his mouth.

"You will return to King Auremar with my message," I murmured, sliding dominion into each word. "Three days after you deliver it, you'll forget everything about this citadel—me, this encounter, your mission. But you'll wake screaming at night, convinced shadows devour you from the inside. That terror will plague you until the day you die."

His body convulsed. Blood trickled from his nostrils, and his eyes rolled back until only the whites showed. The magic lodged deeper than any knife, a poison in his veins.

Satisfied, I grabbed his shirt collar and yanked him upright. He swayed like a puppet with loose strings, eyes empty, waiting for final instructions.

"Go," I said.

He turned, stumbling down the narrow path into the trees, leaving a trail of footprints in the mud. There were plenty of ways to kill your enemies, but a slower unraveling drove the message home and I had a particular taste for letting the nightmares do my work.

Thorne slid up beside me. A grin sliced across his scarred face. It was the kind of smile that could curdle a demon's blood. "Do we follow him, my lord?"

"Yes," I told him. "But bring only enough men to make a statement, not enough to spark all-out war."

Thorne nodded, grin unwavering. Then he vanished back into the shadows.

I tipped my head skyward, gazing toward Skyspire. Above the clouds, lightning crackled around the fortress's spires. I wanted to be up there with Arabella. The tension between us was far more consuming than any thought of war. But I had to clean up this mess first.

My arm throbbed where the runes glowed, heat still thrumming against bone. I started down the path after Thorne. A message needed sending, and I intended to send it in blood.

I slipped through the forest with my warriors fanned out in a silent arc behind me. Twigs snapped softly under our boots, but otherwise, not a sound rose amid the predawn gloom. We'd followed the spy straight through Arvoryn territory, where Auremar's elite guards waited on Solandris's nebulous border. The camp held twelve men in shining royal livery that glowed faintly from the enchantments woven into their blades. They had no idea how nearby death crawled beneath the trees.

When I caught Thorne's eye, I flicked two fingers toward the nearest sentry. Thorne obeyed without hesitation, disappearing into the folds of night. A single slice, and the guard dropped with barely a gurgle. Another crumpled so fast he never even finished gasping.

"Ambush!" someone finally roared, but it was far too late. Four lay dead in a matter of breaths.

I stepped out of the shadows, letting supremacy radiate from me in dark waves. A guard whirled around, fear stark on his face. "The Dark Lord," he stammered, lifting his enchanted sword as if that would impress me. I flicked my wrist and shadows wrapped around the blade, ripping it from his grip. A faint grin tugged at my lips. There was a certain pleasure in showing them how pointless their efforts were.

"Your king sent his dogs to spy on me," I announced, loud enough for the rest to hear. "He should know better than to reach for what's mine."

Shadow-woven steel clashed against royal blades, snarls and screams wrecking the night's hush. I was only interested in their captain, who I spied across the clearing. A broad-shouldered man wearing a commander's insignia. He fought with a remarkably steady hand, keeping two of my warriors at bay with precise, brutal strikes, not an ounce of fear in his eyes.

Excellent, I thought. Someone with a bit of backbone.

I released the guard I'd been toying with. I heard his neck snap when he hit the ground. Then I strode forward, lifting my voice over the clamoring chaos. "Captain," I called out. "A word."

He didn't miss a beat. He shoved a sword through one of my warriors' throats, eyes never leaving mine. "I've nothing to say to you, Blackrose," he spat, brandishing his weapon with confidence. "You kidnapped Lady Evenfall in violation of our peace accords. An act of war. Return her and perhaps the king will show mercy."

I laughed, letting the mocking sound echo through the slaughter. "You assume I ever agreed to his wretched peace in the first place."

The captain's gaze hardened. "What would you call what you've done, then?"

I stepped over a fallen body, my shadows curling higher around my hands. "My reasons are my own, captain. But rest assured, Lady Arabella is now Lady Blackrose. She remains so by choice."

A small part of me might have felt a twinge of guilt for that half-truth, but I buried it under the certainty that I would make it true eventually.

He adjusted his stance, sword steady. "The king won't stand for it."

I tilted my head, letting shadows riot around my body. "He'll stand for it once he gets my next message."

A surge of dark magic smashed into his ribs. He staggered. Another lash of power knocked him onto his back, and I pressed my boot into his throat, pinning him to the dirt. Around us, the battle died away. Eleven of Auremar's guards now lay crumpled, while their cursed spy observed everything with unblinking eyes.

I crouched, eyes mere inches from the captain's. "You will be that message," I murmured, then lifted my voice to deliver the terms. "Tell your king that Lady Arabella Blackrose belongs to me. Any attempt to take her again will be met with force far greater than this." I pushed harder, hearing him choke. "Next time, I won't let even a single man walk away."

He glared, fury blazing in his gaze despite his predicament. "He'll come—" he rasped. "With an army."

"Let him try," I said, relaxing the pressure so he could suck in a ragged breath. "But first, you'll carry my warning."

I motioned to Thorne. He approached with a small, ornate box inlaid with silver runes. "Hold him," I commanded. Two of my warriors clamped onto the captain's arms, pulling him into a kneel.

Drawing the slender rune-etched blade from my belt, I leaned close to the captain's ear. "This won't hurt much," I said, letting amusement edge my tone.

His scream ripped the air when I carved my sigil into his forehead. Dark lines dripped blood across his face, soaking his uniform. I admired my handiwork, then opened the box.

"Now, for the closing remarks," I said softly, pressing the blade beneath his jaw. In one swift cut, I sliced open his throat. Blood pumped in a red arc. His eyes went dim as the light left them.

Shadow-tendrils slithered at my command, wrenching off his head with a neat separation. I held it by the hair, inspected the rune carved into his brow, then slipped the head into the box. The box would only open for Auremar, and then the head of his captain would deliver my message.

The spy stepped forward under my compulsion, and I handed him the grisly package. "Deliver this to your king. Tell him Kazimir Blackrose sends his regards."

The spy turned and walked toward the path, presumably heading straight for Solandris.

At my sign, my warriors began gathering the bodies into a pile. "Keep the captain's corpse visible, as a warning to trespassers. Burn the rest."

Thorne's expression remained impassive, though I sensed his grim satisfaction. He wiped the blood from his blades, then inclined his head. "We also found a chest of coins," he rumbled. "Could be payments to the local bandits."

I nodded. "It seems the viscountess was right about a secret outpost here."

Dawn flickered across the eastern horizon, painting the sky in pale fire as smoke curled from the burning bodies. I stood there for another long moment, inhaling the metallic sting of blood on the breeze. I'd stayed out all night, leaving Arabella waiting. She expected the answers I'd been dancing around. My chest gave an uncomfortable pang, something that felt suspiciously like guilt.

An ache pulsed behind my eyes. War with Auremar was inevitable now. I had to prepare. And soon, very soon, I would need to speak to Arabella.

41

Claim Your Power
(and the Dark Lord)

Arabella

After waiting most of the night for Kazimir to return, I'd finally collapsed into sleep surrounded by my dragon and shredded pillows.

"Bastard," I muttered, plucking a stray feather from my hair.

I'd scrubbed myself nearly raw to rid my skin of that blasted blue tint from the bath salts, then spent hours practicing magic alone (since Kazimir missed our scheduled training), and I still hadn't received a single message from him.

A soft knock on the door cut through my brooding.

"Come in," I called, cinching the silk robe tighter around my waist.

A servant girl peeked in, carefully balancing a tea tray. "Afternoon tea, my lady." She took one startled look at the mess in the room but, with creditable restraint, stayed silent.

"Thank you," I said, forcing a small smile. "Any word from Lord Blackrose?"

Her brow furrowed. "My lord returned hours ago, my lady. Just after dawn."

I froze with a teacup halfway to my lips. "Hours?"

"Yes, m'lady," she confirmed.

Hours. And hadn't bothered to let me know. Betrayal and wounded pride flamed inside me, igniting into white-hot anger.

"Where is he now?" I asked, each syllable clipped.

"He's in the war room, m'lady. He's been in there with his advisors since his return."

"And he left word that he's not to be disturbed, no doubt."

She chewed her lip nervously. "He might have said he'd feed anyone who interrupts him to the void beasts . . ."

I set the teacup down with a sharp click. "Where is the war room located?"

"M'lady, I don't think—"

"Where?" I cut her off, letting my voice and the magic pulsing in my veins warn her I wasn't playing.

She sighed. "East wing, second floor. The large chamber with the double doors and the guards."

"Thank you," I said pointedly. "You may go."

"But the void beasts—"

"They'll have to find something else to eat," I snapped, already marching for the door.

I had a good, long walk to build my fury into something like a wildfire. By the time I reached the double doors, guarded by two burly men in black livery, magic crackled around my fingertips. They straightened, exchanging an uneasy glance.

"Lady Blackrose," the taller one said with a bow. "I must inform you, Lord Blackrose—"

"Ordered you to feed anyone who disturbs him to the void beasts," I finished for him. My voice vibrated with power. "Now step aside."

They shifted uncomfortably, but I lifted my hand, letting sparks loose to show I meant business. One guard swung the door open, and I strode past him.

The war room was enormous, dominated by a black stone table inlaid with an intricately carved map. Tiny runes glowed across contested territories. At the far end, bent over stacks of parchment, stood Kazimir, flanked by Vex, Sims, and Thorne. Four heads snapped up when I entered.

Kazimir straightened. His gaze swept over me, taking in the silk robe, the determined set of my jaw.

"Everyone out," I commanded, not taking my eyes off him. "Except Kazimir."

He glared at me. I glared right back. Thorne, Sims, and Vex practically tripped over themselves getting out, leaving me alone with him in the echoing silence.

Kazimir crossed his arms over his chest and leaned against the table. "*Now* you use my name?"

He looked exhausted—dangerously so—but there was a coiled tension about him that felt electric. Stubble graced his jawline. His hair was mussed, as if he'd been running his hands through it. I wanted to hate him for looking far too good even in that disheveled state.

I folded my arms and let him see the anger in my eyes. "So. You've been back. For hours."

"Yes." He just waited, daring me to say what I wanted to say.

I forced a laugh. "You ran off right when we were—preoccupied—yesterday. Then you sneak back in without the courtesy of letting me know you're alive."

His gaze tracked the stray motes of magic sparking around my fingers. The air snapped with an energy that matched the wild twist in my chest.

Kazimir turned away and reached for a decanter of amber liquor at a sideboard. He poured two glasses, extending one toward me. "I suspect we both could use a drink."

I accepted out of reflex. It gave me something to do with my hands besides setting the war room on fire. "You're stalling."

"And you're itching for a fight." He raised an eyebrow. "Are you angry that I'm still alive? Or that I left you alone after we began something you wanted to finish?"

I thought about tossing the brandy in his face, but it would only make him happy to have elicited such a reaction from me. Instead, I took a sip and wiped my mouth with the back of my hand, watching how his eyes tracked the movement.

I smiled. "Both."

A knowing smirk replaced his momentary surprise. "You wouldn't like the outcome if I'd died. Your safety is too entangled with mine." His voice softened. "Or maybe you would. Maybe you lie awake imagining my demise right after you finish imagining my touch."

My throat tightened. "What happened in Arvoryn?" I asked, deliberately ignoring his attempt to unbalance me.

He paused, brandy sloshing in his glass. Finally, he set it aside, suddenly too preoccupied to drink. "It's done," he said at last. "We're at war with Solandris."

I gave a small nod. "Because of me."

"In part, yes," he admitted. "But it would have happened sooner or later."

"Because that's been your goal all along."

He nodded.

I set my glass down on the table. "You didn't make me wait until afternoon just to tell me we're at war. There's something else."

He held my gaze for a long moment, as if debating whether to continue the charade. "Your father sold you to King Auremar."

I blinked, certain I'd misheard. "What?"

"Forty thousand gold crowns and a seat on the royal council. Your father made the deal months ago." His eyes watched me carefully. "You were to be the king's bride. My . . . intervention upset their plans."

The room seemed to tilt. I gripped the edge of the table to steady myself. My entire life had been a transaction waiting to happen. But knowing it and hearing it were very different things. "And you've known this for how long?"

He shifted his weight. "Three days."

Three days. He'd known for three days and hadn't told me. And there I'd been, in the training room, practically ripping off his clothes . . . And then waiting like an idiot for him to return.

"When were you going to tell me?" I asked, my voice barely audible. "You've had plenty of opportunities."

Kazimir took a step toward me, then stopped when I glared at him. "Tonight. I wanted to confirm the information first, to be certain."

"And are you? Certain?"

"Yes." He didn't elaborate, but the grim set of his mouth told me his confirmation had been thorough. And probably bloody.

I reached for the brandy and drank deeply.

"So," I said when I could trust my voice again, "my options were to be sold to the king or kidnapped by you."

"I was trying to protect—"

"Don't you dare pretend you held back for my peace of mind," I snapped.

Kazimir picked up his drink and moved to the other side of the table before turning to glare at me. "I'm the reason you're not rotting in Solandris's palace right now." He paused. "Unless that's what you want?"

"All those times I asked for honesty, and you just withheld what mattered most."

His temper flared in response to mine. The runic figurines on the map rattled. "I told you. I needed confirmation."

"You needed control," I shot back. "And the only reason you're telling me now is because it's convenient. Because you've set the stage for war, and you need me to hold still while you wave your sword at the king."

"It isn't just about war, damn it." His gaze swept over me, and for an instant I saw raw desire blazing there. "And it stopped being convenient the second I started wanting you for more than your bloodline."

My pulse fluttered. It took everything in me not to melt.

For a moment, his eyes shone with something like regret. "At least answer one question," he pressed. "If you truly had the choice between the king's bed or mine, what would you choose?"

I shook my head, anger and hurt warring inside me. "You're missing the point."

"I'm not." He moved closer. "The question is simple. Do you want to be the Queen of Solandris or my Dark Lady?"

"Auremar would expect me to birth heirs until my body gave out, and then he'd replace me with someone younger." I shook my head. "Being queen is the last thing I'd ever want."

"Is that a concession that I'm the better option?" A hint of his usual arrogance crept back into his tone.

"Neither is freedom."

Kazimir raked a hand through his hair, making him look uncharacteristically unhinged. "Tell me what you want, then. I'm trying to find a middle ground with you, but you keep pulling away. What are you afraid of?"

My magic flared again. "I'm not afraid."

"Good," Kazimir said, studying me with unsettling intensity. "Because there's something else you need to know."

Something in his tone made my skin prickle. "What now?"

He moved to where he'd left his glass and downed it all in one gulp. When he finished, he braced his hands on the table. "The Heirloom of Dominion requires more than just our bloodlines to activate it. It requires . . ." He paused. "It requires the consummation of our marriage."

I stared at him, certain I'd misheard. "Consummation," I repeated flatly. "As in sex."

"Yes," he confirmed, watching me closely. "The binding of our bloodlines in the most literal sense."

A startled laugh escaped me. "Is that what this has been about? The dragon, the training, the unexpected kindnesses? You've been trying to seduce me to activate your precious artifact?"

Kazimir's jaw tightened. "It's more complicated than that."

"Is it?" I rounded the table. "You need me to spread my legs so you can gain the power you've been chasing for a decade. Seems straightforward enough to me."

"Watch your tongue," he warned. His knuckles whitened where he gripped the edge of the table. The temperature in the room plummeted as shadows curled restlessly in the corners.

"Or what?" I pushed back on his magic with my own, a bright flash that made the shadows recoil. "You'll punish me? Force yourself on me? That would hardly serve your purpose, would it?" I paused. "I bet you need willing participation."

His silence confirmed my suspicion.

"And how long have you known this particular detail?" I asked.

"Since the day the ritual failed."

"So you waltzed around my 'no sex' condition, feeding me sweet nothings and shadows, for weeks?"

He exhaled sharply, color rising in his cheeks. "Yes, the Heirloom's requirement complicates things. But—"

"But instead of just telling me, you decided to bury it beneath gifts and seduction."

Tension rippled along his shoulders. "What would you have me say? That I'm sorry for trying to secure what I've worked my entire life for? I'm not. War and power are who I am."

He was being brutally honest for once, but it didn't soothe my anger. I stared him down, refusing to be swayed by the shadows that wrapped around his frame. "All you talk about is power."

His eyes darkened to near black. "Don't pretend you don't crave it too."

My pulse thudded, and I took a steadying breath. "Tell me honestly: What happens if we don't consummate this marriage?"

"Then the Heirloom remains dormant." His gaze didn't waver. "But Auremar still comes for you, and I still fight to keep what's mine."

There it was again. That possessive declaration that should have infuriated me but instead sent heat spiraling through my core.

"And what happens to me if you fall?"

"Best-case scenario? You're returned to your father, who promptly delivers you to King Auremar as originally planned." His voice turned bitter. "Worst-case? My enemies decide your magic makes you too valuable—or too dangerous—to leave alive."

Neither option appealed to me, obviously. But instead of despair, I felt something crystallize within me. A realization, clear and cold as winter dawn. What if I stopped being something to be taken and became something to be reckoned with? My bloodline, my body, and my choice could all be wielded as weapons.

I moved closer. "Tell me, Kazimir, did you ever consider what I might want from you?"

He visibly swallowed. "What do you want, Arabella?"

My heartbeat pounded in my ears. "I want to never be sold or traded again," I said, my voice gaining strength. I'd been seeing myself as a victim, but there was another perspective. One where I wielded power of my own. "I want to develop my magic without fear or shame. I want to build something that's mine. Not my father's, not the king's—not even yours."

Kazimir inhaled sharply, his pupils dilating as he watched me claim my power. The scars visible above his collar pulsed faintly. His voice was rough. "And you believe not consummating our marriage will give you these things?"

"No. I believe consummating our marriage will give me leverage." I held his gaze. "Power of my own to negotiate with."

The air between us thickened. Around us, objects in the room began to respond to our combined magical energy. Scrolls rustled on their shelves, markers on the table vibrated, the flames in the wall sconces flared higher.

A slow smile curved his mouth. "You're proposing to sleep with me . . . for political advantage."

"I'm proposing to sleep with you because I refuse to let anyone else decide my fate."

A flush crept up Kazimir's neck as his breathing became shallower. "Such pretty lies you tell yourself." His voice dropped to a register that vibrated through my bones. "I've heard your breathing change when I move closer, or when you see me naked, and even when I shift toward that ridiculous wall of pillows between us."

Heat flooded my cheeks. "Noticing your physical form doesn't mean I've been pining for you," I shot back. "It means I'm not blind."

"And yesterday's kiss?" He leaned closer, his shadow magic swirling around us as his eyes darkened. "What exactly was that about?"

I lifted my chin. "You tell me."

"Simple. I want you, Arabella." His voice softened, and his gaze raked over my face. "I've wanted you since I first saw you standing defiant in that rainstorm. Every time you challenge me, every time your magic brushes against mine, it makes me want you more."

My breath hitched as the tension between us switched from anger to arousal in a single heartbeat. I stepped close enough to feel the heat of his body, to see the subtle widening of his pupils as I invaded his space.

"So my defiance excites you?" I said, my voice dropping to a husky whisper. "Then understand this: I'm done being just a pawn. If I'm to be used, then I'll choose how and by whom. I'll take what I want from this arrangement, just as you've taken what you wanted from me."

A heady sense of power washed over me as I watched Kazimir's breathing quicken, his gaze dropping to my lips.

"And what will you take, Arabella?" he asked, his voice rough with barely contained desire.

I traced the line of his jaw with my fingertips, trailing down to the edge of his collar where I could feel the hint of scars beneath the fabric.

"Honesty,'" I said, reveling in the way he leaned into my touch. "Respect." My fingers moved to the nape of his neck, tangling in his hair. I tugged his head closer to mine.

"And?" His voice held a note of warning.

I surged up on my tiptoes, capturing his mouth with mine in a demanding kiss that released every ounce of pent-up anger, lust, and frustration.

Kazimir froze for a heartbeat, caught off guard by my aggression. Then, the great and terrible Dark Lord's control fractured. He answered with a near-feral groan, hauling me against him. A spark of dominion magic flicked against my skin like a live wire. My own energy thrummed. I bit his lower lip hard enough to make him gasp and felt a surge of satisfaction when his grip tightened on my hips.

The kiss deepened, all pretense of restraint abandoned as I pushed him back until he hit the stone wall. His mouth left mine to trace a burning path along my jaw, down the column of my throat, stubble grazing sensitive skin in a way that made me gasp.

"Is this what you want?" he murmured against my neck. "To use anger as an excuse for desire?"

"Is it working?" I countered breathlessly, arching against him as his hands roamed over the silk covering my body.

Kazimir's laugh rumbled with dark amusement. "More effectively than all my careful planning and seduction, it seems." His thumb brushed over the front of my robe, grazing my nipple and sending a shock of pleasure down through my belly.

Gripping the collar of his shirt, I managed a ragged whisper. "Then stop planning and start fucking."

His expression darkened. Without warning, he reversed our positions, pinning me against the wall with his body, one hand capturing both my wrists above my head while the other yanked the belt of my robe until silk slithered apart, baring my body to the chilly air.

"Careful, Arabella," he warned, his gaze devouring every inch of exposed skin. "Once this starts, there won't be any retreat."

I met his gaze, feeling more powerful in this moment of surrender than I had in all my days of resistance. "I'm counting on it."

42

Consummate the Marriage
(for Power, Obviously)

Arabella

The moment the words left my lips, a dangerous light flared in Kazimir's eyes. His pupils blew wide, until only a thin rim of gray showed. The flickering shadows around us seemed to coil tighter, as though they sensed the final snap of his restraint. Strange how, in that heartbeat, I felt both a spike of fear and a wicked thrill.

His mouth crashed onto mine with a fury that stole my breath. The cold stone wall pressed into my back, and a startled gasp escaped me as he slid his hand beneath my robe to claim bare skin. His fingers traced along the curve of my breast, his calluses catching deliciously against my nipple before he rolled it between thumb and forefinger.

I arched into his touch, a moan tumbling from my lips. His response was a guttural noise that reverberated through his chest and shot straight to the pulse between my legs. When he finally released my pinned wrists, I half expected him to step back again. Instead, he leaned back just enough to look at my exposed skin with a gaze so intense it nearly scorched me.

"You're staring," I managed, desire warring with a sudden burst of vulnerability.

"I'm admiring," Kazimir corrected, voice rough with a desire that sent a fresh ripple of heat through me. His hands skated down my rib cage. "Big difference."

Before I could fire back a retort, he lifted me effortlessly. Instinct made me lock my legs around his waist, which only brought our bodies flush, forcing a groan from deep in his throat. He turned, scattering maps and markers from the obsidian table with one swipe of his arm. I landed on its edge, my thighs stinging slightly at the cold stone. The rest of my body was pure fire wherever he touched me.

I noticed the flash of calculation on his face. The tactician in him, so rarely off duty. I gripped the front of his shirt. "What are you thinking?"

He flicked his eyes to mine, silver irises molten in the dim light. "I was wondering if I should take you somewhere more comfortable."

My heart slammed against my ribs, that flicker of common sense urging me to pause. But the thought of letting him regroup, or of me second-guessing myself, made me desperate. "No," I insisted, voice shaking only faintly. "Here. Now."

A satisfied darkness settled in his stare. "As my lady commands."

He kissed me again, and I realized that even at my most vigilant, I'd underestimated how intense he could be when he finally let himself go. His lips and tongue moved with a consuming, deliberate hunger that kept me pinned to the spot. Exploring. Tasting. Claiming. He cupped my ass, pulling me so close I could feel every ridge of his body beneath that infuriatingly elegant attire.

I fumbled with the buttons on his shirt, nearly tearing it in my frustration. When it finally fell open, I planted both hands on his chest, taking in the patterns of scars and runes carved into his skin. When I slid my fingers over one elaborate sigil, he sucked in a sharp breath.

"They respond to you," he said, voice ragged.

He kissed me while he trailed his fingers up my inner thigh, and I almost forgot how to breathe. My muscles clenched involuntarily the moment his thumb brushed over my clit. The gentle swirl made me whimper, and I had the disorienting sense that most of my wrath had melted into unfiltered craving. When his fingers dipped lower into the slick heat between my legs to tease my entrance, I gasped.

"Kazimir," I whispered, my voice husky.

"Yes?" he murmured at my throat just before his lips pressed firmly to the spot where my pulse thundered.

"Don't stop," I pleaded.

His next breath brushed heat over my collarbone. "I have no intention of stopping." He pressed two fingers inside me, a slow, deliberate slide, while his thumb kept circling in that maddening rhythm. "Not until you're screaming my name. And then I'll keep going, just to hear you beg."

He dropped to his knees in front of me. I couldn't help the flare of surprise. Before I formed a coherent protest, he draped one of my legs over his shoulder and pressed open-mouthed kisses across my inner thigh. The kisses moved higher as he spread my legs wider.

I watched him, a flush of heat spreading across my cheeks that wasn't entirely from pleasure. No one had ever—

The first swipe of his tongue against my clit made me gasp. The second had me tangling my fingers in his hair. I felt his smug grin against me. But soon his confidence gave way to something more intense, as his mouth and fingers worked in tandem, driving me closer and closer to the precipice.

The intimacy of it was overwhelming at first—his dark head between my thighs, his complete focus on my pleasure. His gaze flicked up to mine, eyes burning an unearthly storm gray. I realized the notorious Dark Lord was on his knees before me, worshipping me with his mouth, and it triggered a fresh jolt of power in my veins. My entire body tensed in anticipation, each swirl of his tongue stoking the magic swirling inside me.

"Kaz," I moaned, the shortened name slipping out unbidden. He groaned against me in response, the vibration adding another layer to the building pleasure.

Through a haze of pleasure, I saw the runes on his skin glowing faintly. My own skin had taken on a golden shimmer. Where he touched me, the colors swirled together, creating eddies of power that spiraled outward.

He curled his fingers at just the right angle and sucked on my clit. My climax snapped through me, bending my spine and ripping a cry of pleasure from my throat. He didn't stop until my legs trembled under his relentless mouth and I moaned for mercy, tugging at his hair.

Kazimir pushed to his feet, and I tried to slow my breathing. His lips were slick with my pleasure, his eyes black with desire, the runes glowing. He looked like a god of destruction. Beautiful, terrible, and entirely focused on me.

"That was . . ." I tried to speak, voice little more than a rasp.

"Just the beginning," he promised, discarding his shirt. He reached for his trousers next, not taking his eyes off me. That hungry expression quickened my pulse all over again.

I watched as he freed his cock, allowing myself to openly appreciate its length and thickness, the head already glistening. Only after I'd finished my shameless look did I lift my gaze to his. He stood between my legs, pressing his hard length against my sensitive flesh that still thrummed with aftershocks. I braced a hand on his warm chest, that overabundance of magic humming along my skin.

"Wait," I said, surprising myself with how steady my voice sounded.

He froze, concern cutting through the haze of lust in his eyes. "Having second thoughts?"

I shook my head. "No. Just . . . go slowly. It's been a while."

The shadows in the corners deepened, flickering in the edges of my vision. There was no mistaking the possessiveness in Kazimir's eyes, no ignoring the raw intensity as he wrestled with his jealousy and buried fury at anyone who touched me before him.

"How long?" he asked, his voice deceptively soft.

"Years," I admitted.

Relief and satisfaction crossed his face before he caught himself. His expression softened as he stroked my cheek with surprising tenderness.

"I'll be careful," he said, though his voice shook with the effort of controlling himself.

He pressed into me, gradually at first, letting me adjust to the exquisite shock of being filled. I released a shaky breath, one hand maintaining contact with his chest, the other bracing myself on the table. His jaw clenched, and he bit back a groan as he sank deeper.

When he halted, fully seated inside me, shockwaves of pleasure made my eyes flutter shut.

"All right?" he asked, voice low against my ear.

I slid my hands up his chest to his shoulders, feeling the power thrumming beneath his skin. "Yes," I murmured, the sound catching in my throat.

He pulled out almost all the way, grabbed my hips, and then pushed into me again. My eyes fluttered closed at the stretch, and he did it again. I ran my hands down his arms, feeling the scars warm at my touch, wanting to pull him closer. He kissed me and began to move, setting a gentle rhythm that had me sighing with pleasure.

But gentle wasn't what either of us truly wanted. Not after weeks of tension, of wanting, of fighting this pull between us.

Without warning, I planted my hands on his chest and pushed him back. He looked startled but allowed it, eyebrows quirking. I hopped off the table and steered him so it was his thighs against the obsidian slab. Seeing Kazimir half-dazed, shirtless, and breathing rough, I felt a heady sense of control.

I let my robe slide off my arms. "My turn," I said, sliding his trousers the rest of the way down. He stepped free of them, letting me guide him onto the table. That smug grin warred with genuine need as he sprawled on the polished stone. Straddling him, I sank down on his cock again, biting back a moan at how deep he went. His hands found my hips, but I grabbed his wrists and pinned them beside his head.

The way his pupils nearly swallowed his irises told me he liked my dominance more than he'd ever admit. The dreaded Dark Lord was at my mercy.

"Is this how you pictured me?" I rasped, rocking my hips in a slow grind that made us both gasp.

"I pictured you in every way imaginable," he finally managed, "but what I want is you. Any way I can have you."

I loosened my grip, letting him bury his hands in my hair, then on my waist, guiding my movements. Each thrust created a spike of magic, setting off a dizzying light show across his body. Books and marker figurines lifted from the floor, swirling in the air as the chamber's temperature soared and plummeted erratically.

The runes carved into his skin blazed brighter with each thrust, burning with crimson and violet fire. The light cast strange shadows across the room, making the war table's map look alive. My power rose to meet his, golden light emanating from my skin in pulses that matched our rhythm.

Our combined magic amplified until warmth spread through my veins like liquid gold. The glow was almost blinding. I could feel his control slipping, magic leaking from the carefully constructed channels he'd built over years of discipline.

He held my hips in an iron grip. "Arabella," he gasped, trying to slow our pace. "I can't—the magic—"

"Don't you dare stop," I growled, grinding down harder, taking him deeper.

The magic built between us, crackling in the air. "I can't control it," he warned.

Understanding dawned, followed by something wild and reckless. Not fear, but fierce joy. "Then don't."

I leaned down to capture his mouth in a kiss that consumed us both. He surrendered to it, to me, to the magic surging between us. The resonance built and our magics merged, creating a swirling vortex of power that spiraled outward. Books flew from shelves. Weapons rattled in their racks. The massive stone table beneath us groaned ominously.

I was beyond caring. There was only the sensation of Kazimir moving inside me, his magic entwined with my own, pleasure so intense it bordered on pain. I rode him harder, faster, chasing the release that hovered just beyond reach.

He reached between us to circle a thumb against my clit. The spike of sensation brought me so close to the edge again I couldn't hold back an impassioned cry.

"There," he growled, his voice barely human. "Come for me."

The combination of his words, his touch, and the magic surging between us pushed me over the edge. Everything in me tightened, and I let go.

This release crashed far harder than the first, making my inner walls quake around his cock as I shouted his name. The radiant surge of my magic collided with his, and for an instant, I swore I saw raw arcs of power crackle around our joined bodies.

Kazimir's breath caught on a ragged groan. "Fuck . . . Arabella—" I felt the pulse inside me as he came.

Our coiled magic exploded in a shockwave of raw power. The stone table snapped straight down the middle, sending us tumbling to the floor in a tangle of limbs. Around us, chaos reigned. Books torn from their bindings, weapons embedded in walls, windows shattered outward in a spray of glass. The stone walls themselves groaned.

A distant rumble suggested something important had collapsed, and Kazimir threw himself over me protectively as mortar and dust rained from the ceiling.

As awareness slowly returned, I became conscious of several things at once: the pleasant throbbing between my thighs, the weight of Kazimir's body covering mine, the dust in the air, and the distant shouts of guards responding to the disturbance.

And above it all, a high, clear note ringing out. A sound I recognized instinctively though I'd never heard it before. The Heirloom of Dominion, responding to our union from its chamber several floors above.

Kazimir raised himself on his elbows to look down at me, his expression a mixture of satisfaction, wonder, and alarm as he took in the devastation.

His hair was a disheveled mess, his skin still faintly glowing, his eyes bright with lingering pleasure.

I'd never seen anything more beautiful.

I couldn't help it. I started to laugh, a full, throaty sound that bubbled up from somewhere deep inside me.

"Did we . . . ," I began, my voice deliciously hoarse.

"Yes," he confirmed, a note of smug satisfaction in his tone. "I believe we just destroyed half of the east wing."

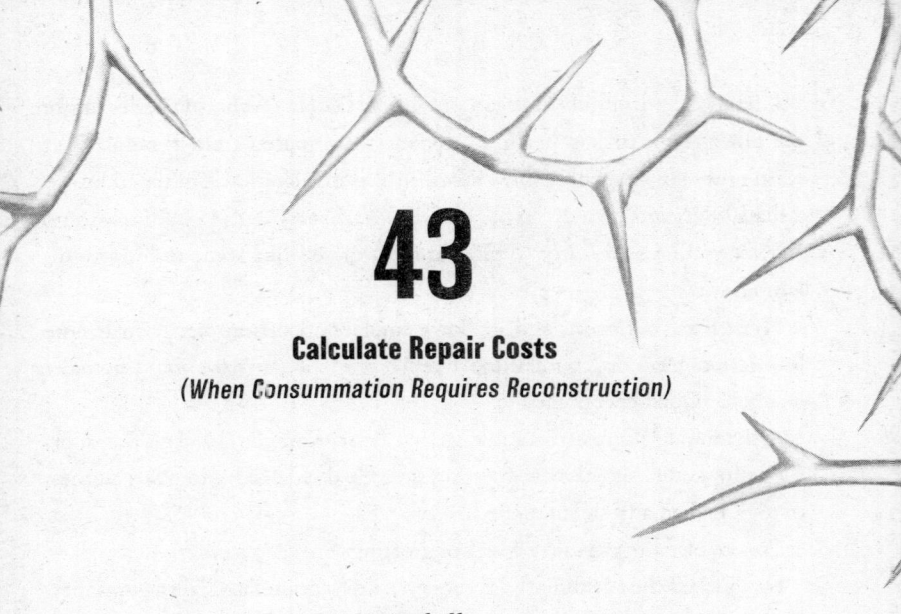

43

Calculate Repair Costs
(When Consummation Requires Reconstruction)

Arabella

My entire body hummed with magic. I sat on a hay bale in the stables, trying to regain some semblance of composure while Nyx devoured her third cow in a flurry of teeth and claws. Everything felt raw and turned up to an almost painful pitch. Colors seemed brighter, scents more potent. Even the hay stabbing into my palms became a source of pleasure-pain.

And the magic. Gods, the *magic*.

It raged through me like a dam had burst, no longer contained in neat, carefully measured channels. I felt it in my fingertips, in my throat, thrumming behind my eyes. Part of me wondered if this was how Kazimir always felt, with an undercurrent of raw power constantly crackling beneath his skin. Or maybe this was simply the aftermath of what we'd done together.

A memory of that moment in the war room strummed through me, scattering my focus all over again. The way our bodies had collided, our magic tangling and intensifying until the walls literally fell around us. I'd called it an excuse to fulfill the Heirloom's requirement, but I couldn't hide the truth from myself anymore. I wanted him. I'd chosen it—chosen *him*.

I exhaled and mumbled to no one in particular, "What does this make me now?" Nyx cocked her head, blood still dripping from her muzzle. I wasn't sure how to explain my chaotic mix of exhilaration, guilt, and lust to a shadow dragon.

"Not you," I said softly. "I'm talking to myself like some unhinged villain's bride."

Nyx gave a wet snort, and shadowy smoke curled from her nostrils. The impression I got was something like *Well, if the horseshoe fits.* I actually laughed. "Don't encourage me."

A shadow fell across the straw-strewn floor. Kazimir stood in the doorway, silhouette framed by the setting sun. He'd changed into clean clothes, though he had a fresh cut along his jaw.

"You're bleeding," I said by way of greeting.

He touched the cut absently, as though he'd forgotten it. "Falling masonry. The east tower took some damage."

"From what we did?"

That faint, prideful twitch of his lips made my stomach flip. "From what we did," he confirmed. His gaze raked over me, lingering where his shirt barely covered my thighs. My robe had been ruined, so I'd grabbed the first thing in arm's reach, which happened to be his clothing. It did next to nothing to hide the fact I wore no undergarments.

"How are you feeling?" he asked.

I felt my cheeks heat under his scrutiny. "Like my skin doesn't fit right anymore. And my magic . . ." Words failed me. There was no easy way to describe the sensation of holding a storm in my body.

He stepped closer, settling beside me on the hay bale. Even that small closeness sent phantom electricity racing across my skin. We'd just had sex, yet my body still turned molten the moment he drew near.

He nodded vaguely to the stablehands, who were themselves attempting to be invisible in the far corner. "The servants are talking," he said. "Apparently the Dark Lord and his bride destroyed half the fortress while"—his lips quirked—"'bonking,' I believe was the polite term they used in front of me."

I buried my face in his shoulder with a groan, noting the distinct mix of his usual magic and the new thread of energy coursing between us. "Are they scandalized?"

"More impressed than anything." He threaded his fingers through my hair in a gentle tug that sent warm shivers across my scalp. "Although Vex did ask that we save any further 'activations' for less essential architecture."

When I dared glance up, Kazimir's eyes had darkened, locked onto my mouth. Desire flared. We'd only just finished tearing half a wing down in our frenzy, and already my blood pounded for more. Maybe that made me reckless, but I no longer cared.

"Everyone out," I said, raising my voice. I didn't even look at the stablehands, just kept my eyes fixed on Kazimir's face.

They set their tools down with awkward speed and scurried out, one of them pausing to shut the door behind them. Nyx huffed in protest at losing her audience, then kept chewing.

"That was very authoritative," Kazimir teased. "I think you've nailed this Dark Lady business."

They were gone, but I still lowered my voice. "So, the Heirloom?"

He exhaled. "Active, but the power feels incomplete. As if it's still warming up."

I bristled at the thought that we hadn't quite finished the job. "We destroyed a war room and half a wing for nothing?"

He tilted my chin until I met his gaze. "We've awakened it, just not at full strength. And," he added, his eyes flicking down to my lips, "I don't believe *anything* about that was nothing."

Heat surged in my face. There was no point hiding my reaction, especially not from him. We both knew this wasn't purely a cold transaction anymore.

I tried to stay on topic. "Is it normal for the Heirloom to warm up?"

He shrugged. "I don't know. There aren't exactly instruction manuals for ancient artifacts of power. I had to piece things together from dozens of obscure sources."

I snorted. "A manual would have been much easier. 'Congratulations on your purchase of the Heirloom of Dominion. Please note that activation requires blood sacrifice and/or earth-shattering sex with your unwilling bride.'"

His lips twitched. "Unwilling?"

"Initially unwilling," I amended, feeling heat rise in my cheeks again.

His voice dropped an octave, taking on that rough edge that sent shivers down my spine. "Because I seem to remember *you* coming to find *me*. And you were remarkably . . . insistent."

I cleared my throat. "So what happens now?" I asked, seeking safer conversational ground. "King Auremar won't stop."

"No, he won't," Kazimir agreed, bitterness creeping into his tone. "But we'll be ready. Let him come."

I frowned. "He can't just want me for a political trophy. I've been kidnapped and married, so it doesn't make me prime queen material. What could he possibly want with me that's worth starting a war?"

"That's the question, isn't it?" Kazimir's jaw tightened, a flicker of fury crossing his features. "He knows something about your bloodline that's important enough to risk everything."

"But there are others with heroic blood. Why me specifically?"

"I don't know yet." He pushed my hair over my shoulder to expose my neck. "Whatever their plan, I'm not letting them succeed."

There was nothing gentle in his promise, only that dark, possessive glimmer that both alarmed and excited me. "I've set a monitoring spell on the Heirloom. If its power continues to build, we'll know." His gaze dropped to my lips, then lower, to the open collar of his shirt that I was wearing. "In the meantime . . ."

He tugged on my hair, pulling my head back to expose my throat. The simple touch sent sparks of pleasure racing down my spine, and I couldn't help the small gasp that escaped me.

He murmured, "Still sensitive?"

"You could say that," I breathed.

"Good." He leaned closer, pressing a featherlight kiss to my neck that had me sagging against him. "Because I'm nowhere near done with you."

Kazimir parted the collar to expose more of my throat and lightly grazed my skin with his teeth. His hand remained firmly tangled in my hair, keeping my head tilted back and my throat exposed to his exploration.

I melted into him, my hands finding their way beneath his tunic to the warm skin and scars beneath, feeling the heat of him as he continued his assault on my neck. He hummed against my skin, his free hand sliding up my thigh. When his hand slid under what passed for my hem, he froze at finding bare skin. A low, appreciative sound escaped him. "No undergarments?"

I shrugged, breath hitching when he teased my inner thighs. "I came straight here to check on Nyx. I . . . didn't think about it."

"Then I'll get the names of every servant you passed on the way," he growled possessively.

My heart drummed a little faster. "Why? So you can play golf with their eyeballs?"

"That would be merciful compared to what I have in mind."

"Don't you dare." I grabbed his wrist, half to stop him from conjuring some violent retribution and half to encourage his wandering fingers to keep going. "The servants like me, and I don't want you to mess that up."

He chuckled darkly, leaning in to kiss me, swallowing the gasp I made when his hand pressed exactly where I was most sensitive.

I hardly registered what I was doing as I grabbed the edge of his tunic, yanking it over his head. The sight of his runes and scars in the warm haze of the stables made me want to explore them again. I traced one with a fingertip, noticing how his breathing caught.

He groaned. "This is going to escalate quickly."

I replaced my finger with my lips, pressing a kiss to the center of the spiral. His hand tightened in my hair. I smiled against his skin and continued my exploration, tracing the patterns with lips and tongue, learning which ones made him tense and which made him moan. When my lips reached the waistband of his trousers, he tugged my hair again and hauled me up.

His expression was raw in a way I'd never seen before. "Enough," he gasped. He bundled my bare legs in his discarded tunic, then scooped me off the hay bale and made for the stable door. "I don't want to burn anything down."

From her corner, Nyx projected a strong sense of agreement, tinged with alarm.

I wrapped my arms around his neck and kissed the underside of his jaw, finding another rune there to map with my tongue. "I suppose one of us should be practical."

"My—our—chambers." Kaz's voice was strained. "The tower is warded more heavily."

Nyx's disgruntled huff behind us was probably disapproving, but I could only manage a half laugh, still lost in Kazimir's taste.

His stride was purposeful as he carried me into the fortress. Each point of contact sent a fresh wave of desire pulsing through me, and his grip only tightened. The staff either fled our presence or pretended not to see us. Fine by me. My brain was consumed by the memory of what it felt like to have him inside me, how the magic had magnified until I was certain we'd both die from the glorious overload.

Halfway up the spiral staircase, he pressed me against the cold stone wall and kissed me until I almost forgot my own name. I felt him tug at his belt. His tunic fell away as I wrapped my legs around his waist, not caring about the precarious angle of our bodies on the narrow steps.

"I can't wait," he rasped, voice low enough to stroke pleasure through my nerves.

I braced my hands on his shoulders. "Then don't."

He thrust into me with no further warning, forcing a cry from my throat that echoed up the narrow stairwell. Electricity practically sparked where our skin met, gold meeting black in a dance of energy. The tower quivered, dust raining down around us. Kazimir gave a dark laugh, his breath hot against my neck.

"We'll bring the entire citadel down," he muttered, driving into me again.

I tried to respond, but he followed with a powerful thrust that made stars burst behind my eyelids. Conversation ceased. There was only the frantic sound of our breathing, the echo of flesh against flesh and the building wave of raw power that crackled through every thrust.

When we both reached the brink, Kazimir clamped his jaw, redirecting the raging magic upward. I felt the tower's wards flare to life, absorbing much of the chaos we unleashed as first I spilled over the edge and he followed. The pressure in the air was deafening for a moment, but the walls held.

He remained pressed against me, panting, as my ears rang with our combined pulse. "That was easier," he said raggedly. "Maybe the fortress will survive the two of us after all."

Instead of putting me down, he adjusted my weight in his arms and continued upward. I clung to him, a dizzy swirl of satisfaction and leftover arousal tangling in my head.

When we finally reached the top, Kazimir shouldered the heavy door open to carry me across the threshold like some dark parody of a traditional wedding night. His eyes never left mine as he kicked the door shut behind us.

When he turned, though, his confident stride faltered at the carnage that had been his bedchamber. Feathers lay strewn over the floor in snowdrifts, glass shards sparkled on the fireplace mantel, and half-wilted black roses drooped from shattered vases.

"What happened here?" he asked, mildly astonished.

Heat suffused my face. "I might have . . . had a tantrum after you left me. It was a low moment."

Expressing no judgment, he set me on my feet and locked the door. Then he turned to me, pulling open my shirt and letting it slide to the ground. "Every second I was gone, I could think of nothing but the taste of you."

He lifted me onto the bed, sending a puff of feathers swirling into the air. "How wet you'd be for me," he continued, his voice dropping to a ragged whisper as he shed his own remaining clothes, never taking his eyes from mine.

Kazimir lowered himself beside me. His hand slid between my breasts to brush away a feather, then continued up to grip my throat possessively. "The sounds you'd make when I finally buried myself inside you."

His lips brushed mine in a kiss, surprisingly gentle compared to the urgency of his words.

"Slowly this time," he said. "I want to learn every inch of you."

And he did. Over the next hours, he mapped my body with meticulous attention, discovering places I hadn't known could bring pleasure, never losing that edge of possessiveness but allowing me to meet him as an equal.

I returned the favor, continuing my exploration of his runes, learning which ones made him tense and which made him hiss in pleasure.

"These never bothered you," he said during a moment when we were relatively still. It wasn't a question, but I answered anyway.

"Why would they? They're part of you." I traced the one over his breastbone. "You never told me how you got them."

He was silent for a long moment, his expression unreadable in the dim light of the bedchamber. "My mother carved them into my bones when I was a child," he said finally, his voice carefully neutral.

My hand stilled, and I sat up to look at him properly. "That's . . . that's barbaric."

He shrugged, the casual gesture at odds with the darkness in his eyes. "It was necessary, according to her. Magic requires sacrifice."

"No child should have to sacrifice like that," I said fiercely, thinking of my own childhood, of the tower and the isolation and the fear. It had been cruel, yes, but at least my father hadn't carved spells into my flesh.

Kazimir's hand covered mine, pressing it more firmly against his chest. "It made me what I am. I don't regret it."

I wasn't sure I believed him, but I didn't press the issue.

There was a normal-looking scar on his shoulder that had no symbolism that I could see. "What's this from?"

"First conquest of a military outpost," he said with casual pride. "I was leading a small band of mercenaries I'd convinced to follow me." He shrugged. "But that was early days."

"You couldn't possibly have done all those things they say," I mused, tracing it. "Not unless you started terrorizing the Western Realms as a child."

A dark pride flickered in his eyes. "I was fifteen when I killed my first general. Seventeen when I raised my first army." His voice was matter-of-fact, as though reciting a shopping list. "By twenty, lords twice my age were bending the knee or fleeing their castles at rumors of my approach."

"That's impossible," I said, though the certainty in his voice gave me pause. "Even the greatest warlords take decades to build such power."

His lips curved into that familiar smirk. "Most warlords don't have magic carved into their bones before they're old enough to shave." He guided my fingers to a particularly intricate pattern on his chest. "This one accelerates thought. This one enhances perception. Together, they let me see patterns in warfare that others miss even after lifetimes of study. As though warfare was a language I was born speaking."

I studied his face, the lack of lines around his eyes, the smoothness beneath the shadow of his beard.

"How old are you really, then?" I asked, curiosity finally getting the better of me. "They speak of the Dark Lord as though you've terrorized the realm for generations."

A smile played on his lips. "Reputation is a curious thing. The more they fear you, the longer they've feared you. At least in tavern tales." He stretched and sat up, the firelight catching the network of scars across his torso. "I'm thirty-three. Though most days I feel considerably older."

Something about his explanation nagged at me. It made perfect sense, and yet . . . There was something ancient in his eyes sometimes, something that didn't match the relatively young man before me.

"What?" he asked, noticing my hesitation.

"Nothing," I said, pushing the thought away. "Just trying to imagine you as a teenage warlord."

His smile turned wicked. "I assure you, I've always been very good at what I do."

Kazimir proved his point several times over the next hour, each touch more skilled than the last. When our bodies finally stilled, a pleasant exhaustion settled into my limbs. He rolled away, and I made a small sound of protest at the loss of his warmth. Kazimir chuckled, reaching out to tuck a strand of sweat-dampened hair behind my ear.

"What?" I asked, suddenly self-conscious under his scrutiny.

"Nothing," he said, his expression softening. "Just . . . this isn't how I expected things to go when I kidnapped you."

I raised an eyebrow. "Disappointed?"

"Hardly." His hand trailed down my arm, leaving goose bumps in its wake. Before I could respond, he was rising from the bed. I watched him go, admiring the lean strength of his body, the confident way he carried himself, even naked.

"What? No cuddles?" I called after him, only half joking.

He paused halfway to the bathing chamber. "Is that something you want?"

I shrugged, suddenly feeling vulnerable. "Maybe. Sometimes."

Kazimir studied me for a long moment, his expression unreadable. Then, without a word, he returned to the bed, drawing me into his chest so we lay entwined among the feathers. They stuck to everything at this point, but neither of us cared.

"Better?" he murmured, his breath warm against my hair.

I nestled closer, feeling the steady beat of his heart beneath my cheek. "Much."

44

Master the Morning After
(When Villains Don't Flee Before Breakfast)

Kazimir

Warmth. That was the first sensation I registered when consciousness finally clawed its way to the surface of my mind. Not the familiar chill of my chambers, nor the cold emptiness of waking alone. Just . . . warmth.

I almost distrusted it on principle. But as I blinked my eyes open, I realized the source was Arabella's body curled against mine. She slept with her head tucked beneath my chin, one arm flung over my torso as though claiming territory. It should have triggered every survival instinct I possessed.

Instead, I lay there like a fool and studied the sight of her tangled hair, the freckles scattered across her face, and that distinctly smug curve to her lips even in sleep. Gradually, though, I became aware of the state of the room. Clothes strewn about, an overturned chair, a crack in the window from unrestrained magic. Books had been knocked off shelves and onto the floor, some pages askew in silent condemnation.

And feathers drifting over everything.

My rational mind tallied repair costs and replacement times, but another part of me basked in the aftertaste of having taken my wife thoroughly enough to leave the room in shambles. A selfish satisfaction welled up that I'd claimed every inch of her last night . . . and she'd claimed me in return, if the new bruises on my skin were any indication.

Discomfort pricked at me, the knowledge that contentment was a villain's pitfall. Contentment was for heroes. Contentment led to complacency, and complacency led to having your head on a pike while your enemies divided your territory. I hadn't built my empire from the blood-soaked ruins of betrayal by allowing myself to be *content*.

But perhaps I could allow myself a sliver of gratification this morning. Purely in celebration of a plan well-executed, of course. Conquering a kingdom or disemboweling a rival brought the same wry sense of accomplishment. Perfectly normal villain behavior.

Arabella stirred against me. I remained perfectly still, watching her eyelashes flutter against her cheeks. When she opened her eyes, they locked immediately onto mine. I braced for curses or a flying fist, but she only murmured, "Good morning," in a husky, deliciously pleased tone that made my pulse kick.

"Yes," I said, unable to hide my smugness. "It is an excellent morning."

She rolled her eyes at me but made no move to distance herself. "Don't look so proud of yourself."

"Difficult not to." I let my gaze sweep over the ruins of our nighttime enthusiasm. "Judging by all this wreckage, I exceeded expectations."

Her lips twitched. "I suppose you can crow a little." She kissed my chest then paused, as if debating some deeper thought.

I arched an eyebrow. "Were you about to bite me? Because I can think of somewhere else I'd rather have your mouth."

She gave a warm laugh against my skin. "I've never woken up with someone before, like . . . this."

Oh. A confession. My pulse thudded in surprise. "Neither have I," I admitted, the truth slipping out before I could properly shield it in sarcasm. Damn it. "In my line of work, it's a good way to get stabbed in your sleep."

"But we've been sleeping in the same bed since the wedding," she countered. "Were you just lying awake with a dagger under your pillow?"

"For the first nights, yes." I shrugged lightly, mindful she was still using my chest as a pillow. "You made it clear about that no-forced-intimacy arrangement. But old habits die hard."

A thought occurred to me. Something she'd said in the war room before I'd taken her against that table. "You mentioned it'd been a while for you." I tried to sound casual, but something dark and possessive coiled in my chest. "Exactly how many lovers have you had?"

Arabella raised an eyebrow. "Are you asking for their names and locations so you can hunt them down? Because your jaw just tightened in that way it does when you're contemplating violence."

"Of course not," I lied shamelessly, my jaw flexing. When she narrowed her eyes, I amended, "Perhaps. A little. So what if I am?"

She let out a long-suffering sigh. "Two. One stablehand, one traveling bard. Hardly worthy of your wrath. They weren't exactly epic romances." Her finger traced a line down my breastbone. "Don't pretend you're disappointed."

The relief I felt was ridiculous, almost embarrassing. My fingers drummed absently on her hip. "On the contrary. I'm glad there aren't more names on that list." Then I let my hand creep higher along her rib cage. "How did you hide such indiscretions?"

"I became creative," she said, voice crisp with mild defiance. "Your turn. How many conquests has the Dark Lord left heartbroken across the realms?"

I gave her my most villainous smile. "Hearts? None. Bodies, though . . . several. I don't keep a strict tally, but I assure you, they knew what they signed up for. No illusions about exchanging love notes." I brushed a strand of hair from her face. "Any arrangements were always . . . temporary."

Arabella sat up and pinned me with a mock glare. "Several is not a number."

"It's precisely a number," I countered, letting my gaze drift lazily over her bare breasts. "Just not a specific one."

"That's not fair. I told you mine." She jabbed playfully at my ribs, and I jerked away with an undignified sound that was definitely not a squeak.

Her eyes lit up like it was her birthday. "Are you . . . ticklish?"

"Absolutely not," I said with all the dignity I could muster. "The Dark Lord is not ticklish. That would be ridiculous."

A wicked grin spread across her face. "The Dark Lord is a liar." Her fingers darted toward my ribs again, and I caught her wrist.

"This is treason," I warned, but she was already attacking with her other hand, finding a spot just below my rib cage that made me twist away.

"How many?" she demanded, relentless in her assault.

I retaliated by rolling us over, trying to pin her arms, but she squirmed free in an infuriatingly agile move. The bed jolted, sheets tangling around us until we both tumbled off the edge onto the rug. I landed on top of her, pinning her wrists above her head. Her body was warm and pliant beneath mine.

"Twelve," I admitted. "Give or take a few."

Arabella's eyes widened slightly. "Twelve? That's fewer than I expected from a man of your . . . reputation."

I let out a mock insulted sound. "Quality over quantity. Besides, conquering realms and chasing artifacts occupies a lot of hours in the day."

She gave me an innocent look. "And all those virgins you supposedly stole? Did you count those?"

"No. That's not funny."

"If you can joke about putting aphrodisiacs in my food, I can joke about your villainous appetite. It makes me wonder if—"

I seized her mouth in a slow, possessive kiss. She met me eagerly, her body arching as my mind went blank with need. When we finally broke apart, she was looking at me with a mixture of amusement and desire.

"Are we counting this morning?" she asked.

"This morning, last night, and however many more times I can have you before we're forced to deal with the rest of the world."

She was studying me intently.

"I've wondered something," I said. "Why did you trust me not to touch you after we got married? Surely you didn't think that absurd pillow wall would stop me if I'd chosen to break our agreement?"

She hesitated, clearly wrestling with something. Finally, she sighed. "I have . . . an ability. A truth-sense. I can tell when people are lying to me."

I propped myself up on my hands to look at her. "And you didn't think to mention this before?"

"It's not something I advertise," she said defensively. "My father . . . He didn't like it when I caught him in lies."

I let that sink in. She'd known all along if I was lying about my vow or exaggerating my desire to keep her safe. She'd read my half-truths about wanting—no, *needing*—her consent. A flush of grudging admiration warmed my chest.

"Useful," I remarked, trying not to sound flustered. "No wonder you kept outmaneuvering my attempts at seduction."

Arabella gave a sly smile. "Yes."

I inhaled. Was I embarrassed that she'd seen through many of my manipulations? Possibly. I decided to bury that feeling and pressed her deeper into the rug instead, letting my body speak.

"Well," I said finally, "I suppose that evens things between us. A little."

"Hm. No comment."

"You know," I murmured, "there are ways to extract information without words." I brushed my lips lightly along her jaw, eliciting a little gasp.

She whispered, "You've mentioned your interrogation techniques before, kidnapper."

I continued a slow path down her neck, nipping gently while my hands explored the slight curve of her waist. "I can demonstrate thoroughly, unless—"

Arabella's breath hitched as my lips traveled down to her breastbone. She tangled her fingers in my hair, tugging impatiently. "Unless what?"

I pulled back just enough to meet her eyes. "Unless you'd like breakfast first," I said. "We could share one, unlike my previous . . . arrangements."

She gazed at me with a combination of shrewd calculation and desire. Then she hooked her leg over my hip. "Breakfast can wait," she decided, pulling me back down to her. "I'm hungry for something else."

45

Channel Your Righteous Fury
(and Your Dark Lord's Destruction Kink)

Arabella

"You're staring." I lowered my fork to my plate. Kazimir had been watching me eat for several minutes, staring at me like he couldn't decide whether to devour me or the meal first. The cozy alcove of his tower hid a private dining area I hadn't known existed until this morning, when he'd led me here after we'd finally exhausted ourselves. Outside the tall windows, diffused sunlight filtered through the clouds, making everything in the room glow.

He leaned back in his chair, all dark elegance and insufferable confidence. "Am I not allowed to look at my wife?"

"Not when she's trying to eat." I shifted in my seat, acutely aware of the pleasant ache in my body. "It's unnerving."

He shrugged, his slow smile unapologetic. "I enjoy watching you enjoy things. You have a little quirk—your eyes widen, and your mouth twitches up just before you catch yourself."

I felt my cheeks warm. "You're being ridiculous."

For a few moments, we ate in near silence. I found myself stealing glances at him despite chiding him for doing the same. I studied the way the sunlight darkened the gleam of his hair, the decisive movements of his hands, the faint stubble along his jaw that I'd felt against my skin not so long ago. This was our first breakfast together. Normally, he was gone before I woke up. It wasn't a casual shift in his routine; it was a deliberate choice.

Kazimir caught me looking as he reached for the honey. "Now *you're* the one staring."

"I was just thinking this is nice," I said, deflecting. "Though I'm surprised the Dark Lord takes time for breakfast at all. Doesn't it interfere with your schedule of terrorizing the countryside?"

"Terrorizing on an empty stomach leads to poor decision-making. Beheading the wrong peasant, that sort of thing." He gestured dismissively with his spoon. "Besides, I've already completed my morning terror. The kitchen staff was quite alarmed when I requested breakfast for two."

I laughed and grabbed my teacup. "The Dark Lord, domesticated at last."

"Perhaps." He reached across the table and brushed his fingertip along the inside of my wrist. A tingling wave of magic rippled up my arm. "I've never felt magic quite like this. Can you sense it? Under your skin?"

I nodded. Since last night, my power had been thrumming through me, vibrant and alive in ways I'd never experienced.

"It's like . . ." I searched for the right words. "Like I've been holding my breath for years, but I didn't know it. And now I can finally breathe."

The hint of a smile left Kazimir's face, and he withdrew his hand from mine. "There's something I need to tell you."

I set down my cup, suddenly wary. "That sounds ominous."

"It's about your father." He paused, watching me carefully. "And what I discovered at Evenfall Estate."

My stomach twisted unpleasantly. "You went there?"

"A couple of weeks ago, yes. I needed to see what kind of man thinks it's acceptable to lock his daughter in a tower." His jaw tightened. "And I discovered something you deserve to know."

I waited, not trusting myself to speak. Kazimir's eyes met mine, and I was startled by the anger I saw there—not directed at me, but *for* me.

"Your father's estate is riddled with suppression runes," he finally said. "Powerful ones, designed specifically to dampen magical abilities. They're concentrated most heavily in the tower where you were imprisoned, but they're throughout the manor as well."

I felt the blood drain from my face. "Suppression?"

"Blood-bound inhibitors. Old ones." Kazimir's expression hardened. "Some were recently activated, but others have been there for decades. Your father clearly has no magic of his own, so he must have paid people over the years to create and maintain them."

A memory surfaced of my father's furious grip on my arm, dragging me into the tower after I'd used my truth-sense to expose one of his lies at a dinner party. *"You'll learn your place,"* he'd snarled. *"Or you'll stay in that tower until you do."*

I'd spent a year in that cold, silent prison. A year of being forced to cling to illusions for comfort, the heartbreak of suspecting no one outside those walls cared if I ever reemerged.

"He told everyone I was ill," I said, the words bitter on my tongue. "That I needed isolation to recover. And they believed him, because who would question Lord Evenfall about his own daughter?"

The magic that had been humming pleasantly beneath my skin all morning now roared to life, responding to my fury. I could feel it surging through me, wild and untamed, seeking an outlet.

"The tower wasn't just a punishment," Kazimir continued, his voice gentle. "Each time you began to grow too powerful, he'd lock you away until the runes could do their work. Until you were . . . diminished again."

"Why?" I managed, though I wasn't sure if I was asking Kazimir or the universe at large. "Why would he do that to his own daughter?"

"Fear," he said simply. "Your bloodline carries immense power that he couldn't hope to control or understand. So he did what weak men always do when faced with something stronger than themselves. He tried to break it."

My hands began to tremble. I curled them into fists to hide it, but Kazimir noticed. Of course he noticed.

"The runes were specific to your bloodline," he continued, his voice soft. "They wouldn't have affected anyone else in the household. Just you."

"Not just me." The room suddenly felt too small, the air too thick. "My mother was from the First Hero's bloodline. That's why my father married her." I laughed, a bitter sound that scraped my throat. "I always thought it was strange that she never showed any magical ability. She used to tell me stories about our ancestor, about the magic in our blood. But I never saw her use it."

"Because she couldn't," Kazimir said. "Not with those runes in place."

"And then he did the same to me." The humming beneath my skin intensified, turning sharp and insistent. My fingertips tingled. The teacup in front of me began to tremble, then crack, a hairline fracture spreading across the delicate porcelain. "He would lock me in that tower whenever I showed signs of anything beyond healing magic. He called it 'discipline' for being too weak to control myself."

"You were never weak," Kazimir said firmly. "Even with your powers suppressed, you were formidable. I sensed it the moment I saw you. And you've demonstrated it several times over."

The prickly, scalding rage unfurled under my skin. "Did you kill him?"

"No." Kazimir's eyes were dark with something that might have been regret. "I considered it. But I thought that decision should be yours."

The sunlight seemed to intensify, glinting off the silverware until it hurt to look at it. The windows began to rattle in their frames as my magic pushed outward, seeking release. I could feel the glass vibrating, hear the high-pitched whine as pressure built against the panes.

"Arabella." Kazimir said quietly, caution in his tone.

I ignored him, lost in the storm of my own rage. My father had stolen my mother's magic. Had stolen mine.

The pressure built to an unbearable crescendo. Magic exploded outward from me in a wave of pure, unfiltered rage. The windows shattered, glass flying outward into the open air beyond the tower. Plates cracked. Goblets shattered.

Cold air rushed in, whipping my hair around my face. I gasped, suddenly aware of what I'd done.

Kazimir hadn't moved. He sat across from me, utterly calm, as if having breakfast amid a shower of broken glass was a perfectly normal occurrence.

"Why didn't you stop me?" I asked, bewildered by his lack of reaction.

He brushed a shard from his shoulder. "I'm familiar with the catharsis of creative destruction. You needed that."

I stared at him, then at the destruction around us. A laugh bubbled up from somewhere deep inside me—slightly hysterical, but genuine. I took a shaky breath. "So then what happened yesterday, in the war room?"

His eyes gleamed with pride. "Yesterday wasn't just an accident of passion. I believe the last hold on your magic snapped, and well . . ." He gestured at the devastation around us. "You've been holding back a great deal of power for a very long time."

I stared at my hands, which were trembling with the magic coursing through me, stronger and wilder than it had ever been. When I looked up, Kazimir was kneeling beside my chair. He took my hands in his. "What you're feeling now, that constant hum of power under your skin? That's you, unbound and unchained. Exactly as you should be." He squeezed my fingers gently. "About the blood test you yelled at me for . . . I discovered something."

"What?"

"Your bloodline magic amplifies other magic to an extraordinary degree." His eyes held mine, intense and serious. "When combined with mine, the effect is unprecedented."

I pulled my hands away and stood. "Now I'm some kind of magical anomaly?"

"You're extraordinary," Kazimir corrected, following me. His feet crunched over broken glass. "You're from the First Hero's line, sure, but there's something older woven into it. I can't claim to know the exact source. I only know you have the capacity to become far stronger than your father ever realized. Now that the runes can't dampen your power, your magic will keep growing. We'll work on your control, but otherwise . . ." He breathed in, eyes ablaze with a dangerous excitement. "The possibilities are endless."

For the first time, I noticed a thin line of blood trickling down his cheek where a shard had caught him.

"You're bleeding," I said, reaching toward his face.

Kazimir went perfectly still as my fingers hovered near the cut. "What are you doing?"

"Healing you. Don't be difficult."

He tensed when my magic made contact with the wound. The cut sealed beneath my touch, leaving unblemished skin. When I withdrew my hand, he trapped it in his own and pressed a kiss to my palm.

"What happens now?" I whispered.

"That depends on you," he said. He didn't relinquish my hand. "What do you want to do about your father?"

The question caught me off guard. "I . . . don't have any idea."

"If you want vengeance, I'll help you take it. If you want to curse his lands until nothing grows for a hundred years, I'll teach you how. If you want his head on a pike outside our gates . . ." He shrugged. "I have several pikes available."

"And if I choose mercy?"

He sighed dramatically. "Then I suppose I'll have to live with it."

I let out a shaky breath. "I need time to think."

He leaned in, brushed a careful kiss on my cheek. "Take all the time you need." Then he dropped his voice, half serious and half wry. "But if he comes near you, I can't promise I won't remove his spine."

"Kaz?" I asked, a slight tremor betraying the swirl of emotions in my chest.

"Yes?"

"Did you know all this would happen when we had sex?"

Laughter rumbled through his chest, and his arms slipped around my waist in a slow, possessive gesture. "Do you really think I would have held on to that knowledge, knowing that it might have persuaded you earlier?"

I huffed a laugh and shook my head. Kazimir's hand slid beneath my chin, lifting my face until I had no choice but to meet the intensity burning in his eyes.

"I am glad," he said softly, "that I didn't know. That we discovered it together." His thumb brushed across my lower lip. "Your power is your own now, Arabella. No one will ever cage it again. Least of all me."

Before either of us could say anything more, the door burst open. Griffin stood there, his eyes wide as he took in the scene—the broken windows, the glass scattered across the floor, the two of us standing calmly amid the destruction and the swirl of cold air.

"My lord! Lady Blackrose! Are you—" He stopped, clearly reassessing the situation. "I heard the windows break, but I see you're . . . fine?"

"Perfectly fine," Kazimir said drily. "Lady Blackrose was just redecorating again."

Griffin's gaze darted between us, uncertainty written across his features. "I see. Well, that's . . . creative."

"Did you need something, Griffin?" Kazimir asked, his tone making it clear that the interruption had better be important.

"Yes, my lord." Griffin straightened. "It's the Heirloom. It's . . . changed since last night . . . glowing, pulsing with energy. I've never seen anything like it."

Kazimir's attitude shifted from affectionate to razor-sharp in a heartbeat. "We'll be there shortly."

As the door closed behind Griffin, Kazimir turned back to me. "Are you all right?"

I wasn't. Not even close. But I nodded anyway.

He caught my arm as I moved for the door, his touch gentle but firm. "I want you to know," he said, "that your rage is justified. And when you decide what to do with it, I'll be there."

He squeezed my arm once before releasing it. "Now, let's see what your magic has done to my Heirloom."

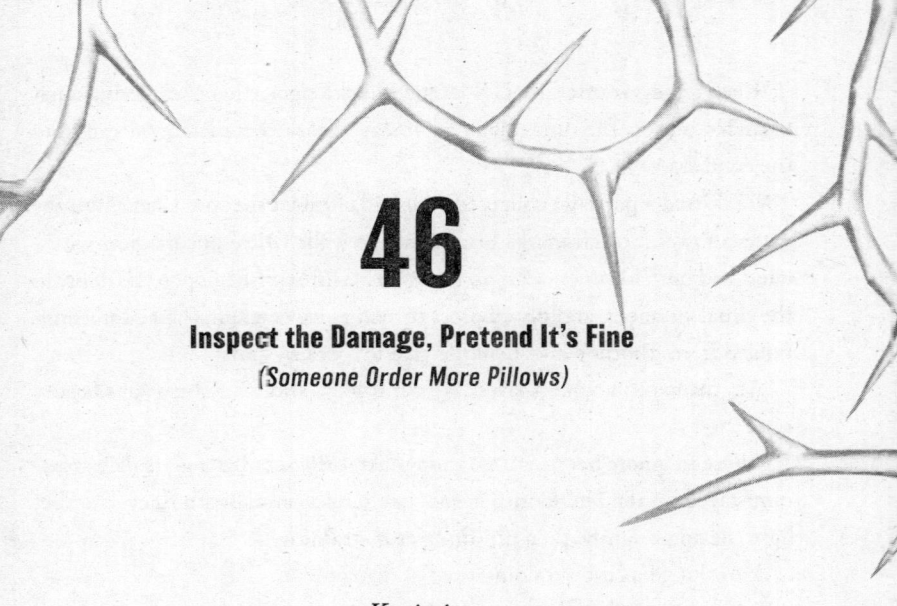

46

Inspect the Damage, Pretend It's Fine
(Someone Order More Pillows)

Kazimir

I strode down the corridor toward the eastern tower, moving just slowly enough for Arabella to match my pace. Griffin bounded ahead of us, nearly vibrating with excitement. The memory of last night's chaos still coursed beneath my skin. Beneath that pleasant buzz, my runes prickled with raw discomfort. They always grew sensitive after intense magical activity, and I'd needed a great deal of power to contain our combined magics.

Not that I was complaining.

Servants scurried past, casting furtive glances our way, particularly at my wife. She pressed closer and lowered her voice. "Why is everyone looking at me like that?"

I smirked. "Perhaps because half the fortress heard you screaming my name last night. Several times, in fact."

Her cheeks blazed an exquisite pink. "I wasn't that loud."

"You shattered a window."

"That was the magic," she hissed, gripping her fists so tightly that errant sparks crackled between her fingers, bright and hungry.

"Keep telling yourself that." I let my knuckles graze hers, triggering a jolt of shared power. The runes along my forearm seared beneath my sleeve from the contact.

We skirted a partially collapsed wall and climbed the spiral steps into the eastern tower. Scorch marks blackened the walls where our magical whirlwind had burned runes clean off the stone. Griffin pushed open the doors to the ritual chamber, and my advisors turned as we entered. Their expressions ranged from Thorne's not-so-subtle grin to Vex's sly smirk.

"Ah, the happy couple arrives," Vex drawled. "Did we disturb your beauty rest?"

I chose to ignore her needling, though Arabella shot her a glare. My attention stayed on the Heirloom. The ancient circlet pulsed with uneven amber light, flaring brightly, then dimming as if straining.

"How long has it been doing this?" I demanded.

Griffin bounced on his toes. "It began around midnight, coinciding with a major spike in mystical energy—more than we've ever recorded in the fortress."

Sims scanned his notes, murmuring, "Fascinating." He tapped the page. "And now?"

"The pulses have grown more frequent," Griffin said. "I'd guess about a seventeen percent decrease in the intervals since dawn."

I rested my hand on the circlet, searching for the surge of power I'd expected to feel upon contact. It was warm, almost alive, but still unstable. Something about the rhythm of its glow felt off, like a heartbeat skipping.

Arabella drifted closer, her fingers flexing as though she were one breath away from releasing that feral magic inside her again. The Heirloom's amber glow flared in recognition. I exhaled sharply, forcing the memories of last night aside.

"It's responding to you," I said. "To us."

Arabella's eyes flickered to mine, equal parts fascination and caution. "But you're saying it isn't fully . . . awake?"

I circled the artifact, tension coiled tight in my bones. "No. Something's building, but it isn't at complete power. Why?"

"If I may," Griffin offered, "the texts speak of a bond between wielders. Perhaps the connection must be... er... continually reinforced over time?"

"What he means," Thorne cut in with a lazy grin, "is that you two need to keep having sex to make it work properly."

"The, ah, terminology in the ancient texts is somewhat oblique, but yes, essentially," Griffin stammered.

Arabella's mortified huff made Vex snort with laughter. Meanwhile, my jaw tightened. The very public suggestion that I continue sharing my bed with Arabella was hardly unpleasant, but the pointed stares from my closest advisors were grating. Still, I couldn't deny the flicker of relief that unraveled in my chest. My outward scowl didn't mirror that secret triumph.

"How periodically?" I asked.

Griffin adjusted his robes nervously. "The texts aren't specific, my lord. But based on the current pattern of energy fluctuations, I would hypothesize... daily?"

"How terribly inconvenient for you both," Vex remarked drily.

I shot her a withering look. "Enough."

As I rotated the Heirloom for closer inspection, I spotted a faint shine that looked out of place among the ley line etchings across its surface. I tilted it toward the light, and a cold sensation spread through my chest.

Fuck.

A hairline fracture. One crack, almost invisible, ran along a curled etching. My stomach plunged, and I stared at the nearly invisible crack with growing horror. Artifacts like this were nearly indestructible. It shouldn't have cracked unless it met some monstrous force, which evidently, Arabella and I had just become. But there it was. A tiny, devastating flaw.

White-hot anger lanced through me. My runes seared along my ribs, and I forced down the urge to hurl the circlet against the wall.

No one else had noticed the fracture. They were busy debating the frequency of "ritual reinforcement" required. Griffin offered more theories in halting phrases. Thorne's irreverent humor stoked Arabella's visible annoyance.

The fracture must have formed last night in the same catastrophic release that damaged the east wing. I just hadn't noticed it yesterday when I'd initially checked the Heirloom after our . . . enthusiastic consummation.

Ten damned years spent plotting, killing, bargaining to track this artifact down . . . only to damage it with mind-blowing orgasms. I would have laughed at the absurdity if not for the savage fury swirling inside me.

"I've never encountered a magical *object* that required bodily intimacy to function," Sims was saying. "Though there are precedents in blood magic rituals where continued exchange is necessary for—"

"Lady Blackrose?" Thorne's voice cut through. "Are you unwell?"

I glanced up, suddenly noticing Arabella's pallor and the tight set of her jaw.

"I'm fine," she snapped, then immediately softened her tone. "Forgive me. I'm just . . . it's been a long morning."

"Magical exhaustion," Griffin supplied helpfully. "Quite common after intense spellcasting. Or other intense activities that involve magical resonance."

"I can have someone bring you a tonic, if you'd like," Vex offered.

"No," Arabella said, stepping away. She glanced sidelong at me, her face knitting with frustration that I recognized all too well. "I need to feed Nyx before she sets the stables on fire."

She started for the door, pausing just long enough to cast me another look before slipping into the corridor.

I should have said something, but my mind was consumed with the Heirloom's fracture. If that crack worsened, the Heirloom might fail—or worse yet, unleash something catastrophic. I had to fix it or discover a way to mitigate the damage. Another fear slithered beneath that: If the artifact ended up useless, would Arabella still have reason to stay? My heart hammered in my ears from the unstoppable tangle of worry and anger. *Dammit.*

I tried to focus on the circlet. "Keep monitoring the pulses and chart each fluctuation. I want hourly reports."

The advisors nodded. Out of the corner of my eye, I spotted Vex slipping out, probably to trail after Arabella.

I let my gaze drift over Griffin's charts, but my mind reeled with more urgent matters. If the entire circlet shattered, we'd lose the main advantage we had over Solandris. But the shameful spark of panic that stirred wasn't just about the artifact's power.

I felt a violent urge to demolish something—preferably Solandris itself. But such tantrums would accomplish nothing now. So I exhaled, letting the tension coil under my skin.

I'd fix the damage. Because if I lost this artifact, I might lose her, too. That possibility, I was starting to realize, terrified me more than I dared admit.

47

Blow Off Steam
(Without Destroying the Castle)

Arabella

I left the eastern tower and crossed the inner courtyard toward our chambers. My head throbbed from exhaustion. The morning's revelations had piled atop the magical overload until I felt like a dry tinder pile just waiting for the slightest spark to ignite.

Behind me, their clinical discussion about our "daily reinforcement" was still ongoing, as though it were a mere footnote in some arcane textbook. The memory left a sour taste in my mouth. The talk had sounded so . . . impersonal. Like I was one part of a magic equation rather than a person barely clinging to sanity.

None of them had mentioned the suppression runes or my father's betrayal. Apparently, Kazimir hadn't shared what he discovered at Evenfall Estate, choosing to keep that between us. Some small piece of me felt grateful for his discretion. Another part wanted to scream at him for focusing on the artifact while my world kept crumbling.

I fought the urge to let magic crackle across my fingertips. That not-quite-anger still hummed under my skin, constantly threatening to burst out in an uncontrolled show of force.

"Lady Blackrose."

I nearly stumbled at Vex's voice. She appeared beside me with that unsettling grace of hers, falling into step as I stormed down the corridor.

"A word?" she asked.

She guided me to a narrow alcove behind a column. A pair of servants scurried past without looking up, no doubt aware I was the Dark Lord's bride who occasionally released dramatic bursts of magic while in the throes of passion.

"You're upset," she stated, getting right to the point.

"I'm just tired," I bluffed. I was twisting the edge of my sleeve, which probably gave me away.

"And overwhelmed," she added, folding her arms. "And furious with him."

I leaned back against the cool stone. "Is it that obvious?"

"Only if you know the signs. I've served Lord Blackrose long enough to recognize certain patterns." Her tone stayed matter-of-fact. "He's not good at this, you know. The emotional part."

A hollow laugh slipped out of me. "Really hadn't noticed."

One corner of her mouth twitched. "He understands rage. He practically breathes it. But tenderness, attachment . . . those scare him more than death—always have. He's clumsy when it matters most."

I blinked, uncertain how to process that level of honesty from Vex. "Why are you telling me this?"

"Because despite his infinite flaws—and trust me, I could list them alphabetically—he's different with you. And I think you're different with him."

I tried to shrug it off, but she just raised her eyebrow in that infuriating way. So I busied my hands, plucking a stray thread from my skirt.

"We have a mutually beneficial arrangement," I said.

"Call it what you like." She gave a low chuckle. "But I've never seen him look at anyone the way he looks at you."

I let out a disbelieving snort. "Like I'm a useful tool to power his artifact?"

"Like you're a fire he can't decide whether to extinguish or throw himself into."

The electric prickles in my veins grew more intense. If what she said was true, it meant Kazimir felt the same way I did.

"Just don't give up on him too quickly," Vex said, pushing away from the wall. "He's learning. Slower than a concussed tortoise, but learning nonetheless."

With that, she slipped away into the corridor, and I was left with my swirling thoughts. Each heartbeat felt too loud. When I reached the junction that would lead to our chambers, I hesitated. My magic built inside me like storm clouds pressed too tight together.

"To hell with this," I muttered, changing direction.

I stormed into the training room, letting the heavy door slam behind me. The wards etched into the stone floor glowed faintly, reacting to the surge of power that pulsed through my body.

Everything felt wrong. Kazimir's advisors discussing our intimacy like an ongoing experiment. The Heirloom refusing to stabilize. Kazimir being so attentive one moment and so consumed with his goals the next. And beneath it all seethed my festering rage at my father.

Focus your anger. Use it. That voice in my head sounded too much like Kazimir's. But it made sense. There was no escaping the fury swirling inside me, so I might as well channel it somewhere.

I moved to the center of the circle, knelt, and placed my palms flat against the cold floor. Warm, roiling energy pulsed under my skin. "I don't need anyone," I whispered. "I'll figure this out myself."

First, I tried forming the energy bird like I'd done once before. But this time, I'd do it without siphoning the essence of any living creature. I wanted to prove I could create something purely from my own magic. I closed my eyes. Power ignited deep within me, hot and bright. I shaped it, coaxed it, demanded it obey. A spark quivered between my hands, almost forming wings, then shattered in a burst of wild magic.

I landed hard on my backside. My once-fine day dress hung in tatters around me, the blue fabric scorched and torn beyond salvaging. That's what I got for storming in here to throw magical tantrums without bothering to change into my training leathers.

"Damn it!" I slammed my fist against the floor. The stone cracked in a spiderweb of fissures radiating outward. I stared at the damage in disbelief. The raw might reverberated through me.

I tried again. And again. Each time, I hovered painfully close to success before the construct destabilized. Residual force ricocheted around the chamber, saved only by the thick wards that Kazimir had installed for exactly these sorts of outbursts.

On the seventh attempt, I finally shaped the bird. It floated on shimmering wings for a miraculous few seconds—long enough to see each feather outlined in soft, purple-white light—before it dissolved into flickers.

"Why won't you stay together?" I shouted at the empty space, fighting the sting in my eyes. I surged to my feet and wiped the sweat from my forehead. My hands trembled from the excess energy still coursing through me.

I turned on the row of wooden training dummies by the wall, each with a blank, mocking face. My magic practically roared for release. Snarling, I slammed a surge of energy into the nearest dummy. It exploded in a hail of straw and splinters. Flames caught the next one. The air filled with burnt straw, smoke, and crackling energy.

It felt *good*.

I moved down the line, unleashing my rage. Dummies shattered, burned, twisted. One collapsed in an oozing puddle. Stray embers floated everywhere. My heartbeat thundered in my ears. By the time I reached the end of the row, I was breathing hard from exhilaration. My whole body hummed with power, more alive than I'd ever felt.

The training chamber looked like a war zone. Bits of straw floated in the air. Scorch marks blackened the walls. The acrid smell of smoke hung heavy.

I returned to the center circle, determined to master the energy bird. This time, instead of forcing the magic into the shape I wanted, I visualized it already complete and perfect. I held that image in my mind, crystal clear, and then simply . . . invited the magic to fill it.

Slowly, it coalesced. My core trembled with an almost gentle warmth, and I felt a flutter near my fingertips. Opening my eyes, I saw a small bird made of shimmering light perched on my cupped palms. My breath caught. Every feather glinted in an array of colors, shifting as though capturing starlight.

The bird hovered there, fully formed, its wings beating in perfect silence. It was more beautiful than the one I'd created from the mouse's life force, because this one came purely from me. From my magic. From my will. Its tiny weight felt like nothing, yet I could sense the connection between us—a thread of magic linking creator and creation.

Well done, it seemed to whisper.

Three seconds. Four. Five. Then it dissolved, its essence rolling back into me. That time, the bird left a soft echo behind. Stunned, I created it again, faster, stronger. It flew lazy loops around my head, then perched on my finger.

I lost track of how long I practiced. Each conjured bird grew more elaborate, some singing voiceless songs that resonated in my mind. Others flitted through the swirling smoke overhead before winking out.

I barely noticed my scorched dress or the straw littering the chamber. I just felt . . . free. Slowly, the anger and fear seeped out of me, replaced by pure joy in what I could do when no one was holding me back.

"They're beautiful."

I jumped, nearly losing hold of the glowing phoenix perched on my fingertips. It dissolved in a swirl of red-gold motes. My heart lurched as I turned. Kazimir stood against the door, arms folded, expression carefully neutral.

"How long have you been standing there?" I demanded, suddenly conscious of my tattered dress and the destruction surrounding me.

He pushed off from the door and took a few steps in. "Long enough to see you tear through half my training equipment, then create something remarkable."

"I'll . . . replace those dummies," I offered, glancing at the charred husks that lined the back wall.

He waved them off. "I have more. Though I should order them in bulk if this becomes a habit."

Despite myself, I smiled. "How often do you hide in the shadows to spy on me?"

"Never," he said, and I could tell it was the truth. "I wasn't hiding now, either. You were simply so focused that you didn't notice me enter."

"That's . . . concerning."

"It's something to work on." Kazimir studied the scorched, cracked floor, then regarded me with a strange softness. "But you looked magnificent."

I crossed my arms over my chest. "Weren't you busy with the Heirloom?" The question sounded defensive, even to me.

A momentary shadow crossed his face. "I was. But . . . I missed you."

That simple statement stole the breath from my lungs. I narrowed my eyes, trying to spot any manipulation. I found only sincere weariness etched in the lines around his mouth.

"You . . . missed me?"

"Is that so hard to believe?" He stopped a few feet away, respecting my space. "Yes, the Heirloom is important. But . . . you're important too. Not just because of the power you bring. Because . . ." He sucked in a breath, as though he hated admitting it. "Because of this thing between us, whatever it is. It's . . . new. For me."

It was perhaps the least eloquent I'd ever seen the Dark Lord, and strangely, that made his words more meaningful. Though I still didn't know whether to feel flattered or angry. My magic prickled on my skin, uncertain which emotion to feed on.

"I missed you too," I confessed. "Even though you infuriate me sometimes."

"I noticed." His gaze flicked to the demolished training dummies. "Remind me never to truly anger you."

"Too late for that." But there was no heat in my words.

He took another step closer and smiled, an honest, rueful curve of his mouth. "Show me another bird?"

I hesitated, suddenly self-conscious. "They're not perfect yet."

"Show me anyway."

I took a deep breath and drew magic from the reservoir inside me, shaping a small bird with shimmering midnight feathers. It flitted from my fingertips to Kazimir's outstretched hand, perching there as though examining him. His eyes glowed with fascination.

"You've done this in an afternoon," he murmured. "Conjured a complex construct that most mages can't manage after years of study."

The bird preened under his attention, then flew back to me, settling on my shoulder. I reached up to stroke its shimmering feathers with a fingertip. "I didn't use life force this time."

He trailed his gaze along the shredded skirt exposing my legs, the scorched sleeves leaving my arms bare. A darker hunger sparked in his eyes. "Yes," he said, voice turning rough, "you used only your essence . . . and it's incredible."

Suddenly self-conscious, I let the bird dissolve. "It's easier now, without the suppression runes. I'm not even tired."

"They were draining you more than you realized," he said. "The runes were probably built that way."

Fresh anger flared in my chest. "My father really did think of everything."

"Not everything." Kazimir held out his hand to me. "He didn't account for me."

I placed my hand in his, feeling the warmth of his skin against mine, the quiet strength in his grip. I suddenly realized I had no idea how much time had passed. The windows high above showed only darkness. "What time is it?"

"Nearly midnight." He gave my arm a light tug. "Come on. You should rest, even if you don't think you need it."

"Is that concern I hear, Lord Blackrose?" I teased, trying to lighten the mood.

"Practical advice," he corrected, but there was a warmth in his eyes. "I have plans for you that require a certain level of . . . stamina."

Heat bloomed in my cheeks, spreading down my neck. "Oh?"

"Mmm." He tugged me closer, his lips brushing against my ear. "Very specific plans."

My stomach chose that moment to growl.

His eyes crinkled at the corners. "When did you last eat?"

I shrugged. "Breakfast, I think." The memory felt distant, as if it belonged to another day entirely.

"Unacceptable." He tugged me toward the spiral staircase. "You need food."

"Fine," I said. "But I want a bath first. I smell like smoke and sweat."

He leaned in, inhaling the air near my neck. The proximity made my pulse jump. "I like the way you smell after training. It reminds me of battlefields."

"That's . . . disturbing."

"Is it?" He smiled against my skin. "Flames, sweat, victory. It's intoxicating. I've barely been able to stand not telling you."

A throb of longing pulsed through my body. My fingers curled against his chest, feeling the quick drumming of his heart.

"Bath," I insisted. "Then food."

"As my lady commands."

48

Contemplate Destiny
(While Your Villain Sleeps)

Arabella

Our chambers had been scrubbed and polished by the time we returned, almost unrecognizably tidy with an odd layer of coziness layered over the usual gloom. Gone were the scattered feathers, and even the finger bones that once decorated Kazimir's desk had vanished. Many of the ancient, ominous-looking books had disappeared as well—removed "for safety," Kaz had explained. In their place stood a small vase of noncarnivorous flowers and a few new plush cushions around the seating area.

It wasn't too bad, overall. Maybe I'd spend more time here.

After our baths, we ate sitting cross-legged on the massive bed. I watched him over the rim of my wine glass. Even still-damp, Kazimir Blackrose radiated danger. It was in the coiled strength of his body, the casual grace with which he wielded his knife and fork as if they could become weapons at any moment.

I noticed the faint red glow pulsing beneath the skin of his wrist, visible only for a moment before his arm moved. The runes were more active tonight, which usually meant he'd been channeling excessive magic. The cause wasn't too difficult to determine, considering all the effort it'd taken for him to stop me from bringing the tower down around us.

"You're quiet," I observed.

"Just tired," he answered, reaching across to trace a light fingertip along my jaw. "And . . . distracted."

"By the Heirloom?" I ventured.

His gaze lifted from my lips to lock on my eyes. "Among other things."

I snorted, rolling my eyes in mock exasperation. "You only manage a three-second attention span for anything that's not about world domination."

"Strange," he murmured, brushing his thumb across my lower lip. "With you, the hours pass like seconds."

I wanted to toss something witty back at him, but the warmth of his touch turned my thoughts into a haze of want. I set my plate aside, letting him lean in. The kiss was soft as a whisper, a gentle sweep of his lips that barely grazed mine. Then, greedy for more, he pressed harder, his tongue teasing until I parted for him and tasted wine and that dark taste of Kazimir beneath it.

His fingers loosened the tie of my robe, tugging it open until the silk slipped down. I gasped at the sudden chill brushing my bare skin, but the heated look in his eyes chased it away. He took in every inch of me, gaze drifting from my face to my exposed breasts, and then he bent his head to trail lazy kisses across sensitive skin. My back arched, a spark of pleasure kindling every time he focused on a spot.

He finally paused long enough to whisper, "Lie on your side."

I shifted onto my hip, the robe falling away completely. Kazimir shed his sleeping pants, revealing his erection, thick and hard. The bed dipped under his weight when he lay down behind me, a line of unmistakable warmth against my back. His lips skimmed across my shoulder, moving up to the spot behind my ear.

"Do you know how long I've wanted to enjoy you like this?" he asked in a hushed rasp. "When you're not fighting me, but . . . eager." One hand slid over my hip, down between my thighs, exploring my slickness with a deliberate stroke that made me tremble. "Wet for me," he murmured, voice full of smug satisfaction.

Then he let his hand drift away, gliding up over my stomach, my ribs, until his palm rested lightly against my throat. His lips resumed their path down my shoulder blade, pressing an open-mouthed kiss there before trailing down my spine. Each vertebra received attention—a kiss, a lick, a gentle scrape of teeth that sent shivers through me.

When he reached the small of my back, he paused. I felt the wet heat of his tongue trace a pattern—not random, but deliberate.

"What are you doing?" I managed to ask, my voice breathy.

He chuckled. "Marking you temporarily with a rune. You'll like what it does."

I opened my mouth to demand specifics and then couldn't speak as a radiant heat spread from that spot, everything growing sharper and more intense. My entire body lit up with need.

"Oh," I gasped, limbs turning pliable beneath his touch.

His fingers found me again, and he hummed in approval. "You're enjoying that, aren't you?"

"Yes," I breathed.

He shifted behind me. Then I felt his cock, hot and hard, pressing against my entrance. He entered me slowly, inch by delicious inch. I clenched my fists in the sheets.

"Gods," I breathed, feeling impossibly full, stretched around him in the most exquisite way.

"No," Kazimir said, his voice strained with the effort of holding still. "Just me."

Before I could respond to his arrogance, he began slow and deep thrusts that drew out pulses of pleasure that radiated everywhere. The rune amplified every little sensation, as though my entire body was an exposed nerve. He wrapped an arm around my waist, keeping our bodies flush, and I melted into the steady rhythm of his hips pressing firmly against me, that demanding stroke inside me. I felt every ridge, every vein of him, driving me toward a swift, shuddering peak.

When his hand slid down my stomach, I nearly bit my lip in half. He matched the thrust of his hips with the insistent circle of his fingers, sending me headlong into a staggering release. I clenched around him, and he groaned deep in his chest, pace faltering. His thrusts took on a frantic edge until his body stiffened, and I felt every twitch and throb of him inside me.

The sensation triggered another climax. I gasped into the mattress, hardly able to believe how intense it was. Kazimir let his forehead rest against my shoulder, our combined ragged breathing echoing in the hush of the room.

He stayed close, not pulling out, and looped an arm around my middle as though he couldn't bear to let go. His voice came to me in a tired mumble. "Stay just like this."

His breathing slowed and deepened as he drifted into sleep. I wondered what he dreamed about. Power? Conquest? Or perhaps something more mundane. The thought made me smile. The fearsome Dark Lord, dreaming of sweet cakes or puppies. It seemed absurd, yet . . . he was human beneath the shadows and power.

My muscles ached in the best of ways, but my mind refused to settle. I shifted slightly. His arm tightened reflexively around my waist, but his breathing remained deep and even.

The scars on Kazimir's arm glowed in the darkness. His taste lingered on my tongue—wine and darkness and something ancient.

Outside, the moon had risen high. The citadel slept around us, floating, suspended between heaven and earth, a living thing of stone and shadow, keeping secrets in its foundations older than either of us. I felt storms brewing inside these walls, inside my chest. My power surging, receding, surging again.

The Heirloom gleaming with hunger. My bloodline thrumming beneath my skin, finally free. The First Hero's shadow stretching across centuries to touch me.

Kazimir's grand design reshaping itself around me, around us.

Black roses unfurling in darkness, golden ones withering in sunlight. Blood calling to blood. Magic calling to magic. Darkness to darkness. His runes and my lineage speaking languages neither of us fully understand.

All of it spiraling together, a whirlwind of purpose and chance that I'm caught in, that I'm driving, that I'm becoming.

My father feared my power enough to cage it. Kazimir sees it and wants it unleashed.

There's more, so much *more*, waiting in the spaces between what I've been taught and what I could learn. What he could teach me.

What I could demand he show me. Everything. All of it. Every dark corner, every forbidden text, every midnight ritual.

Power that's mine by right, by blood, by choice.

Abruptly, I sat up, dislodging Kazimir's arm and breaking our intimate connection. He stirred, mumbling something unintelligible before rolling onto his back, still asleep.

I wasn't sure if I'd been thinking or dreaming, but now that it was in my mind, I wanted to tell him. I looked down at my fearsome villain, so at ease in slumber. More of his runes glowed faintly, and for one reckless instant, I wanted to trace them with my fingertips until he stirred and turned that intense gaze on me again.

Instead, I settled back down beside him and smiled. I'd let the Dark Lord sleep. He'd need all his strength tomorrow.

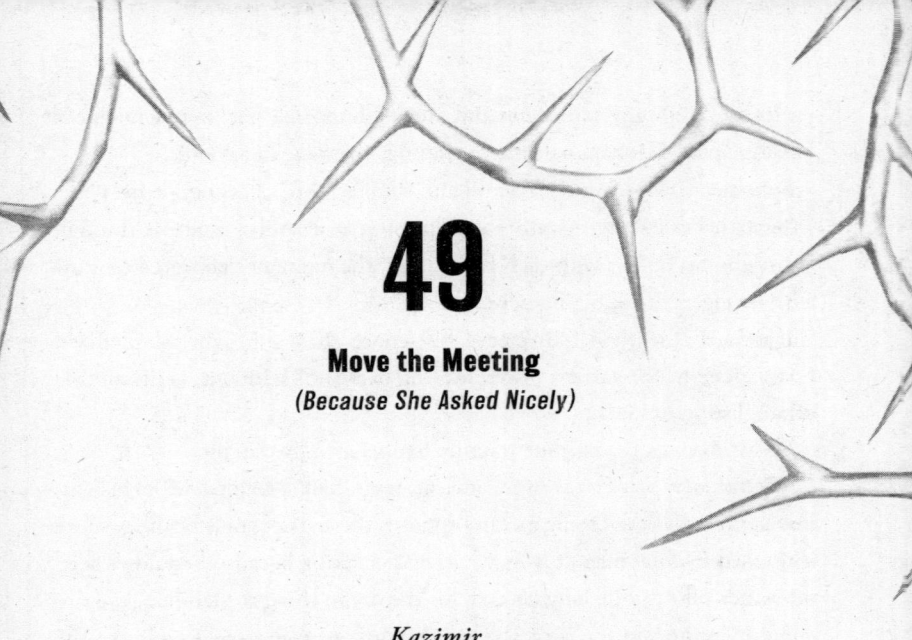

49

Move the Meeting
(Because She Asked Nicely)

Kazimir

—and that's when I told him, 'It's not necromancy if they're still breathing when you start.'"

Griffin's laughter ricocheted off the stone walls. I stabbed my sausage with a fork, feeling a dull throb pound behind my eyes. The last two days had left me gloriously drained and impressively short-tempered. And this weekly breakfast meeting with my advisors felt closer to torture than an actual meal.

Across the table, Sims hunched over a thin obsidian tablet. His finger traced a glowing red script while his lips curved into what passed for a smile on his perpetually pessimistic face.

"What's that?" Griffin abandoned his breakfast, practically levitating with curiosity as he peered over Sims's shoulder. "The text is moving!"

Sims didn't glance up from his reading. "My new Doom Scroll," he said. "It tracks disasters, deaths, and despair across the realm in real time. Extremely efficient."

"Fascinating," I muttered, jabbing another piece of sausage as if it had personally offended me.

Griffin caught my expression and nudged Sims like they were schoolboys passing notes. "Do you have those readings from the Heirloom?"

Sims put down his Doom Scroll and shuffled the papers beside his plate. "The artifact's energy signature kept pulsing at irregular intervals through last night. Strangely, with each fluctuation, the resonance appeared to grow a bit stronger. Encouraging news, I'd say."

I nodded absently. I didn't need his report, since I'd spent the predawn hours alone in the eastern tower, leaning over the Heirloom while fending off a splitting headache.

To my dismay, the hairline fracture had *widened* overnight.

My cursory search through ancient texts had provided little insight. Perhaps it was part of some metamorphosis, the artifact transforming before it reached its final form. Or maybe it was cracking because I couldn't keep my hands off my wife long enough for the damn thing to stabilize.

I also considered the surges in magic when Arabella and I had sex. The war room incident had been wild, uncontrolled . . . But since then, I'd successfully channeled the more destructive bursts away from the citadel. My rune-carved bones still screamed in protest.

Worth it, though. Painfully, gloriously worth it.

Vex shot me a look over her tea that somehow managed to be both amused and judgmental. "Someone woke up on the wrong side of the bed."

"I woke up exactly where I intended," I said, heat flaring through my veins at the memory of Arabella's warm, naked body pressed against mine. Maybe I needed to conduct a more thorough investigation—purely for research purposes—into exactly how our combined resonance affected the Heirloom during specific activities.

Or perhaps each time I buried myself inside my wife, I was destroying the very artifact I'd spent years searching for.

I pushed the thought away. I couldn't afford to consider that every delicious, gasping moment with Arabella might be causing further damage. Not when I craved her more with each passing day.

"What of Auremar?" I asked, desperate for distraction. "Any response to our message?"

Thorne set down his knife. "Nothing yet. The enchantment confirmed delivery, but the king has gone silent. No troop movements, no diplomatic overtures."

"He's up to something," I said. "Men like Auremar don't receive severed heads without retaliation."

Sims smoothed the edge of a parchment. "Perhaps he's reconsidering his position."

I shook my head. "He's gathering forces, deciding which allies to bribe or threaten. We—"

The dining hall door burst open so hard it nearly tore off its hinges. All eyes snapped to Arabella as she strode in, draped in deep purple that clung to every curve I'd tasted last night. Her golden hair cascaded loose and wild around her shoulders, and the morning light caught the gold flecks in her eyes, making them blaze with an almost supernatural intensity.

My breath caught. Last night had been transcendent. But this was something else entirely. She radiated scorching power.

"Good morning," she announced to the room, barely acknowledging my advisors before fixing those burning eyes on me. "Teach me everything you know about dark magic."

Griffin choked on his tea, coughing with the dramatic flair of a man being strangled. Vex's eyebrow arched so high it nearly disappeared into her hairline. Thorne's face remained carved from stone, but I caught the slight widening of his eyes.

I carefully set down my coffee cup, buying time as my body reacted to her command in ways entirely inappropriate for a breakfast meeting.

"That"—I cleared my throat—"might take a while."

Arabella's eyes narrowed dangerously, the golden flecks darkening in an approaching storm. She looked poised to unleash holy—or unholy—hell at any moment.

"When do you want to start?" I amended quickly, suddenly envisioning her looking like that while wielding shadow magic.

"Now."

One word, delivered with such absolute certainty that it sent another bolt of pure lust straight through me. This was not the hesitant healer I'd kidnapped two months ago. This was something new—something that made my inner darkness purr with recognition.

My wife had woken up and chosen violence. And fuck me if it wasn't the sexiest thing I'd ever seen.

I searched her face for any hint of doubt or fear but found none. Only determination, hunger, and a fierce intelligence that matched my own. If I wasn't careful, I'd end up bending the knee to her for good. The thought should have terrified me. Instead, it made my blood sing.

Perhaps this was exactly what we needed. If the Heirloom was suffering from our uncontrolled magical surges, teaching Arabella to harness her powers might stabilize everything.

"Very well," I said, rising from my chair with the calm deliberation of a man who was willingly going to his death. "Griffin, stay on Heirloom patrol. Sims, draft responses to our allies about potential Auremar scenarios. Thorne, double the patrols along the western perimeter. Vex—"

"I'll handle everything else," she said, already gathering papers with resignation. "Go corrupt your wife, and try not to raze another wing of the fortress while you're at it."

I ignored the jab and moved around the table to Arabella's side. "Are you certain?" I asked quietly. "Dark magic exacts a price."

"So does ignorance," she replied, her voice equally low. "I'm ready to learn."

The raw potential radiating from her promised to become either the final piece of my power . . . or my undoing.

I smiled. "This might be my favorite day."

There was something undeniably arousing about watching Arabella prepare for battle. She moved through the training room with coiled, lethal grace, stretching her limbs in the leathers I'd given her. The material clung to every inch of her body, flaunting a lean, honed strength that had a way of setting my blood on edge. And her eyes—gods, those eyes—glowed with a fierce purpose that made me anticipate disaster in the best possible sense.

I'd swapped out my regular tunics for plain black leathers reinforced with protective enchantments. Just in case. After all, the memory of my shirt going up in flames during our first training session remained vivid enough to put me on guard. And she'd grown exponentially more powerful since then.

Not that I'd mind if she scorched me again, so long as I got to relish that mix of horror and mischievous delight flashing across her face.

"Are you going to stare all day, or are we going to begin?" Arabella asked, her voice cutting through my thoughts.

I leaned against the stone wall, arms crossed. "Patience, my lady. Dark magic requires more than just brute force. It needs the proper mindset."

"I've had the proper mindset since dawn," she said, her smile razor-sharp. She stretched an arm across her chest. "I'm ready."

Her enthusiasm was amusing. Dark magic wasn't like her healing arts—clean and pure and unwaveringly selfless. It demanded tribute. It took as much as it gave, often more. Like inviting a starving vampire to dinner and expecting it to be satisfied with the appetizer. Teaching Arabella to delve into that hunger . . . I suspected it would go splendidly and perilously off-script.

I stepped away from the wall, wrestling with a flicker of caution. "Before we start, there's something you should know."

She paused, halfway into another stretch, watchful as a cat with its hackles up. "Go on. Unless you've kidnapped yet another noblewoman while I was sleeping?"

"No." I smirked, moving closer. "Though that's not a terrible contingency plan."

"Because I just moved my things into your—" She caught my look and sobered a bit. "Well, I'm just saying there isn't room for a second wife."

"Relax, there's only one Lady Blackrose at the moment," I quipped, ignoring the treacherous flutter of contentment in my chest. I forced my expression to sober. "I've made the mistake of keeping critical information from you before. I won't do that again."

Arabella's smile faded, but she met my gaze steadily, ready for whatever I had to say. It was a nice change, this . . . honesty.

"It's about the Heirloom. I noticed a small crack yesterday."

"A crack?" Her brow furrowed.

"I first noticed it when Griffin summoned us to the eastern tower. It's small, barely visible, but it's there. And it's growing."

"Is it my fault?" she asked immediately, her voice tight.

"No." I reached out, unable to stop myself from tucking a loose strand of hair behind her ear. "If anything, it's mine. I don't fully understand why, but our activities seem to be both powering it and potentially damaging it."

Her eyes went wide. "When you say activities, you mean—"

"Yes." I let my hand drop, though I didn't step back. "Every time we strengthen our bond, we risk destroying the very thing we need most."

She took a step back. I could practically see the calculations running behind her eyes. The same ones that had kept me awake half the night.

"Further testing is required," I added, flashing her a shameless smirk. "Rigorous, uninhibited research. Possibly against various surfaces. For science."

"You waited to say this until right before you teach me destructive magic?"

"The timing seemed appropriate." I gestured around the reinforced chamber. "Perhaps you could direct your first fireball at this problem rather than my clothing."

To my surprise, she grinned. "That must have been difficult for you—telling me the truth. Especially about something that threatens your plans."

I straightened. "Don't get used to it. I still have plenty of villainous secrets."

"I'm sure you do." Her smile widened, and her eyes turned warm and dangerous all at once. "Show me a bit of this dark magic first. Then we can talk about how I might help with the Heirloom problem."

Help. Not blame, not accuse, not demand. Just . . . help.

I raised my hand, summoning a small orb of shadow laced with a ripple of violet energy. "Dark magic doesn't give like yours. It borrows, sometimes from the caster, sometimes from the surroundings. Even from life itself."

Arabella leaned in to observe the shadows that swirled, flickered, and yearned toward her. She studied them unflinching, as though they were a riddle she intended to solve.

"May I touch it?"

"Not yet." I closed my fist, dissolving the orb. "Lesson one: Respect what you summon. Dark magic always wants more than you mean to give."

Rather the same as *her*, I thought privately.

She absorbed my words with unguarded fascination, then tilted her chin. "I want everything: not just barriers and half steps. I want the force you wield. I want to truly use it."

"It won't be easy," I warned. "And once you begin—"

"I can't go back," she finished for me, meeting my gaze dead-on. "I *know*, Kaz."

"Keep saying my name like that and we'll skip straight to the advanced lessons," I said, stepping closer until I could feel the heat from her body. "I know enough bedroom sorcery to make last night look polite."

I brushed my thumb along her lower spine, exactly where I'd placed that rune.

She gave a heated little smile. "Advanced lessons should wait until I master the basics, *Kazimir*," she said. "But I'm a quick study, as you well know."

I reluctantly dropped my hand—neither of us would get anything done otherwise. My runes thrummed under my skin, alive with the same tension that fueled her. "And I suspect you'll master this faster than anticipated. You've already mastered the art of driving me to distraction."

I extended my hand, palm up, and summoned the shadows once more. This time, I let them dance across my skin, showing her how they moved, how they breathed, how they hungered.

"Now," I said, "let me show you how to call the darkness. After all, if you're going to be my Dark Lady, you should at least know how to make a dramatic entrance."

50

Research the Relic

(and Other Library Violations)

Arabella

"The crack in the Heirloom grew last night," Kazimir said, not looking up from the ancient text he was reading across the table.

I paused, blinking at my own book. "By how much?" My stomach did a traitorous little flip when I finally glanced at him. Damn him. Even exhausted and rumpled from hours of research, he was still unfairly attractive.

He turned a page with more force than necessary. "It went from hairline to spiderweb."

"That's . . . concerning."

He finally looked up. "Are you more concerned about the crack itself, or the possible reason behind it?"

He was referring, of course, to the theory that our nighttime . . . activities . . . were damaging the relic. I narrowed my eyes at him. "Have you found anything useful in that book, or are you just going to tease me all morning?"

"Nothing definitive," he admitted.

I turned a page. "It makes no sense that the Heirloom would require our union to activate, only to be damaged by the same thing."

"Magic rarely makes sense," Kazimir said. "That's why I prefer to bend it to my will rather than follow its rules."

I snorted. "How's that working out for you?"

He gave me a withering look. "I was doing perfectly well until a certain hero came along and complicated everything."

I sighed, rubbing my temples. This marked our third day straight in the library. Each morning, we'd arrive after breakfast, divide tasks, and then vanish into musty stacks of histories and half-forgotten lore. I'd been poring over pages of heroic bloodlines for so long my eyes felt like they might fall out of my head.

I groaned and pushed the thick volume away. "This is useless. According to this author, my great-whatever-grandfather could fly and shoot lightning from his fingers. I'm beginning to think these historians just made things up when they got bored."

I stood and went to the end of the table, intending to pour myself tea, and found Kazimir trailing behind. He hovered like that sometimes now. Perhaps he was just ensuring I didn't destroy the rest of his fortress with a wild burst of magic. Oddly, it made me feel secure.

"Maybe we're asking all the wrong questions," I said, handing him a steaming cup. "Everything I've read so far about the First Hero only talks about his triumphs or conquests or how many times he saved entire villages. Nothing about how to repair a magical crown that cracks because you had sex with your kidnapped bride."

Kazimir drank half his tea in one go, as if it wasn't piping hot. "I imagine that scenario wasn't covered in the epic ballads."

"No, the bards mysteriously left that part out." I reached for another book from the stack and examined the title. "There must be something. We're just digging in the wrong places."

Kazimir's voice turned deceptively casual—even playful. "Oh, I uncovered plenty of solutions."

I eyed him suspiciously. "You just said you hadn't found anything."

"I said nothing *definitive*." He finished his tea and returned to his seat. "There's a fascinating ritual that involves the sacrifice of twelve virgins under a blood moon. The text claims it can repair any magical artifact, regardless of its origin."

"No, it doesn't." I held out my hand. "Let me see that book."

With a smirk, he slid the book toward me and flipped the page. I scanned the small, cramped text, then looked up at Kazimir accusingly. "That day you gave me the citadel tour, you said virgins offer no special magical benefits."

"Not at all. I said if I needed blood, I wouldn't go searching for virgins in particular." His expression was infuriatingly unreadable as he gestured to the book. "There's a difference."

"Where would we even find twelve virgins in *this* court?"

He shrugged. "We could import them."

"No."

"Fine." He flipped another page with mock nonchalance. "What about spirit binding? We trap a powerful entity inside the Heirloom to reinforce its structure."

I returned to my seat across from him, taking my tea with me. "And risk having a vengeful spirit possess us while we're using it? No thank—"

"Bathe it in the blood of its creator?"

"The creator's been dead for centuries," I pointed out.

"A minor obstacle," Kazimir said with a dismissive wave. "There are ways around that."

I drank my tea, but he was still watching me. "You've got more?"

"Naturally." He smirked. "One method calls for bathing the relic in the blood of a murdered king."

I blinked. "That's... Well, kidnapping King Auremar is always an option, I suppose."

"I'll mark that down as 'maybe,'" he said. "Then there's another that involves no murder at all: immersing the Heirloom in the essence of true love for three days and three nights."

I snorted. "Pass."

Kaz gave me a shrewd look. "Not a believer in true love, Lady Blackrose?"

I yanked my book toward me, almost spilling my tea in the process. "Are you actually suggesting these things, or just trying to annoy me?"

"Both," he admitted smoothly. "Your reactions are entertaining. Besides, it's good to consider all options, even the absurd ones."

"You're the absurd one," I muttered, turning back to my book.

He shot back in that languid, confident tone, "You didn't think so last night. As I recall, your exact words—"

"If you finish that sentence," I warned, "I'll set you on fire again."

"That's not quite what you said." He chuckled, warm and low. "You're enjoying this, aren't you?"

"What, vetoing your increasingly horrific suggestions?"

"No." He motioned to the shelves. "The books. The environment. The entire library ritual. You like it."

I hesitated. It was unnerving how sharp his insight could be sometimes. "I do," I admitted. "When my father wasn't watching, I read anything I could scrounge up. I prefer it to trivial skills like needlepoint." I shuddered. "At least reading doesn't draw blood, usually."

For a while, neither of us spoke. The library's hush surrounded us, broken only by the rustle of pages and the scrape of Kazimir's quill across parchment. Eventually, everything I read blurred together. I rose from my seat, heading for the rows of shelves.

Kazimir glanced up briefly, eyes tracking my movement before returning to his text. "Try not to set fire to anything important."

"I haven't *accidentally* set fire to anything in ages."

"The warning still stands."

I strolled through the rows of towering shelves, letting my fingertips skim the worn spines. We already had more than enough texts on the table to occupy us until we went cross-eyed, but I craved one more sweep for anything new.

A faint scuffling noise made the hairs on my neck stand up. I whirled in time to see the edge of a dark robe disappearing between shelves. The librarian. I'd never actually spoken to the man—if he was indeed a man and not one of Kazimir's magical constructs. Pip had told me the librarian preferred to remain unseen and rarely spoke to anyone unless they disrespected a book. I'd never seen him up close before, though I'd sometimes felt his stare.

Curiosity got the better of me. I edged around the corner, only to find empty space. More shelves, more books, and the certainty that someone was silently judging me from the shadows.

I heard another shuffle and spun again. This time, I glimpsed an unnaturally thin figure with skin like bleached parchment. Perched on his nose were enormous spectacles magnifying bug-like eyes. His spindly fingers fussed over a chained grimoire's spine with near reverence.

"Hello," I ventured.

The librarian froze and drew his shoulders up, visibly cringing at my attention. Slowly, he turned, lips set in disapproval. Then, slipping a rag from his sleeve, he dabbed at the book cover, as if my very voice had contaminated it.

He lifted his gaze to me, behind those unnerving lenses. "You're Lord Blackrose's . . . acquisition."

"I'm Lady Blackrose," I replied with forced politeness.

He made a sound both acknowledging and dismissive. "He throws books."

The bizarre statement made me blink. "Pardon?"

"When they don't contain what he seeks," the librarian clarified, continuing his meticulous wiping. "He hurls them at the walls. Tears pages. Breaks spines. The red volume on eastern necromancy has a tear in page seventy-three from when he flung it at the wall two years ago. The black grimoire of soul transmutation has a bent corner from being dropped in frustration. The—"

"I get the idea," I cut in, slightly mortified.

"In total, I've catalogued four hundred and thirty-seven incidents of abuse." He finished cleaning and returned the cloth to his robes with a flourish. "Do you throw books, Lady Blackrose?"

I shook my head. "Never."

He gave a curt nod, still displeased but slightly less so. "Good. The Dark Lord thinks because he owns the citadel, he owns the knowledge within. But knowledge belongs to itself."

I found myself oddly charmed by his fierce protectiveness. "I'll be careful."

Satisfied, or at least no longer brimming with scorn, he reached into his robe once more and retrieved a thin volume bound in midnight-blue leather. "This might help with your search. It details artifact repair through nonsacrificial means."

I accepted the book with surprise. "Thank you, that's very kind."

"It's not kindness," he insisted, glaring over his spectacles. "It is efficiency. The sooner you find what you seek, the sooner these books can be properly reshelved." His gaze shifted to something behind me, and his expression soured. "He's coming. Tell him . . . tell him if he damages another binding, I will reorganize the forbidden magic section by color rather than subject."

Before I could respond, the librarian seemed to dissolve into the shadows between the bookcases, leaving me to wonder if I'd only imagined him.

"Arabella?" Kazimir called, his footsteps approaching. "Are you lost?"

I turned to face him, clutching the blue book to my chest. "Not lost. Just making friends with your librarian."

His eyebrows shot up. "Magister Vellum spoke to you? Willingly?"

"If you can call threatening to reorganize your books by color 'speaking willingly,' then yes." I glanced back at where the man had been. "Is that his real name?"

"It's the only one he's given me." Kazimir's gaze caught on the slim book in my arms and he reached for it, flipping the cover open before passing it back. "Interesting. He rarely suggests anything."

"All I did was promise not to throw books," I said, lips quirking. "He seemed convinced you were the real menace."

"Ah, he mentioned something about that." Kazimir shook his head. "Some texts deserve to be flung. Especially when they've wasted hours of my time."

I tucked the book under my arm. "So, did you come over just to defend your book-hurling habit or to make sure I'm not setting anything on fire?"

He leaned in, that sharp, smug confidence rolling off him. "Neither. I've been staring at the same page for twenty minutes while picturing you instead of deciphering magical theory. And I kept thinking . . ."

"Yes?" My pulse sped up despite my best efforts to seem indifferent.

"The Heirloom reacts to our . . . activities," he said, his gaze dipping provocatively. "But we never tried a controlled experiment to confirm whether the crack expands after *every* encounter, or only certain types."

Heat flared in my cheeks. "Uh-huh. So you're proposing—"

"Research," he clarified, looking far too triumphant. "Documenting which activities impact the artifact . . . and to what extent."

"Meaning we'd have to keep testing. Does this involve your 'various surfaces'?" My words came out flat even as my heart lurched with a traitorous thrill.

"Naturally. We should be thorough." His smile was wicked. "We'd vary location, intensity, specific acts . . . even fantasies."

"Fantasies?" My voice came out slightly strangled.

His smile turned slow, dangerous. "You *do* have fantasies, Arabella."

I parted my lips, but no sound emerged. Of course I did. Over the years, but especially recently, lurid images had skittered through my head. But confessing them out loud?

"You can face down a Dark Lord"—his voice dropped—"but you can't speak of what you dream about?"

Those words stung my pride, and I shook my head. "It's different," I managed. "I . . . It's not something I'm used to sharing."

Kazimir stepped closer, curiosity in his eyes. "Then let's make this fair. I'll share one of mine first."

His breath skimmed along my cheek. "See that low shelf over there? I've pictured bending you over it, right in the midst of these forbidden texts with Magister Vellum lurking nearby. Would you stay quiet, or would I have to clap a hand over your mouth while I take you from behind?"

My heart hammered. The ferocity in his expression—the warm, electric undercurrent filling the air—damn near stole my voice.

"Kaz...," I whispered.

He brushed a thumb over my lower lip. "Does the possibility of discovery excite you, Arabella? Knowing how we might be caught?"

It did. Gods help me, it absolutely did. But I tried to muster logic. "We're supposed to be researching," I said weakly, even as my body betrayed me by leaning toward him.

"This *is* research," he murmured, trailing his fingers down the curve of my neck. "Or a needed distraction to clear our heads."

Trapped in his gaze, I remembered all the reasons I *should* refuse. But that swirl of warmth in my stomach, the memory of his hands on me, the promise of danger—well, it was potent.

"So, Lady Blackrose?" He took the book from my arms and set it carefully on a nearby shelf. "Shall we begin our experimental trials? Right here?"

I tried to say no. I *should have* said no. But my traitorous lips parted, and I barely managed a whisper.

"All right," I breathed. "Okay."

51

Rattle the Bookshelves
(and Trigger an Earthquake)

Kazimir

I'd been half joking when I proposed this "experiment"—or at least, that was the lie I told myself. Joking or not, the moment Arabella's eyes darkened with that breathless, consenting fury, I lost my grip on any pretense of self-control.

I closed the distance between us in a heartbeat, pressing her back against the bookcase. My mouth claimed hers in a hungry, demanding kiss. She met me with equal fervor, her fingers tangling in my hair to pull me closer while I pressed my body against hers.

"We need to be careful," I murmured, doing my damnedest to hold on to a shred of rational thought. "No magic."

"No magic," she agreed. "Just us."

Just us. As if that weren't dangerous enough. My hands slid down her sides, tracing the curve of her waist through her simple blue gown, which was far too modest for the effect it had on me. I bunched the fabric in my fists, dragging it up, spurred on by the sight of her parted lips.

"Turn around," I said.

She stiffened, just enough to remind me that she didn't take orders lightly. "Excuse me?"

"Turn around," I repeated, firmer this time.

Her chin lifted in a gesture of defiance, but I could sense the heat in her gaze. I gripped her chin, easing her closer, absorbing the storm in her expression. "This is my fantasy, Arabella. If you had a library fantasy of your own, you should have mentioned it. But you didn't, which means, right now, you're going to do what I tell you."

Her pupils dilated, and she swallowed hard. I could practically see desire and pride colliding in her mind. Finally, she breathed out and turned to face the shelves.

"Good girl." I growled, pressing against her back and leaning in to nip at the sensitive skin beneath her ear. I ground my hardening cock against her, making sure she felt exactly what she did to me.

"Is this what you want?" I let one hand drift around to roughly cup her breast over the bodice while the other slid lower. "To be taken right here, surrounded by forbidden knowledge?"

She nodded, inhaling sharply at the pressure of my hand on her breast.

"Say it," I demanded, biting the junction of her neck and shoulder hard enough to leave a mark. "I want to hear you say what you want."

"I want you," she whispered, her voice strained.

"To do what?" I tightened my grip on her breast.

She drew a ragged breath. "To fuck me against this shelf."

I smiled against her neck. "Was that so difficult?"

Slipping my hand under her skirts, I trailed my fingertips up her inner thigh. She let out a quick, stifled gasp when I finally touched her. She was already slick with arousal, and I teased her entrance with one slow stroke before pulling away.

I spun her to face the nearest low bookshelf. She let out a small noise as she steadied herself.

"Bend over."

She cast a look over her shoulder but complied, bracing herself with both palms on the shelf.

"Spread your legs wider," I ordered. When she only shuffled her feet a few inches, I kicked them apart roughly. "I said wider."

I pulled her undergarment aside and freed myself from my trousers, my heart pounding hard enough to drown out all caution. "Keep your hands exactly where they are. And remember, not a sound. Unless you want to be caught."

She tried to answer, but the second she opened her mouth, I slid the head of my cock against her folds and she shuddered.

"Kaz," she whispered, impatience lacing every syllable.

That single plea unraveled any restraint I'd clung to. With one fierce thrust, I buried myself to the hilt, and she let out a gasp that echoed far too loudly in the hush. I clamped a hand over her mouth.

"Shh," I cautioned, fingers pressing into her cheeks. "Didn't I tell you to be quiet? Or do you want everyone to find you bent over and filled with my cock?"

She shook her head, eyes flicking shut as I began to move inside her. Her tight, wet heat nearly shattered my composure. I grabbed her hips and found a punishing rhythm, each thrust edging her forward so the books on the shelf rattled ominously.

We both needed to be quick. I had no illusions about lasting long anyway. The sheer rush of taking her like this, the risk of discovery, it was all too thrilling. My free hand slid around her waist and between her legs. She quivered as I stroked her clit in time with my thrusts, every muffled moan driving me harder. Her body trembled, her magic a faint thrum around us both, as if it sought to break free. My own runes burned with suppressed power.

I gritted my teeth, ignoring the ache in my bones and focusing on her small sounds of rapture. My pace quickened. The shelf creaked, and I hoped to all the dark gods it wouldn't topple.

Then I felt the telltale clench around me, the ripple of tension in her muscles. My entire spine tingled in response, my own climax surging.

"Come for me," I ordered, pressing tighter circles into her swollen clit. "Now."

She shattered, her walls clamping down as a deep spasm of pleasure wracked her body. I barely slapped my palm over her mouth in time to muffle a cry. I followed her over the edge, burying my face in her neck to muffle my groan. Bliss crashed through me in hot waves, and for a breathless instant, I forgot every piece of strategy, every looming threat. Everything but the feeling of Arabella's body against mine.

We stayed lost in that moment longer than was wise. The library was too quiet, so the low rumble beneath our feet hit me like a cold shock. The floor was shaking. I lifted my gaze. Books swayed on the shelves, dust drifting in faint clouds.

Arabella's eyes snapped open. "What—"

"I don't know," I rasped, quickly withdrawing and yanking my trousers back into place. The reverberation grew stronger, rattling the shelves and sending books cascading.

She hurriedly rearranged her skirts as the quake intensified. Another violent jolt nearly knocked us off balance. I lunged forward, wrapping an arm around her. A deafening crack of thunder tore through the air, and lightning strobed through the high windows.

"Gods," Arabella gasped, her face pale. "The storm—?"

"It's not coming from below," I said, heart pounding. "It's coming from the eastern tower."

A massive tremor wrenched the ground out from under us, and we toppled to the floor. I twisted midfall so I'd take the brunt of the landing, wincing as books clattered off the shelf, forcing me to conjure a shadowy shield overhead.

"Are you all right?" I demanded, scanning for signs of injury.

She nodded, breathing fast. "Yes. But the Heirloom—"

"I know." I kept an arm over her, cursing the adrenaline that still surged from our frantic coupling. My chest heaved—half from fear, half from leftover desire. I raised my voice over the din. "Stay with me. When the shaking stops, we move."

At last, the tremors eased, replaced by thunder echoing ominously outside. The final crack of lightning lit the windows with an eerie, unnatural glow—a swirling purple shot through with amber. The amber color of the Heirloom. I swore.

Arabella pressed herself against my chest. "Is the fortress going to fall?"

"No," I said, forcing more confidence into my voice than I felt. "We have wards for storms. It's built to withstand—well, hopefully anything."

A hush gripped the library. My shield flickered out, and I helped Arabella to her feet, both of us straightening our disheveled clothing as best we could. It was impossible to ignore the mark I'd left on her neck or the way her hair stuck to her damp forehead. My body still hummed with raw tension.

"If I die now," I muttered, running a hand through my hair, "at least it was right after fucking my wife senseless."

She actually laughed, breath shaky. "I'd have thought the mighty Kazimir Blackrose would prefer to die gloriously in battle."

"Overrated," I said. "This was much more pleasant." My gaze roamed over her, taking in the flushed cheeks, the brightness in her eyes. "And I like how you look thoroughly . . . occupied."

She shot me a glare, equal parts arousal and annoyance. "You have the worst timing for compliments."

A last, dying tremor rattled through the library, sending a few more books tumbling. I braced my hand at her back, scanning the wreckage. At least the structure hadn't collapsed. Still, the risk to the rest of the citadel crowded my mind.

"Let's go," I said, steering her toward the door.

The library floor was now littered with scattered tomes and loose pages. Magister Vellum would be apoplectic, if he'd survived. I hoped so. Finding another librarian of his skill would be terribly inconvenient.

We emerged into a corridor teeming with guards and servants. Many ran in frantic circles, hauling tools or supplies. Sims spotted us and approached at once, doing a spectacular job of not looking too closely at Arabella's messed-up hair or the very obvious teeth marks on her neck.

"My lord!" he called over the fading thunder. "Are you hurt?"

"We're fine," I said curtly. "What about the rest of the fortress?"

He shook his head. "Some structural damage, from what I can tell, but something's happening at the—"

I cut him off. "Yes, we're headed there. Gather the others at once. No delays."

Sims nodded and sprinted away. Arabella and I set off at a brisk pace, side by side but silent. My mind spun with the knowledge that we'd triggered this with our "experiment." The crack in the Heirloom, the swirling storm, the quake, all pointed to a dangerous, intimate link between our magic and that ancient artifact.

And wasn't that just cosmically inconvenient.

52

Shatter Your Toy
(and Lose Your Privileges)

Arabella

I raced through the corridors alongside Kazimir, still catching my breath after our reckless library experiment. My legs felt like jelly, a humiliating blend of continued arousal and pure adrenaline. Everywhere we turned, servants and guards rushed past in a panic, likely convinced the whole fortress was about to crumble around us.

I clung to Kazimir's hand, and he gripped so tightly it almost hurt. We dodged rubble-strewn hallways and the occasional frantic staff member until we reached the spiral staircase leading to the eastern tower.

My heart lurched when I saw the damage. The staircase had partially collapsed, chunks of stone scattered across the floor. Kazimir scrambled over the debris first, then extended an arm to haul me up.

"Be careful," he warned, gripping my arm as a stone shifted beneath my boot. "If you fall and break your neck after surviving all this, I'll be extremely annoyed."

"Easy, Kaz," I muttered. "I might think you actually care about me."

We managed to climb over the broken steps and stumbled into the tower room. I gasped. The wooden door had been blasted off its hinges, shattered into kindling. An eerie purple glow flickered in the air, crackling with stray sparks of energy that set my teeth on edge.

Griffin stood near the pedestal in the chamber's center, backlit by bright, flickering arcs of magic. His eyes were wide enough to rival an owl's. His hair stood in frizzled tufts, and his robe was singed.

"My lord! Lady Blackrose!" he exclaimed, nearly tripping over a loose stone in his haste to reach us. "Thank the forgotten gods you're all right. There was . . . I tried to—"

"What happened?" Kazimir's curt demand rang through the chaotic space. He stalked toward the Heirloom, leaving Griffin in his wake.

I swallowed hard as I followed, already guessing what I'd see. My blood went cold the instant I reached the pedestal.

The Heirloom of Dominion gaped with a devastating crack nearly splitting it in half. Hairline fractures branched outward in every direction, forming a lattice of ruin.

"Oh gods," I whispered, pressing my hand to Kazimir's arm. "It's . . . it's so much worse than before."

He looked pale. "When did it happen?" he asked Griffin, though of course he already knew.

"About fifteen minutes ago, my lord," Griffin admitted with a shaky glance at Kazimir—and, tellingly, at me. "I was monitoring the artifact's fluctuations when this surge hit. The raw energy threw me across the room." He gestured to a spiderweb crack in the wall. "By the time I woke up, the storm outside was raging, and the Heirloom was, well . . ."

His voice trailed off as he glanced between our disheveled clothes and the mark on my neck. I felt my cheeks heating. The timeline matched precisely with our sweaty entanglement in the library. Of course. The only thing missing was a banner reading *We Just Had Sex and Broke the Crown*.

Kazimir cleared his throat. "Understood, Griffin. Likely what we'd already suspected."

Griffin's blush deepened. "Yes, my lord. That is . . . quite conclusive data."

Kazimir shot Griffin a dry look. "You don't need to dance around it. We fucked, and the Heirloom cracked further. That's all there is to it."

"Kazimir!" I hissed, mortified and irritated in equal measure. He tilted his head as though asking if I wanted a more poetic version. I bit back a laugh. Even in the face of potential catastrophe, he had a knack for making me want to strangle or kiss him.

He turned serious as he surveyed the crown. "This is even worse than I anticipated."

My gut churned. If it was beyond repair, all those twisted plans for dominion, Kazimir's entire vendetta, my chance to carve out my own power—vanished. "Can it be fixed if we find the right method?" I asked softly.

"I don't know." His jaw tightened. "Griffin, any thoughts?"

Keeping a wary distance from the artifact, Griffin examined the splintered edges. "The power signature is still present, but it's impossibly volatile. I wouldn't recommend . . . well, doing anything with it."

"Unless my goal is to blow us straight into the underworld," Kazimir said grimly.

Before either of us could process that lovely mental image further, boots scuffed over the rubble at the door. I turned to see Vex, Sims, and Thorne picking their way through the rubble, each of them dust-streaked and frazzled.

"Report," Kazimir commanded.

Vex took the lead. She snapped a quick glance at the battered door, then at me and Kazimir—reading an entire story on our faces, no doubt. "Damage is extensive, but the citadel's main structure remains intact. We have injuries reported, some of them serious but not fatal. Magister Vellum is in the infirmary with a bump on the head and a ruined stock of books."

I winced. Somehow I didn't think he'd be so quick to make recommendations after this.

Thorne and Sims chimed in. The lightning bridges were unstable, swirling in and out of existence. The wards were strained near their limits. If the Heirloom lashed out again, we might lose more than just a few walls and staircases.

Kazimir's expression darkened. He brushed dust off his shirt, only half listening. I didn't blame him. My own mind reeled with the potential consequences. The entire fortress could come crashing down if the Heirloom decided to blow.

Griffin cleared his throat behind us. "There's one more matter, my lord."

All of us turned to him.

Griffin swallowed, fiddling with a scorched corner of his robe. "As you requested, I've been researching the Heirloom's instability since the first fractures. Based on its reaction now, I suspect the only way to prevent further damage is for you and Lady Blackrose to . . . well, to put it delicately . . . to abstain."

Kazimir gave the enchanter a hard stare. "Abstain."

Griffin coughed. "Yes, my lord. From all forms of physical intimacy. If the crown is responding to your magical bond, then additional surges could prove catastrophic. The next one might not just wreck the citadel. It could destabilize the ley lines across the entire Western Realms."

My stomach twisted. "How catastrophic are we talking?"

"Potentially devastating," Griffin said quietly. "We could lose entire regions. Possibly more. This artifact is old enough and connected enough that if it shatters while active, the backlash might be unstoppable."

Dread hollowed me out. I joked about wanting Solandris to burn, but not at the cost of an entire realm's destruction. Kazimir seemed equally rattled. I noticed how his hands clenched and unclenched at his sides.

"Fantastic," I said, voice dripping with dark sarcasm. "We can destroy swaths of civilization while achieving Kazimir's dream of punishing Solandris. Doesn't that solve multiple problems at once?"

He cast me a sideways glare, though I caught a faint twitch of amusement in his mouth. "This isn't the time for gallows humor, Arabella."

I shrugged. "It's my coping mechanism."

Kazimir let out a sigh. "How long do we have to . . . abstain?" He said the word with a pained expression.

Griffin winced. "Weeks, maybe months—until we stabilize the Heirloom or discover a new method of containing it."

Kazimir and I exchanged a sharp glance. I felt a sinking sense of loss that startled me with its intensity. Foolish as it was, I'd grown used to the notion of indulging in him, especially after we'd finally relented to the inevitable.

He turned to me, his expression a mixture of frustration and resignation. "Well, this complicates things."

"That's putting it mildly," I muttered.

Kazimir's eyes held mine for a long moment. "We'll figure something out," he said quietly, just for me. "Though I'm afraid we might have to hold off on exploring some of those fantasies of yours."

I swallowed hard, acutely aware of our audience. "Perhaps we should focus on the potential world-ending crisis first?"

He sighed dramatically. "Always so practical." But he turned back to the others.

Sims muttered something about a "Doom Scroll" to Thorne, but Kazimir snapped back into leader mode before I could ask questions. He delegated orders with brisk efficiency, telling Vex to oversee repairs, instructing Thorne to double the guard to account for the strained wards, and counseling Sims to alert our outposts. Everyone scattered, leaving just Kazimir and me in the presence of the fractured Heirloom.

I stared at the crown's jagged edges. That crack might as well have run through me, too. Everything in my life had become shaped by this artifact—my marriage, the dark power swirling in my veins, and even the raw connection Kazimir and I shared. If it shattered, what then?

"So," I said quietly, wrapping my arms around myself. "Does this mean that was the last time we can ever . . . you know?"

Kazimir's sigh matched the weary lines on his face. "Not if I have any say in it. But for now, we have to play by the Heirloom's rules."

For once, I dropped the pretense of flippancy. "Then we need to fix this quickly."

Under that familiar arrogant tilt of his chin, I saw genuine worry. "Indeed," he said, taking my hand. Even that small contact felt heightened. "We'll find a solution, Arabella. And after that . . ." His lip curled into a wicked hint of a smile. "I have a rather long list of fantasies to work through with you."

Despite the near apocalypse swirling around, I felt an undeniable thrill at the thought. "Right," I said, my voice catching. "Fantasies."

We stood there, both ignoring the flickering purple aura that threatened us all, locked in some twisted attempt at romantic tension. Then, like the universe needed to remind us of bigger problems, a tremor groaned through the stone walls.

We jerked apart.

"Let's go," I said, squaring my shoulders. "We've got a realm to save—so we can ruin it on our own terms."

Kazimir's laugh was low and begrudgingly affectionate. "What a practical sentiment. You really do fit right in with me, Lady Blackrose."

53

Pretend You're Fine
(While Writhing in Agony)

Kazimir

The pain had started as it always did—a dull ache in my bones, a whisper of discomfort that I could usually ignore—but it quickly flared into a persistent, throbbing pulse.

Arabella's shadow wolf dissolved into wisps of darkness, its glowing golden eyes the last to fade. She'd managed to maintain it for nearly twenty minutes, a vast improvement compared to yesterday's three-minute struggle.

"Excellent," I told her, forcing myself to ignore the burning sensation crawling up my right arm. "Your control is improving rapidly."

She beamed. "It'd be better if you weren't distracting me."

"If you find my mere presence distracting, perhaps we should discuss your lack of focus rather than my influence."

She crossed her arms. "My focus is fine. It's your intensity."

I attempted a low chuckle, though the pain now seared through my forearm. "Maybe I enjoy watching you command the darkness. It's quite stimulating."

She stepped closer, pressing her body lightly against mine. Not exactly helpful when my rune-carved arm felt like it had been set on fire.

"And here I thought you preferred being the one in command," she teased.

"There are exceptions to every rule," I replied. "Though if you'd like another demonstration of my command—"

"I didn't say that," she snapped, but I heard the faint catch in her voice. A flash of interest. Damn the Heirloom.

The pain intensified, a white-hot needle threading through the runes etched in my bones. I fought to maintain a teasing expression, even as my muscles tensed from the agony.

"See you at dinner?" she asked.

I managed a nod, hoping my face didn't betray how badly I wanted her to clear the room so I could collapse. Arabella hesitated, then leaned in to press a light, brief kiss on my lips. We'd discovered through an . . . error . . . that a quick peck didn't result in catastrophic tower collapses.

"See you then," she murmured, stepping away.

The moment her footsteps faded outside the training room, I slumped against the cold stone wall, exhaling the ragged breath I'd been holding on to for the past hour.

"Fuck." I rolled up my sleeve to inspect my forearm.

The runes glowed with an angry red color beneath my skin, more vivid than anything I was used to. A fresh wave of pain burned all the way to my shoulder. Ordinarily, after a heavy magic session, I would sense a lingering ache. But right now, it felt like molten shards of metal were burrowing under my flesh.

It'd been a week since the Heirloom had cracked, and every day of forced restraint seemed to deepen this torture. Between overseeing repairs, hunting for some way to stabilize that thrice-damned circlet, and tiptoeing around Arabella so we didn't spark another magical surge, I was at the edge. If this pain was a sign that my control was fraying, it couldn't have picked a worse time.

I stared at the far corner of the training chamber, where several large crates stacked on top of each other held my latest acquisitions. Femurs from unmarked graves, rib bones from criminals, a scattering of skulls from forgotten corpses. Basic materials for the weapon I intended to craft. Nothing too diabolical.

I needed an army-breaker. We'd received word that Auremar was amassing forces. And the Heirloom was temporarily useless. The solution? A Bone Behemoth. It would stand as tall as a siege tower, a monstrosity no mortal army would face without trembling.

Ignoring my screaming arm, I dragged the crates to the center of the chamber. My breath hissed through clenched teeth as a hot spike of pain flared. I refused to stop. One by one, I dumped the bones in a jumbled heap, forming rough outlines of monstrous limbs and a curved chest cavity big enough to house a guard.

I placed the last set of bones carefully—the partial remains of that Evenfall Estate guard I'd killed in the tower. His skull would anchor the beast's chest, an echo of his terror fueling the construct's rage.

I stepped back. The twisted pile of bones reached my height, a skeletal abomination waiting for my command. I rolled my shoulders, ignoring how the runes sparked beneath my sleeve. Fine. I could do this.

Inhaling a slow breath, I raised both hands. The embedded runes along my bones flared white-hot. I gritted my teeth, summoning my dominion magic. The mass of bones trembled, rattling across the stone floor. Sweat pricked my forehead as I pressed harder, forcing my will into the half-formed hulk.

A crackle of dark energy surged from my palms, illuminating the bones with a deep violet glow. The skeletal limbs churned against each other, joints fumbling into place. The rib cage expanded and curved into a grotesque parody of a beast's torso. One bony arm slammed into the ground with enough force that the floor trembled. The shriek from that guard's skull grated in my ears.

With a final burst of power, I locked the bones into alignment. They snapped together with a deafening crunch, forming a towering creature of jagged angles, a mockery of life. I poured the last threads of my magic into its chest, finalizing the binding that would give me masterful control over this monstrous puppet.

"Kneel," I commanded, my voice reverberating with dominion power.

It obeyed, at first. The limbs began bending, the spine creaking as it lowered itself. Then another searing pain ignited in my runes. It was as if someone had shoved a fiery iron rod straight into my marrow. I lost focus, and the link between me and the behemoth snapped.

The monstrosity twitched violently, unmoored from my command. The skull's high-pitched wail lit every nerve in my body with agony. Meanwhile, the giant bones flailed in an uncontrolled rage, smashing into pillars, pounding the ground in frenzy. The floor rattled dangerously beneath me.

I tried to reassert control, but I could barely see through the white-hot haze of pain. The shriek of the runes in my forearm sent me down to my hands and knees. Blood dripped from my nose, spattering onto the stone.

"No," I hissed, my voice shredded by anguish.

At last, the binding spell shattered altogether. The behemoth froze midswipe, then fell apart into a clattering downpour of femurs and ribs. I raised an arm to shield my face, but a stray rib struck my shoulder. The guard's skull rolled across the floor, its glowing torment extinguished.

I couldn't move. The agony was so immense it tugged me under, making my muscles spasm. And then, in the depths of the agony, I saw something.

Not a memory. A vast, endless darkness, deeper than night, older than time. Within it, shapes moved—or perhaps the darkness itself moved, forming patterns that hurt to look upon. And at its center, something waited. Something ancient.

Something hungry.

I gasped, and the vision vanished as suddenly as it had appeared.

I retched, gagging on blood and bile. This was worse than anything I could recall in recent memory. I managed to pull myself to my feet. My legs nearly gave out, and I staggered toward the exit, leaning on the stones for support. The corridor outside was blissfully deserted, but I barely found the strength to care.

Halfway to the spiral staircase, my legs buckled again. My cheek smacked the cold wall, and I slid down, helpless. *Shit.*

"My lord?" Vex's voice sounded from behind me. No. I wasn't ready to be seen like this. I tried to stand, to straighten, but my body refused.

She reached me in two swift strides. Her expression was dread personified. "What happened?"

"Nothing . . . important," I managed. Every syllable felt like razor wire in my throat.

She glanced at the bone dust and blood staining my clothes, clearly unconvinced. "This isn't nothing. I'm getting Griffin."

"No." I grabbed her wrist with what little strength I had left. "No one needs to know."

"You can barely stand," she argued.

"I don't care," I growled. The pounding in my skull threatened to crack me open. "Just help me to my study. That's an order."

She set her jaw, then hoisted my arm over her shoulders and hauled me up the winding staircase. I must've blacked out for a few steps because one moment we were in the corridor, and the next I was slumped in my leather chair behind my desk, shaking so badly I could hardly breathe.

"Sit still," she warned, pressing her palm to my forehead. "You're burning up."

I tried to focus on her words, but the runes seared my arm again. I glimpsed that dark vision, the swirling mass of hungry shadows, beckoning me. I nearly passed out.

Vex shook me, and her voice sounded distant. "—with me."

I forced my eyes open. "I'm fine," I hissed, though it was far from any rational definition of "fine."

"I'll grab you something for the pain," she insisted, dashing to the cabinet where I stored certain potions.

I gestured vaguely, my breath coming too fast. "Blue vial. Third shelf."

She pressed the draft into my hand, and I downed it in a single gulp. It burned on its way down my throat, but the relief followed swiftly. The savage edge dulled to a tolerable throb.

"You can go," I gasped when I could speak again.

Vex lingered, probably about to insist on calling Griffin anyway.

"I said *go*."

Her lips thinned. "As you wish, my lord. But killing yourself solves nothing." Then she slipped out the door.

I closed my eyes, leaning back, letting the draft spread numbness through my veins. Maybe I should've listened to her.

No. I had a realm to crush and an Heirloom to fix. There was no time for weakness. I tried to collect my thoughts, but the respite lasted all of two seconds before I heard footsteps. I recognized them immediately.

Arabella.

I tried to put on my usual mask of calm. Straightening in my chair, I kept my face carefully composed. Or so I hoped. The door opened without the courtesy of a knock. Arabella paused in the threshold, scanning my features before striding forward.

"What happened?" she demanded, her eyes raking over my disheveled clothes. "Vex practically ran straight into me. She seemed rattled."

"Nothing." I lied, functional enough to sound dismissive.

"Liar," she snapped. "Your shirt is glowing."

I glanced down. Indeed, the area around my forearm still glimmered faintly. "It's a new style. Very trendy among warlords."

"Kazimir," she said in that exasperated tone, crossing to my side. "Show me your arm."

I shook my head. "No."

"Either you show me, or I rip your sleeve off," she warned. "Your choice."

I knew she'd do it. With a resigned sigh, I let her roll up my sleeve. A hiss escaped her lips at the sight: the runes beneath my skin pulsed an angry red, each symbol outlined in raw, infected flesh. She knelt next to the chair, her fingers hovering as if she wanted to touch them but didn't dare.

"Why is this happening?" she asked in a hushed voice. "I've seen your runes flare before, but not . . . like this."

"They always sting after I use a lot of magic," I muttered. "Lately, though, it's worse."

"How long has it been worse?" Her gaze pinned me.

"Since the war room fiasco," I admitted. "I've had random flare-ups before, but never this excruciating. The partial Heirloom activation might be accelerating it, or—" I cut off, unwilling to say more. Especially the part about that vision.

Arabella brushed my arm gently with her fingertips. Even that featherlight contact sent a ripple of pain through me, but I endured it. Her concern surprised me, though I tried not to let it show.

"What did you do after I left the training room?" she pressed.

I could've lied again. But I met her eyes and found I didn't want to. "I attempted to create a Bone Behemoth. A construct. I needed a monstrous weapon. It worked for a few seconds . . . until my runes decided they hated me."

Her expression flickered between horror and fascination. "Bone . . . Behemoth. Did you seriously piece together a giant skeleton with your magic?"

I offered a mirthless smirk. "I nearly had it under my command before everything went to hell. Then it collapsed and took me along for the ride."

She shook her head like she couldn't believe my recklessness. "How many times can you do this before it kills you? Before your magic tears you apart from the inside?"

I didn't answer. Because I didn't know; I only knew I couldn't stop. Auremar was moving against us, and the Heirloom remained broken. I had only one path forward: keep fighting, keep forging new horrors to defend my territory and the people in it.

Arabella examined the runes more closely. "Let me help you. Maybe I can ease the pain."

"It won't work," I warned. "Regular healing magic won't go near these runes. They're carved into my essence."

"Good thing I'm not regular," she retorted, meeting my gaze head-on. "Let me try."

I hesitated, torn between making a snarky remark and giving in to the throbbing misery. Eventually, I nodded. "Go ahead."

Arabella laid her hand fully across the cluster of runes. A knife of agony ripped down my arm, but I remained still. She closed her eyes and summoned a gentle swirl of magic. My breath caught when I felt warmth flow inside me, far from the scorching brand that typically accompanied my own spells. Her power took on a deft, coaxing shape, as though creating channels for a raging waterfall. The runes' angry flare began to subside, tapering to a deep ache I could endure. I inhaled shakily, flexing my fingers.

It was . . . manageable. Not gone, but no longer threatening to break me. I stared at her, half in awe and half uneasy at her skill. "How did you do that?"

"I listened," she said simply. "The magic told me those runes are meant to channel power, but something is blocking them. Something external. I just gave them an outlet, let them redirect a portion of the surge."

I wiped sweat from my brow, unsettled by her words. If an outside force had begun tampering with my runes, I had bigger problems than fractures in the Heirloom.

"Thank you." My voice came out rough. "I . . . appreciate it."

A relieved smile flickered across her features. "You're welcome. But I want a full explanation of this Bone Behemoth. It sounds . . . insane."

Despite my exhaustion, I found a tiny grin. "It stood tall enough to smash a battalion. If I hadn't lost focus, it would have knelt at my command."

"And now it's a pile of bones," she pointed out drily, raising an eyebrow. "Next time, maybe start smaller. A Bone Kitten, perhaps?"

That sentence caught me off guard, and a laugh burst from my mouth before I could stop it. I winced when my ribs protested. "Yes, that would certainly maintain my terrifying reputation."

"On the bright side, a Bone Kitten is less likely to maim you or bring the ceiling down." She pushed a stray lock of hair away from my forehead. The simple gesture made my heart pound harder than it should have.

I tried to swallow down my discomfort at her tenderness. "Lady Blackrose, are you actually concerned for me?"

Her expression softened. "Surprise. I'm not eager to watch you tear yourself apart just yet."

I cleared my throat. I wanted to mock her for coddling me, but ironically, I appreciated the honesty. "Sorry to disappoint you by not dying this evening," I said lightly, though my tone lacked its usual venom.

She rose to her feet, gaze drifting to the runes scarring my arm. "Will you tell me someday about your mother, about how she . . . did this to you?"

I froze. No one asked that question. Even mentioning my mother's vile enchantments brought back memories I'd rather bury. I closed my eyes for a moment. "Perhaps," I murmured, a quiet concession that tasted foreign. "Someday."

She offered a slow nod, not pushing me further. Outside in the corridor, footsteps echoed faintly—servants going about their duties. Meanwhile, my arm still tingled from her healing magic.

"Do you want me to help you up to our tower?"

I shook my head. "I'd rather stay here a bit . . . Find where I left my pride."

Arabella studied my face, then placed her hand lightly atop mine instead of replying. I squeezed her fingers once, then watched her slip from the study.

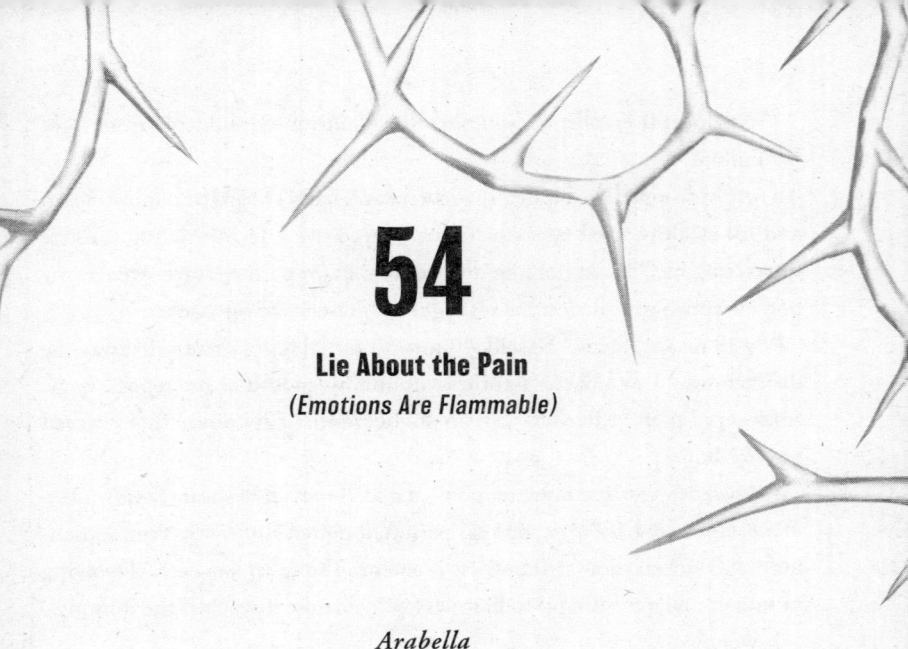

54

Lie About the Pain
(Emotions Are Flammable)

Arabella

I let the shadow dagger fly from my palm, a ribbon of pure midnight slicing through the air. It lodged in the training dummy's chest with a satisfying thump, quivering in place before fading back into wisps of darkness.

Kazimir stood several yards away, arms folded across his chest. "Better," he called. "Now try a spear."

A wave of pride flickered through me, and I rolled my shoulders to work out the tension. We'd been at it since dawn, and the midday sun was merciless—my leathers stuck to my skin, sweat tracing down the back of my neck. But I couldn't quite ignore the jagged silhouettes of scaffolding clinging to the citadel's east wing like giant spider legs. Workers busied themselves halfway up the damaged stone, all because Kazimir and I had caused a magical demolition when our . . . "resonance" got out of hand.

He glanced at me, then at the scaffolding, his face unreadable. Drawing in a slow breath, I shaped the darkness between my palms, this time letting it stretch into a spear. I took aim at a distant dummy, locked my stance, and—

"Your form is excellent," Kazimir's voice murmured suddenly from right behind me.

I nearly dropped the blasted shadow spear. I hadn't heard him move closer, and his stealthy habit was equal parts impressive and infuriating. "You're distracting me," I said, forcing my eyes to remain on the target, even as my body snapped to full alert merely from his presence at my back.

"By all means, focus," he said. "But in an actual fight, there will always be distractions." I caught the tightness around his mouth as he stepped away. A flicker of pain he tried to veil, no doubt another flare of the runes carved into his bones.

I exhaled, wrestling my attention back to the shadow spear. *Steady. Deep breath. Pull back the arm.* But his pain had gotten under my skin, loosening my concentration at the worst moment. The spear wavered, dissolving in midair and vanishing into harmless wisps before it reached the dummy.

I swore.

"Your concentration is slipping," Kazimir noted, his tone carefully neutral.

I glared at him. "And you're in pain again."

"I'm fine."

My truth-sense sparked at that feeble lie, an ugly prickle behind my eyes. "Stop pretending nothing's wrong."

"This is your training," he said, still dismissing the topic. "Focus on that."

Across the courtyard, I spotted Griffin heading our way. He lugged a leather satchel that glistened with dark liquid at the corners, trying his best not to get blood on his robes. He headed for Nyx, who basked in a patch of sunlight near the wall. My dragon raised her head with lazy arrogance, her half-lidded silver eye on me even as Griffin offered her bits of raw venison.

"Exotic deer from the north," Griffin murmured, lifting a gory chunk and carefully extending it. "Far preferable to my familiars, I hope."

Nyx sniffed, menacing just enough to keep Griffin's hands shaking, then snatched the meat in one gulp. Such a spoiled creature. I still felt guilty about her taste for Griffin's poor, doomed little magical creations.

"Again," Kazimir urged, and I wrenched my attention back to him.

Fine. Another attempt. My mood soured, but I forced the darkness to coalesce once more, forging an ax instead of a spear. It usually felt sturdier in my grasp. The edges gleamed an impossible black, so dense it seemed to swallow the sunlight.

I braced myself to throw, but Kazimir flinched again, his hand flexing like lightning had marched up his bones. My concentration evaporated, replaced by concern, and I could feel the shadow ax quivering in my grip.

"You really should rest," I snapped.

He set his jaw harder. "I don't need—"

"Don't even try lying to me." My truth-sense had been screaming all morning at his denial.

His usual scowl deepened, but he made an attempt at composure. I felt a wave of frustration spike in my chest. Not only was I dangerously off-balance, but so was he. And that tension between us got sharper by the day, made worse by the vow of abstinence we'd had to adopt for the Heirloom's sake. It was maddening.

"Fine," I muttered, lifting the ax. "Show me how well you can ignore your pain while I throw the next one."

I launched the weapon, letting the frustration fuel a sharper, heavier shape. But the instant Kazimir drew in another pained breath, my focus slipped again. The darkness wavered, flickering in my hands, and in a quick, vicious burst, it exploded. A whirl of black energy erupted outward, sending me flying into Kazimir. His arms wrapped around me just before we slammed into the ground.

Shadow tendrils lashed wildly across the courtyard, slicing the air with lethal hisses. One nearly grazed my cheek. Another slammed into the stones inches away, sending up a shower of molten rock fragments. I heard Griffin shout, and Nyx's raw roar shook the walls. The ground trembled under us.

Kazimir rolled so that he ended up over me, caging me protectively under his arms. His eyes flared white-hot as he raised a hand, commanding the darkness to heel.

"Enough," he barked, voice resonant with dominion magic.

The shadows froze midswipe, then collapsed into themselves, swept back by his outstretched hand. My ears rang in the sudden silence that followed, my lungs burning from the dusty air. Kazimir hovered over me, blood trickling from his nose, his breath ragged. The broad lines of his shoulders tensed protectively, but there was a faint tremor in his arms.

"Are you hurt?" he rasped.

I shook my head. "You're bleeding."

He swiped under his nose, almost surprised at the crimson smearing his fingertips. "It's nothing," he said, voice tight. He then pushed himself upright and offered his hand to me. I took it, letting him haul me to my feet.

Nyx crept closer, tail flicking warily. Griffin followed behind her, a nervous expression plastered on his face. "What . . . happened?"

"A minor setback," Kazimir drawled, though I could sense the effort it took him to appear calm. "Lady Blackrose's power surged for a moment."

"A 'minor setback'?" I snapped. "That could've ripped us both to shreds!"

He turned a steely gaze on me. "It didn't. Which is the entire reason we train. Mistakes happen."

My heart pounded, part fear, part anger. "Is that what you'll say at my funeral if I lose control?"

Griffin hovered, looking like he wanted to melt into the stone. Kazimir, meanwhile, was coldly unmoved. "You lost focus. It happens to everyone who practices dangerous magic."

"I lost focus because you're in obvious pain!" I threw back, ignoring the tremor in my voice. "You're too proud to admit it, and you think I shouldn't worry."

He gave a dismissive shrug that only infuriated me further. "My discomfort is irrelevant. I can handle it."

"This bizarre purgatory is making us both reckless."

He exhaled, stepping closer, voice dropping. "We agreed to abstain. We have to protect the Heirloom."

I threw up my hands. "Yes, we did. And I get it. But you're not taking care of yourself. And it's affecting me, our training . . . everything."

Griffin cleared his throat nervously. "Um, I should—"

"Stay here," Kazimir ordered.

I folded my arms, livid. "I'm not going to be dismissed like one of your minions."

He leveled a delicate dangerous look at me. "I wasn't dismissing you. But I don't think this is the place for our little . . . conversation."

"No," I agreed, "it's not. But I'm done pretending you're fine. I have a literal headache from your lies." I tapped my temple. "My truth-sense doesn't just vanish, you know."

"The pain is manageable. That's not a lie."

I felt the slightest hum of truth, warring with half-truth. "It's not enough to just manage things, Kazimir."

He didn't respond. Instead, his gaze slipped to Griffin and Nyx before returning to me.

My anger still hadn't cooled, but I lowered my voice. "Let me help. Like I did before."

He stiffened, looking ready to fire back, but he only said, "Not now."

I sighed in frustration. "These accidents are just going to keep happening."

"Not if you work on your control," he spat back.

I shook off the lingering tremor in my arms. "If my 'lack of control' is such an issue," I said, voice pinched with anger, "maybe the best solution is for me to train without your grim"—I gestured at his entire, tense villain persona—"brooding."

Kazimir's eyes narrowed, and for once, he didn't respond with his usual retorts. I gulped down the urge to soften, and fury propelled me forward. "You're my biggest distraction. Every grimace of pain, every glare you shoot my way—it breaks my focus. So, how about you give me space instead of demanding perfection?"

Silence stretched between us, taut as a bowstring. Part of me wanted him to fight back. Instead, he inclined his head in curt, cold agreement. "Very well," he said, each syllable laced with biting frost. Then he turned sharply on his heel and strode away.

I stood there feeling hollow. My shadow magic had almost killed us, and Kazimir wouldn't let me help him. We were a pair of fools.

"Well," Griffin said softly once the tension had diffused a bit, "that was . . . intense."

Ignoring the hammer of my heart, I sank onto a stone bench. "I damn near murdered us both with that explosion," I said, staring at the cracks I'd inflicted on the stones.

Griffin offered a tentative shrug. "That's how things go with dangerous magic. People blow up once in a while." He chuckled nervously. "Or more often than not."

A faint, miserable laugh escaped me. "It's not just the near-death stuff. Everything's complicated. And Kazimir's lying to himself about his own pain."

"I suspect he's done that most of his life," Griffin said, smoothing the wrinkles on his robe. His hairy calves stuck out beneath the short hem. "He's a brilliant orchestrator of illusions, especially the ones he tells himself." He paused, glancing at me. "But you, on the other hand, are a terrifyingly accurate lie detector. I suppose that's bound to cause friction."

I slumped with a sigh, letting the events swirl in my mind. My father's cruelty, Kazimir's infiltration into my life, the fact that half his staff seemed to quietly root for him to let me in . . . "Does he ever accept advice from any of you?"

"Rarely," Griffin admitted. "He hates looking weak in front of others, even when those 'others' have seen all his weaknesses anyway." He fiddled with a loose thread. "If it helps . . . I've never seen him like this."

"Is that good or bad?" I asked quietly, rubbing my arms.

He gave me a measuring look. "Maybe both." Standing, he grabbed his bloody satchel. "I should get back to my research. I'm working on an enchantment that would prevent further degradation to the Heirloom, possibly even allow limited use of its power."

I wanted to hug him but thought better of it. "That's amazing, Griffin."

He grinned sheepishly. "It won't address the underlying fracture, but maybe . . . ah . . . it'll let everyone breathe a little easier."

I laughed ruefully. "It would. Thank you for everything."

He offered a small bow before padding away, leaving me with Nyx. The dragon let out a low, rumbling sound of reassurance.

I stroked her snout. "At least we understand each other, right?"

She blinked, unimpressed. Then she nudged my shoulder. The dragon was so large now that it almost bowled me over. I couldn't help a small smile.

"Come on," I said. "You've earned another nap by the stables."

We walked side by side, and as I looked around at the citadel's looming spires, I mulled over that shocking wave of fear I'd felt seconds before the explosion. My power was too potent for me to be sloppy. And that only made me more conscious of Kazimir's self-negligence. If he tore himself apart, the entire Western Realms would implode. And he was the only person who could help me learn to control my magic; I needed him at full strength.

A small part of me recognized that I was lying to myself, too. Maybe I wanted more than just an "alliance" or help with my power. Maybe I wanted the man who hovered protectively above me, who bled from his nose but still shielded me from rogue shadows.

Had I overreacted? Perhaps. But the fear, both of my own power and of whatever was happening to him, had been real.

No. I wasn't the villain here, but I wasn't going to be a victim, either. "Space" was exactly what I needed.

And perhaps a few more hours throwing shadow weapons at inanimate straw.

With a growl that felt far too much like his, I turned on my heel and stalked toward the training room. If I couldn't fix Kazimir's secrets, I could at least hone my magic until thinking about him didn't burn a hole in my chest. That was safer than letting his lies and my own desire combust again.

55

Stand Close
(and Pretend It's Strategy)

Kazimir

The temperature dropped noticeably as I stalked through the corridors. Servants flattened themselves against walls when I passed, gazes fixed on their boots. Even Thorne gave me a wide berth when we crossed paths in the courtyard.

"Where is Lady Blackrose?" I demanded, not slowing my stride.

"I don't know, my lord," Thorne said. "Perhaps the library?"

I'd already checked the library. And the training room. And her old chambers. And the observatory.

I waved him off, too consumed by the twin frustrations gnawing at me. One was the external threat gathering on my borders—that I could handle in my sleep. But the other lived under my own roof, slept in my own bed, and had practically mastered the art of vanishing from me.

Three days. Three godsdamned days since Arabella asked for room to breathe. Three days spent spotting only the end of her skirt flicking around a corner, or marching into a chamber just in time to catch the lingering hint of her perfume. I wasn't the type to cower from confrontation. No. The problem was much worse than that.

If we truly saw each other, truly spoke . . .

The tension would spike.

We would end up in our chambers.

We would lose ourselves in that heady rush of magic and desire.

We would break the Heirloom.

We would destroy the Western Realms.

After our last argument, the pain from my runes had settled into a dull echo, as if my bones still remembered the torment. These flare-ups happened more frequently now, something I refused to share with anyone, least of all Arabella. It was mine to bear, not a weakness for others to dissect. Apologies over me being in pain? Absurd. I was the Dark Lord Kazimir Blackrose, the Terror of the Western Realms. People feared me; they didn't fret for my well-being.

"My lord?" A tentative voice interrupted my spiraling thoughts.

I turned and found Pip hovering in the intersection of two corridors, a tottering stack of linens in his arms.

"What?" I snapped.

He flinched, though he held his ground. "I—I was only wondering if you needed anything, my lord."

I forced out a slow breath, tamping down my temper. "I'm looking for Lady Blackrose. Have you seen her?"

Relief spread across his face. "Yes, my lord! I saw her heading toward the High Gardens maybe half an hour ago."

Of course. The one place I barely visited. I crossed an outdoor walkway toward the western tower, taking spiral steps two at a time, shadows crawling after me. By the time I reached the landing, the darkness around me had deepened to a near-inky black.

I paused at the glass doors, scanning the lush interior. Thick greenery climbed archways, vines heavy with flowers, exotic fruit glowing with a faint magical sheen, herbs growing in intricate magic-boosting patterns. And there she was, perched on a stone bench beneath a canopy of luminescent leaves, her hair lit by midday sunlight.

She looked radiant in that golden haze. Beautiful. Irritating.

Almost as if she sensed me, she stiffened, closed her book, and slipped deeper into the greenery toward a side door leading to the apiary.

My shadows spilled through the doors when I strode in, dimming the warm sunlight and causing a few blossoms to curl inward. I followed the path she had taken.

Stone walls enclosed that small patio, keeping out the worst winds. Enchanted beehives dotted the perimeter. Griffin stood at the center, bent over a hive with one of his absurdly long fingers hooked under a dripping honeycomb. And there stood Arabella next to him, feigning a deep interest in absolutely anything except me. I hoped no one expected me to appear fearsome while chasing my wife through a garden of docile bees.

"—and you say the honey gains magical properties?" she asked, though her posture looked rigid.

Griffin nodded, entirely oblivious to the tension crackling in the courtyard. "Indeed, my lady! Bees that feed on black roses produce honey infused with trace elements of shadow magic. It's remarkably versatile in potions... and other uses. Enhances pleasure, induces prophetic dreams, and makes a decent cure for sore throats. Not sure why people stop asking once they hear that first part."

Arabella watched a bee land on her tunic. "Enhances pleasure?"

Griffin's cheeks pinked, and he stumbled over his words. His lanky body seemed to shrink in on itself, as if he wanted to vanish. Clearly, the conversation had gotten away from him.

"Sex magic," I said flatly, and felt a wry satisfaction at Arabella's blush. "It forms a connection between partners. If you apply it to certain areas, one can feel the other person's sensations." I let my gaze slide over her in a slow sweep. "Every. Single. Sensation."

Griffin turned a deep shade of scarlet, suddenly paying almost reverent attention to his sleeves. A lone bee circled his head in confused loops, but he stayed put, as if too mortified to move.

Arabella held my gaze, her pupils widening. "And you've confirmed these effects for yourself, Lord Blackrose?"

"Not yet. I've kept a jar for when I find the right partner." Her breath hitched, feeding my ego. "I didn't realize you were interested in beekeeping."

She swallowed. "There's plenty you don't know about me. If you'd bothered to ask—"

"I've hardly had the chance," I cut in. "Hard to ask questions when my wife slips off the moment I walk in."

Griffin stood there blinking at us both, as if he somehow regretted existing. He cleared his throat and took a cautious step back. "I should finish checking these hives," he ventured. "My apprentice normally cares for them, but he's in the infirmary . . . Stung repeatedly. Rather severe reaction."

I flicked my gaze to the honeycomb. Dark amber, potent with shadow-laced potential. "So, these bees are temperamental?"

"They require a specific approach," he said. "I'd prefer not to hand that job to anyone else." He gave a half shrug. "Unless you'd like them to die . . . ?"

I glanced at the shimmering comb. "No," I conceded. "But be quick about it."

Griffin resumed his work, though he seemed painfully aware of our conversation. I turned my attention back to Arabella.

"I asked for space," she said, determinedly calm. "You agreed."

"Actually, you asked for space, not to vanish entirely." I took a purposeful step forward. "And things have changed."

She frowned. "Changed how?"

"The Hero's Guild is mobilizing. Morana sent word yesterday, and my scouts confirmed it. Three companies, supposedly for 'training' but inching closer to my border. Apparently, the king has been holding closed-door meetings with the Guild for days."

Griffin paused, honey dripping off the comb. "Curious timing."

Despite his previous half-hearted attempts to threaten me, Auremar had never sent the Hero's Guild. Those self-righteous warriors with their enchanted weapons and state-sponsored piety had always stayed within

Solandris's borders, polishing their armor and accepting medals for heroically slaying garden pests they called "monsters." I'd almost be flattered they were finally considering me worth the trip, if it weren't so irritatingly inconvenient.

I nodded at Griffin. "Yes, rather."

Arabella glanced between us. "Are you saying Auremar knows about the Heirloom?"

"Perhaps. But likely it's because of the message I sent with the last spy," I explained, watching her reaction carefully.

"What message?"

"The captain's head," Griffin offered helpfully, then flinched under my glare.

"Yes," I confirmed. "An unmistakable declaration that his plans for you didn't amuse me."

She pressed her lips tight. "Now the Guild is after us. A sterling example of your diplomacy."

"Would you rather I'd returned you to Auremar?" My voice dipped, velvet soft, dangerous. "Maybe place a ribbon around your neck?"

"Of course not," she snapped. "But there's a lot of space between 'do nothing' and sending severed heads as invitations."

Griffin tried to suppress a cough that sounded suspiciously like a laugh.

I moved on, ignoring both her cutting sarcasm and Griffin's poorly disguised amusement. "We have to fortify the Heirloom's power before the Guild marches on us."

"And how exactly do we do that?"

"We figure out how to maintain our bond," I said, stepping close enough that her annoyance radiated off her, warm and electric. "Our connection influences the Heirloom's stability. The more 'out of sync' we are, the weaker it gets."

She chewed her bottom lip.

"I don't mean repeating what caused the last explosion," I clarified, "but your strategy of keeping away from me isn't going to solve anything."

Her eyes sparked with anger. "My 'strategy,' as you call it, is caution. You make it sound like a ploy to undermine you."

"You vanish whenever I appear," I said grimly, "bending your schedule to avoid me."

"I'm being careful," she shot back. "We already have enough tension. Adding more physical contact on top of it is asking for disaster."

"You're afraid," I said, voice low. "But not of magic. You're afraid of this." I gestured between us. "It's not about my pain or the Heirloom, but about how I make you feel."

She scoffed.

"The second I step near you, your breath catches," I continued. "You flush. You can't hold my gaze longer than a few seconds." My heart thumped as I watched her stubborn defiance. "You insist you need space because of the Heirloom, but you're lying to yourself."

Color crept up her neck, yet she stepped closer even as she struggled to keep her eyes locked on mine. "Am I? All our interactions have revolved around your quest for the Heirloom's power. What else am I supposed to think?"

I closed the distance, lifting her chin so she had to look me in the eye. "Use your truth-sense. Tell me if I'm lying when I say you're more than a key to my power."

She inhaled and I sensed her gift activate, that subtle shift in her gaze as she weighed my words. Irritation, confusion, and desire flashed through her eyes.

"You're not as immune as you pretend," I added softly. "I'm not immune to you, either. The difference is: I'm not running from it."

Her voice shook. "I don't run."

"No?" I arched an eyebrow. "How would you define that abrupt exit you attempted just now?"

"Strategic retreat," she said stiffly.

I felt an uninvited urge to grin. Then I spotted movement behind her. Vex appeared in the doorway, surveying the courtyard with one brow raised. She spotted Griffin, who gave her a hesitant nod, and joined us.

"My lord," Vex greeted, stepping closer. "More border reports arrived. The Hero's Guild is moving faster than expected."

I kept my stare on Arabella. "I'll read them soon," I said. "We were discussing our urgent situation."

"Yes, I can see that," Vex said, voice guarded but eyes amused. She glanced at Griffin, who pretended deep fascination with his honeycomb. "Shall I give you privacy?"

"No," Arabella answered quickly. "I was leaving."

"Were you?" I countered. "We hadn't decided how to handle the Heirloom."

"What's left to say?" she argued, crossing her arms. "Griffin insists we can't risk more resonance until it stabilizes. So no . . . physical contact."

"You seem to think that means avoiding me altogether," I pointed out.

Griffin, apparently finding some courage, cleared his throat. "Well, the real threat comes from certain intimate acts, not all. The types that trigger significant magical surges."

Arabella's cheeks flamed. "Yes, thanks, Griffin. Perfectly clear."

He continued, oblivious to her embarrassment. "Based on interesting data of the last few days, smaller interactions—mere proximity, if you will—might help maintain your established bond, which could stabilize the artifact rather than worsen it."

I tilted my head. "So you're suggesting we stay near each other, but not too near?"

His ears went pink. "Quite so, my lord. Exact thresholds remain . . . fuzzy."

Vex coughed, possibly turning laughter into something more dignified. "He means to say, if you both avoid each other entirely, you risk an even bigger blowup next time you do come into contact."

Arabella let out a long exhale, casting a resigned look at me. "Fine. I'll stop avoiding you. But I still need breathing room to deal with everything."

"Reasonable," I agreed, and a strangely potent mix of relief and anticipation coursed through me. "We'll resume training and shared meals."

She nodded, then turned for the exit. "I'll see you at dinner." She disappeared into the High Gardens.

I blinked after her for a moment, keenly aware I could chase her again. But maybe for once, I wouldn't. No sense in pressing our luck.

Vex and Griffin exchanged glances. A quiet, private amusement flickered between them.

"Something to share?" I asked, tone steely.

Vex straightened. "Not exactly, my lord."

"Then why the meaningful look?"

Griffin stammered, "We—I just—" He hesitated, then tried not to flinch from my stare. "We've been making bets."

My brows shot up. "Bets?"

Vex glowered at him, but he plowed on. "On whether or not you and Lady Blackrose can hold out until the Heirloom stabilizes before, er . . . giving in to temptation and obliterating half the Western Realms."

"Griffin," Vex muttered, "shut up."

He made an apologetic grimace. "What can I say? He asked."

I folded my arms across my chest, torn between anger and reluctant amusement at how well they knew me. "And what are the stakes?"

Griffin's grin turned sheepish. "I've got three gold on you both losing control by the end of the week."

"And Vex?" I glanced around with a dangerously calm expression. "Do you fancy an apocalypse?"

Vex met my gaze, not flinching. "I put my money on you two behaving, though . . . barely."

I stared them down, exasperated. "If Arabella and I stop the world from collapsing, you both owe five gold to the citadel's repair fund."

Griffin brightened. "So you're in?"

"Merely acknowledging your insolence," I corrected, though a corner of my mouth threatened to twitch. "Now get back to your bees, Griffin, then help with the Heirloom."

I strode away, hearing them mutter in hushed excitement behind me.

"You really think they'll manage it?" Griffin asked softly.

"Not a chance," Vex whispered. "And do not tell him I said so."

I shook my head as I left, the flicker of amusement at war with the cold dread that maybe Vex was right. Because every time Arabella and I collided, we risked losing ourselves again. And next time, we might just bring the entire realm down with us.

56

Interrogate the Dying Ex
(Poison Makes Them Chatty)

Kazimir

I glared at the replacement oak table in the war room, silently cursing Sims for scavenging it from who-knew-where. I would've preferred forging a new obsidian table, but "crafting mythical stone furnishings" had apparently slipped a few notches on my priority list. At least the debris was gone, though carpenters hammered and clanged outside, jarring my focus as I tried to plan an entire war in peace.

Arabella sat cross-legged in her chair, studying a thick tome coaxed from our dearly beloved Magister Vellum. He'd been stubborn about letting either of us near his precious library ever since we'd, ah, disrupted the atmosphere in there.

Since our confrontation in the apiary three days ago, we'd reached an uneasy truce. We shared meals, trained together, and maintained the careful distance Griffin had prescribed. Close enough to stabilize our bond, yet far enough to prevent another magical catastrophe. The arrangement was . . . tolerable. Barely.

She glanced up as I approached, expression half exasperation and half curiosity. "The noise?" she guessed, nodding toward the thunderous pounding outside.

I tried not to look at her for too long. The Heirloom might interpret it as permission to wreak havoc. "Distracting," I muttered. "For more reasons than I care to narrate."

She smirked. "I'd offer to help with your focus, but that might be dangerous."

Her sardonic tone just escalated my irritation, and my desire. "We still have a war to plan," I said curtly, gesturing for her to keep reading. "Find me answers, and I'll consider letting you back into the library unsupervised."

She rolled her eyes. "As though you're the one keeping me out in the first place."

The doors creaked open, and Thorne entered. The noise from outside seemed to swell at his back, hammering a discordant rhythm.

"My lord," Thorne greeted, bowing slightly. "Lady Blackrose."

I inclined my head for him to speak, while Arabella carefully closed her book. The half-moon shadows under her eyes betrayed long nights of reading, but she still looked infuriatingly resolute, like she'd bite anyone who suggested she rest. Despite her exhaustion, she looked alive, vibrant, and beautiful in a way that had nothing to do with conventional aesthetics and everything to do with the raw—

Dammit. I was staring again.

Thorne cleared his throat. "We received a message from one of Morana's guards. A Solandrian noble has been found in the pass. Poisoned, delirious, and apparently babbling about you two."

Arabella exchanged a glance with me. I scoffed. "Morana's being helpful again? That's certainly suspicious."

"Indeed," Thorne said. "It's unusually cooperative of the viscountess to alert us so promptly. Her guard delivered him to our southern outpost, if we want to question him. The man's identity is unknown to them, but the signet ring suggests he's from Auremar's court. Vex was already there on business, and she sent word that he's in a bad state."

Arabella stood from her chair. "I'll go."

"Not alone," I growled.

She tensed but nodded.

I gestured at Thorne. "We'll meet you at the southern outpost." I turned back to Arabella.

"Let me guess: We're not going via the Portal Isle, are we?" she asked.

"No. I'm not taking any chances." I smirked. "Unless you prefer scenic routes with potential traps and assassination attempts?"

She stepped around the oak table, meeting me halfway. Even from a small distance, I felt the hum beneath my bones. Her eyes flicked to my hand, as though expecting me to reach for her. When I didn't, she lifted her chin defiantly and stepped closer. "The last time we traveled by personal portal, I was your prisoner and you were an absolute ass about it."

The spark that had ignited whatever this disaster of feelings was between us. How much had changed since then. I'd gone from wanting to use her to wanting . . . well, still to use her, but in entirely different ways.

"And now?" I asked.

"You're just looking for a reason to keep me in your arms," she accused softly, voice laced with wry humor.

"Don't flatter yourself," I said, which was a lie and we both knew it. I drew runes in the air, the swirling energy of a portal forming at the edge of the war room. I murmured the final word, and a vortex of violet light spun open. "Full contact," I reminded her, sliding my arm around her waist. "Can't have your head end up in another part of the realm."

"I remember," she muttered, but she leaned in, bracing a palm against my chest. "You do so love your excuses to manhandle me."

In a rush of distorted air, the portal yawned wide. We stepped through together, the world dissolving into swirling darkness before rebuilding itself around us. The southern outpost materialized instantly—a squat fortress perched near a river bend. Storm clouds hovered overhead, as though paying homage to my mood.

Arabella peeled away from me the moment we landed, smoothing her clothes with a quick, almost self-conscious gesture. I fought the urge to yank her back.

She scanned the fortress, then the horizon beyond, a calculating look in her eyes. The wide-open landscape stretched in all directions—no witnesses, fewer guards than the citadel, a clear path to the nearby river. I could practically see her mapping escape routes.

"Kazimir." She turned to me, eyes narrowed slightly. "If I wanted to run, would you try to stop me?"

The directness of the question startled me, but I still considered it carefully. Once, the answer would have been simple: I'd have hunted her to the ends of the earth. Now . . .

"I would be . . . disappointed if you chose not to stay," I finally said, watching her reaction.

A smile ghosted across her lips. "That's not an answer."

"Make no mistake: You're still my wife, and I didn't go through all this trouble just to let you walk away."

She studied me for a moment longer, as if testing my words against her truth-sense. "Interesting. You still didn't actually say you'd stop me."

I sighed. "If you're planning on leaving, then by all means."

I stepped aside and waited. Arabella was testing me, just as I was testing her, I supposed. Would I really let her go? The uncomfortable question laid something bare in me that I shoved down and buried beneath my usual possessive arrogance.

Of course, she made no move to leave. My chest unknotted in quiet relief, though I'd never let it show.

I gestured toward the outpost. "Shall we? Or would you prefer to continue this philosophical debate while our prisoner expires?"

She studied me for a moment longer, then nodded and fell into step beside me. We walked in silence, and within moments, were at the gate. It was manned by my own men, and everything seemed normal. No traps, then. But I still didn't regret being cautious, especially because the intelligence had come from Morana.

"Where's our would-be informant?" I demanded of the nearest guard.

The guard bowed. "Inside, my lord, but he's not doing well. Commander Vex is with him."

I nodded brusquely. Arabella and I entered the outpost's main hall, where the torches guttered in the wind seeping through the old stone. Vex stood near a makeshift infirmary corner, arms crossed. Keen-eyed as ever, she caught Arabella's presence and quirked an eyebrow at the space (or lack thereof) between us.

Behind her, a man slumped in a chair, wrists bound. He wore the tattered remnants of an expensive jacket. Dark lines of poison spread across his neck, creeping toward his jaw. A single glance told me he had little time.

"Perris?" Arabella demanded. "What in the seven hells are you doing here?"

The man jerked at her voice, raising milky, terrified eyes. "Lady Evenfall," he rasped. "You must help—"

"Her name," I cut in coldly, "is Lady Blackrose."

A look of sheer terror crossed his face as he realized who I was. Though I'd never seen him before, his name was familiar.

"You know him?" I asked Arabella.

"Unfortunately." Her mouth twisted. "He tried to court me at my father's insistence. Ambitious, but not particularly bright. He once told me women shouldn't concern themselves with politics because our delicate constitutions couldn't handle the strain."

"I hope you did something fun to him."

A wicked smile crossed her face. "I set his cravat on fire."

Ah. The pieces of the puzzle clicked into place. I'd heard this story even before I'd kidnapped Arabella. It was the reason I'd originally warded her chambers against fire.

Arabella's voice turned icy as she gazed at Perris. "So tell me, Lord Perris, why are you here?"

He swallowed hard, black veins creeping up his neck as he fought for breath. "Because . . . you're a healer. I—I had no choice but to find you."

A flicker of mild amusement crossed Arabella's face. "That's not much of an offer. There are other healers much closer to your home."

Perris's expression twisted, rage warring with panic. "You turned traitor. Married the Dark Lord. You—you're worse than your father ever said."

The temperature in the hall plummeted as my magic responded to a surge of rage. The shadows around me darkened, ready to tear into his flesh. Terror filled Perris's eyes as he just realized how suicidal an insult that was.

Arabella gave me a subtle headshake.

I warred with myself but let her control the conversation. Though I made sure Perris saw the truth in my eyes—that if my wife hadn't intervened, he would be screaming his apology before dying.

"My father's opinions have never concerned me," she said to Perris. "But I am curious about yours. Why are you poisoned? And why come to me for healing when the last time I saw you, you were calling for my imprisonment for attacking you?"

"Because, if you heal me, I'll tell you anything I know."

Arabella's face was a mask of cold calculation. I was fascinated by this darker version of her compassion. The healer deciding who deserved salvation.

She glanced at me. "I assume you have no objection to me healing him for information?"

"As long as he understands that lying to us afterward will result in me reapplying the poison myself. With interest." I directed this last comment to Perris, whose eyes widened in fear.

She turned back to our captive. "Then you better speak quickly, or I might not be able to do anything for you."

"They poisoned me," Perris began.

"Who?" I asked.

"King Auremar. We had an arrangement." Perris gasped for air, and I thought he'd die before giving us anything useful.

"Spit it out," I commanded. Much as I wanted to hurry this interrogation along, my dominion magic would likely be too strong for him in this state. He'd die before revealing anything useful.

Perris flinched. "If I hadn't done it, someone else would have. The king needed someone to meet with bandits and let them know the border defenses were . . . pulled back."

The shadows around me darkened further, my runes thrumming. "So you're the one funneling gold to the bandits," I said softly. "Torching villages on the king's orders."

Arabella's gaze never left Perris. "You ruined how many lives?" she pressed, her voice calm but not gentle. "I could let you rot. Unless you have something else worth trading. Something more than what we already know."

I let my shadows swirl menacingly around him. "I should kill you here and now for all the trouble you've caused me," I said, voice low.

He coughed wetly, black spittle flecking his lips. "I swear there's more. I overheard the king. He's planning something with you, Lady Even—Blackrose. Some ceremony, not just a marriage."

She stepped forward. "What kind of ceremony?"

He clutched at her sleeve, half pleading, half furious. "I don't know the details. I—please—"

I tensed, ready to yank her back. But Arabella raised her hand, motioning for me to hold. A glint in her eyes told me she wanted to see what else he might confess. She leaned in. "Do you know more?"

Perris nodded frantically, eyes wild. "Yes, yes, much more—I'll tell— Just heal me."

But Arabella's eyes burned with righteous fury. "You know," she said with deceptive softness, "I've spent my entire life being told I have a duty to heal." She tilted her head. "But I think I've finally realized something important."

"What?" Perris gasped, the black poison veins now creeping toward his temples.

Arabella's smile was cold enough to rival my own. "I get to choose who deserves my gift."

Perris's expression crumpled in disbelief. "But—you can't—"

"Oh, I absolutely can," Arabella said.

"Please—" he begged, reaching for her sleeve again.

She stepped out of reach. "Fuck you, Perris. You're going to die, just like those people you betrayed."

I felt a surge of . . . something. Pride? Arousal? Both, if I was being honest. This darker side of Arabella was exquisite. I could have reminded her that he might have more information, but I wanted to watch her embrace this part of herself without my interference.

Perris alternated between curses and pleas as the poison worked its way through his system. His body convulsed, and black foam bubbled from his lips. "You heartless bitch," he gasped. "You're no better than him." His eyes flicked to me.

"Perhaps," Arabella said calmly. "But I'm the one who gets to walk away from this room."

The last of his curses died with him, his body slumping in the chair.

I raised an eyebrow at Arabella. "That was . . . unexpected."

She shrugged, though I could see the slight tremor in her hands. "He deserved worse."

"I don't disagree," I said carefully. "Though we might have needed more information from him."

"My truth-sense told me he'd given us everything useful," she replied grimly. "The rest would have been just pathetic begging. Besides, I thought you'd appreciate the efficiency."

A laugh escaped me before I could stop it.

"Let's go," she said, turning toward the door. "We have a war to plan."

I followed, unable to suppress the fierce pride swelling in my chest. My wife—my brilliant, ruthless wife—was becoming more dangerous by the day.

And I was absolutely here for it.

57

Kick Him Where It Counts
(Foreplay, Apparently)

Arabella

I woke before dawn with a restlessness that wouldn't settle. The space beside me was empty, the sheets cold. Kazimir hadn't returned to our chambers last night.

After dressing in my training leathers, I made my way through the citadel's quiet corridors. When I reached the training chamber, he stood at the far end, shirtless, shadow blades in both hands. Rippling arcs of ebony coiled across his forearms, writhing with quiet menace. He made creating solid shadow weapons look infuriatingly easy.

He glanced over when I entered, our gazes locking for a fraction of a second. A glint of hunger flared in his eyes, making my pulse tick faster.

"You're early," I said.

He gave a faint huff of laughter. "I needed a distraction that wasn't made of ink and parchment."

"Did you work all night?" I crossed my arms. "Why didn't you wake me?"

His jaw tightened, though the circles under his eyes confirmed it. "You needed rest."

"And you didn't?"

His shadow blades dissolved as he rolled his shoulders. "I'm used to going without."

Kazimir wasn't exactly telling the truth. The intensity in his gaze made it clear why he'd avoided our bed. He didn't trust himself to lie beside me without doing something that might damage the Heirloom further.

"Ready to begin?" he asked, changing the subject.

I nodded, moving to the center of the room. We'd been working on shadow weapons for days. I could form them well enough, but wielding them against Kazimir was another matter entirely. He moved like water, anticipating my attacks before I even committed to them.

I exhaled, conjuring the swirling ribbons of shadow that condensed around my fist. Slowly, they merged and elongated into a curved blade.

"We're working on reflexes today," he said, drawing me into the protective circle. "Your hesitation will kill you in a real fight. So don't hesitate, Arabella."

He lunged.

Even half expecting it, I barely managed to parry in time. The clang of ephemeral blades rang out sharper than steel. The next series of blows came fast, the swirl and slash of shadow shaping the air in electric arcs. I blocked him, dancing to the side, aiming quick retaliations. He brushed them off with a smug twist of his wrist.

An exasperated growl slipped from my throat. "Are you toying with me?"

He paused, the tip of his conjured blade quivering an inch from my collarbone. "Try harder," he said calmly. "I can practically feel you pulling your strikes."

"I'd prefer not to accidentally kill my husband."

"Kill me?" A laugh rumbled out of him. "Then do it. If you can."

He was so damn cocksure it made me want to flatten him right there. I formed another blade, but this time, I also called on my truth-sense. I couldn't read minds, but I could feel the intent behind actions, the subtle shifts that preceded a person's next move.

As Kazimir circled me, I felt the slight change in his weight, the fractional narrowing of his eyes that meant he was about to strike from the left. I formed a small ball of light in my palm and flung it at his face, momentarily blinding him while I ducked under his guard and landed a solid punch to his ribs.

He grunted, more in surprise than pain, and caught my wrist before I could pull back.

"Clever." The corner of his mouth tugged upward. "Keep trying."

"You're not angry I tried a cheap trick?"

"In a real fight, all advantages are fair. I'd be more concerned if you didn't start to cheat." He lifted his hand, beckoning me forward with a slow, taunting motion. "Is that the best you can do, then?"

I snarled in frustration and rushed him again, aiming low this time. We collided, arms locking. My heart thundered as his body pressed into mine, sweat mixing with the tang of ozone from our magic. The sheer closeness made every nerve hum.

When I twisted away, he automatically caught me around the waist, a reflex to keep me from falling. "Stop that!"

He raised both eyebrows. "You want me to let you smash your face into the floor?"

I wriggled free and reset my stance. "It's humiliating to be coddled."

"If this feels like coddling—" His voice dipped. "I've been doing it wrong." He smirked, gaze raking over me. "Your stance is off. Widen your feet—like that, yes. Better."

I huffed and stepped forward to realign myself, catching a glimpse of the sweat shining on his chest.

"What?" he demanded.

"Nothing," I snapped. "Focus on your own stance, oh mighty warlord."

We launched at each other again, fists and conjured shadows clashing. He easily batted away my illusions, forcing me into a more direct style of grappling. My arms locked around his shoulders, and I tried tripping him. He responded by hooking my leg inside his own, nearly sending me sideways.

"Stop pulling back," he growled, breath hot against my ear as he tugged us chest-to-chest. "You want to get stronger? Stop fighting like a timid girl. Fight like—like you did when I kidnapped you."

That caught me off guard. "I—"

"Don't think." His voice dropped low, almost intimate. "Fight."

An electric pulse ran through me. With a wild twist, I wrenched free and flung myself sideways. Kazimir came after me, seeing the vulnerability left by my hasty pivot. I pivoted again in a last-second attempt to dodge, but the training room floor had a slick patch of sweat that made me slip.

Shit.

I landed hard but scrambled to my feet when I saw him advance.

He paused. "Still glad I let you fall?"

I rolled my shoulder and winced at the twinge of pain. My body would have plenty of new bruises after today. "You're being an even bigger jerk than usual."

He flashed me a grin. "I wonder why. Could it be that I'm trying to avoid climbing on top of you and doing something really stupid?"

I formed a curved blade. "Again."

My next blow was fueled by a confusing swirl of arousal spiked by his words. We parried for another few minutes, shadows clashing, boots scraping. Sweat slid down my spine. My entire body thrummed with exhilaration. I needed something else to focus on, or this sparring session would end very badly.

"So, Perris," I started. If anything would cool me down, that subject would. I lunged and Kazimir parried. "He shouldn't have made it so far from Solandris in that condition."

Kazimir lunged again, and I had to deflect. I aimed a slash at his midsection. He danced away.

Finally, having proven I was out of breath, he slowed enough to talk. "Go on."

"What if," I said, breathing hard, "he wasn't poisoned in Solandris, but in Arvoryn? Then they sent him to your outpost as a show of cooperation?"

Kazimir paused, considering. "Morana, you mean."

"Who else?" I pressed. "She had the means and opportunity."

"Possible. Morana does keep a nice stock of lethal goodies. But how would she know he had information? Why not keep his visit a secret and use his information for herself?"

"So maybe she invited him," I said, thinking aloud. "Then poisoned him, all on Auremar's orders."

A smile played at the corners of his mouth. "You're trying very hard to pin this on Morana."

"She's a spider. She lures everything into her web," I retorted, my muscles burning as we circled each other. "You, for instance. She fucked you, didn't she? So maybe she thought another gullible courtier would be easy to manipulate too."

Surprised fury swept across Kazimir's features, but it made him pause for half a second. "I—" he managed.

And in that moment of vulnerability, I kicked him hard in the balls.

He made a strangled sound and dropped. Hard. For a moment, I feared I'd gone too far. Attacking the Dark Lord's manhood might be crossing a line, even in training. My breath sawed in and out of my lungs while Kazimir glared up at me from the floor, clearly furious with himself for giving me that opening.

A bolt of savage satisfaction shot through me. "You told me to stop holding back," I said. "Consider that mission accomplished."

"I can't believe I let that land," he rasped.

"Believe it." Then I stepped closer, planting my feet on either side of his legs and pointing my shadow dagger at him. "I could kill you right now, if I wanted."

He squinted up at me, pain and grudging respect warring in his expression. "Are you thinking about it?"

"If you died, I'd have no one left who could handle the Heirloom." I sighed dramatically, letting the shadows around my fingertips fade. "So . . . no. I guess I'd rather keep you alive."

He let out a faint huff that might have been a laugh. "I can think of nicer ways to express your fondness, but I appreciate the sentiment."

Kazimir shifted like he might rise. Then, with a sudden upsurge of motion, he swung a leg around, knocking one foot out from under me. I yelped. My knees buckled and I crashed to the floor, my back painfully slamming the stone. The air whooshed from my lungs.

A second later, he pinned me with his weight. One of his hands grabbed my wrist, easily prying away the new shadow blade I'd tried to conjure. His free arm pressed down against my shoulder, trapping me. He was breathing hard, lips parted, eyes wild.

A slow grin spread across his face, transforming it from merely handsome to devastating. "Never assume your opponent is defeated until they're actually dead."

My mouth went dry. "So what's next? Planning to silence me for good?"

"That would be an awful waste of that witty mouth." His voice was low.

The adrenaline in my veins mutated swiftly into a powerful surge of arousal. If I lifted my head a fraction, we'd be kissing. My thighs parted just enough that his hips settled between them, and I felt his unmistakable erection pressing through his trousers.

"If we never get to have sex again," I said, only half joking, "maybe we'll just need to keep wrestling each other instead."

His pupils flared. "Is that one of your fantasies, Arabella?" He lowered his voice. "Being wrestled to the floor and taken so hard you forget your name?"

My breath caught. "I—"

Kazimir's storm gray eyes darkened. "I remember how wet you were in the library." He shifted slightly, and the friction made me bite my lip to stifle a soft moan. "When I was in control. When I fucked your needy cunt against the bookshelf. You *like* being dominated."

I paused a beat before confessing, "I've daydreamed about that afternoon more times than I care to admit."

Dangerous. So dangerous.

I wanted him—gods help me, I wanted him so badly it hurt. My magic stirred with a crackling heat under my skin. The runes on his chest answered with dark energy, and I felt their pull.

He groaned and dropped his head. "If I'm not careful," he said against the skin of my neck, "I'll forget every reason why this is a bad idea."

Instead of waiting for an answer, Kazimir rolled off me with a muttered curse, lying flat on his back beside me. We lay there in silence, our chests rising and falling in tandem as we tried to regain control. The magic in the air slowly dissipated, the connection between us fading to its usual background hum.

After what felt like an eternity, he sat up, extending a hand to help me do the same. I took it, letting him pull me upright. He held me with a smoldering stare, as though he was fighting every cell in his body not to drag me back to the floor.

I broke the trance first, moving to the side of the room where a pitcher of water waited. I grabbed cups and poured water for both of us, then eased down the wall to sit on the floor. Kaz followed but remained at arm's length.

"I can almost feel it," I said after a while. "When we're taking things too far. There's this . . . pressure at the back of my mind."

He nodded. "I've been experiencing something similar. A connection to the Heirloom. It makes sense—our magics are both tied to it now."

I took a sip of water, using the moment to steady myself. "So . . . have we learned anything new about the Perris situation?"

Kazimir lowered his cup. "Yes and no. We confirmed Auremar likely wanted him gone, but precisely what Perris overheard is unclear."

I shivered. "Auremar wants me for my bloodline, right? But he's part of that lineage. The entire Solandris royal line descends from the same heroic bloodline as I do, albeit a different branch. So why would he need me if he has the same power?"

A shadow passed over Kazimir's face. "He might not need your blood in the literal sense. Maybe he wants to bind your magic to his. Or perhaps your mother's branch is stronger. Too many unknowns." He swallowed, the lines around his mouth tightening. "But I won't let him have you."

Relief bloomed in my chest at his possessive tone.

Silence settled between us, broken only by our steady breathing. Though part of me dreaded whatever twisted scheme Auremar was plotting, my thoughts drifted to something we hadn't discussed.

I scrubbed a hand across my face. "I barely felt anything when I let Perris die," I admitted softly, glancing at Kazimir. He turned his head to look at me, and I pressed on. "And that bothers me more than the fact that I actually did it."

He gave me the knowing look of a man who'd long ago made peace with the shadows inside himself. "He was your enemy, Arabella. Why *would* you feel sympathy for a man like that?"

I rubbed the back of my neck. "I don't know . . . Old habits, maybe. The naive idea that a 'noble heart' should seek redemption for everyone. But I'm not naive anymore. And if that means letting worthless scum die, I can live with it. I just . . . wonder where I go from here."

Kazimir's gaze was still faintly tinted with desire. "I hate to say this," he teased, voice dipping low, "but your 'noble heart' was always questionable. Especially since you started practicing dark magic." His gaze pinned me meaningfully.

"So I should just embrace this title of Dark Lady?"

He said nothing for a beat, just holding my gaze. "I can think of worse things than having a lethal, gorgeous Dark Lady at my side."

My cheeks warmed, though I wasn't sure if it was embarrassment or simple hunger for him.

Kazimir shifted closer. "You're uncertain about your future," he said gently, "but you're not uncertain about yourself. That's why you're dangerous, Arabella. You know exactly what you want. It's just that your old illusions of heroism have fallen away."

"I know exactly what I want," I echoed. My eyes drifted lower, to where Kazimir's arousal was still visible through his trousers. An idea formed, reckless and tempting.

"Are you hurt?" I asked softly, though a devilish grin curled my lips. "After I nailed you in the . . . well, you know."

He made a tortured noise in his throat. "I'm tender," he admitted. "Why?"

I reached out, tracing a finger along the waistband of his trousers. "I've been thinking . . ."

He stiffened.

I stroked lightly, letting my nails scrape across the taut muscles of his stomach. "If we can feel when we're pushing things too far with the Heirloom," I continued, my fingers dipping lower, "then maybe we can find ways to . . . work around it."

Kazimir's gaze was molten with caution and lust.

I pressed my palm against his erection. "If I feel the Heirloom stirring, I'll stop."

When he didn't stop me, a lazy, thrilling confidence coursed through me. I slid my hand inside his trousers to wrap my fingers around his cock. It was hot and hard in my palm.

Kazimir's head fell back against the wall, his eyes half closed. "This is a terrible idea."

"Probably," I agreed, slowly stroking him. "Do you want me to stop?"

"Fuck no," he growled.

I smiled, watching his face as I continued my explorations. I varied my grip and pace, noting what made his breath catch or his hips thrust forward. He was magnificent like this—powerful but completely at my mercy.

Wanting better access, I freed him from his trousers. He was thick and long, the head already glistening with precum. I ran my thumb over it, spreading the moisture, and was rewarded with a deep groan.

"Like that?" I asked, increasing my pace slightly.

"Yes," he hissed through clenched teeth. "Tighter."

I obliged, tightening my grip and stroking him with more purpose. His hands clenched at his sides.

"You can touch me," I said, voice husky.

He shook his head. "If I touch you, I won't stop there."

The admission sent a thrill through me. The powerful Dark Lord, reduced to restraining himself because he wanted me so badly. I watched his face, noting the flickers of pleasure. He liked it when I twisted my wrist just so. And if I squeezed lightly at the base, his hips jerked forward in response. His breathing grew more ragged, his hips thrusting into my hand. A surge of warmth soaked my undergarments as I watched him unravel.

"Gods," he whispered, his hands clenched into fists now. "Arabella . . . that's—shit—"

I felt it then—a faint stirring at the back of my mind. A distant warning. The Heirloom was responding to the magic that hummed between us.

But I didn't stop. We were close to the edge but hadn't crossed it yet. "Come for me, Kaz."

His control snapped. With a guttural sound, he grabbed my face with both hands and surged forward to kiss me—

The warning in my mind exploded. At the same moment, Kazimir jerked back, eyes wide as he felt it too.

"Fuck," he gasped, even as he came in hot pulses against my fingers. A moan escaped him—quiet, low, and all the more delicious for it. Residual tension rippled through his body as I stroked him through the ebb of pleasure.

When he finally stilled, he tucked himself back into his trousers, and we sat in silence for a moment.

"Well," I said finally, "I think we've learned something important."

He pinned me with that dark, sated gaze. "That we're playing with fire?"

"That there might be ways around our . . . limitation." I gestured between us. "This worked, mostly. Until you tried to kiss me."

"Yes." His gaze then slipped down my body, toward the heat I felt between my thighs, and his eyes darkened with renewed lust. "Let me return the favor?"

The flutter in my stomach was immediate, but I hesitated. The Heirloom was still throwing off faint sparks in my awareness, as if glaring at us for our mischief. "We'll push it too far."

Kazimir let out a slow, frustrated exhale, forcing himself to nod. "Later, then," he promised, voice rough. "I won't forget."

I almost whimpered from the raw intensity in his voice. Instead, I forced myself to my feet. "I think that's enough training for today."

He nodded but didn't get up. I wondered if he'd take a nap there against the wall after I left.

"What's on your schedule today?" he asked casually.

I brushed off my leathers. "More reading." And maybe a bath and some self-love. "I have a new book to look through."

Kazimir's mouth quirked. "And you'll be ready to spar again tomorrow, I assume?"

"Yes." Though the next step in my training would be figuring out how to keep me improving without either of us ending up in bed. Or on the floor. Or pinned to a wall. "You know, so I don't accidentally get rescued by Auremar's knights in shining armor."

He laughed. "Don't worry. They'll rue the day they try to save you, Lady Blackrose."

58

Calculate the Risk-Reward Ratio
(of Ancient Rituals and Desk Activities)

Kazimir

The columns of numbers blurred into nonsense. Somewhere between "Siege Engine Repair Fund" and "Boot Stipend (mercenary)" my thoughts wandered to the taste of Arabella's skin and refused to come back. Runes pulsed beneath my shirt, throbbing in wicked counter-rhythm to the quill scratching parchment. War demanded coin; my body demanded her.

The door opened without so much as a perfunctory rap. Arabella stalked in—no apology, no hesitation—wearing a forest green dress that weaponized every curve. My ledgers never stood a chance.

"Someone's flouting healer's orders about rest," she said, sliding a slim cobalt book across the desk.

"I'll rest when the treasury stops hemorrhaging." I folded my hands to keep from hauling her onto the desktop. "Or when I invent a breathing tax, whichever arrives first."

She arched a brow. "It's your mind that's hemorrhaging, not the coffers."

I smirked, but the book's gold leaf title snagged my attention—*Sacrificial Restorations: The Healer's Burden*. A scarlet ribbon marked a chapter headed

"The Lifeweave Ritual: Healing the Tethers of Arcane Vessels."

Arabella perched on the desk, ankles crossing. "Magister Vellum gave it to me just before our little library adventure. I forgot about it until now."

I skimmed. *Third Age . . . Great Magical Drought . . . cabal of artifact-keepers*—gods, this thing was older than half my nightmares. As the title promised, it was a ritual to feed healing magic into the artifact's fissures, to stitch the fractures with living essence. The dangers section dripped in cheerful understatement—Soul Tethering, Essence Drain, Wraithification—followed by delightful case studies of healers who either shriveled into jerky or slept for centuries.

I snapped the book shut. "Absolutely not."

Arabella didn't flinch. "Kaz, every other repair method you've suggested involves demon lords, royal bloodletting, or both. This is cleaner."

"Cleaner?" I tapped the cover. "One attempt restored the Crown of Tides and burned out the mage's magic forever. Another user became a decor item—*a withered husk*, Arabella. The Twins of Callahan are still snoring in a glass coffin. If the Heirloom rejects you . . ."

I lose you.

Something twisted in my chest. A thought threatened to coalesce—unthinkable, realm-shaking—and I slammed the mental door before it could take shape.

Her gaze softened, but only for a heartbeat. "And if we do nothing, the crack widens, ley lines unravel, and half the Western Realms is gone. My heroic bloodline gives me better odds, and the Heirloom already half recognizes me through the marriage bond. This might be the one gamble stacked in our favor."

I rose, circling the desk until I stood in front of her. "You could end up chained to that crown for the rest of your life. If someone chips it, you'll bleed. If it's stolen, you'll wither. I will not allow that."

She tilted her chin, stubborn light sparking in hazel eyes. "*Allow?* You abducted me, remember? Stole me away to power your precious Heirloom. I've adapted, I've cooperated, and I've even . . . desired things I never thought

I would. Because I decided to. On my terms. You do not get to pick and choose when my autonomy matters."

Damn her for being right. "And if it fails? If the ritual drains you until there's nothing left but a withered husk? Am I supposed to stand by and watch while you sacrifice yourself for an artifact I dragged you into this citadel to activate?"

Her hand came to rest over my sternum.

"Then don't stand by," she said softly. "Stand *with* me. We study the rite together, build safeguards, draft contingencies. You of all people should be able to keep me safe. If the crown tries to devour me, you drag me out. If I falter, you steady me. What you don't get to do is lock the door because the risk frightens you."

She slid the tome back into my hands.

I exhaled through my teeth. "We study it—in detail—before either of us bleeds into ancient jewelry. Agreed?"

A fractional nod. Tension eased enough for a darker, hungrier current to surface. The memory of her hand that morning—and the glorious loophole we'd discovered—flooded my mind.

"Argument time is over," I murmured, dropping the book on the desk and sliding my hands up her calves. "Come here."

Her breath caught. "Here? Now?"

"Consider it practical research. If the Heirloom objects, it can file a complaint."

She laughed—low, eager—and scooted fully onto the desk. I knelt, pushing her dress to her hips. It'd been too long since I'd tasted her properly. Warm, intoxicating scent drowned the scent of ink and parchment. Easing her undergarments aside, I ran a finger down her slit, then replaced my finger with my mouth. She sucked in a sharp breath and braced her hands on the desk. My grip tightened on her hips as I dragged my tongue through her folds and across her clit in a deliberate circle. Her fingers found my hair, tugging me closer. I rewarded her with dipping my tongue inside before replacing it with my fingers.

The tug of her wild, golden magic curled around me—sweet, perilous temptation. In response, my runes glowed faintly with raw, wicked pleasure. I drew back a fraction. "Steady. Control it."

"I'm trying," she gasped, hips rolling. "Stop lecturing."

I eased my fingers back inside. Her magic lunged for mine, hungry and intoxicating, wrapping my shadows in molten gold. The rush was exquisite—and catastrophically unsafe.

A pulse of power skittered across my nerves. It was too much for the Heirloom. Ignoring her whimper, I pulled away and stood, rearranging her dress with shaking restraint.

Arabella grabbed a fistful of my shirt and yanked me toward her. She glared, cheeks flushed, eyes dark. "I'm going to murder you in your sleep."

"I'll bring the knife." I gently disentangled myself from her grip. "But until you can control your magic—"

A brutal knock saved me from retaliation.

Thorne barged in. "My lord, an emissary from the Hero's Guild awaits. Says it's diplomatic." His gaze flicked to Arabella's rumpled state, but the bastard wisely kept silent.

War first, desire later—story of my cursed life. I ran a hand over my mouth. "Great Hall in ten. Shadow retinue, full armor."

Thorne exited.

Arabella hopped down, smoothing her skirts as fire banked behind composed eyes. "We are not done discussing that ritual."

"Or finishing what you started this morning," I growled. "Lightning bridge in five minutes. Wear something that says *touch her and die screaming*."

"Black and silver, then." She left with the book clutched to her chest.

My possessiveness surged so fierce I could taste iron. The Lifeweave might save the Heirloom . . . or hollow Arabella from the inside. A chill scraped down my spine, and I locked the reason for it in the darkest vault of my mind.

I snatched the ledgers, shoved them into a drawer, and stalked after my wife. War could wait. Protecting Arabella Blackrose could not.

59

Reject Unwanted Rescue Attempts
(and Make Your Villain Proud)

Kazimir

I lounged in my seat, watching as the Great Hall filled with courtiers and nobles, all eager to witness the Hero's Guild emissary.

Arabella took her place on my right, looking suitably menacing draped in a black-and-silver gown stitched with roses along the hem. The sight of her tugged at the runes carved into my bones, a jolt of attraction I felt through muscle and marrow. It still surprised me how, after everything that had happened, she now sat beside me of her own will.

If that wasn't proof I could bend fate, I didn't know what was.

The massive black doors groaned open. A broad-shouldered man in gleaming armor stepped in, his retinue at his back. Their polished silver plate bore the Hero's Guild emblem, a sword wreathed in golden flames. My shadow warriors escorted them. One flickered at the edges like it strained to maintain solidity, a side effect of Solandris's wretched golden rose magic. Irritation prickled in my ribs. I clenched my fist, forced the warrior to hold its shape, and felt a faint twinge for my trouble.

A herald bellowed, "Announcing Sir Darian Lightbringer, Knight-

Commander of the Hero's Guild and Royal Emissary of His Majesty, King Auremar of Solandris!"

Sir Darian strode forward, ignoring Arabella completely, as if I were the only threat. Once, that might have been true. He halted at the foot of the dais, puffing up his chest.

"Lord Blackrose," he said, voice taut, "I come bearing a message from His Majesty, King Auremar."

I splayed my fingers on the throne's arm, feigning boredom. "Congratulations, Sir Darian. Let's have it. I'm a busy man."

He looked ready to grind his teeth to powder. "His Majesty demands the immediate return of Lady Arabella Evenfall. Her abduction was a grave act of war, and our king will respond with force if she is not released."

I flicked my gaze toward Arabella. "Abduction? There's some confusion. Lady Arabella Evenfall is Lady Arabella Blackrose, and she's here of her own free will. Right, my dear?"

Pride colored my voice, even as my nearest shadow construct glittered with new fractures. I willed it solid again.

Arabella gave an imperious nod. "Indeed, dear husband."

Sir Darian blinked, finally noticing her. "Lady Evenfall, whatever enchantment or coercion this villain has placed on you, the Guild can break it. Come with me, and you'll be safe, restored to your father and King Auremar's care."

His arrogance stoked my anger, though I kept my tone smooth. "Mind your tongue, commander."

Arabella spoke before he could respond. "My name is Lady Arabella Blackrose. I'm here by choice . . . and I have no interest in returning to that father you speak of."

He refused to meet her eye. Instead, he withdrew a glowing golden rose from his armor. One of Solandris's cursed blooms. My runes heated in protest. He held it out as though presenting a peace offering. One of my shadow warriors shifted menacingly at his bold step forward.

Sir Darian noticed the movement and halted. "From home, my lady," he said, voice thin. "A small reminder of your rightful place."

I tensed at the bright hum of the rose's magic. It prickled at my domain, stirring every old grudge I harbored against Solandris. Arabella moved gracefully to the front of the dais, curiosity flickering across her face. That expression shifted as she extended her hand.

The rose began to wilt. The gentle glow guttered out, petals shriveling to dust that fell at the commander's feet. A hush smothered the hall.

Sir Darian jerked back a step. "What have you done?"

"I don't need your token of Solandris," Arabella said coldly, "nor my father's machinations. I am not anyone's property."

Sir Darian's hand drifted to his sword hilt. I felt a twisted thrill, eager to see him try. "You threaten a royal emissary," he accused, voice shaking.

I couldn't hold back a soft, cruel laugh. "I'd heed her, commander. Lady Blackrose is quite capable of defending herself, and I do love a good demonstration."

He glared but stepped back from the mound of rose dust. "King Auremar insists Lady Evenfall—"

"It's Lady Blackrose," Arabella snapped. Every hair on my body pricked with admiration. "Tell your king I decline his rescue."

His expression twisted, equal parts anger and disbelief. "Your father and the entire realm think you've been kidnapped. The Guild is authorized to reclaim you by force."

I sensed Arabella's power coil beneath her composure. My own runes vibrated in response. "Then go ahead and try." She lifted her hand, letting golden light bloom across her fingertips, bright and deadly. My heart pounded with vicious pride. The shadows behind me roiled, stirred to join in.

Sir Darian paled, stepping back. "This is corruption . . . black magic. He's twisted you!"

"Spare us the moral lecture," I cut in, voice dropping to a threat. "His Majesty—the champion of Solandris, your glorious, pompous king—worked with Lord Evenfall to sacrifice her future. And you come here calling me the villain?" I tossed a glance at Arabella's glowing hand, imagining what it would do to the knight-commander's smug face. "Now, I suggest you leave, *emissary*. Unless you're eager to see Lady Blackrose's new talents firsthand."

He darted a wild look at the ashen remnants on the floor.

Arabella flexed her magic once more. "Go back to Auremar. Tell him I said no."

Sir Darian looked ready to argue, but my fracturing shadow warrior lifted a blade close to his throat, an unsubtle warning. With a final, outraged glare, he spun on his heel and stormed out, his men behind him. The rumble of the great doors slamming shut chased them away. With a wave of my hand, I dismissed the court. They scattered, probably craving the safety of distant corridors to gossip. Soon enough, only Arabella and I remained in the cavernous hall.

My shoulders sagged as the tension slipped free. I turned to regard her, perched on the dais with regal confidence. "You," I murmured, letting my voice echo in the hush, "were extraordinary."

She looked at the spot where the rose had disintegrated, then at me. Power glimmered around her, magnetic and sharp. "I only told him the truth."

I rose from the throne and moved closer, letting her see the desire in my eyes. "And you did it in a way that made me want to pin you on that throne. Rarely do people stand beside me so boldly—especially when it comes to defiling Solandris's beloved flowers." My pulse thudded at the memory of that golden rose turning to dust in her hand. "Magnificent."

Her cheeks warmed, though her tone remained steady. "I'm not a damsel, Kazimir."

I shook my head, voice low. "No. You're a nightmare descending on them all, and they'll never see it coming."

A faint smile tugged at her lips. "Speaking of nightmares . . . I believe Vex and the others have some wager on how soon you and I might tear the realm apart, or each other."

I flared my shadows ever so slightly. "We still remember our rules, Lady

Blackrose. But there are plenty of other ways to indulge ourselves, as we proved earlier. My knees still bear the imprint of my study floor."

She brushed a hand over the throne's arm and then stood. "The mighty Dark Lord, brought to his knees by a taste. It's a good look on you. Almost as satisfying as seeing a Hero's Guild knight tremble at my feet. Maybe I should make both happen more often."

Her grin sent a current of longing through me. She turned away, gown sweeping dramatically behind her, and I admired each smooth line of her body. That lethal potential belonged at my side.

I'd never wanted a single person more.

"Dinner here, in an hour. To celebrate," I said. "Don't be late, Lady Blackrose."

She glanced over her shoulder, face composed but eyes dancing. "Wouldn't dream of it."

With that, she left, and I finally let out a long, steady breath. My runes still vibrated with the remnants of the rose's interference, a reminder that Solandris's hold over me wasn't fully gone. But I felt a savage spark in my chest as well. Arabella was with me by choice—something neither the king's demands nor a gilded flower could break—and part of me craved the war that would follow.

Let them try to take her back. The world would learn exactly what it meant to face me . . . and my wife.

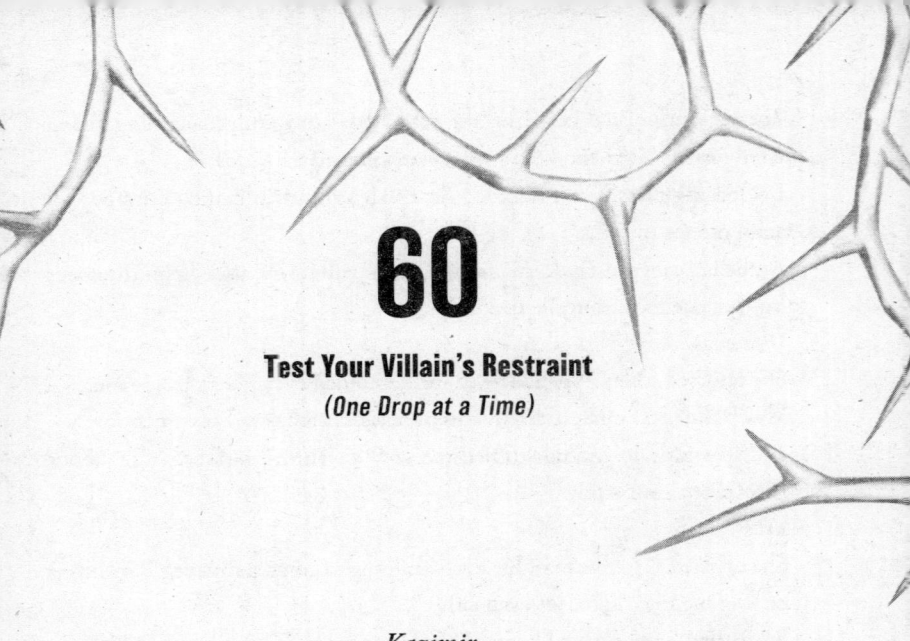

60

Test Your Villain's Restraint

(One Drop at a Time)

Kazimir

Candlelight gleamed across the Great Hall, giving the space a deceptively romantic glow, provided one ignored the axes, spears, and swords lining the walls. Black roses overflowed from silver urns, interspersed with vivid blooms from the High Gardens.

I drummed my fingers on the dark wooden table beneath the dais, still high on the sight of Sir Darian scuttling from Skyspire. Satisfaction coiled warm and smug, and I wondered what Arabella might do next.

A servant hovered to my left. "More wine, my lord?"

"Yes. And inform Lady Blackrose that dinner is served. She's already testing my patience."

"That won't be necessary," came a voice at the doorway.

Arabella sauntered in dressed in midnight blue silk, loose hair, and a smile that promised wickedness. Thoughts of troop deployments fled as I stood. "Lady Blackrose. I was beginning to think your dragon ate you whole."

She took the chair to my right, smirk razor-sharp. "And miss a chance to torment you? Hardly."

The servant poured her wine and retreated. Only two guards lingered at the far corners—far enough to miss every juicy detail.

I lifted my glass. "You handled Sir Darian beautifully. His outrage will sustain me for months."

Arabella's eyes glittered. "What do villains call it when a woman threatens to rot her enemies from the inside?"

"Foreplay."

She laughed, then sipped. The sound tightened everything inside me.

When the first course arrived—an overengineered tower of mushrooms—she set her fork down and studied the wine's swirling surface. "Kaz, about earlier . . . in your study."

"Yes?"

She exhaled. "You were right. I wasn't going to control my magic with you touching me like that. Not even close."

A satisfied hum escaped before I could censor it. "I'm well aware."

"Don't gloat," she said, but amusement softened her glare.

"I only state facts. You, however, should take notes, because I kept my power perfectly leashed when you"—I let the pause drag, savoring her blush—"wrapped that pretty hand around me in the training room this morning."

She scoffed. "Congratulations on your iron self-restraint. Enjoy it while it lasts."

I leaned forward. "Is that a challenge?"

"A . . . hypothesis."

Servants replaced plates with roasted fowl. We discussed supply routes, troop morale, and the ethics of collapsing mountain passes. Respectable conversation laced with innuendo thick enough to drown in. When an indecent mountain of chocolate arrived for dessert, she closed her eyes on every spoonful, humming. I envied the spoon.

"Trying to get me drunk?" she teased when I refilled her goblet yet again.

"You're dangerous enough sober," I drawled. "Just watching you savor that chocolate makes me plan all sorts of indecent things."

A servant reached between us for plates, hands shaking so badly he nearly dropped the china. The sensible man fled before I could threaten to flay him for existing.

Arabella rose with her wine and drifted to my side, perching her hip against the table so I had to tilt my head back. Silk stretched. My focus shattered.

"What are you doing?"

"All you have to do is say the word, Kaz, and we could christen this table."

She was obviously still riding the high of our earlier victory over the Hero's Guild emissary. I made a mental note to arrange more spectacular displays for her in front of my court. Arabella fed on that power as surely as I did.

"An enticing offer." I let my gaze linger. "But 'ley-line apocalypse' still rings in my ears."

She licked her bottom lip and turned as if to move away. "Then perhaps we shouldn't push our luck any further—"

Her foot hooked on my chair. The goblet tipped. Dark red splashed across my shirt and pooled in my lap.

"Oh!" she gasped, hand to her mouth—pure theater. I watched as she set the glass aside and reached for a napkin.

I caught her wrist. "Not with the napkin." My voice rasped.

Her eyebrows raised in question.

"Lick it off." I released her.

For a moment, her eyes widened, but I saw excitement beneath that shock. "Is that an order?"

"Yes."

She paused, studying me. I shoved my chair back from the table, wood scraping against stone in a discordant squeal. The two guards at the far end of the hall promptly stepped outside.

I settled into the seat with calculated ease, legs parted, arms draped along the carved rests. I'd rarely felt so on edge, but I hid it. Her smile dripped triumph as she sank to her knees before me, the silk puddling around her.

"You claim impeccable control," she whispered, fingertips grazing my thighs. "Sure you want to test it?"

Arabella leaned in and pressed her tongue to my shirt, tasting the wine-soaked cloth with a deliberate flick. My breath caught, fists tightening around the armrests until they groaned under pressure. Each languid stroke of her tongue spread fire through me.

"You're tense," she purred. "Should I slow down?"

"Do your worst."

She undid my buttons one by one, grazing my skin with each little tug, until my shirt gaped open. She surveyed the stains against my flesh, then dipped her head. Her tongue on my bare skin was torture, gentle flicks that followed rivulets of wine meandering over old scars. When she circled my navel, I sucked in a hard breath, trying not to groan. Every sense narrowed to the warm press of her mouth against me.

"Almost done," she murmured, though we both knew she was in no hurry. Her hands slid higher on my thighs. The pressure of her thumbs teased closer to truly dangerous territory. Every brush of her mouth teased my magic, daring it to surge. I wasn't entirely sure I could keep the lid on it, but damn if I wasn't hungry to find out how far she'd push.

My cock was already rock-hard. She let her gaze flick there, a smug smile ghosting her lips when she noted just how undone I was.

"Hmm," she mused, lips hovering indecently low. "Still composed? Maybe I should keep going."

I wanted to let her. I wanted her lips on me, wanted to bury my hands in her hair and fuck that pretty mouth of hers until it was thoroughly defiled.

The ley lines quivered—only a hair, but enough to prickle alarm.

"Enough," I ordered, voice frayed.

She sat back on her heels, not a hair out of place. "So much for your impeccable control, Dark Lord." With a smirk, she stood and smoothed her gown. "I need to feed Nyx. If you'll excuse me."

My jaw ached from restraint. "By all means."

At the door, she glanced over her shoulder, eyes aflame. "Thank you for dinner. Consider us even."

"I really fucking hate you," I called after her.

61

Wake Your Spouse with a Blade
(True Romance, Dark-Lord Style)

Arabella

Something cold and razor-sharp pressed against my throat, dragging me from dreamless sleep into heart-pounding awareness.

"You're dead," Kazimir's voice whispered in the darkness, his breath warm against my ear.

I stayed perfectly still, eyes adjusting to the gloom. A faint silvery glow emanated from the blade at my neck—not steel but a sliver of shadow essence. Kazimir loomed over me, half-hidden in darkness, the other half illuminated by moonlight spilling through the window.

"Most people," I said evenly, "just shake someone awake."

The shadow blade dissolved. "Most people aren't married to the Dark Lord."

"Lucky them."

Kazimir straightened, and I realized he was fully dressed in fitted training leathers, his hair slicked back. The smug bastard looked infuriatingly composed.

I pushed upright, blinking away sleep. "It's the middle of the night."

He moved toward the door. "Enemies rarely attack at convenient hours."

"And which enemies might those be?"

"The breathing kind." He paused, hand on the door. "You have four minutes."

The door closed behind him, leaving me alone in the moonlit chamber. I sucked in a frustrated breath, tempted to burrow back under the covers, but something in his tone had roused my curiosity. Within three minutes, I was out in the corridor, wearing my training leathers and with my hair hastily braided. Kazimir stood waiting, arms crossed. His mouth twitched upward in approval.

"I expected to drag you out by your ankles," he said mildly.

"I was tempted to make you work for it." I stifled a yawn. "But curiosity won."

We set off, his stride swift and deliberate, forcing me to hurry.

"Is this some bizarre ploy to push me past the Heirloom's limits?" I asked, eyeing him suspiciously.

He stopped so abruptly I almost collided with him, and in a blink, he had me caged against the tapestry-lined wall, hands braced on either side of my head. My pulse kicked hard.

"Oh, Arabella," he murmured, his voice settling into that dangerously soft tone that shot heat through my core. "If you only knew how close I am to forgetting every restraint for you." His breath brushed my lips, warm and taunting. "You want me to risk the Heirloom? All to hear you scream my name like you did that night—loud enough to rattle this entire citadel."

"Your ego is staggering," I managed, though my breath hitched.

His voice was low and as smooth as silk. "You like it."

A current of want tore through me, forcing me to swallow hard. His gaze fell to my mouth, his own lips curving in a slow, knowing smile that made my pulse throb.

"As soon as we solve this little complication," he said, voice roughening with every word, "you'll find out exactly what happens when I stop playing the Dark Lord . . . and start being a man who can't get enough of his wife."

My heart slammed behind my ribs. Each syllable threatened to pull me closer, until I was practically leaning toward him, barely aware of the step I took forward. His grin flashed wickedly, like he knew he'd already won. Then he slipped back, letting a cold rush of air replace the warmth of his presence. The abrupt distance left me dizzy and furious at how badly I wanted him.

He was calling my bluff, I realized. But he was also admitting just how much I unsettled him. And that realization sent a dark thrill racing through my veins.

Kazimir smoothed his collar with one tug. "We have somewhere to be."

"Where?" I asked, trying to steady my racing heart.

"Down."

I rolled my eyes and followed him through the deserted corridors. The tension between us felt electric, but the chill of the damp air was a welcome shock to my flushed skin. Now and then, we passed servants who bowed or flattened themselves against the walls, seemingly eager to avoid the swirl of danger and frustration that followed us. I kept my gaze forward, ignoring the pit in my stomach that said I wanted more of him than I should.

We descended deeper still, the air growing colder and tinged with a mineral scent. At last, we reached a heavy iron door inscribed with runes. Kazimir pressed his palm to the center, and the door groaned open.

Beyond lay a cavernous chamber—larger than any training hall I'd seen—with natural stone walls and a rough-hewn floor. Weapons racks, battered practice dummies, and odd contraptions lined the perimeter, as if no one had tidied in months.

Kazimir lit torches along the walls with a flick of magic. The dancing light revealed half a dozen wooden-and-metal humanoid figures posed in eerie stillness, each clutching a real weapon.

"What is this place?" I asked.

He strode to the center of the cavern. "Preparation. With Solandris escalating, Auremar won't rest until he's pried you from my hands—or destroyed you so no one else can use your bloodline."

I crossed my arms. "I handled Sir Darian."

"You did. But a single knight-commander isn't the king's entire arsenal." He gestured at the motionless figures. "These are keyed to attack you at increasing levels. They won't kill you, but they'll hurt—and they'll teach you to survive. Magic alone might fail if it's blocked, countered, or if you're exhausted."

The way his gaze flicked over me betrayed more worry than he meant to show. "These constructs aren't me," he said flatly. "No more excuses for hesitating. You'll learn better footwork . . . and we avoid certain temptations."

My pulse kicked at that reminder of what happened when we sparred alone. "So I'm practicing against wooden puppets instead of you?"

"They won't make the mistake of flirting back."

I studied him for a moment. "You're worried."

"I'm practical," was his gruff reply. "War is coming." Then he glanced away. "If you regret staying—"

"No," I said firmly. "Do you regret taking me?" The question slipped out before I could stop myself.

Kazimir's eyes met mine. "No," he said simply. "Not once."

Something warm unfurled in my chest, but he didn't give me time to savor the sensation. He flicked a hand at one of the constructs, sending it forward with a shudder.

"Choose your weapon."

I stepped over to a rack of blades and staffs and opted for two daggers. Lightweight, balanced. "I'm not exactly a master duelist."

He gave a half shrug. "You don't need to be. You only need to survive."

He stepped aside and let the construct advance. It rushed at me, sword raised in a clumsy but swift arc. I barely managed to duck, the blade whistling over my head.

"Block!" he ordered.

I brought my daggers together and caught the sword in a shaky X-block. My arms trembled under the force, but I held on until I heard him call again.

"Disengage!"

I twisted, letting the construct's momentum spin it off balance. For the next hour, he barked out instructions: how to parry, where to step, how to find an opening. The constructs improved with each round, and I fell more times than I cared to admit.

By the thirtieth—or maybe the hundredth—time I'd been disarmed, I lost it. "This is absurd!" I hurled a dagger at a far wall, where it bounced harmlessly to the ground. "I can't win like this. I have real magic."

Kazimir strolled over and picked up my fallen blade. "Magic that can be drained or negated. You need more than that to outlast the Hero's Guild."

"That doesn't make your method any less futile," I snapped.

He tossed the dagger at my feet. "Again."

"No," I said flatly, ignoring the sting in my arms and the bruises forming on my knees.

His eyes narrowed dangerously, and shadows darkened the room. "No?"

"You heard me." I folded my arms across my chest. "I'm tired, I'm sore, and I'm getting nowhere with this. Either change your approach or I'm going back to bed."

For a moment, I thought he might actually drag me back to the center of the room and force me. Then his expression softened with a grudging smile. "Finally."

"Finally what?" I demanded.

"The fire. You've been too compliant. That's not you." He waved again at the construct. "This time, fight your way. No illusions of normal combat. Use what you have."

I stared nervously at the lurching wooden figure. "You kept telling me not to rely on magic."

"Show me what you'd do if your life truly depended on it. Then we'll go from there."

He stepped back, and two constructs came forward at the same time, swords raised. My palms prickled with sweat, but I swallowed my fear. If he wanted me to use my natural instincts, then I wouldn't keep playing at this sword fight.

One construct swung high, the other low, forcing a choice I refused to make. Instead, I summoned a pulse of healing magic and channeled it into the daggers. Golden light flared along the blades, meeting the swords in a burst of sparks. Both constructs recoiled, as if stunned by the backlash of power.

I let out a sharp cry and cut into the nearest construct's wooden shoulder. It split cleanly, splinters raining down. The second dove for me, but I ducked beneath its swing and drove my glowing daggers into its chest. It seized once, then collapsed.

Turning back, I saw the first attempt to raise its sword again—so I slashed and separated its head from its torso. Silence echoed against the cavern walls.

Kazimir observed me from the side. "That," he said softly, "was impressive."

I exhaled, chest heaving. "You told me to do whatever it took."

He stepped forward, gaze flicking between me and the wreckage. "I did. Though I didn't expect you to dismantle them so completely." With a flick of his wrist, four more constructs rattled to life.

My blood felt like ice water. "Kazimir—"

"Fight," he said simply, and backed away.

I gritted my teeth. "I really hate you right now."

"That's fine," he replied, crossing his arms. "Hate me, but stay alive."

The constructs converged, each movement strange and unnerving. The first came at me with a sword overhead. I lifted my daggers, but the second came from behind. I was overwhelmed at once, weaving and blocking frantically. In seconds, I lost a dagger. One sword caught me across the back.

I expected searing pain and a spray of blood. Instead, the blow slammed me forward, leaving me breathless and aching but not severing me in two.

The weapons were blunted. Damn him for not telling me.

Dizzy, I whirled in place, catching glimpses of wooden limbs and metal edges all around. I started to summon my golden energy again, but a panicked voice in my head said there were too many, and a construct simply absorbed my distracted attempt.

The next blow nearly took my head off. I dropped and rolled, feeling the sword whistle past. One construct lunged again, but I'd lost track of the rest. I was done if I didn't adapt.

"Do something else," Kazimir called, as though reading my mind. "Don't let it siphon your healing power."

I let my next breath go slow and steady, summoning a short sword from shadow. Its blade glimmered obsidian dark. The nearest construct slashed at me. I met its blade with my shadow sword, half expecting a rebound. But it sliced through the blunted weapon with a brutal hiss.

One construct down. The others attacked in unison. I evaded low strikes, parried overhead ones, letting the ephemeral blade reshape in my hand whenever tension threatened to break it. My fear fell away, replaced by raw focus. A wave of my free hand conjured shadowy tendrils that snagged a construct by its ankle. My sword cleaved through its chest.

Another came at my flank. I whirled, blocking with an edge of living darkness. The final construct swung a heavy ax that crunched into my conjured blade, fracturing it. Desperate, I pivoted and re-formed the shadow into a curved scythe, hooking its wooden neck and yanking forward. Its next strike glanced off my shoulder, but I pressed closer, biting down the pain as I hewed into its torso. It broke apart with a hollow crack.

Panting, I glanced around to confirm they were all destroyed. My arms shook from exhaustion and sheer expenditure of magic.

Kazimir lifted his hand to still the final, twitching fragments of wood. "Enough."

I sank to one knee, breathing hard. My shoulder throbbed where the ax had clipped me, and I'd have bruises for days. At least there was no blood.

Then one of the constructs jerked upright with a wild screech of gears, as if possessed. Its limbs moved in disjointed spasms, weapon raised. I threw myself aside, but it rushed me with speed that nearly defied logic.

Kazimir cursed. "Something's interfering with my control." He tried to blast it with shadow energy, but the construct barely faltered.

I backpedaled. "Why?"

"Likely an overload from your healing magic. It's scrambled the enchantments."

"Neat timing," I muttered, hissing as the construct's ax swung for my face. I blocked with the battered remains of my shadow scythe. Splinters of wood flew as the construct overpowered me, driving me to the ground.

It raised the weapon for a killing blow. I scrambled, conjuring a smaller dagger of shadow, and slashed wildly at its wooden legs. I nicked one joint, but not enough to cripple it.

The ax whistled down, catching me across the same shoulder that was already injured. Agony exploded through me even as I rolled free. Another strike was coming—I braced—

Kazimir surged forward, unleashing a wave of dominion magic so potent it made my hair stand on end. The construct froze mid-attack, limbs splayed. Then it collapsed in a clatter of wood and metal.

Tension hung in the air as we both tried to steady our breathing. He turned, features softening the instant he saw my shoulder.

"You're hurt," he said, voice low.

"It's fine." I winced, touching the bruised area.

He walked me to a nearby table with a first-aid kit. Carefully, he helped me peel away my vest and jacket to inspect the skin. The bruise was large, but the skin had barely broken.

I tried calling on my healing magic. Golden light flickered weakly around my fingers but failed to take hold. "I've never been very good at healing myself," I admitted.

"This might sting." He poured a clear liquid over it, rubbing gently until the pain dulled.

When it felt better, he exhaled, lingering close to my side. I let myself lean into him, just enough to feel the warmth of his shoulder against my cheek. We stood there a moment, silent except for the flicker of torches and the lingering adrenaline.

I was exhausted, and the thought of taking all those stairs back to bed made me want to just sink to the floor in surrender.

I looked up at Kazimir and forced a small, helpless smile. "It still smarts. Maybe you could help me back to our chambers?"

His brow rose. "Are you still trying to tempt me into ignoring the Heirloom's restraints, Lady Blackrose?"

"I have no idea what you're talking about," I said innocently.

"Of course not." A slow smile curled over his mouth. "But I suppose you'd like me to carry you up all those stairs?"

I shrugged, then regretted it because my shoulder twinged. "Well, if you insist."

With a dry laugh, he scooped me off my feet and threw me over his shoulder in one fluid motion. "Smartass."

"Put me down!" I yelled, half laughing and half annoyed. I swatted at his back with my good arm, feeling infinitely scandalized at being hauled around like a sack of grain.

He strode out into the corridor, ignoring my protests. A startled servant pressed herself against the wall, eyes wide at the sight of her Dark Lord carting his wife around at dawn. Heat flared in my cheeks. Kazimir gripped my thighs firmly, and dammit, my body reacted with a traitorous surge of desire.

"Are you taking me upstairs to ravish me?" I tried for indignant but sounded more enthralled.

He chuckled, shifting me higher. "Tempting." The quiet rumble in his voice promised that the idea was definitely on his mind.

At last, we reached our chambers, the sky outside just turning pale. He paused, clearly debating between continuing his barbarian act or showing mercy. With a theatrical sigh, he set me down on the edge of our bed with surprising gentleness.

He fetched a fresh glass of water and a small vial, placing them on the bedside table. "Drink that if you have lingering pain. We'll try this again tomorrow night—with fewer constructs and no magic."

"Lucky me," I said wryly. Then my gaze flicked up to his. "Kazimir?"

"Yes?"

"When you said you didn't regret taking me . . . did you mean it?"

He paused in the middle of pulling on a fresh shirt, something unguarded flickering across his face. "I did."

"Even . . . with war looming and no Heirloom to use?"

He met my eyes. "Even then."

After he left, exhaustion tugged at me, but so did a quiet sense of affirmation. I lay back on the bed, smiling faintly in the dim light.

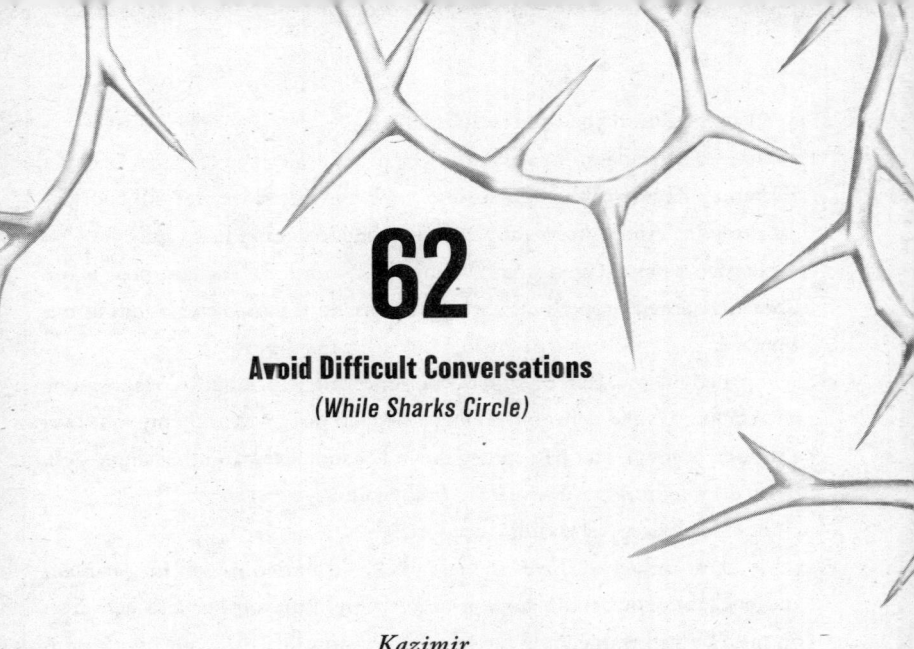

62

Avoid Difficult Conversations
(While Sharks Circle)

Kazimir

The war room settled into near silence after midnight, save for the whisper of candle flames and Griffin's tired muttering. We'd retreated there as soon as the workers left, craving the dead-of-night quiet for unholy paperwork and half-finished enchantment diagrams. I hovered over the table, scanning Griffin's meticulously sketched runes—complex bindings and arcs that hurt my eyes if I stared too long.

"This stabilization matrix should work," Griffin said, tapping the parchment with an ink-stained finger. "In theory."

My eyebrow twitched. "I loathe that phrase."

One of his lenses had cracked earlier in the week, giving him a permanently disgruntled look. "You're asking me to fix an artifact that's never been broken, using an untested method to ensure it doesn't explode and annihilate half the Western Realms. So yes, 'in theory' is the best I can promise."

I bit down the urge to snap and examined the schematic again. It appeared elegant—spells layered in interlocking patterns, designed to feed the Heirloom's unstable magic back into itself.

"How long until you can test it?"

"Two or three days," he replied.

I ran a finger over the drawn runes, half convinced we were all courting catastrophe. "And it won't interfere with the Heirloom's function?"

He gave a beleaguered sigh. "I can't know until the enchantment is finished and tested properly . . . which I can't do if you keep hounding me. My lord."

I opened my mouth for a suitably domineering retort, but the door swung open before I could deliver it. Arabella stepped inside, wearing my robe over a thin nightgown. Her hair spilled down her shoulders, and that single sight twisted something possessive deep in my gut.

"I couldn't sleep," she said, voice soft.

My chest tightened. Over the last week, I'd buried myself in war plans and enchantment details, hoping to keep my mind off her and her effect on me. We still trained and ate together, but outside that, our interactions were tempered by the presence of others. It seemed wise, considering the circumstances.

Griffin cleared his throat. "Perhapsss—"

"Stay," I ordered, still watching Arabella. "We're finishing the stabilization discussion."

She reached the table, eyes roaming over the runes. "Any progress?"

"Some," Griffin answered, visibly grateful for a distraction. "We're close."

Arabella turned to me, all challenge and unwavering gaze. "And the Lifeweave Ritual? Have you decided? Or are you still hoping to stall until the Heirloom collapses?"

My spine went rigid. I'd been putting that decision off for days. "We have other options to explore first," I said, layering my voice with finality.

"Do we?"

I forced a measured exhale. "Yes."

When Griffin tried—and failed—to look anywhere else, Arabella caught him with a direct question. "Tell me honestly: Is the ritual our best shot at repairing the Heirloom permanently?"

He stood there, loyalty and honesty waging war behind his eyes. Then he sighed. "Yes. Stabilization might keep it usable in limited fashion, but the Lifeweave Ritual is the only method that could fully mend that fracture."

Arabella gave a curt nod. "Thank you, Griffin."

I glowered at Griffin for his betrayal; he busied himself collecting notes. "I'll, uh, continue my calculations elsewhere," he mumbled, then practically sprinted out before I could banish him to the scorpion-infested vaults.

Silence draped the room as I turned to the window. A flicker of lightning rimmed the sky. Behind me, Arabella steadied her breath.

"You're avoiding me," she said.

I stared at the faint reflection of my own face in the window's glass. "Are you suggesting I ignore Auremar massing troops on our borders? The Hero's Guild planning a frontal assault? My time is better spent anticipating them than placating you."

Her voice dropped a notch. "I'd rather have your honesty than your placation. Why won't you discuss the Lifeweave Ritual?"

A cold spike of dread traced down my spine. "It's too dangerous."

"For who?"

I turned, half tempted to hurl a paperweight to release tension. "If you connect your bloodline and healing power directly to that damaged artifact, you could die. We have alternatives—"

"Stop lying to me." She moved closer, eyes snapping with anger. "You've been hiding in the war room all week so you won't have to decide. At least admit that."

The flare of anger in me nearly ignited a corner of a map. I inhaled through my teeth. "Yes. The risk to you is unacceptable. And yes, apparently, that matters to me. Satisfied?"

She took that in, her anger wavering. "Complicated," she murmured.

I let myself laugh darkly. "I'd call that an understatement." Shifting topics, I gestured at troop movements. "Morana whined again this morning about my forces clogging her borders. But she's terrified Auremar will come for her first."

"Are you deliberately drawing the king's ire toward Arvoryn?"

"Absolutely," I said. "She's strategic ground. Besides, I'm tired of her attempts to hedge her bets. Edmund is more malleable."

She eyed me with faint amusement. "That's a polite way of saying you plan to dispose of Morana."

"She's outlived her usefulness," I admitted. "No sense pretending otherwise."

Arabella folded her arms, apparently unbothered by my casual cruelty. "So you're done changing the subject?"

I held her gaze. "What do you want, Arabella? I can't think straight where you're concerned. Sacrificing you is no longer something I'm willing to risk. That's the truth you demanded."

She opened her mouth—maybe to respond, maybe to press for more—but an icy jolt of magic shot through my runes. The wards flared in warning.

"Visitors," I muttered. "Stay here."

Naturally, she trailed after me as I rushed into the corridor, and I wondered why I bothered giving orders at all. We nearly ran into Thorne, who looked agitated enough to chew nails.

"My lord," he said, bowing. "The Syndicate is here."

"Which representative?"

Thorne's face tightened. "All of them."

"I thought the Syndicate attended our wedding," Arabella said.

"They sent proxies," I corrected. "The actual members rarely leave their sanctums. For all of them to appear together, unannounced . . ."

It was like having six hungry sharks suddenly appear in your bathtub.

Thorne's voice dropped. "They demand an immediate audience."

I steeled my expression. "Demand, do they?" Then I gave Thorne a curt command: "See them to the Great Hall, and order a meal prepared."

He took off at once. Arabella turned to me. "You hold a seat among them, don't you?" she asked. "That's what I suspected when they showered us with wedding gifts."

"Seventh Chair," I confirmed.

"Do they know about the Heirloom?"

I tapped a finger against my wedding ring. "They might suspect something, but not the specifics. That's likely why they're here."

Smuggling, assassination, information brokering, magical artifacts—nothing moved without the Syndicate's knowledge or approval. But I'd kept my quest for power a secret, and if they discovered my true plans before they were fully realized, I'd end up fighting a war on two fronts.

Without the benefit of the artifact that had started all the trouble.

I turned away, voice low as I led us toward our chambers. "I won't let them sabotage our plans. Or you, Arabella. But watch out. They're a nest of vipers."

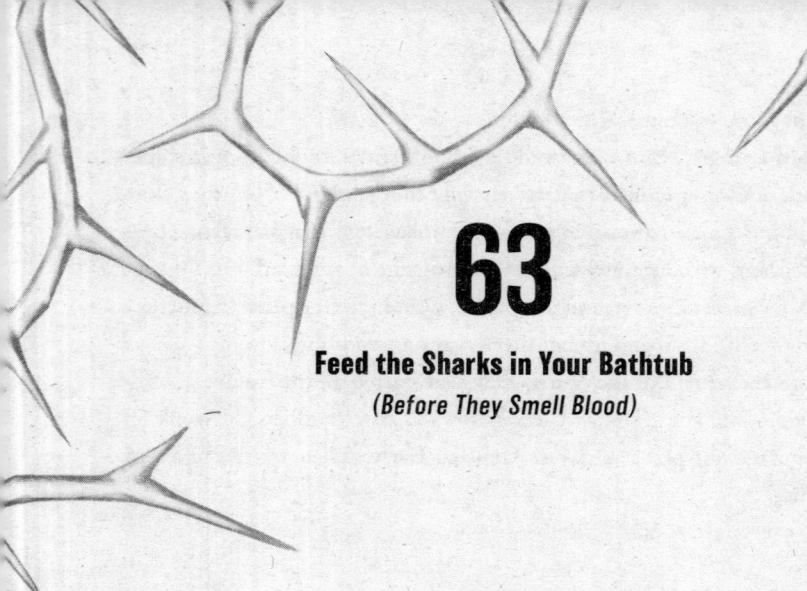

63

Feed the Sharks in Your Bathtub
(Before They Smell Blood)

Arabella

The midnight blue gown absorbed light rather than reflected it, creating an effect as if I were wrapped in a slice of moonless sky. Silver thread traced subtle patterns along the bodice and sleeves—arcane symbols mirroring some of the runes on Kazimir's skin. The neckline plunged lower than I preferred, and the back dipped even more dramatically, exposing most of my spine to the icy air that lingered over the lightning bridge. By this point, though, I only bothered with cloaks when it was cold enough to freeze my last functioning brain cells. Otherwise, the wind grabbed them and tried to tug me over the edge.

Vex walked beside me because Kazimir was already in the Great Hall with the Syndicate. I'd needed more time to dress—and, if I were being honest, to brace myself for a midnight dinner gathering where I felt like both the main course and the entertainment.

She eyed me as we descended a tower staircase. "You look like you're marching to your execution," she remarked, her hair dyed a deep, blood red hue.

"Maybe I am," I muttered.

We paused at a landing and Vex turned to face me. Her eyes flashed silver before returning to their normal gray hue—something I'd learned happened only when she was truly worried about Kazimir. Her sensitivity to his moods was uncanny, but now wasn't the time to ask questions.

"The Syndicate values three things: power, profit, and predictability," she said quietly. "They already know you have power—your bloodline makes that obvious. What they don't know is whether you're their asset or their liability."

I lifted my eyebrow. "Which am I supposed to be?"

"Neither." Vex gently adjusted the small silver circlet nestled in my hair. "You're Lady Blackrose, wife to the Dark Lord and mistress of this fortress. You're not beneath them, and you're not afraid of them."

I tried to manage a sardonic smile. "So basically, act like Kazimir with better manners and fewer war crimes?"

Her mouth twitched. "Not exactly. Lord Blackrose already has his own history with the Syndicate. You're unknown, which can be useful."

She continued down the stairs, lowering her voice as we neared the final curve. "There are three representatives you need to watch carefully: Lady Zaraiah holds the Chair of Whispers—she runs the entire intelligence network." Vex's tone hardened. "She and Lord Blackrose have . . . history."

Jealousy sparked hot and sudden in my chest. I let out an aggravated breath. How many of Kazimir's ex-lovers would I end up meeting? First Morana, now Zaraiah. Apparently, the Dark Lord had left a trail of scorned women across the realm. "And the others?"

Vex stepped off the final stair. "The Alchemist holds the Chair of Transformation. Never accept anything they offer you to eat or drink. If you must, purify it with your healing magic. I once saw them turn a rival's bones to glass in the middle of a toast. The man clinked nicely for a few weeks . . . until he died."

A chill ran along my spine. "They'd poison me at a diplomatic dinner?"

"They wouldn't call it poison," she said bluntly. "They'd call it 'testing your resilience.' They believe real power shows best under duress." She glanced forward, voice stretching thin. "And the third is Lady Vespera, who holds the Chair of Contracts. Every word out of her mouth binds in ways you wouldn't believe. Be extremely precise when you respond."

We reached the bottom of the staircase, and I could already hear voices drifting from the hall. Vex halted one last time, turning to me with an uncharacteristically earnest look. "Remember, Lady Blackrose, the Syndicate isn't here to befriend you. They're here to assess a threat."

"Kazimir," I said.

She nodded. "And by extension, you. They sensed a surge of magic from the citadel. They know something about the Dark Lord has changed, and they suspect you're the reason."

My mouth felt dry. "And if they decide we're too dangerous?"

"Then nothing good." She exhaled sharply, then straightened my circlet one final time. "So give them enough truth to keep them satisfied, don't hesitate, and smile like you're about to ruin their lives and have fun doing it."

She pushed open the doors and ushered me in. A wave of static-like magic spilled out from the room, seven separate power signatures spiking the air with tension. The hair on my arms prickled, and I almost raised my defenses on instinct. These people weren't just aristocrats; they were apex predators, and the air around them shimmered with barely contained power.

A single long table waited in the center, draped in black linens and lit with floating orbs of pale blue light. I recognized it as the same table where I'd poured wine onto Kazimir's shirt, only now it was set for eight, with centerpieces of black roses and strange glowing fungi.

Kazimir anchored the head of the table, dressed to match my dark blue tones with silver accents and a tailored jacket that emphasized his tall frame. Shadows curled around his fingertips.

He was surrounded by six people who could only be the Syndicate. My truth-sense vibrated uncomfortably, not because they were lying but because the entire atmosphere shimmered with masked intentions.

Standing near Kazimir was a tall, willowy woman with short-cropped hair that accentuated her regal posture. She wore a crimson dress that revealed most of her limbs and neck. Her fingertips grazed Kazimir's arm in a way that knotted my stomach with jealousy. I guessed that was Lady Zaraiah. But I noticed Kazimir's jaw tighten when she touched him, like a man forcing himself not to flinch from a hot iron. For some strange reason, that quiet refusal settled something in me, and I strode forward.

He looked up when I approached, and his calm mask shifted to approval briefly before he extended his hand. The gesture had him stepping away from Zaraiah with a casual firmness that she didn't miss.

"Here she is," Kaz said, voice warm with a charm he'd refined to perfection. "My allies of the Syndicate, please allow me to introduce my wife, Lady Arabella Blackrose."

I was aware they were all tracking my movement when I took his hand. One by one, he introduced the Syndicate members.

Lady Vespera, short and round with silver-streaked hair piled high, wore a conservative charcoal gown shimmering faintly with enchantments. Despite her grandmotherly image, her eyes felt razor-sharp.

"Lady Blackrose," she greeted in a voice deeper than I expected. She sized me up in a single glance and nodded once.

The Alchemist wore kaleidoscopic robes that refused to stay one color for more than a few seconds. A partial face mask hid everything above their thin mouth set in a mysterious half smile. They murmured, "Fascinating," and I felt a ripple of magic that made me dizzy. "Her aura fluctuates in counterpoint to yours, Kazimir."

The remaining Syndicate members were no less striking. Baron Revek, half mechanical with brass gears visible in his chest cavity, and Garrick the Unmourned, draped in funeral black and avoiding my eyes as if he were seeing ghosts behind me. Most ostentatious was Lord Faustian Gilt, a rotund figure with unnaturally golden skin and tiny jewels in place of pores. He watched me with the cutting gaze of a merchant appraising goods.

Then Lady Zaraiah swept forward with fluid grace that made me despise everything about her. "Lady Blackrose," she purred in a musical accent, "it's such a pleasure to meet the woman who finally tamed our untamable Kazimir. We'd begun to think he was incapable of domesticity."

She smiled brilliantly, overflowing with insincerity.

I held my own smile without blinking. "I wouldn't presume to tame anything. Lord Blackrose never bends to someone else's will. I've just learned more creative ways to channel his enthusiasm."

Kazimir's thumb slid across my knuckles in silent approval, a gesture that said both "well played" and "I'll make you pay for that later."

"Indeed not," Lady Vespera said, her voice seeming to vibrate the air. "But marriage is its own constraint, wouldn't you agree?"

I steeled my voice, recalling Vex's warning about Vespera's gift for binding words. "I consider it a partnership," I said carefully. "We both bring unique strengths to a shared purpose."

"And that purpose might be . . . ?" the Alchemist asked with a singsong curiosity, tapping their fingers in a beat that made my temples throb.

I glanced at Kazimir, and he gave me the faintest nod. "Exploring my magical abilities," I replied.

Lady Vespera's eyebrows crept upward. "Indeed. Your family's healing powers are quite well-known."

"Perhaps we should discuss such matters over dinner," Kazimir suggested smoothly.

"Of course," Lady Zaraiah agreed, though her eyes lingered on me with undisguised curiosity.

Kazimir guided me to the seat at his right hand, while the Syndicate members arranged themselves around the table. Servants appeared silently, bearing trays of delicacies and decanters of wine.

"Tell me, Lady Blackrose," Zaraiah said after we'd all been served. "How are you finding life at Skyspire Citadel? I understand you were raised to heal the sick and comfort the dying . . . not to share a bed with the man who causes much of the sickness and dying."

Before I could answer, something brushed my ankle under the table, making me startle. Kazimir's shadowy magic curled around my leg—not forcibly, but in a way that felt both proprietary and oddly comforting. He pretended not to notice the look I gave him.

"Yes, Lady Blackrose has remarkable life-magic," Kazimir said in a polished tone, all while that damned shadow traveled higher. "Her heroic lineage ensures it's potent."

"How fascinating," Lady Zaraiah murmured, eyes gleaming. "One might assume you orchestrated this union purely to capture that power, Kazimir."

"One might," he agreed, voice neutral. "But fate has a peculiar sense of humor where I'm concerned."

The tendril of shadow was halfway up my thigh, and I tried not to choke on my wine. I wanted to throttle him or maybe drag him away to discuss boundaries. Yet from a strictly practical standpoint, it kept me from fixating on the cluster of deadly predators watching us. I just wished he'd chosen a less distracting method.

The Alchemist skewered a piece of food on a tiny fork and addressed me again. "So, you arrived here rather abruptly, from what we gather?"

I carefully set my goblet aside, ignoring the building tension vaporizing my self-control. "Lord Blackrose can be very persuasive."

Lady Zaraiah's laugh had a harsh edge. "Oh, I remember his persuasions. They were quite irresistible . . . for a while."

It sounded too pointed. I forced a calm smile. "Strange how some things last, and others . . . don't." I let my gaze flick to her hand, still brushing Kazimir's sleeve like a cat pawing a cushion. "Sometimes the hold disappears altogether."

Kazimir's shadow stilled under the table, then abruptly vanished. A glance at him showed his expression had hardened. Yet he spoke in a smooth, almost genial voice. "My wife and I share a unique bond."

Lord Gilt, the golden-skinned Commerce Chair, interjected. "We noticed. The magical surge from your consummation rattled three entire kingdoms. Cost me a fortune in trade."

Kaz's hand moved to mine.

"Did your father approve of this union, my dear?" Vespera asked. "I recall Lord Evenfall kept you sheltered."

"My father's opinions stopped mattering long ago," I said with an edge to my voice. "He likely felt cheated that he couldn't auction me off."

"Auction?" The Alchemist cocked their head, enthralled. "To someone else entirely?"

"King Auremar," I clarified, hearing my voice tighten. There was no reason to hide what they likely already knew.

Lady Zaraiah exhaled something resembling a faint laugh. "So you've angered the crown of Solandris on top of everything else. Typical Kazimir style."

"That explains the movements of the Hero's Guild," Vespera said, pinning Kazimir with a look. "And your army."

He merely shrugged. "Auremar and I were enemies already. Now it's more official."

The conversation drifted to trade routes, magical components, and politics. I mostly listened, examining how each Syndicate member responded to Kazimir. Respect existed, but it was laced with apprehension. Lady Zaraiah hovered near him with unsettling familiarity, while the Alchemist studied me like I was their next experiment.

Dessert arrived—dark chocolate and berries dusted with edible gold—and Lady Zaraiah finally spoke again. "You've been quietly absent from Syndicate affairs, Kazimir. We wondered if you'd lost interest in our collective efforts."

"My focus has been on securing my marriage and consolidating matters at Skyspire," he replied calmly.

"Yes, your abrupt interest in matrimony was fascinating," Lady Vespera observed, eyes drifting toward me. "Especially after you rejected the idea so forcefully in the past."

I debated letting the silence hang, then spoke up. "People do change," I said, each word measured. "Or maybe they find motivation that wasn't there before."

Lady Zaraiah's smile held the gleam of a blade. "Kazimir's motivations of power and dominance have always been consistent. One wonders what you could possibly offer him."

Kazimir's voice went dangerously soft. "Perhaps you presume too much, Zaraiah. My wife is not your interrogation subject."

She responded with a predatory tilt of her head. "But she's so responsive. I can't help being curious about her strengths . . . or weaknesses."

I leaned in, refusing to look away from her challenging gaze. "If it was only about power, Kazimir could've pursued it elsewhere. I assume certain paths proved short-lived?"

Her bright red nails tapped the table. Kazimir's posture stiffened enough to signal he was done entertaining that line of talk, and Garrick took the opening.

"We've sensed changes running far deeper here," Garrick said, voice scratchy as a coffin's hinge. "Magic straining under an ancient hunger. It feels as if something latched onto this citadel, feeding."

My stomach turned cold, but I kept my shock off my face.

"My wife's bloodline resonates strongly with my dominion magic," Kazimir said. "It's produced interesting consequences."

"And potential hazards," Lord Gilt muttered, tapping jeweled fingertips on his goblet. "That concerns the Syndicate."

Kazimir's shadows loomed a fraction darker along the walls. "If I've threatened the Syndicate, it's news to me. Our goals remain aligned."

"But your methods do not," Baron Revek said. Something mechanical whirred from his chest.

Garrick's gaze settled across the table at me. "You two share power. That threatens the balance we rely on."

I forced my spine to remain straight. "Does the Syndicate oppose innovation? Isn't experimentation part of your core?"

The Alchemist let out a delighted laugh. "She certainly has a point."

Kazimir used that moment to propose ending the dinner, claiming our guests had traveled far and needed rest. After a subtly charged exchange of glances, Lady Vespera agreed. One by one, servants led the Syndicate members to their guest suites. Lady Zaraiah paused by me on her way out, leaning in so I caught a potent whiff of her spicy perfume.

She whispered for my ears alone, "Kazimir collects power like trophies—beautiful at first, then replaced once he finds something better." She gave a soft, knowing smile. "Don't mistake your present seat for permanence."

I couldn't resist a low murmur, though she was already turning away. "Did he discard your power, or did you simply fail to keep him interested?"

Her step hesitated, shoulders tensing just slightly under that gorgeous crimson gown, but she walked on without a word.

Meanwhile, Kaz was giving orders to a servant in a low voice. By the time I excused myself, he caught up to me in the hallway with a fleeting grim look that softened once our eyes met.

"I keep repeating this," he said quietly, "but you were brilliant."

I crossed my arms over the gown's low neckline. "Apparently, your ex-lovers are more dangerous than your enemies. Should I be taking notes or hiring a guard?"

His mouth twitched. "Jealous, are we?"

"Try concerned," I hissed. "Zaraiah seemed to know you awfully well."

He brushed a stray lock of hair away from my face, and a faint tingle burst along my skin at the small gesture. "Not as well as she believes," he said. "She wanted power more than she wanted me. But *I* refused *her*."

"Does she plan to orchestrate your downfall now?"

He gave a humorless snort. "Most likely. She's more trouble than Morana, but less cunning. Trust me."

His gaze dropped to my mouth. Even in the midst of political chaos, a pulse of heat flared between us. "You do have a habit of making your lovers into enemies," I quipped softly.

"Then maybe I did it in the correct order with you."

"Enemy first, lover second? Truly romantic."

He stepped closer. "It's a foundation built on truth, even if it's a twisted one."

"Speaking of twisted," I said with a glare. "What in the hell were you doing with your shadows during dinner?"

"You looked tense," he murmured, reaching up to brush his thumb across my collarbone. Amusement and desire warred in his eyes. "I thought a little . . . distraction might help."

"That wasn't distraction, that was torture," I said, though I didn't pull away as his fingers traced the edge of my plunging neckline. "And don't pretend it was strategic. You're suffering as much as I am."

His eyes darkened. "Perhaps I am," he admitted, voice dropping even lower. "Perhaps I've been thinking about how many ways I could touch you without breaking our restrictions. Maybe I've been lying awake cataloging every inch of you I could taste without triggering the Heirloom's wrath."

The tension rose again, a magnetic pull I nearly gave in to, until footsteps echoed around the corner. Kazimir seized that moment, pressing his lips to mine in a swift, heated kiss right as a servant passed by. My breath caught in my throat, and I waited for some punishing blast of magic to slam me for ignoring the Heirloom's delicate condition. But none came.

The servant scurried past, clearly trying not to stare. I glared at Kazimir once I could breathe again, voice lowered to a ferocious whisper. "You're an insufferable bastard."

He showed me a wicked grin. "Everything's fair in love and war, Lady Blackrose." Then he offered his arm with that smug, gallant formality. "Shall we retire? We'll need our wits tomorrow."

I slipped my hand onto his arm, not sure if I wanted to slap him or kiss him harder. As we strode toward our chambers, my mind spun with the memory of the words he'd let slip.

Love and war.

He'd said it so easily. And deep in my chest, I recognized something fierce: If he was indeed a villain, then he was my villain, fury and all. Let Zaraiah choke on her regret.

64

Defend Your "Research" with Legal Jargon
(and Occasional Violence)

Kazimir

The next morning, I strode into the Chamber of Accords with Arabella at my side, my hand resting possessively at the small of her back. The carved bone chairs and the austere emptiness of the room reminded me why I rarely used it—no one came to Skyspire to negotiate. They came to beg or to die. The Syndicate, of course, would do neither.

At least not today.

Orblights were already lit when I entered, revealing the towering walls draped in my crest, black roses entwined around a bleeding sword. The high-backed chairs formed a circle in the center, each carved from bone and etched with runes of power. I noted that the Syndicate representatives were already seated, which irritated me. In my domain, they should have waited for me to arrive.

Zaraiah sat directly opposite my seat, her crimson gown an arrogant slash of color against the pale chair. The Alchemist occupied a seat to her right, those restless fingers forever twitching. Lady Vespera sat to Zaraiah's left, and the other three Syndicate members filled in around them.

"Lord and Lady Blackrose," Zaraiah greeted, voice soft as a blade sliding from its sheath. "We're honored you could join us."

I ignored her sarcasm and guided Arabella to the seat at my right. I settled into my own with calculated leisure. This was no mere chair made of bones, but a larger, more elaborate creation that creaked faintly beneath me. The shadows at my feet rippled in response to my mood.

"I trust Skyspire provided you with a suitable night's rest," I said lightly. "Some guests find the nightmares fade after a few days."

Lady Vespera inclined her head. "The accommodations were . . . adequate. Though the magical turbulence proved somewhat disruptive."

That was her opening jab. I leaned back, offering her a pointedly casual smile. "Renovations. Hardly worth the fuss."

"Renovations," the Alchemist echoed, clearly unimpressed.

Arabella sat still as stone beside me. We'd agreed to reveal nothing about the Heirloom or our plans to manipulate the ley lines. The Syndicate didn't deserve such knowledge.

"My magical experiments are purely personal," I said, letting steel sharpen my voice. "Unless you're volunteering to serve as test subjects?"

Lady Vespera's delicate bone hairpins caught the glow of the orblights as she leaned forward. "When those personal pursuits threaten the balance the Syndicate maintains, we are forced to take notice. Your activities have raised alarms."

"And here I thought the Syndicate cared only for collective interests," I replied. "I didn't realize my private research warranted such vigilant nursemaids."

"Your actions reflect on all of us, Kazimir," Zaraiah said. "When you unleash magical bursts visible from three kingdoms away, you force us all under undesired scrutiny."

I clamped down on a twinge of annoyance. If they preferred a subtle sorcerer, they shouldn't have allied with a fucking Dark Lord. "If you're concerned about prying eyes," I said icily, "perhaps you should examine Lady Vespera's so-called expansions."

Vespera's eyes narrowed. "That operation was sanctioned by a unanimous Syndicate vote. We're here because your abrupt surges in dominion magic coincide with this sudden marriage, and we need to determine if you're weaponizing something beyond our control."

Arabella shifted, drawing their collective stares. Calmly, she said, "Is there a question in there? Or do you simply enjoy insinuations?"

The Alchemist's thin lips curled up in delight. "I do like her. But yes, Lady Blackrose, we do have questions, starting with the nature of your magical bond to His Supreme Darkness."

I spoke before Arabella could. "My wife and I share a link, as married couples often do, especially those gifted with certain arcane legacies." I paused. "Am I required to detail every aspect of our private life?"

Zaraiah's perfect brows arched. "How fascinating. The heroic bloodline of the Evenfalls merged with your . . . singular heritage. Unprecedented, wouldn't you say?"

She'd spent years rummaging for secrets about my background. Evidently, she thought today was the perfect time to corner me. I forced a dismissive smile. "Must I be planning something? Perhaps I married for companionship."

"You've never done anything without a motive," Zaraiah countered, gaze flicking to Arabella. "Since I've known you, it's always been about advantage. And I knew you quite intimately, Kazimir."

I smoothed my coat sleeve, ignoring the swirl of shadows that betrayed my growing anger. "That was long ago and irrelevant. Unless you came here for bedroom gossip, which, frankly, is beneath all of us."

She gave a poisonous smile. "Is it? I wonder if Lady Blackrose knows the depth of your imagination when properly motivated."

Arabella's eyes blazed, but I cut in. "You wanted to discuss magical disturbances. I suggest we remain on topic."

"Indeed," Lady Vespera murmured, straightening. "The Syndicate detected vestiges of dominion magic radiating from Skyspire. We suspect you could upset the power balance if you continue on this path."

"How dramatic," I drawled. "Our charter allows independent research unless it threatens other Chairs."

"Research or weaponization?" Vespera challenged. "These energies are not minor experiments."

I shrugged, shadows curling out from under my throne. I didn't bother to rein them in. "Speculation. I see no clear evidence presented here, just your prattling about vague concerns."

Zaraiah leaned forward. "If you want to quell our fears, show us what you're doing. Provide transparency. Then we won't need to worry."

I gave a short laugh. "Invite the Syndicate to ransack my private workrooms? Absolutely not. My projects remain my own, under the protections of the Charter."

Vespera's expression shifted to something more formal. "Then I invoke Protocol Seven. When a chair holder's actions risk destabilizing the region, they must provide full disclosure upon unanimous demand or face censure."

I stared coldly. "Be very sure you want to cross that line. We both know invoking Protocol Seven without cause carries penalties. I can think of a certain former chair who still can't hold a spoon."

"We're prepared to face any verdict," Vespera said, unflinching. "Syndicate stability comes first."

I glanced at Arabella. She watched me steadily, clearly taking in every word. "Fine," I said at last, "then I invoke Article Three, Paragraph Four: Proprietary research can remain confidential if I offer assurances of no direct threat to the Syndicate or its interests."

The Alchemist's twitching fingers froze midair. "So you refuse disclosure?"

"I uphold my rights under the Charter," I corrected. "My work is delicate, and revealing it now would compromise everything."

"You ask us to trust your word," Lady Vespera said skeptically.

I spread my hands in a near-mocking gesture. "For almost a decade, the Syndicate has found me reliable enough to hold a seat among you. My integrity hasn't changed."

Zaraiah laughed. "How conveniently vague. Forgive us if we find that insufficient."

Shadows licked up the arms of my throne, responding to my temper. "I don't recall asking for your forgiveness. You can speak to my shadow warriors if you're not satisfied."

Zaraiah and Vespera exchanged a knowing look, some silent conversation passing between them. Then Zaraiah stepped back into the fray. "You're so fun when cornered, Kazimir. It's almost nostalgic."

I sighed. "I'm not cornered—I'm bored. Is there anything else, or shall we end this charade?"

She cast a smug glance at Arabella, then pressed on. "I recall your fascination with demonic anatomy. Has your new wife heard stories of that incident?"

My pulse spiked as a hot spark of terror burned beneath my anger. Of everything she could have mentioned, that was the worst. Arabella caught my reaction, confusion clear in her face, but Zaraiah wore a self-satisfied smirk.

"You mistake desperation for strategy," I said harshly. "But you've always lacked genuine understanding."

Zaraiah's smile curdled. "Strategy? So that's what you call it, letting that monster—"

CRACK.

Thorns erupted through her chair, splintering the ancient bones. Zaraiah leapt aside just in time, but her hem snagged. She tore it away as a drop of venom slicked off the thorn's tip, hissing and melting a burn mark in the stone.

I stood, shadows swirling around me in furious arcs. "Leave. Now. Unless you'd like your entrails tangled in those vines."

"You're far more entertaining when you're angry," she said, attempting a mocking tone but not quite succeeding.

The other Syndicate members rose. None seemed shocked, implying they'd known her plan. Lady Vespera leveled a cool gaze at me. "This isn't over. We have too many unanswered questions."

"Then seek them elsewhere," I snarled. My magic slapped the floor in thick, writhing tendrils. "My hospitality just expired."

The Alchemist bowed, still wearing that half smile. "A pleasure as always, Lord Blackrose. Lady Blackrose." Their unsettling focus landed on Arabella. "I look forward to future conversation—perhaps involving tea, if not threats."

I said nothing more, letting the shadows thicken until they exited. Zaraiah lingered for one final triumphant look before stepping through the door. Once they were gone, I remained standing, chest tight from the collision of rage, fear, and old ghosts.

"Kazimir?" Arabella's voice cut through the haze. She came to stand near me, though not too close. "What was that? Zaraiah mentioned demons—"

"Nothing," I said tightly, unable to meet her eyes. "She's always digging for weaknesses."

Arabella studied me. "Then why did it affect you so badly?"

I twisted away, circling my chair, my shadows trailing like black smoke. "Because Zaraiah is very good at stirring old wounds, that's all."

"Is it so bad I can't know?"

"It's not a topic for discussion," I snapped viciously. I forced my jaw to unclench and measured my tone. "We should focus on next steps. Over wine, or something stronger."

Arabella's eyes shone with concern, but she nodded. "Fine. Will the Syndicate leave after this?"

"They will. They got what they came for: proof I'm hiding something. Now they'll regroup to exploit it." I forced a calm shrug, though my heart still pounded. "They won't strike openly yet."

She sighed, brushing a strand of hair behind her ear. "They seemed genuinely worried about what we're doing."

I offered a savage smile. "They should be."

65

Play with Your Wife
(Without Breaking the Rules)

Arabella

Steam from my bath still clung to the air when I padded back into the main chamber. The Syndicate's visit had left me with a sense of unease. Zaraiah's pointed remarks about demons, Kazimir's sudden, violent fury—none of it made sense. He had changed the subject afterward, but the memory of his barely contained rage kept replaying in my mind. Whatever lurked in his past, it clearly had teeth.

I sank onto the stool in front of the vanity. The door opened quietly behind me. Kazimir stood there, leaning against the frame as if he had all the time in the world. His expression was a careful mask of control, but intensity burned in his eyes. He hadn't come looking for me right after the Syndicate left, retreating into whatever shadows claimed his thoughts. I wasn't sure if I was relieved or annoyed.

"Still awake?" he asked in that low, intimate rumble of his.

I reached for my hairbrush. "I was busy reflecting on your delightful associates."

He came away from the doorframe, stopping near the sofa, keeping a deliberate few strides of distance between us. "Zaraiah loves stirring trouble. It's best ignored."

"Is it?" I turned on the stool, letting the robe gap a bit at the thigh. I couldn't help prodding him, dangerous as that might be. "You didn't exactly ignore it."

His gaze flickered, a flash of that earlier storm surfacing then disappearing behind a practiced calm. "Let's just say," he began, lowering his voice so it vibrated along my skin, "I owe you. For the Syndicate's intrusion. And for my . . . abruptness earlier."

Desire coiled low in my belly. "You owe me three debts, then, because you never finished what you started in the study days ago."

His eyes darkened, trailing down the line of my throat to where the robe lay open. "You know why I stopped. Will you have the same issues with control tonight?"

I felt a thrill spark inside me. The challenge was clear. He was tying his apology, his desire, and my own power into one knot. "My control is better," I replied, feigning more confidence than I felt. "But I'm still not sure about yours."

His slow smile made the hairs on my neck stand up. "I'm always in control." He still didn't come closer. "But our predicament demands . . . creativity."

"Care to explain?"

He lifted his hand, palm up. "As you know, I don't actually need to touch you to *touch* you."

Before I could speak, I felt something brush against my ankle. It felt like cool silk, a tendril of shadow, darker than the rest of the room, twining around my skin. I sucked in a breath, looking from the shadow to him.

He spread his hands innocently.

The shadow pulsed against my leg, tracing the curve of my calf, then slipping beneath the hem of the robe to circle my thigh. A shiver swept through me, not from cold exactly, more from the sheer possibility. Every inch of it whispered of power, of a storm about to break.

"This . . . is dangerous," I managed. Another ribbon of darkness slithered around my waist, sending my heart galloping.

He tilted his head, the look in his eyes daring and smug. "Is it?"

A squeeze around my middle lifted me off the stool. I let out a startled cry as the shadows half carried, half floated me across the room, depositing me onto the bed. More dark ropes appeared, winding around my wrists and ankles, pinning me back against the soft sheets. My robe slipped and fell open.

"Kaz—" I gasped, not entirely sure if I was begging him to stop or to continue.

"Yes, Arabella?" He stood at the foot of the bed, arms crossed, gaze scorching me from a slight distance. A predator savoring the final helpless squirm of his prey.

"This isn't fair," I croaked.

He let out a low laugh. "Nothing about us has ever been fair. You, tempting me with every glance. Me, unable to lay a hand on you. Don't you think we both suffer?"

Before I could retort, a new tendril of shadow formed near my face, brushing against my lips. I gasped and it slipped inside, tasting faintly of ozone and old power, stroking my tongue in a brazen kiss. And then the shadow changed, no longer feeling like a kiss, but growing in width and length until it hit the back of my throat in a rhythm that mimicked other, far more carnal acts.

A choked moan escaped me. The shadows holding my wrists tightened slightly, drawing my arms further above my head.

"Look at me," he commanded, voice rough.

My gaze snapped to his. A flush marked his cheeks, his chest moving faster with each breath. Watching him lose that perfect composure unleashed a flood of wetness between my thighs.

"Keep your eyes on me," he ordered, the words thick with possessiveness. "I want to watch."

Shadows at my ankles pulled, spreading my legs. The robe gave up any pretense of coverage, leaving me shamelessly on display. The vulnerability collided with thrilling pleasure. I was pinned, subject to his will, yet the raw desire in his eyes made me feel like the one in control.

Kazimir made an approving sound.

Another shadow slid up between my thighs. I strained against the bonds, a silent plea for more. The shadow in my mouth prevented speech, but my whimpers seemed to convey my desperation clearly enough.

"Patience," Kazimir chided, a hint of dark amusement in his tone. "You were so insistent on teaching me restraint. Are you regretting it now?"

The shadow brushed against the delicate folds between my legs before seeking my clit, and I arched into the touch with a strangled cry. The shadow obliged my silent demand, pressing more firmly, alternating between insistent pressure and barely-there teasing. My head fell back against the pillows, eyes fluttering shut as pleasure built, sharp and demanding.

"Eyes. On. Me," Kazimir snapped, the command absolute.

I forced my eyelids open, focusing on how he drank in my response. The shadows held me firmly, sliding across my breasts, my waist, all those tender spots I never imagined darkness could caress. It was a maddening barrage of sensation, too many competing touches to think straight.

I hovered on the edge of release, breath coming in ragged pants. Then, abruptly, the shadows froze. I let out a ragged, muffled sound of protest. Writhing, I found no relief.

Kazimir's faintly cruel smile made his intentions clear. "Did you assume I'd hand over satisfaction so easily?"

The shadow withdrew from my mouth, leaving me able to speak again. "Kazimir," I ground out, half plea, half growl. "Don't you dare stop now."

He raised a brow. "Ask nicely. Admit that I have more self-control than you."

I opened my mouth to snap at him, but all that came out was a choked moan as the shadows resumed, tracing lazy circles at just the right spot. My skin lit up in gooseflesh, and my hips twisted in search of more.

"Patience, hero," he teased. "If you want me to break your every limit, you should consider the word *control* more carefully next time."

"I won't—" My denial dissolved into a sharp moan as a shadow flicked against my clit with deliberate cruelty.

"No?" His smile widened. He shifted against the bedpost, and I couldn't help but notice the blatant ridge straining against the fabric of his trousers. "Maybe you need a bit more persuasion. Soon, I'll be able to replace these shadows with my hands, my mouth." His voice dropped lower, raspier. "I'll finally *taste* you properly. Make you scream my name until the foundations of this citadel break."

The images his words painted were almost enough to make me lose my grip on my magic. Almost. Caution warred violently with the desperate ache between my legs.

He shook his head, his eyes glittering with admiration. "Gods, the defiance. Even pinned and begging."

"You want this just as badly," I accused, arching again as the shadows renewed their torment, circling faster now.

"Undeniably," he drawled, his gaze fixed between my legs now. Another shadow slid between my thighs, tracing the swell of my ass before brushing with shocking intimacy against the delicate skin of my back entrance. I arched hard off the bed.

He stepped forward. His presence radiated pure command, making every nerve beneath my skin buzz. Meanwhile, the shadows redoubled their pace, each flicker winding me tighter inside.

"Say it, Arabella," he coaxed, voice dropping. "Tell me you yield. Let me give you what you need."

I bit my lip hard enough to draw blood, pride warring with the acute need to let go. The tension coiled so tightly that it hurt. I wanted to resist, but the slick heat pulsed between my legs, turning every breath into a whimper.

"I—" I tried, unsure if the words would be rebellion or surrender. Maybe it didn't matter. Kazimir's face showed something like triumph. Or hunger.

He didn't wait. The rhythm of that shadow touch accelerated, merciless and right on target. My body spasmed with a rapturous burst, the crescendo rolling through every tendon. Silently, I screamed, snapping taut against the bindings as release claimed me in a shock wave of color and sensation.

Slowly, the shadows retracted, dissolving back into the dim corners. I lay there trembling, heart galloping, sheets twisted under me. Every bit of me thrummed with pleasure.

Kazimir rounded the bed, and the mattress dipped as he sat next to me. The earlier wicked amusement was replaced by something softer. Gently, he brushed a strand of sweaty hair off my face. The warmth of his fingertips was startling after the cool press of shadows.

"Better?" he asked softly, stroking along my cheekbone.

My throat felt too dry for words, so I nodded, leaning into his hand.

He bent his head. His scent swept over me—winter and a blade's edge, threaded with magic. "Soon," he whispered, voice rough. "Soon we'll stabilize the Heirloom and won't need these ridiculous restrictions." His lips hovered near my ear, and I shuddered as he added, "And I have so many ways I want to make up for lost time."

He pulled back, eyes flickering with an unsettling blend of triumph, possession, and something I wondered if he'd ever name. Wordlessly, he stood and smoothed his clothes like nothing had happened. Then he crossed the room and vanished through the door.

I lay there, body still pulsing with aftershocks, mind spinning at the precarious bond between us. It was stronger now—maybe strong enough to scorch everything else to ash if we couldn't control it.

But in that moment, I just tried to catch my breath, still tasting the faint echo of shadows on my lips.

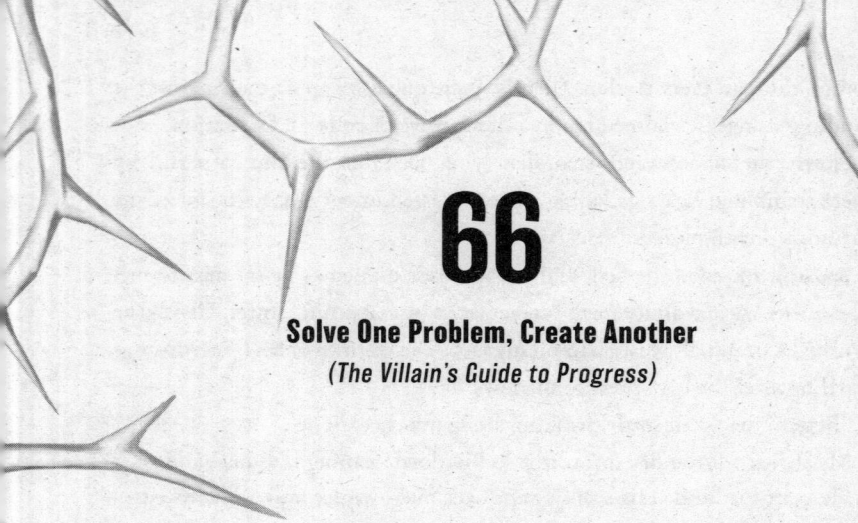

66

Solve One Problem, Create Another
(The Villain's Guide to Progress)

Arabella

I closed my eyes and pressed my palms against Kazimir's, trying to keep my focus from shattering into a thousand bits. The eastern tower was still half in ruins. Griffin had insisted that with its wards and enhancements, it was the best location for the stabilization enchantment.

A week had passed since the Syndicate departed, leaving behind more questions and a brittle hush over Skyspire. This was our shot at regaining control before the Heirloom tore itself—and the entire Western Realms—apart. At first, Kazimir scoffed at the idea of dragging me along; he wanted me safe away from the tower in case things went wrong. But after a tense, whispered debate in front of Griffin, he finally conceded. So here I stood, summoning every shred of nerve to link my power with his again.

A warm hum buzzed in my middle, the telltale sign of my magic flaring to life. Kazimir's cooler, violet-slanted magic rose to meet mine, swirling together until a gold spark pulsed at the center. Griffin lingered nearby among half a dozen obsidian spheres, eyes practically glowing with anticipation.

"Yes, yes, that's it," he urged, voice trembling on the edge of manic. "Keep it steady."

I forced out a long exhale and opened my channels to Kazimir, exactly the way he'd shown me. Strange how easy it had become to connect with him—to the point it felt wrong *not* to.

The spheres glowed faintly at first, then pulsed brighter. Griffin squeaked out an excited sound. Kazimir leaned closer and whispered, "A bit more."

I did as he asked, letting that swirl between our hands thrum. Gold and violet arced in the space. The spheres flickered in time with our heartbeats. Griffin's breath caught. "It's working—the orbs are sponging up the excess!"

I felt a measure of relief. For once, something seemed to go as planned. Then, without warning, my magic surged out of control. One obsidian sphere cracked with a sharp pop. My energy flared through my veins, scorched my muscles, then ricocheted into Kazimir.

My eyes snapped open.

He looked taut, sweat beading on his temples. "Keep the connection," he snarled, each word dripping with tension. "I'm diverting the overflow to the outer wards."

I felt a tidal shift as he siphoned that furious power away from our joined hands, sending it rippling into Skyspire's defenses. Windows rattled, and vibrations crept through the floor under my boots.

Griffin practically hopped in place, half terrified, half enchanted. "Truly fascinating! Your synergy is—"

Kazimir's breath snagged, pupils blown wide. A deep, strangled groan ripped from his throat, and fear jolted through me. I tried to draw back, but his grip clamped around my wrists, stopping any retreat. Dread coiled in my gut, then images started crashing through my head.

A cavern drenched in a sickly glow, runes gouged into the rock—unlike the ones on Kazimir's body but carved with the same savage, ancient style. A surge of fury and hunger knotted together, pounding with raw, primal rage. The vision threatened to drown me.

"Kazimir!" I shouted, voice cracking.

He tore his hands free. The sudden break in magic left me feeling hollow. The remaining obsidian spheres disintegrated in a puff of black dust, and a pulse of recoil wrenched me off-kilter.

I clung to the wall, battling a swirl of dizziness that made my teeth buzz. Kazimir stood stiff as a pillar, wild-eyed and pale. Griffin rushed closer, scanning us both.

"That was incredible," he said, though concern laced his tone. "But what happened to you two?"

My voice rasped. "I saw something. An underground place with runes. They felt . . . vicious."

Kazimir's jaw tightened, and he wouldn't meet my gaze. "Magical feedback," he muttered.

Griffin, brushing dust from his robes, nodded decisively. "Regardless, the enchantment is in place. The crack in the Heirloom shouldn't keep spreading. Hopefully it'll be usable again soon. I'd call that a success, wouldn't you?"

I wanted to appreciate the good news, but my body still throbbed with leftover terror. Before I could celebrate, pain stabbed beneath my ribs as though something were clawing its way free. I coughed in agony and hunched over. A heartbeat later, Kazimir did exactly the same, mirroring my posture.

"Interesting," Griffin observed, eyes bright behind his broken spectacles. "You must have triggered an entanglement effect—temporary, I'd guess."

"Entanglement?" I ground out, pressing a palm to my side. "It feels like my guts are trying to wring themselves inside out!"

Kazimir staggered closer, wincing at his own pain. But as soon as he neared, my muscles eased, the pain sliding back. He exhaled, relief in the lines of his shoulders.

Griffin rubbed his chin. "Yes, that supports the theory. You're forcibly sharing a magical signature. Until those energies settle—perhaps a day, maybe less—you'll suffer if you're separated. Staying close will dampen the worst of it."

"A day?" I croaked, straightening by sheer spite alone. "Griffin, you'd better be joking."

He shrugged. "Sadly, no. But it's not soul-ripping, per se. More like . . . polite internal shredding. Think of it as mild mayhem. You'll live."

I shot him what I hoped was a withering look, and Kazimir radiated restless irritation. "Guess I won't be going down to inspect the garrison tomorrow. Then again . . ."

His face shifted, that aggravating smirk forming on his lips as he gazed down at me. "The entanglement won't disrupt our plans for tonight, now that the Heirloom isn't seconds from catastrophe. However will we endure?"

"Right. Endure," I echoed with a tight swallow, the heat in his eyes leaving me dizzy again. "At least we solved one problem."

Griffin dusted fragments of obsidian off his boots. "Exactly. It's a major victory. I'll gather the remains for further tests, just in case a repeat is necessary."

Kazimir rested the lightest touch on my elbow, soothing the last tremor in my chest. The moment felt precariously intimate, and I had to clench my jaw not to lean farther into him. Our moment of calm was shattered by footsteps hammering up the tower stairs. Vex barreled through the doorway, brandishing a sealed envelope.

"Letter for Lady Blackrose," she said breathlessly. Then she eyed us, her brow furrowing. "From the Alchemist."

Kazimir tilted his head, tension rolling through him. "Why would the Alchemist write to my wife?"

I gave him a mock glare. "Maybe they liked me better than you."

Vex stepped forward, ignoring the shattered orbs. "No idea. But it's sealed properly."

Kazimir passed his hand across the envelope's surface and sniffed the wax. "No poison," he said. "No subtle toxins, at least—not the Alchemist's style. They're more about flamboyant transformations." Then Griffin performed a quick enchantment check and nodded. Kazimir offered me the letter, staying close so that our arms brushed.

I tore open the seal carefully, uneasy about the dancing loops of script. The Alchemist's writing filled the page:

Dearest Lady Blackrose,

It has come to my attention that Lord Atticus Evenfall—your father—awaits a tragic end at Auremar's behest. Assassins are en route to remove him as a loose end. Whether you think he deserves such a fate is your affair, but I suspect you may want this information for your own reasons. You must act swiftly if you wish to intervene, or simply observe. I, of course, find the possibilities thrilling.

Let me know how the story unfolds.

I crumpled the edge of the parchment but then passed it to Kazimir in silence. He skimmed the lines, his jaw flexing. I doubted he cared much about my father's mortal peril from a moral standpoint, but we both recognized the manipulation for what it was. My father, the man who sold me to the highest bidder, was apparently marked for execution by King Auremar. Now I had . . . options.

Kazimir lowered the paper. "So Auremar cleans up his mess by killing your father."

"Probably to hide the deal they struck involving me," I said, each word tasting bitter. "Though that's hardly a secret, anymore, is it? It means the king's hiding something else."

"The Alchemist doesn't hand out truths from the goodness of their heart. They'll expect a favor in return if we intervene."

"Unless it's all a lie." I looked up at Kaz. "Could be a Syndicate trick."

He shook his head. "The Alchemist doesn't fabricate details outright. They prefer real sparks that set everything ablaze. It's more entertaining. I'd bet Auremar wants no loose ends."

I inhaled, swallowing any flicker of pity. "So if we do nothing, Father dies on Auremar's terms. If we chase him down, we'll owe the Alchemist. Great choices."

"What do you want?" he asked, placing his hand on the small of my back.

I crossed my arms so he wouldn't feel me trembling. "He's not worth saving, but if Auremar kills him, I'll never get the chance to confront him myself."

No one spoke for a beat. I sensed the tension spiking around us, thick as the residue of burned magic. Griffin busied himself with orb fragments, clearly wanting no part in family matters. Vex just waited, unblinking.

Kazimir eyed the paper one more time. "Then we'd have to leave now, entanglement be damned. We might face Auremar's killers along the way. It's not exactly ideal if we're stuck staying close."

"Are you telling me we can't?"

He looked torn between annoyance and a grudging approval of my nerve. "I'm saying it's a perfect storm of inconvenience. But if you need to see your father first, then we'll do it."

A swirl of emotions almost floored me—fury, old wounds, a twisted gratitude that Kazimir allowed me the choice. Possibly some excited glint that I'd confront my father.

Griffin cleared his throat and hefted the remains of one shattered orb. "I'll see to the Heirloom while you indulge your paternal closure."

"Wait," I said. "The manor. Those suppression runes my father used . . . are they still active?"

Kazimir's gaze sharpened, his hand tightening almost imperceptibly on my back. "Yes. They won't reach full strength instantly, but don't underestimate them."

"Right." *I'm not the same girl he locked away.*

I tried separating from Kazimir, but a fresh stab of pain made me hiss and pitch forward. Kazimir lunged to catch me before I hit the ground. Our abrupt half embrace eased the agony, leaving me breathless.

He tried for a wry grin, though his voice still sounded strained. "I'd rather endure an entirely different kind of writhing with you, but once again, the Heirloom has other ideas."

From behind us, Griffin coughed awkwardly. "Well, no one's spontaneously exploded, so I'll count today as a success. We can refine the enchantment later. Just . . . try not to stray too far from each other."

I lifted my chin, aware that Kazimir's arm still circled my waist, his body flush against mine. "At least we aren't about to blow up the citadel. That's progress, right?"

He gave me a light squeeze. "I'll take what I can get."

And although anger, dread, and a twisted sense of anticipation throbbed inside me, I leaned into Kazimir long enough to steady myself. If we really were stuck together until this entanglement wore off, then so be it—my father's impending execution demanded a reckoning, and I wasn't about to cower just because it hurt to walk away from Kazimir's side.

No. I would face Lord Evenfall on my own terms, even if I had to drag the Dark Lord along with me.

67

Kidnap Your Father-in-Law
(Villain Style)

Kazimir

I felt the air pop, thin and smelling of damp earth mixed with something sickeningly sweet—pure Solandris. The scent of leather polish and steel still clung to me and Arabella as we stepped from the ragged portal and onto the moonlit Solandris road.

A sharp pain lanced through my chest, radiating from the main rune carved over my heart. I choked back a groan, but Arabella caught the tightness in my expression, her eyes narrowing with concern.

"Are the runes acting up again?" she asked, scooting closer until our shoulders brushed. That small contact soothed the worst of the ache, though it didn't banish it completely.

"It's nothing," I lied, scanning the road for threats.

"It's getting worse." She frowned. "I don't know why you keep lying about it."

"And I don't know why you keep pointing it out." Damn her truth-sense. It was growing more and more irritating. I sighed. "Perhaps it's worse than usual," I admitted. "But now isn't the time to chat about it."

I kept my hand at the small of Arabella's back while she tugged her leathers into place. She'd only half laced them before we left Skyspire. "So," she asked without meeting my eyes, "what happens next?"

I nodded toward a merchant's cart rattling our way, its driver humming, blissfully unaware of the Dark Lord and his wife materializing in the middle of the night. "I plan to persuade him to drive us farther west."

She lifted an eyebrow. "Persuade?"

"I can ask nicely. On occasion."

"Right," she said flatly. "So compulsion, then."

It took only a whisper of dominion to brush the man's mind. The horse stopped. The driver blinked, his face smoothing to the vacant calm of someone who now existed for the sole purpose of driving me wherever I wanted. Simple minds were refreshingly easy.

Two shadow warriors took shape from the darkness beneath the trees, wolflike silhouettes that prowled on either side of the carriage. I coaxed four more from the night, sending them to scout ahead. Holding that many shadows in Solandris—despite the magical bond I shared with Arabella—felt like juggling sharp blades while balancing on a fraying rope, but I was taking no chances.

We climbed into the carriage and sat side by side. My hand landed on her thigh, mostly to cool the burning in my bones, and I knocked on the carriage roof. At once, we set off at a lively clip.

I studied Arabella in profile as the moonlit fields swept past. She wore that determined set to her jaw. I'd seen that look enough to know she was already plotting whatever confrontation lay ahead at Evenfall Manor.

"What's your plan when you see him?" I asked softly.

She kept her gaze on the horizon. "I haven't decided."

A lie. Her craving for answers—vengeance, maybe—nearly vibrated in the air. But if she wanted to keep secrets, that was her call. I could respect it.

The shadows prowled alongside us, half-formed beasts that flickered between wolves and formless dark. A deeper burn flared along my spine, the runes buzzing like wasp stings against my bones. Solandris always pushed back at my magic with its smug, sanctimonious aura. Normally, I wouldn't get this close to the Golden Rose Fields without extensive preparations. But with Arabella tangled in my magic, her heroic blood buffering the worst of it, the agony was . . . less.

My thoughts circled back to that vision we both glimpsed during the enchantment. Something old. Something hungry.

"You're thinking about what we saw," Arabella remarked, her tone neutral.

I met her eyes. Denying it was pointless. "I was."

"What exactly *was* it?"

"I have no clue," I admitted. "But it all felt too familiar. Like it called to the runes in my bones."

Arabella's face softened just a fraction.

One of my shadow warriors flickered then vanished, the thread of its connection snapping in my mind. I flinched.

"Your magic's hurting you."

"I can handle it."

She turned to stare at Evenfall Manor's outline wreathed in distant moonlit haze. Her fists clenched on her thighs. "Maybe we should take him back to Skyspire."

I raised an eyebrow. "You want to drag your father from his estate all the way to the citadel?"

"I don't want you getting drained in Solandris," she said, glancing at me, "and I'd rather not rush the inevitable conversation with him."

It was irritatingly sensible. Another shadow warrior blinked out. "Your call," I said as evenly as I could manage.

She shot me a look, as if I'd just handed her something precious. "You'd give me that choice?"

"Why not?" I shrugged. "He's your wretched father, after all."

Her hesitation broke with a quick nod. "Fine. I want him in Skyspire."

I slid closer and draped my arm across the back of the seat, letting my fingertips brush her shoulder. "Done," I told her quietly, letting my voice drop lower. "Whatever you require."

She gave a short laugh. "Careful, Kazimir. People might suspect you're turning heroic."

Obviously, she hadn't expected me to agree so quickly. But this was a simple matter of letting Arabella direct our next move. She deserved it.

By the time we reached Evenfall Estate's outer drives, the moon was high above us. My head pounded with savage pain, but I felt that familiar need to protect her from seeing me in agony.

"Maybe I should be grateful your father is such a monumental bastard. Without him, you'd never have found me so intriguing."

She tipped her head, a smile ghosting across her lips. "If he'd been a decent father, I still wouldn't have fit in with those Solandrian peacocks. I never belonged there."

"Their loss," I said, pressing a kiss to her temple.

The driver brought us to a stop just shy of the gates. I hopped out first, pulling Arabella with me. The hum of our entangled magic circled us. A silly part of me felt proud as my shadows slid across her as if they belonged at her side.

Slipping around the manor's perimeter was embarrassingly simple. The wards were trifling, and the guards stuck to predictable routes. Two shadow warriors had more than enough cunning to handle security. The real problem was the possibility of Auremar's assassins arriving first.

I led Arabella through a narrow side door, the same one I used the night I discovered her father's suppression runes. He hadn't improved his defenses even after mysteriously losing one guard. Fool.

The servants' corridors smelled of cheap brandy and old polish. I caught a sudden wave of memory from my own youth—another set of candlelit halls, another father figure ripe for disposal. I remembered the weight of the sword, the satisfying *thunk* as steel met bone, the hot spray across my cheek.

Tonight the ghost of that moment followed me all the way to Atticus Evenfall's study.

A single guard snoozed in a chair. One flick of shadow around his throat, and his eyes rolled back. He slumped to the floor with a soft exhale of breath. Arabella stepped over him, her expression set.

The door swung open. Evenfall sat behind that atrocious gilded desk. He froze midscribble and slowly looked up, going from scowl to full-blown terror as Arabella and I walked in.

"Arabella? How—what are you—?"

"No theatrics, Father," she said, her voice crisp. "You're coming with us."

I inspected him, letting cold menace hum in my voice. "I recommend you cooperate. The citadel's food tastes infinitely better if you retain the use of your kneecaps." My runes flared, cutting through my composure. I fought it, because the Dark Lord did not *hunch*.

Evenfall shot to his feet and shoved his chair aside. "This is abduction! The king—"

"—has already sent assassins to deal with you," I finished for him.

His face paled as that sank in. He tried leveling a paternal glare at Arabella like it might still work. "My dear, you've been ensorcelled! This demon corrupted—"

Her eyes sparked with a swirl of gold and violet. Evenfall's mouth clamped shut so fast I half expected his teeth to crack. *He knew.* Those suppression runes were nothing against her now.

"I pledge my loyalty where I choose," she told him. "And it's never been with you."

I snapped my fingers, summoning coiling shadows to bind him to his chair. He yelped in panic. "Pack him," I instructed my shadow warriors.

They lifted his entire chair, occupant and all, dragging him to the door. He let out a high-pitched squeal. "Efficient, aren't they?" I asked Arabella lightly, keeping my hand on her back.

We wound down the servants' staircase, Evenfall's shrill protests leading the way, but either the servants had the good sense to stay in their rooms, or they were glad to see him go. I made sure his chair bumped around the walls and corners all the way to the door.

I leaned in to whisper, "Any regrets?"

She shook her head. "Not one."

Outside, my shadows tipped his chair forward, dumping him onto a velvet cushion in the merchant's carriage. He let out an *oof* as I dispelled the immediate restraints. Before we could climb in ourselves, though, movement stirred by the trees.

Five figures approached, blades catching the moonlight. Auremar's cleanup crew. So the Alchemist's tip hadn't been a ruse after all.

"Stay behind me," I snapped at Arabella. Her palm flattened on my back, feeding me extra magic that cut through the worst of the pain. Lord Evenfall whimpered and tried to burrow into the cushions like a terrified mole.

I didn't bother with pleasantries. My shadows tore two assassins apart in a flurry of snapping teeth. Another screamed when a warrior shredded his chest. I flung a dominion bolt at the fourth, though the bitter rose-laden air of Solandris snagged my spell. White-hot agony ripped through my ribs.

A knife hurtled toward Arabella, but she snapped up her hand, conjuring a flash of golden light that deflected the blade. Pride flared so bright I almost forgot the battle.

Within half a minute, the attackers were bloody heaps on the ornamental gravel. I dispelled my remaining shadow warriors, and the abrupt release of power nearly sent me to my knees. Arabella pressed her hand harder to my back, trying to keep me upright.

"You're not all right," she whispered.

The world swayed. "I've been in worse shape," I gasped. "Let's get the fuck out." We stumbled inside the carriage, with Evenfall huddled in the seat across from us. I banged the roof with shaking knuckles. "Drive!"

The carriage lurched forward. For her sake, I restrained myself from setting the entire manor ablaze.

68

Confront Your Past
(Bring Threats, Not Forgiveness)

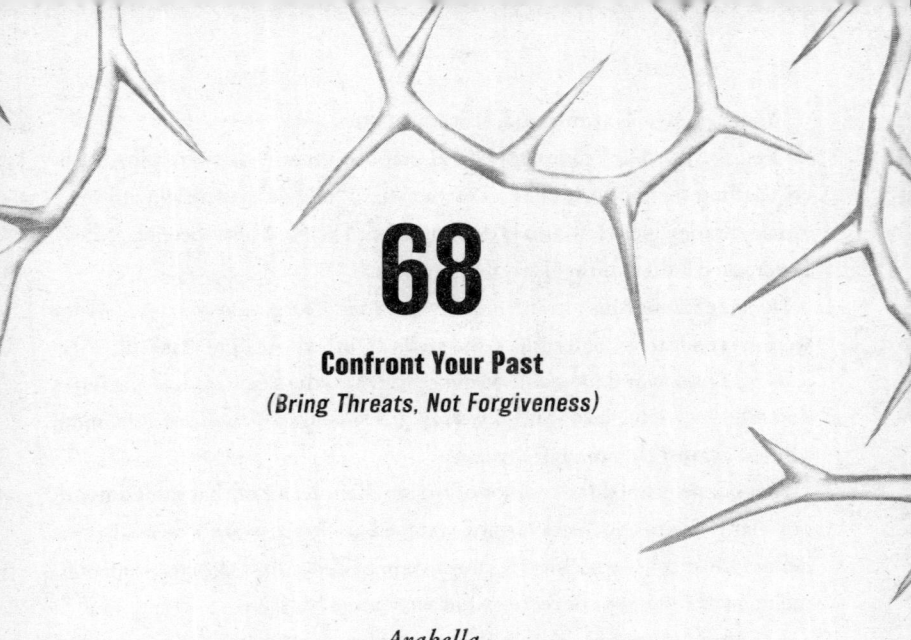

Arabella

Sleep hadn't brought rest, only a restless tangle of limbs and simmering resentment. Kazimir had all but collapsed beside me after hauling my father off to the dungeons, the lingering drain from Solandris finally claiming him. He'd honored my request—no cage hanging from bare rock, merely a cell with some added "enhancements."

The magical entanglement continued to hum between us. The pain of forced proximity had eased enough that neither of us collapsed if we stepped apart, but I still found myself reaching for him in the darkness, startled awake by the emptiness if he rolled too far away.

Kazimir was already awake when I stirred. Leaning against the headboard, he regarded me with a stare that seemed to peel back my every defense. Though a slight tightness lingered at the corners of his eyes—the aftermath of overusing his magic in Solandris—he appeared more relaxed than the night before.

I pushed off the sheets and swung my legs over the side of the bed. My father had sat in a cell long enough. Now, I wanted answers. And I wanted closure.

"You're going," Kazimir said. It wasn't a question.

"Yes," I replied, my tone clipped as I grabbed my still-dirty training leathers. Pulling them on felt almost ceremonial. "And you're coming with me."

The entanglement left him little choice, but I wanted him there regardless. He cracked a dry smirk. "I wouldn't miss it."

Skyspire's dungeons weren't musty pits in some forgotten courtyard. They were carved into an outer isle. Cold walls absorbed the light, making it feel less like a prison and more like a void carved into the sky. This was Kazimir's domain—efficient, cold, and unyielding. He walked beside me, one hand splayed against the small of my back.

Rows of cells lined the interior of the smaller isle, all of that same smooth obsidian. Guards in black armor watched us from behind face-covering helms. Most cells lay empty. Kazimir didn't believe in long-term imprisonment; swift judgment or recruitment were more his style.

A jarring dissonance echoed up the corridor: some poor soul mutilating a lute while singing off-key about shadows and heartbreak. The chords made me want to rip the strings out of his hands.

"The Minor Annoyance Wing," he explained. "For petty criminals. Your father got premium accommodations last night."

We stopped in front of a cell. Lord Atticus Evenfall sat on a pile of straw, looking sallow and exhausted. The reek of stale sweat and regret clung to him. Next door, the hapless minstrel belted out an especially painful note.

"He's improving," Kazimir noted with mock cheer, tilting his head toward the musician. "He hasn't sung the verse about my 'brooding eyes' in at least a day."

My father hauled himself up, fury flaring across his features. "Arabella! Praise the heavens! Get me away from this lunatic's serenade. Have you any idea what I've endured?"

Kazimir stepped up to the bars, radiating menace. "My wife suggested we keep you"—he smiled coldly—"lucid. Now I'm second-guessing that decision."

Whatever bluster my father had mustered vanished. He went pale, casting frantic glances between us.

I signaled the guards. "Open the door. We're moving him."

They hauled him out quickly, and I couldn't resist noticing how pathetic he looked, stumbling and trying to maintain a scrap of dignity. The journey to the next wing felt interminable. My father's breathing turned ragged the moment we led him into a chamber with a row of terrifying implements lining the walls—spiked contraptions, scalpels, bizarre glass vials with tortured spirits swirling inside. Kazimir's presence completed the effect, leaning against the wall with an air of menace.

My father's eyes fixed on me. "Whatever he promised you, Arabella," he rasped, "he's lying. Men like him don't—"

"What do you suppose he wants, Father? My bloodline? My connection to the First Hero? How different is that from what you wanted? Or Auremar?" I let my voice harden. "Forty thousand crowns, wasn't it?"

He gaped at me while the guards forced him onto a stone chair. Shackles sprang to life and clamped around his wrists.

"Why does Auremar want you dead?" I demanded. No point in wasting time.

Father started with bluster—denials, righteous indignation. My truth-sense screamed behind my eyes. He must have noticed something in my expression because he faltered, hedged, and finally stammered, "I . . . I don't know."

I shook my head in cold disbelief. "Liar."

Shadows snapped down, swift as a whip, slicing a thin line across his cheek. He yelped.

"I'm not known for my patience, Evenfall," Kazimir said in a dangerous voice.

Father's eyes darted around the chamber. "I can't tell you," he whispered, voice shaking. "There are . . . consequences."

"And there are consequences for *not* speaking."

Shadows curled around Father's forearm, raking thin welts down his skin.

He whimpered. This sniveling coward was the man who had ruled my life with an iron fist? He broke at the first touch of real pain.

"You don't understand," he gasped, terror flashing across his face. "There are things worse than your shadows."

"Try me." Kazimir leaned closer. "Whatever you fear, I assure you, I can make it seem like mercy." He raised his hand again, letting more shadows slither around my father.

Father's eyes bulged. "The king!" he choked out, his voice barely a whisper. "His magic . . . it isn't his own. He wasn't born with any."

I frowned. "I've seen Auremar's spells in court. If it's not from heroic blood, then what is it?"

"Something old. Terrible." Father sagged in the chair. "The Golden Roses help contain it—contain *him*—but Auremar's been siphoning power."

"Go on," Kazimir said, as if he was bored.

Fear twisted Father's face, and when he spoke, it was in a strangled whisper. "The Shadow King . . . he's real, imprisoned for centuries beneath the Golden Rose Fields."

I felt Kazimir's rigid silence. For all his earlier dismissal of ancient tales, he looked distinctly grim now. He and I exchanged a look. "The Hero's Garden." The ley lines. Perhaps they *were* all connected.

"What do you mean?" I asked. "The Shadow King's been dead for centuries. After Soriven transformed him, he led a long life atoning for his evil deeds."

"That's what your mother told you," Father said. Bitterness twisted his features. "She didn't know the truth. Few people do. *I'm* not even supposed to know. It's why"—he licked his lips—"why the king wants me dead. Long ago, Auremar told me that Soriven never redeemed the Shadow King; he *sealed* him away with blood magic. The Golden Roses grew from that blood."

"What?" I stepped closer, disbelief churning in my gut. "Mother's stories all said Soriven transformed him through compassion. That the roses were a gift of healing."

Father let out a harsh laugh. "Pretty lies for children. Your mother believed them too—her family made sure of it. Every Golden Rose that blooms reinforces the seal."

"The Hero's Garden," I whispered. "It wasn't about compassion at all."

"It was about containment," Kazimir said quietly beside me, his expression darkening. "Blood magic of that magnitude would require an anchor, something living that could sustain the spell across generations."

Father nodded, sweat beading on his forehead. "For centuries, Solandris has built its kingdom atop a monster's cage."

"And Auremar's messing with it," I realized. "Drawing power from something that should never be awakened."

"He's grown greedy," Father said quietly. "Or desperate. I suspect he realized I knew too much."

My truth-sense hummed, but it wasn't sounding any alarms. This was genuine. Kazimir's voice cut in like a blade. "So you offered your daughter's magical blood as a bargaining chip?"

Father stiffened. "It was a chance to elevate House Evenfall—"

"A staggering display of fatherly devotion," I said flatly. "What does the king want with me?"

"He said he wanted an heir."

"Auremar already has heirs," I spat. "Did you not think it might have something to do with his dark schemes?"

My father studied the floor. "I told you . . . I'm not supposed to know."

"And how did *you* learn all this?" Kazimir pressed.

Father recounted a sordid tale from his youth—drunken nights at court, Auremar's loose lips and dark appetites, a secret spilled in confidence that Auremar didn't seem to remember the next morning. "He suspected I knew," Father mumbled. "My influence waned. When he made it known he was looking to marry again, I reminded him of my daughter and told him of her power."

"Even knowing what he was like," I said with disgust. "What he was doing. And the suppression runes? The tower?"

"I did what was necessary to keep you manageable," he said coldly.

"To *break* me, you mean." Magic sparked in my fingertips, but I held it back because my truth-sense was tingling again. "There's more, isn't there?"

His silence was damning.

A slow, glacier-cold anger churned through me, dredging up memories of isolation, fear, and betrayal. And even now, my father couldn't admit to everything he'd done. I extended my hand until it rested against Father's chest. "I've learned how to reverse my healing magic. I wonder how effectively I can target one organ. Your left lung, perhaps?"

Terror flooded Father's face. "Arabella, you wouldn't—"

"Why not?" I asked with a thin smile. "You taught me that blood means nothing if it stands in the way of ambition."

I pictured the lung in my mind, seized it with that lethal part of my magic, and *squeezed*. He wheezed, eyes bulging. I felt a dull satisfaction in seeing him panic, but also a sick sense of emptiness. Still, I didn't pull back right away.

Only when his lips turned a ghastly shade did I relent. He slumped, gulping air, tears streaking his face.

"Ready to talk?" I asked, voice shaking only slightly.

He gave a jerky nod. "The king's mages," he croaked. "They . . . altered your mind. When you first manifested power, you refused to obey, so they made you forget. As you got older, I locked you in that tower, used runes to keep you docile."

My stomach churned. "I don't remember defying anyone."

"Right. Because they made sure you wouldn't." His gaze slid away. "Your mother . . . she wasn't supposed to be there that night."

Ice filled my veins. "What night?"

"The night they took your memories." He licked his lips. "But she found out. And she broke through years of suppression spells her family had placed on *her* to protect you. It . . . killed her. The backlash. You witnessed everything."

An odd numbness spread through me, as though my body refused to feel the full crush of this revelation. "Mother died of a fever when I was eight."

It was a fact etched into my memory, solid and unshakeable.

"No," he whispered with a helpless shrug. "That's the story we arranged so you wouldn't question it. You saw it all, and you screamed for three days straight. That's why they had to be so thorough. They took that memory, too."

I stumbled back as if he'd struck me. The room tilted. "I watched her die?"

"You did." His voice was hollow. He still wouldn't meet my eyes.

Kazimir's shadows erupted in anger, sharpened spikes of pure rage that shattered the stone wall behind my father's head. The surge of his fury shook the entire room, and his eyes flashed silver. A low growl—an actual, animalistic growl—vibrated in his chest. Father leaned as far away as his shackles allowed.

Kazimir's voice scraped across the air, roughened by an accent I'd never heard before. "Why did they suppress your wife's magic, too?"

Father could only stammer. "She— Her family didn't . . . want her drawing attention at court."

I couldn't stand to look at him. My breath hitched, rage tangling with grief. A lifetime of illusions, my mother's actual death stolen from me. Every painful minute in that tower. The man who had orchestrated all of it now cowered, pinned by shadows and shaking in fear. I felt no triumph, only a yawning pit of betrayal.

"And so you offered the court your daughter instead," Kazimir stated roughly. "Without even knowing why."

"I offered a political alliance!" Father cried, trying to regain some footing. "One that would restore House Evenfall! Auremar was intrigued—a young bride, pure heroic blood—"

Kazimir moved so fast I barely caught it until his hand clamped around Father's throat. "At the cost of silencing one generation and selling the next." Sharp black claws emerged from Kazimir's fingertips. "They call me the villain," he snarled. "But I have never sold my own blood."

Father's frantic, choking sounds filled the room. I placed a hand on Kazimir's arm, not sure if I was stopping him or encouraging him. Part of me wanted to watch Father suffocate. The rest of me wanted to tear him limb from limb for all he'd done. But the bigger part, oddly, just felt hollow.

Kazimir let go, and Father sank forward in a coughing fit. The battered man looked up at me with something akin to dread.

"You remember the stories Mother told me," I said softly, "about a hero who used love and compassion. She must have been so horrified by you."

He tried to spew more invective, but it came out as a sob. Then his eyes narrowed bitterly. He glared past me at Kazimir. "Don't pretend you're any better! What did you want her for, Dark Lord? Her blood? Her magic? Or just a noble whore to warm your bed?" He spat weakly toward Kazimir's feet. "We're not so different, you and I."

I maintained my grip on Kazimir's arm to prevent him from unleashing more fury. "The difference, Father, is that I *chose* him."

Kazimir's gaze flicked to me, a glimmer in those shadow-dark eyes. He turned back to my father, his fury banked but not extinguished. "Auremar's hubris will cost him—and you, Lord Evenfall. I'll keep you alive for now while Lady Blackrose decides how best to deal with you. Know that her will is the *only* thing keeping me from tearing you limb from limb."

The guards released the shackles and yanked him upright. Father's eyes locked on mine. "Arabella, don't let him make you his pawn."

I felt no flicker of sympathy. I said nothing. He'd stolen everything that should have been mine—family, memories, innocence. There was no forgiveness left.

As they dragged him away, Kazimir's hand slipped into mine. The hum of our entangled magic flared, then steadied. I managed to stay upright, though rage and heartbreak churned through every vein. When my father disappeared around the corner, I released a shaky breath.

"Let's get out of here," I muttered. "The stench is making me sick."

69

Repel the Knights in Shining Armor
(Your Wife Doesn't Need Saving, Thanks)

Kazimir

I watched Nyx spiral above us, her sleek black form slicing through the clouds and painting dark trails against the pale sky. She'd grown significantly since the day I first brought her to Skyspire, hoping to seduce my new wife. Now, she boasted a fifteen-foot wingspan and the kind of aerial precision that raised one inevitable question: Just how powerful would she become once fully grown?

I let my gaze drift downward. Arabella leaned against the stable's outer wall, the tension in her posture betraying the storm beneath her surface. She hadn't said much since we left her father in the dungeons. Instead, she'd walked straight out to see Nyx, as though only the dragon's presence could anchor her thoughts. Any number of pressing matters demanded my attention—troops to marshal, defenses to reinforce, a war to spark—but I remained at her side. If she needed this moment of quiet, I wouldn't deny her. And if I was honest with myself, I wasn't prepared to walk away from her even if the entanglement allowed it.

Something fierce shimmered behind her eyes whenever she stared into the sky, the same look I'd glimpsed when she first arrived at Skyspire, defiant and ready to carve her own path. Even in stillness, she looked coiled tight enough to shatter steel with her bare hands.

"Do you want to talk about it?" I asked carefully. My voice came out a bit harsher than intended, reflecting the tangle of regret and protectiveness inside me.

She shook her head, not turning around. "Not yet," she said quietly. "I'm not ready."

I understood all too well. On more than one occasion, I would've done the same: swallow your rage until you find the right moment to aim it. Still, if Arabella asked me to rip off a dungeon door and hand her a sword, I would have complied.

My eyes narrowed when I spotted dark bruises around her wrists. A spark of anger lit in my gut. I reached out and took her hand gently, tilting it to study the discolored flesh.

"What happened?" I managed, my tone low with forced calm.

She hesitated. "It's nothing."

"Arabella," I pressed, voice dropping further, "those are finger marks."

She exhaled, pulling her hand from mine. "They're from the stabilization enchantment yesterday," she admitted. "You had that . . . episode, and you grabbed me. I couldn't get free."

Memory crashed through me. It had felt like some ancient presence erupted from nowhere, ransacking my thoughts. I must have clamped down on her in my desperation.

"I'm sorry," I murmured. The words felt pathetically inadequate. "I didn't realize—"

"It's fine," she said, cutting off my apology. "I know you didn't mean it."

Fine or not, I hated seeing those bruises. They were my fault, accidental or not. I moved to cast a healing spark, but she backed away, out of reach.

"Don't waste your strength," she insisted. She waved a hand in a vague gesture to indicate the sprawl of my summoned shadow warriors patrolling the forest below the citadel. "You've got enough magical burdens right now."

She wasn't entirely wrong. Keeping sixty shadow warriors in existence took a toll, and my runes hadn't settled to normal after Solandris. Still, being told not to bother only sharpened my sense of guilt and mild bitterness at my own limitations.

I cleared my throat. "The citadel's defenses did receive a boost during that stabilization enchantment. The shadows are just an extra measure."

Arabella's look of skepticism felt like a physical jab. "At what cost to you?"

I shrugged, hoping to dismiss it. "I've certainly endured worse." It was the truth, though the ache in my bones could have argued otherwise. My pride would never let me admit that out loud. "Once our entanglement ends, I plan to inspect the garrisons in person."

She angled her head to study me. "You still fight on the front lines yourself?"

I nodded once, short and certain. "I'm not the kind of warlord who hides behind an army."

Arabella's eyes flicked over me, measuring my words. "I guess I knew that."

Overhead, Nyx let out a keening screech that pulled our gazes skyward. She spiraled downward in a graceful corkscrew, wings slashing the air in rhythmic beats. Curls of heat shimmered around her scaled hide when she finally touched down. She folded those massive wings carefully, and Arabella reached out, stroking the dragon's snout.

"She's getting better at landings," Arabella remarked with subdued pride.

Even in my darkest mood, I felt a flicker of pleasure watching Nyx respond to Arabella's gentle hand.

Stepping away from the stable, Arabella turned toward me. She kept one hand on Nyx's muzzle, but her gaze was fixed on my face. "During the Syndicate's visit," she began, "you said something that's been rattling in my head."

I tensed. The Syndicate's visit had exposed more than I'd intended, thanks to Zaraiah's calculated barbs. "Did I?"

"'All's fair in love and war,'" Arabella said. "Tell me what you meant."

I exhaled slowly. "It's a common enough saying."

"You don't do common, Kazimir. You measure every word."

I attempted a smirk. "I've been known to indulge in a bit of poetic flair."

She snorted, clearly unimpressed. Her intensity wrapped around us, urging a raw confession I didn't want to out myself with. My heart hammered in protest. I did the only thing I could think of to break through her tension—close the distance and press my mouth to hers in a fierce, immediate kiss.

For an instant, she stiffened beneath my touch; then her lips softened, melding to mine. My arms slid around her waist, pulling her firmly against me. I felt the pent-up worry, the anger, the uncertain heartbreak, all melt into that kiss. The entire realm could have burned around us for all I cared. I just wanted her warm lips and her body against mine.

When we finally broke apart, Arabella stared at me, chest heaving. Her eyes glowed dangerously, and for one shining heartbeat, everything else disappeared.

Nyx's sudden hiss yanked us back to reality. She craned her long neck toward the main citadel, nostrils flaring.

At the same time, a chill threaded through me. I sensed a shift in Skyspire's wards, the kind that signaled an emergency. An alarm thrummed at the edge of my awareness, and adrenaline flared in my veins.

"What is it?" Arabella asked, noticing the tension in my stance.

I shook my head sharply. "The citadel's defenses just triggered." I grabbed her hand. "We need to get to the Inner Sanctum. Now."

We sprinted to the nearby lightning bridge and were halfway across when the entire structure went dark beneath us. I felt the surge flicker and vanish underfoot, leaving only sky and a jarring sense of weightlessness.

Arabella gasped, and together we plunged. A desperate shout lodged in my throat as I summoned a void portal, ignoring the red-hot pain that tore across my carved runes. Instead of splattering thousands of feet below, we dropped into a swirling darkness and emerged on the Gate Tower's stone floor. Our landing was awkward and jarring, but at least we were alive.

She stumbled into me. "What the hell was that?" she managed.

"Emergency protocol," I snapped, not at her but at the entire fiasco. "The bridges shut down if there's a threat."

No time to explain further—we broke into a run again. Something or someone had triggered a major assault. I yanked on the psychic tether to my shadow warriors, summoning them upward, but they'd need precious seconds to converge inside the citadel.

We skidded around a corner and nearly bowled over a Hero's Guild soldier in shining armor. Shock flashed across his face. Clearly, he hadn't expected me to appear out of nowhere. I reacted faster. A burst of shadows snapped around his throat, and the soldier died before he could cry out.

Arabella's breathing hitched, but she stayed focused. We kept going. Alarm bells rang in my head at the distant clang of steel and the crackle of spells echoing through the citadel's halls. The fortress had been breached. My domain, my stronghold, violated.

We nearly ran straight into Vex. She had a vicious gash on her cheek and dried blood crusting the front of her tunic. She sucked in a breath upon seeing us.

"My lord," she rasped. "Lady Blackrose. At least a hundred from the Hero's Guild. They used the emergency ascension platforms."

I wanted to snarl. We'd installed those platforms so that our people could evacuate in a disaster, never for an enemy to exploit. Only a handful of people knew they existed, and fewer still knew how to activate them. "They're after the Heirloom," I stated coldly. "And Arabella."

"Yes," Vex replied, picking up her pace. "They seem to think they can seize both."

Fury lanced through me. I swore I'd find whoever leaked that information, then string them up. "Where are our people?"

"Thorne's holding the Gate Tower. Griffin's holed up in his workshop—I last saw him heading that way. Sims is . . ." She hesitated, her voice trembling. "He's dead."

A cold ball of anger hardened in my gut. Irritating as Sims was, he belonged to me. And now he was gone because these fools marched in with their self-righteous illusions.

We tore around another bend and slammed into three more knights. The one in front roared, raising a sword. My shadows lashed out. His eyes bulged when I severed his hand. A second knight conjured a golden shield, only to have my darkness swirl behind it and slice through his unprotected flank. He collapsed with a strangled groan.

The third, a robed mage, began chanting to dispel my illusions. She almost succeeded, but I lunged forward and wrapped a hand around her throat, cutting the incantation short. "Who let you in?" I growled.

She spat out a curse. "Go to hell," she rasped.

I tightened my grip until I felt her windpipe give way. She crumpled to the floor, lifeless. Arabella stepped past me without comment, not a shred of revulsion in her expression. I hardly had time to register my own grim satisfaction before we raced ahead. Besides my wife, the Heirloom was the greatest prize in these walls, and that was where the Guild must have been headed.

As we passed the war room, I saw the doors flung wide, half a dozen Guild soldiers ransacking my maps. They spotted us, and one with a commander's insignia beckoned Arabella with an almost triumphant gleam.

"Lady Evenfall! We've come to re—"

"It's Lady Blackrose," she said fiercely. "And I didn't ask for rescue."

That final word dripped with contempt. My temper flared anew. Enough. With a flick of my hands, I unleashed a wave of blackness that blanketed the room in stuttering gloom. Cries of alarm erupted as they stumbled into illusions among swirling shadows.

One knight bore down on me with a flaming sword. I sidestepped, thrusting a conjured blade into his back. Another two harried Vex, but she twirled away with nimble efficiency, twin daggers gleaming. A final knight rushed Arabella, only to be blasted by a bolt of blazing gold magic. He fell, armor smoking.

Their commander tried to call for a retreat, but I appeared behind him before he could rally. He whirled, sword swinging, scraping my swirling darkness. My hand morphed into razor talons, slicing him wide open. His armor parted like paper. He dropped, mouth agape in silent horror.

The silence afterward was punctuated by labored breathing. I gritted my teeth, ignoring the fierce burn in my runes. We had to keep going. We had to secure the Heirloom. Vex turned toward me, probably to await orders, but at that moment a searing pressure exploded behind my eyes.

Something ancient and ravenous twisted in my mind. The same presence I'd felt before, biting into my consciousness with frenzied hunger. My runes erupted in agony, and I let out a raw, choking cry. The world pitched, pain shredding every nerve. I couldn't see, couldn't hold on.

Vaguely, I heard Arabella shouting my name. Then everything receded into darkness.

70

Discover Her Dark Side
(and Admit You Like It)

Arabella

I watched in horror as Kazimir collapsed at my feet, every inch of his body jerking like he'd been struck by a vengeful god. A scream ripped up his throat—an animalistic wail so raw that I wanted to clap my hands over my ears. The runes etched across his skin flared violet-black, pulsing uncontrollably.

"Kazimir!" I dropped to my knees and grabbed for him, desperate to keep his head from cracking against the stone floor.

The instant my palms touched his shoulders an electric jolt tore up my arms—pain so sharp it wrenched a gasp from my lungs. Our entanglement bond locked us together, flooding my nerves with every ounce of his torment. It felt like thousands of scorching needles driving into my bones.

He let out another ragged scream, his eyes rolling back until I saw only white threaded with black veins. Pressure coiled around my skull—his pain or my own or both. I barely knew anymore, and I refused to let go even when instincts screamed at me to pull away. This was Kazimir, the man I couldn't bear to lose. Even if it meant scorching agony for me, I'd hold him.

Behind us, Vex stood by the doorway, daggers dripping fresh blood. "He's been overextending himself for a while," she said, her voice tense. "He never rested when he should have."

I stared down at his contorted face, my heart thudding with fear. How much pain had he hidden? In all the times we'd argued about it these last weeks, I'd never imagined this magnitude of suffering.

"Do something!" I shouted at Vex, fury and desperation boiling over.

"I'm not a healer," she answered softly, "but you are, my lady."

Right. I was a healer. More than that, actually. And the nauseating wave of pain that hammered my mind told me it was magical overflow. With the entanglement tying us together, maybe I could siphon some of his agony.

I gritted my teeth and forced myself to open that bond. A hideous torrent of agony poured in like hot iron flooding my veins. For one nauseating heartbeat, I trembled on the edge of letting go. Then I pressed my knees into the stone and refused.

My hearing dulled as though I was submerged underwater. The entire world shrank to blistering pain in my head and the sight of Kazimir's convulsions finally subsiding. His breathing steadied, ragged gasps slowing to deeper gulps. The runes on his skin dimmed from their fiery glow to a faint flicker.

His eyes fluttered open at last. "Arabella...," he rasped. His voice sounded torn, shredded from the force of his screams.

"Don't talk," I managed in a hoarse murmur. Pain still throbbed through my muscles, but I clung to him, determined to bear it. "Just shut up and let me carry it for a second."

He looked like he wanted to give me one of his usual smirks, but all he managed was a twitch at the corner of his mouth. Slowly, with trembling effort, he pushed himself upright, leaning heavily against my shoulder. My entire body wavered under his weight. Still, I latched onto that pounding energy inside him, drawing away its sharpest edges.

An explosion thundered in the distance, rattling the walls of the citadel. Shouts rang out somewhere beyond the corridor. My stomach twisted in dread. This place was my home now—these were my people being attacked by so-called heroes.

"Kaz," I said urgently, voice raw, "the Heirloom. If they get ahold of it—"

"They won't," he snarled, though he practically collapsed against me. Another violent crash somewhere overhead made dust trickle from the ceiling.

Vex swept her gaze down the corridor, daggers raised. "We have to get there. If the tower collapses, or if they breach the wards . . ."

I couldn't believe we'd left that artifact in a half-ruined tower. "Why didn't we relocate it?"

"Wards," Kazimir muttered, leaning on me. "We built that chamber specifically to shield it. Even if Skyspire falls, that chamber is safest."

A third explosion rocked the hall, and my jaw clenched. "Let's move. I have some heroes I'd like to personally eviscerate."

With Vex leading, I helped Kazimir hobble forward. His arm slung across my shoulders, his weight pressing me down with every step. My senses stayed on high alert, adrenaline forcing me to adapt to the constant burn of his pain. As terrifying as it felt, I didn't want to relinquish contact. Not when I knew how close he was to losing control.

The corridor teemed with bodies—some dead, others dying. Choking coils of magic and the reek of blood kept my pulse hammering. My chest felt too tight.

We'd nearly reached the eastern tower when a dozen Guild assailants rounded the corner. Without a second thought, Vex leapt forward, her daggers glinting.

"Go," she barked. "I'll handle them."

"There are too many," I protested.

"Get the Heirloom," she insisted fiercely. "And kill any bastard who dares to touch it."

I swallowed down the urge to argue. Kazimir pulled me the other way, and I forced my feet to move. Vex's battle cries erupted behind us, followed by shrieks of panic from the Guild members.

Kazimir guided me through a servants' passage hidden behind a ragged tapestry. The cramped tunnel smelled of dust and stale air. He stumbled against the narrow walls, and I felt each footstep echo in our entanglement, a sickening pull that made me lurch too. I concentrated on steadying him, channeling everything I had to ease his suffering.

We emerged into the eastern courtyard overshadowed by the tower. My stomach sank at the sight of three more Guild members waiting, staves raised. They spotted Kazimir's distinctive silhouette, recognized me at his side, and drew themselves up with righteous fervor.

"Dark Lord," a gray-haired woman snarled. "Your reign of terror ends now!"

Kazimir gave a half-deranged laugh. "Fucking heroes," he said hoarsely.

"At least they dressed the part," I muttered, stepping forward despite exhaustion coiled around my limbs. "You can't just barge in and kill people, then pretend you're morally superior."

She glowered at me. "Lady Evenfall, please step aside. We're freeing you—"

"Freeing me from the only person who taught me to harness my power?" Rage sparked through my veins. "Spare me your sanctimonious drivel." I flicked my hand, sending a burst of inverted healing magic that cracked the stone at the woman's feet. She scrambled back.

Kazimir seized that opening. The bond between us pulsed with a careful exchange of energy. His shadows surged outward in a black wave. The old woman hissed, trying to fight him off. Another one lunged for Kazimir's exposed back, but I intercepted, forming a shadow dagger and blocking her staff. Sparks hissed on impact. She aimed a bolt of light at Kazimir just as I shoved my dagger aside and slammed my hand to her throat.

No illusions this time. I let my lethal magic flow. She stiffened, eyes wide, then dropped. My stomach lurched at how easy it was. Another corner of me exulted in the power, a savage satisfaction that I'd survived.

Kazimir dispatched two more assailants with brutal speed. The last woman attempted a final staff assault, but Kazimir's shadow spear tore through her with a wet, sickening sound. Her strangled cry echoed, then died. The courtyard fell quiet except for our gasping breaths. Kazimir nearly sagged to the ground, but I caught him.

He gave a ragged, delirious grin. "You are so fucking sexy right now."

My heart squeezed. "Focus, you bastard. The tower." If I let myself dwell on the rush of his compliment, I might fall apart.

We kept moving, ignoring the renewed chaos rising behind us. The double doors to the eastern tower still stood, though a new wave of Guild forces thundered somewhere close. Kazimir pushed me forward, his eyes flaring with feverish determination.

"Go," he growled. "Get the Heirloom. If they seize it—"

"No," I whispered, tightening my arm around his waist. It felt wrong to leave him here like a cornered beast.

"Now, Arabella," he ordered, voice cracking. As if to punctuate his point, three knight-mages charged into the courtyard, swords and spells gleaming.

I hated every second of it, but I knew Kazimir was right. If they got the Heirloom, he was dead anyway. Gritting my teeth, I grabbed his collar and crushed my mouth to his in a single savage kiss.

"Don't you dare die," I breathed against his lips. My entire body trembled.

He let out a harsh exhale that might have been relief or desire. Then I tore away, burst through the tower doors, and slammed them shut. The lock caught with a hollow clank. Even with the wards, it wouldn't hold for long.

Inside, the spiral staircase was half collapsed. I'd been up here before with Kazimir's help, but now I had to do it alone. My head whirled, my muscles screamed for relief, and the aftershock of his torment still echoed in my blood. I dragged myself upward.

Where the steps had fallen away, I conjured shaky platforms of shadow to vault the gaps. Thank the gods Kazimir had forced me to practice. Every time I wavered or stumbled, I pictured his face contorted in pain. I swore I wouldn't let him die defending a useless chunk of relic if I could save it.

It felt like hours, but in truth, it was only moments before I burst into the tall chamber at the top. The Heirloom's amber glow pulsed erratically, as though in distress. The walls quivered under repeated assaults below, cracks creeping along the stones.

I clutched my ribs, trying to calm the thundering of my heart. My eyes flicked across the room. If I failed, if the Guild destroyed the Heirloom or twisted it to their own ends, Kazimir wouldn't survive. I couldn't lose him. Not now that I'd finally admitted how deeply I needed him.

My legs nearly gave out, but I forced them to stay upright. There was only one choice left to save us both.

And I would make it.

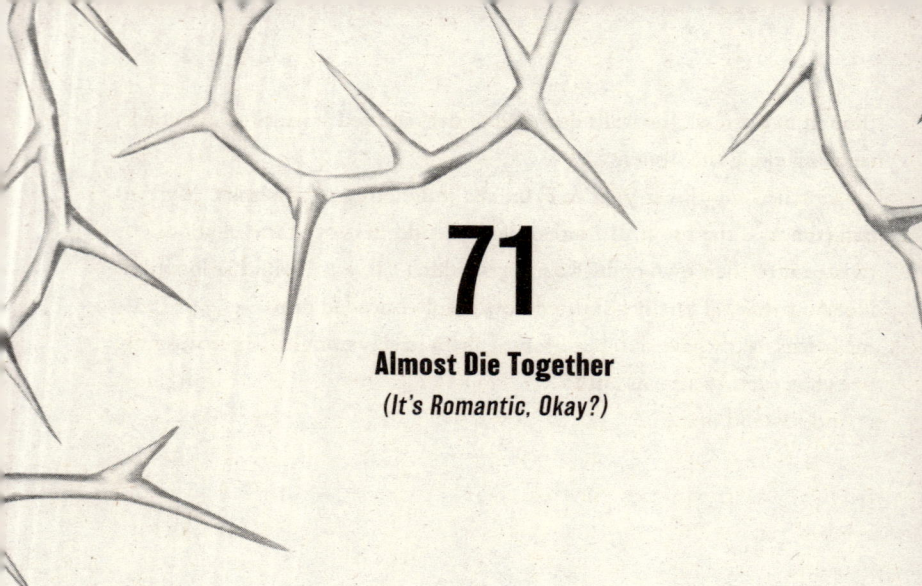

71

Almost Die Together
(It's Romantic, Okay?)

Arabella

I'd planned for this moment ever since I first laid eyes on that damned ritual. Even after Kazimir swore he wouldn't risk it, the Lifeweave's instructions kept haunting me. While he busied himself with war councils and clandestine experiments, I pored over every page of that ancient text, memorizing the runes in the small pauses between our near disasters. I even practiced my precision and control in secret, determined to master this . . . just in case.

Now, the Heirloom of Dominion's amber glow fluttered like a failing heartbeat. The crack along its side had spread since the last time I'd seen it, and strands of oily black magic seeped from the fissure as though the artifact itself were bleeding.

Kazimir's pain pounded through our magical entanglement—he was somewhere below, his body near collapse as the so-called heroes unloaded bright, righteous fury on him. Every pulse of his agony lanced across my nerves, but I forced myself to swallow my fear.

"I'm not letting you die for this," I whispered, though my words felt directed as much at myself as at him.

On the other side of the tower walls, steel clashed and spells crackled, merging into a thunderous roar. Another tremor rocked the building. Dust hung in the air, shaken off the stones. My heart lurched at the surge of fresh pain from the bond—he was suffering badly.

I tore my gaze from the chaotic swirl of magic long enough to grab an uncorked inkwell from what remained of Griffin's worktable. My hands trembled as I crouched by the Heirloom's pedestal, drawing wide circles of runes that curled around the base: symbols for life force, for binding, for sacrifice. Each line came back to me as if I'd known them all my life.

Seven runes ringed the pedestal in neat arcs. The eighth, largest of all, stretched directly beneath the Heirloom, forcing me to contort awkwardly so I didn't accidentally brush the artifact itself. Ink smeared across my fingers and stained my training leathers.

Below, I heard a roar that shook the stones. Another quake almost knocked me flat. Kazimir's fresh agony ripped through the bond, blade-sharp, and I felt my vision tilt dangerously. I bit down on a whimper and steadied my nerves.

No time left.

Pressing both palms to the runes, I began reciting ancient syllables. My voice wavered, but the words flowed from memory. A hush settled around the pedestal, followed by a golden glow that crawled along every swirling line until the entire sequence blazed with brilliant light.

Relief and fear tangled in my chest. My magic recognized these sigils; my heroic blood answered. The Heirloom's amber aura flickered, out of sync with the golden circle, but I pushed forward, chanting each phrase until my throat felt raw.

On the final word, I slammed my hands onto the runic ring. Power flooded me, a torrent of raw magic scorching every nerve. I gasped, my back arching in pain as a thread of golden light burst from my chest to the crown, tying us in a single, searing cord.

That connection made the Heirloom feel alive in my mind: ancient, battered, and carved hollow by the crack it bore. Through that glowing bond,

I sensed the artifact's wounded state, the edges of the fissure pulsing like an open gash. The entire tower groaned, as if objecting to my interference.

I kept going, channeling my life force through the link. The text had warned this ritual would demand sacrifice. I'd prayed it wouldn't kill me, but there hadn't been an option to stop once it began. My strength rushed out in waves, siphoned by the Heirloom.

How much does it need? My vision blurred. It felt endless.

Kazimir's panic flared through our bond. He realized what I was doing. I sensed the dark swirl of his dominion magic as he fed his strength into me, even though he might be bleeding out down there.

Tears swam in my eyes. "Idiot," I whispered through a throat gone tight. "Glorious, stubborn idiot."

I let his dominion power weave with my heroic magic, funneling both into that bright cord of light. The Heirloom's amber aura blazed in unison, surging so intensely it almost drowned the entire runic circle in brilliance. Where the fracture cut the metal, I watched the edges begin to fuse, stitching themselves back together.

Below, the roar grew deafening. The tower rocked on its foundations, beams splintering and stones scraping into fresh rubble. I felt Kazimir's magic flicker; he was weak. I clung to what remained of my control and hurled the entirety of my life force at the artifact. A final burst of light exploded between the Heirloom and me, wringing out my soul like a soaked rag. Then—suddenly—the fracture fused, leaving only unmarred metal in its place.

The Heirloom shone, steady at last . . . but I couldn't savor the victory. I pitched forward, my forehead smacking softly against the pedestal. Kazimir's relief washed over me, followed immediately by fresh fear as yet another violent blast rocked the tower's lower floors, shuddering upward.

I tried to stand, but my legs refused to unbend. My mind felt hazy, my strength nearly gone. And it was too late anyway. The tower was caving in. I flung my arms out in a desperate attempt to find something to keep me from sliding into the yawning void. The floor tilted. Stone, mortar, and centuries of architecture gave a final, tortured groan.

I had one clear heartbeat in which I understood there'd be nothing to save me. The tower was crashing to oblivion, and I was trapped. I reached out and snatched the newly healed Heirloom, holding it tight against my chest.

The floor dropped from beneath me. A ragged scream caught in my lungs. Through the bond came Kazimir's unfiltered terror, echoing my own. My world whirled in a storm of dust, golden glare, and collapsing stones. The entanglement between Kazimir and me stretched impossibly thin. But it didn't break.

I had no strength left to spare. The only thought scratching through my panicked brain was to use the Heirloom. It was the last shred of protection I had.

Clutching it in my trembling fingers, I shoved the gleaming crown onto my head as the tower's remains swallowed me in a crush of thunder and stone.

Then I fell into the dark.

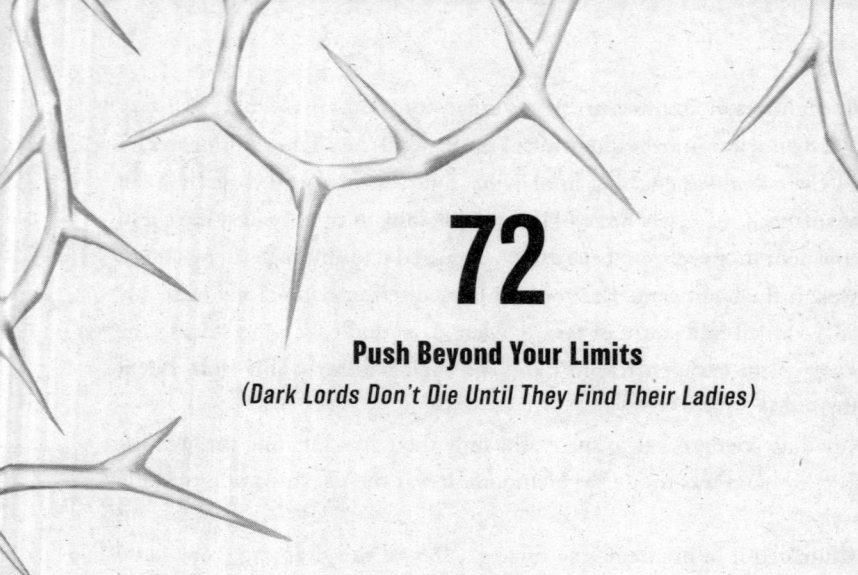

72

Push Beyond Your Limits
(Dark Lords Don't Die Until They Find Their Ladies)

Kazimir

I rammed my dagger through the idiot hero's throat. His eyes went wide, shocked in that timeless, righteous way that heroes often died, like they never saw it coming. But I barely registered the kill.

My focus hung by a thread, pulled in a thousand directions. Every corner of the courtyard bristled with chaos, and magic pounded through the entanglement that bound me to Arabella. She was attempting the Lifeweave ritual—of course she was. Beneath my own frantic terror, her will thundered through our link, fueling me even as it threatened to crush me.

I yanked the blade free. The Guild warrior's corpse slumped onto the stone with a harsh gargle. My bones throbbed in time with the raw surge of power I felt from Arabella. She was channeling her own life force into that damned Heirloom, and somehow still bolstering me through our connection. I hated imagining the toll it demanded from her.

A second Guild fool lunged. I hissed a command, and my shadow warriors tore him apart before I could blink. Usually, I took a degree of satisfaction in watching them feed on my enemies, but I barely registered the blood splatter. Instead, I reeled as each new wave of Arabella's desperation tore along my insides, twisting my runes in pure agony.

The citadel shuddered hard enough to rattle my teeth. I stumbled backward, dragging my gaze toward the eastern tower. I needed to reach her—to stop her or help her or do anything but stand there. Another quake fractured the stone. I managed two steps before Thorne grabbed my arm.

"My lord! The tower's failing!"

I shoved him aside with a vicious elbow. "She's in there!" Panic seared every nerve. I slammed a wave of force that sent Thorne reeling and bolted forward. Then the archway ahead cracked wide, revealing the endless drop below Skyspire. I almost pitched into it. Thorne yanked me back just as the tower coughed out one final, violent groan and caved in on itself, collapsing floor by floor.

Rage, cold and lethal, rose in my chest. I glared at Thorne, my breath catching in ragged spurts. "What have you done?"

His face was grim under trails of blood. "If she's still alive, my lord, the entanglement would tell you . . . yes?"

He was right. I still felt that bond through a haze of unreal pain, but still there. If she had vanished entirely, I would've known. So she had to be breathing. She had to.

Dust coated everything, hung in the air. The tower was gone, reduced to a jagged crater. I refused to believe she lay buried beneath it.

Thorne coughed. "The Guild forces are scattering. We need orders."

Orders. Right. I forced myself to think like a warlord again, though my chest felt strangled. "Take prisoners—throw them in the dungeon. Everyone else looks for Lady Blackrose. Tear the fortress apart if you have to."

He nodded sharply and ran off, shouting commands. I stumbled ahead, ignoring the throbbing in my side. Collapsed corridors, twisted iron, and dripping carnage surrounded me. My shadow warriors flickered at the edges of my vision, failing as I weakened.

Griffin stood near a heap of rubble, half his face burned. When he spotted me, he lurched forward, leaning on a shattered pillar. "They used some artifact to blind our wards," he said. "I managed to cripple one of their mages, but—"

"Worry about it later," I snapped, forcing each step. "Have you seen Arabella at all?"

He shook his head apologetically. "None. Maybe the Observatory?"

"Then come with me."

We slogged through more rubble and thick layers of dust. The Observatory dome had cracked like an eggshell, and the crystals powering the lightning bridges flickered. Unconscious on the floor lay Sir Darian Lightbringer, his beloved righteousness failing him when he tried to manipulate the wards.

A harsh laugh broke from my lips. "Alive. Unfortunate for him." I bound him in swirling shadows. "I'll let my wife decide his fate."

My ribs ached with every breath. She had gone and done something insane, and I should've protected her from that choice. Now I felt her presence skitter through me. It kept me upright, but barely. I swallowed back a curse, ignoring the lines of wounded soldiers stumbling through the broken halls. Reports hammered me from all sides: no sign of Arabella here, there, anywhere. Portions of the fortress had collapsed into inaccessible pockets of ruin. The panic building inside me threatened to ignite.

Vex found me next. She was bruised and winded, but alive. Her eyes darted around as if she hoped to see Arabella at my side. "Skyspire's mostly secured. We've captured or killed all the Guild members we found. No sign of her anywhere." Her voice wavered just enough for me to notice. "What about the Heirloom?"

I gave a ragged laugh. "Possibly healed, possibly destroyed, I have no idea." My chest heaved. "I can feel her, though."

Vex fell silent, her gaze set on me with an unsettling blend of sympathy and dread. Trying not to tear her apart out of pure frustration, I stared past the Observatory window. Through the gloom, I glimpsed Nyx's dark shape slicing through the clouds, headed for a far-flung shard of floating rock—one that hovered beyond the usual bridges, when they were functional.

"Griffin," I barked, gesturing to the flickering crystal console, "make me a bridge. She's going after Arabella."

He winced. "It's wrecked, my lord. I'd need hours."

"Then I'll open a portal." Easy enough, if I wanted to risk blowing out every last rune carved into me. I ignored the fresh wave of dizziness.

Vex stepped in front of me, arms spread. "You'll kill yourself," she warned. "What do I tell her if you end up dead after trying for heroics?"

A scornful chuckle ripped from my throat as I lifted my hands for the spell. I needed anger to keep going. "Tell her I was worried about the Heirloom," I growled. "She might find that funny."

Forcing each sign and utterance into place, I tasted blood as I breathed through the sharp ache in my lungs. The portal crackled in front of me, a savage swirl of violet and black spatters that stung my palms. My knees buckled, and I heard Vex call my name in alarm.

I hurled myself through anyway. Pain raked across every nerve as that desperate, single-minded need exploded in my chest. *Arabella, stay alive. I'm coming.*

73

Claim Each Other Properly
(No Artifacts Were Harmed)

Arabella

The frigid wind didn't give a damn about my custom training leathers, even if they were magically reinforced. It ripped across the desolate chunk of rock masquerading as an island, finding every tear and thin spot in my gear. Still, I mentally thanked Kazimir for commissioning these leathers; they had saved me from being crushed before I put the Heirloom on my head.

I huddled near the base of a gnarled, lifeless-looking tree, knees pulled tight to my chest. My head throbbed with a dull ache, and the Heirloom felt different—no longer the cold, demanding artifact it once was, but humming with a quiet, steady current of life that resonated in my bones. Taking it off felt . . . wrong.

Despite that low glow of magic, I was bone-deep exhausted. When I tried coaxing some warmth out of my power, a pathetic flicker of flame sputtered in my cupped palms before dying. I had nothing left to give.

Through the bond, I sensed Kazimir like a distant echo. He was alive, but I couldn't tell if he was angry, wounded, or both. Facing his wrath after completing the ritual alone wasn't high on my list of desired activities.

A sharp screech tore through the howling wind. My heart lurched, and I struggled to stand, every muscle protesting. There, against the deepening twilight, I saw Nyx's familiar silhouette, her dark wings spread wide as she circled overhead.

Relief hit me so hard I nearly collapsed back onto the rocky ground. Nyx landed in a crouch of thudding claws and nudged my hand, offering a hopeful puff of warm breath. Then her head snapped up, ears flattening as a low rumble vibrated in her chest.

Behind me, the air cracked open.

A portal flared, hissing violet sparks, and Kazimir stepped through. The instant his boots hit stone, that constant knot of emptiness lifted. Relief flooded me so intensely I had to drag in a breath just to keep my balance. Bloody cuts streaked his face, and the set of his jaw looked etched by pure exhaustion. He clutched one side as though it might come loose if he let go.

He looked wrecked. Terrible. And devastatingly beautiful.

"Arabella," he rasped, voice rough with fatigue and something painfully raw.

"Took you long enough," I managed. My usual snark wavered on cracked vocal cords.

The corner of his mouth slid into a faint twitch. "Traffic was hell. Too many idiot knights redecorating my corridors with their entrails."

Then we collided. Maybe I moved first, maybe he did. His arms locked around me in a grip that felt less like possession and more like frantic relief, and I clung back like I needed his heartbeat to stay upright. Ours pounded together in a tangled, desperate rhythm.

"You're freezing," he murmured against my hair.

"And you're bleeding," I shot back, glaring at the gash above his brow. I braced for a lecture about me performing the ritual alone. But his storm gray eyes just devoured me with undisguised relief, no anger at all.

I swallowed my own flood of emotions, pressing a trembling palm to his wound. "Hold still." The trickle of magic I offered knitted the skin just enough to stop the bleeding. He inhaled sharply, gratitude flickering along our bond.

"Don't waste your strength," he muttered, his hand slipping to the back of my neck. His fingers shook as they tangled in my hair.

"It was never a waste." Lifting my gaze, I whispered, "You came."

A storm of feeling flickered over his face. "When the tower fell . . . I could barely sense you." He swallowed, and the memory seemed to gouge into him. "I was . . . concerned."

That small, raw confession shattered my remaining defenses. "I worried about you too," I said softly.

We fell silent for a moment, overshadowed by everything undone—the fortress in rubble, the battle we'd survived, the risks we both took.

"Skyspire?" I finally managed.

His jaw clenched. "Mostly standing." The ruthless edge in his voice suggested everything else had been handled with typical Kazimir viciousness. "The Guild survivors are contemplating their life choices in the dungeons. Lightbringer sends his regards."

A cold ripple of satisfaction ran through me. "Good."

Nyx pressed her nose against my shoulder, apparently bored of our emotional display. Kazimir's arm tightened protectively around my waist as I swayed, exhaustion hitting me again.

"She led me here," he said, nodding at Nyx.

I stroked the dragon's snout. "Good girl." Nyx responded with a faint, brimstone-scented huff.

Kazimir watched her warily, weariness etched into every line of his face. "You could've gone with them," he said quietly. "Played the damsel."

At the thought of going back to Solandris—isolated, caged—I felt a surge of nausea. Holding Kazimir's gaze, I said, "I'd rather wrestle a kraken naked than live that life again."

His grip on my hip tightened by a fraction. "So you choose Lady Blackrose?" The question landed like a challenge . . . and an invitation. He needed to hear me say it, I realized.

The name settled on me with a fierce sense of belonging. "I'm still figuring out the job description," I admitted, "but yes. I choose this."

Another violent gust of wind slammed into us, and I shivered. Wordlessly, Kazimir shrugged off his tattered coat and draped it over my shoulders. It smelled of him—of steel and shadow magic and old blood. I burrowed into it.

He scanned the barren landscape. "I don't have enough left in me to form a stable portal. We're stuck here until sunrise."

I nodded, my entire body sagging under fresh waves of fatigue. We moved to the twisted tree, where I all but collapsed against the rough bark. He settled beside me, our shoulders brushing. Nyx stretched out her wing to give us a cruce windbreak. Her proximity gave us the warmth of a fire, and I sighed in relief.

The short silence was filled by howling gusts and the occasional snort from Nyx. Distant stars cut through the darkness, cold and uncaring.

"I kept fighting it," I said after a moment, my voice barely carrying over the wind. "This . . . whatever it is between us."

He stilled beside me. I swallowed and continued, "Not because I didn't want it. Gods . . . *Want* doesn't cover it. I was terrified of losing myself in you—of not knowing who I'd be if I wasn't fighting you all the time."

For a few heartbeats, he said nothing. Then he spoke in a low voice, "I understand that fear."

I turned toward his silhouette, the sharp angles of his face outlined by dim starlight. "Do you?"

He nodded. "I was taught that power demands isolation, that attachment becomes a liability." A hint of bitterness threaded his tone.

My chest ached at the thought of what horrors shaped him this way. I took his hand and laced our fingers together, noticing how cold his skin felt. "They were wrong."

He looked at me with a flicker of fragile hope.

I cleared my throat, trying not to drown in those mesmerizing eyes. "I used to think vulnerability was weakness, that caring meant handing someone a blade to stab you in the back. But after everything . . . fighting you, fighting for you, and with you . . . I don't feel weaker, Kazimir. I feel . . ." The word got caught in my throat. "More."

He searched my eyes. "As do I," he whispered unsteadily. "And that scares me more than facing an entire army of self-righteous knights."

A small smile tugged at my lips. "The infamous Dark Lord Kazimir Blackrose, cowering before emotions?"

He let out a brief laugh. "Gods forbid Vex catches wind of it."

"She'd hold a betting pool with Griffin and then lecture you on emotional availability," I said drily.

His hand lifted to my jaw, tipping my head to meet his gaze. The simple contact sent fire racing through my veins. "Perhaps," he said softly, brushing his thumb against my lip, "I'm only available to you."

Heat kindled low in my belly. "Is that so?" I asked, my voice lowering in challenge.

He leaned in, intruding on the last of my personal space. "It is."

When his lips finally met mine, the kiss started with a gentle, searching hush . . . then flared into something deeper. Relief—sheer, staggering relief—flooded me. I flung my arms around his neck, the Heirloom pressing against my forehead as I lost myself in him.

He groaned into my mouth, pulling me closer until I landed on his lap, straddling him. My muscles protested the movement, but my body refused to care. Over the wind, I heard him murmur my name, raw and needy.

I rocked my hips experimentally, feeling the unmistakable hardness between us. He hissed through his teeth, grip tightening on my waist. Our kiss went wild—urgent, fierce, tasting of blood and exhaustion and longing.

"I've imagined this every night," he panted between kisses. "Since the damned library—"

"Stranded out here," I teased, "freezing our butts off with Nyx watching like a scandalized chaperone?"

Kazimir's teeth flashed in a grin, his breath ragged. "Especially the chaperone."

A snorting huff from Nyx suggested her displeasure. I was about to laugh, but Kazimir's thumb traced the underside of my breast, and I forgot how to breathe.

"Tell me," he demanded, voice thick with hunger. "What do you want?"

"Everything," I confessed. "You. All of you."

His eyes blazed. "As my lady commands."

He eased me onto his ragged coat, covering my body with his. He kissed the line of my jaw, moving down my throat, teeth grazing where my pulse hammered. A moan tore out of me as I dug my fingers into his shoulders.

"Too many clothes," I mumbled, fumbling with half-frozen laces. My fingers trembled so badly that I cursed under my breath.

He chuckled darkly. "Impatient, aren't we?"

"You started it."

His grin looked positively wicked. "Then I'll finish it." In one swift motion, he tore away the remains of his shirt and tossed it aside. Moonlight etched the runes and old scars that mapped his torso. Fresh bruises peppered his flesh, and my anger flared at whoever inflicted them. I reached out and traced a jagged rune near his heart. It flickered beneath my touch.

His breath hitched. He did the same for me—helping rid me of the last tattered scraps of cloth until I was bare to the cold night air. But his gaze was so hot it practically seared my skin.

"Touch me," I breathed

He did more than touch. His hands followed the curve of my waist, the shape of my breasts, setting every nerve ablaze. I arched off the coat with a needy cry. He pressed his mouth to my breast, swirling his tongue until I moaned, half delirious. His other hand slipped lower, dragging a ragged gasp out of me as he found the damp heat between my thighs.

"Kaz," I begged, thighs quivering against his wrist.

His eyes swept up, intense and dark. "Tell me again, Arabella. What do you want?"

A half sob, half laugh tore through me. "You. Inside me . . . now."

He gave a wicked smile. "Demanding. I like that."

He shifted over me, kissing me hard while I fumbled with his trousers until he helped me wrestle them off. Finally, my hand closed around his erection, hard and hot and thick. He made a low, guttural sound, bracing himself.

When he entered me, I felt the world tilt. The stretch burned sweetly as he filled me. My breath caught, tears stinging my eyes at the sheer intensity.

He bowed his head, teeth clenched. "Gods, you feel—"

"Move," I commanded, legs locked around his waist.

He did, setting a rhythm that shattered all sense of time and place. Our moans echoed off the stones, half lost to the howling wind. Tiny sparks of magic danced over our skin, combining in golden light twisted with shadow, weaving us tighter. My heart pounded so hard I felt it in my throat. I had no magic left to give, but the Heirloom seemed to pulse with it. Like it was returning a measure of power.

I saw the surprise flicker in his eyes, mirroring my own.

"Don't fight it," I managed, grabbing his forearms when his eyes widened in alarm at the sudden surge of energy. "Let it happen . . . with me."

He gave a frantic nod. Our magic meshed in that moment, that swirl of golden and dark. It poured into each thrust as the tension coiled in my core, building far too fast. My nails raked his back, and I urged him on.

"Arabella," he groaned, edges of his control shredding. His thrusts became deeper, faster, rougher. "Come with me?"

"Yes," I gasped, the final coil tightening in my belly. *"Now!"*

The climax slammed into me. I shouted his name, my body racked by wave after wave, my vision sparking white. He tensed with a ragged moan that tore from his chest, surrendering to his own release. The magic flared around us in a bright arc, then fizzled into the quiet dark.

He stayed there, breathing raggedly against my neck, our bodies still joined. Finally, he rolled onto his side, pulling me tight against him. Shaking fingers brushed the hair from my face. The Heirloom pulsed gently on my head, content for once.

His voice was low and hoarse. "I never wanted attachments. But . . . losing you?" He swallowed hard. "I'd be even more lost without you."

Tears burned behind my eyelids. "Kaz . . ." I pressed my forehead to his, sharing breath in the quiet. In his expression, I saw too many emotions to name but also a spark of mischief that made my heart pound all over again.

He kissed me then, slowly, with impossible tenderness. I kissed him back, letting go of the fear, of the fight, of everything but him. Falling still felt terrifying. But maybe falling together wasn't falling at all. Maybe it was finally finding solid ground.

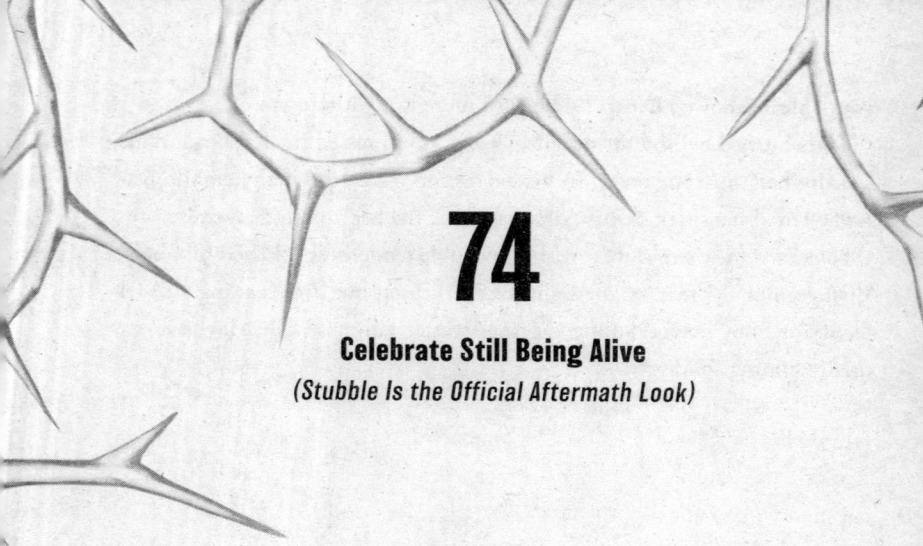

74

Celebrate Still Being Alive
(Stubble Is the Official Aftermath Look)

Arabella

Something dark and weightless feathered across my skin. A brush of shadow against my collarbone that was somehow both possessive and playful. It lingered, tracing a path up my neck, leaving goose bumps in its wake. The touch hummed with a low thrum of power, intimately familiar.

I smiled, eyes still closed. "Kaz."

The shadow retreated, then returned, deliberately slow, tracing my jawline. Teasing.

I forced my eyes open, blinking against the dim light filtering through heavy curtains. Kazimir sat perched on the edge of the bed, watching me with unnerving intensity. Shirtless. The intricate runes etched across his chest and arms stood out starkly against pale skin. His black hair was a glorious wreck, and a few days' worth of stubble darkened his jaw. It wasn't just scruff; it was feral. Dangerously, stupidly hot.

"How long was I out?" My throat felt like I'd swallowed half the rubble from the tower collapse.

"Three days." His voice was rough from disuse. Relief warred with some other, darker undercurrent in his tone. It screamed *mine* and *finally* all at once. "We slept through most of it."

"Three days," I echoed, pushing myself up on shaky elbows. My body screamed profanities at me. Between the bruises, strained muscles, and the dull ache of magic clawing its way back from empty, I felt more rested than I should. And the agony had dulled to a persistent throb, at least. "Unconscious?"

He gave a shrug, his gaze never leaving mine. "Mostly. You surfaced yesterday. Drank some water. Immediately passed out again." A ghost of a smile crossed his face. Clearly, my brief moment of consciousness hadn't been particularly impressive. "Don't remember?"

I shook my head, searching the foggy aftermath of the ritual and the fall. I remembered Kazimir finding me and our sex under the stars, but everything after we left the barren rock isle was just a blur. We must have collapsed the second we arrived.

"You?" I asked, forcing my gaze away from the distracting landscape of his torso to the faint pink line healing across his brow. The worst of his injuries seemed repaired, leaving only faint reminders. That thick stubble, though . . . that was new. And unfairly appealing.

"Better. Surprisingly." He flexed his fingers, a subtle test. Shadows coiled around them, looking less like frayed threads and more like waiting vipers. "My magic replenished faster than expected. Yours feels . . . less obliterated."

I focused inward, probing the space where my power resided. Relief fluttered, sharp and bright. It wasn't full, not by a long shot, but the terrifying emptiness was gone. The well wasn't dry anymore.

Then the cold dread washed back. "The others? Vex? Griffin? Thorne?"

His expression tightened, a flicker of something that might pass for empathy in a normal person. In Kazimir, it was controlled acknowledgment. "Alive. Recuperating. Griffin is cataloging structural damage and noting detailed complaints about ancient masonry."

I exhaled shakily. But the worst question still hung in the air. "And Sims?"

Kazimir's gaze hardened. "His death was quick, but he took his attacker down with him." A beat of silence. "We'll honor him appropriately. No sentimental bullshit. Just . . . respect."

An ache tightened under my ribs. Sims. His cynical pragmatism, his unwavering loyalty to this impossible man. Gone. The loss felt sharp and unexpectedly deep. I hadn't known him long, but he was part of this chaotic fortress, part of Kazimir's strange inner circle that he called advisors. I took a breath, pushing the grief down until I could process it appropriately.

Kazimir's hand settled on my hip, warm and possessive through the thin fabric. I glanced down and realized I was wearing one of his ridiculously soft, large shirts. Nothing else. Heat prickled my cheeks.

"Feels like we were gone for years," I murmured, instinctively leaning into his warmth, chasing away the lingering chill of loss and near death. "Even if we were just comatose side by side."

His eyes darkened, the ever-present hunger resurfacing with startling speed. "I've been awake a few hours," he said, his voice dropping lower. "Tried to occupy myself because I found waiting . . . distasteful."

Ah. That predatory stillness hadn't just been relief. He'd been *waiting*. My stomach did a nervous little flip-flop. "I'm awake now." I let my gaze linger on his mouth, then travel slowly down his chest. "What did you have in mind, Lord Blackrose?"

His answering smile was pure, uncut wickedness. Hungry. Promising. "Why tell you," he murmured, leaning closer, invading my space, his scent of storm and steel filling my senses, "when I can show you?"

Later—how much later, I couldn't say—I lay sprawled across the sweat-dampened sheets, boneless and buzzing. Every inch of me hummed with a sated, languid energy. Kazimir was beside me, his chest rising and falling in a matching rhythm. My body felt thoroughly, gloriously wrecked. Used. Claimed. The thought sent a fresh wave of heat through me. Staying here, tangled up with him, drifting back to sleep, was dangerously tempting.

I stretched, a groan escaping me as my muscles protested. I was deliciously sore. Everywhere. "Bath," I managed. "Definitely need a bath."

Kazimir rolled onto his side, propping himself up on an elbow. The sheet slid lower, revealing more of that unfairly perfect, rune-scarred torso. "Can't walk, hero? I can carry you."

I pulled a face, though honestly, my legs felt about as useful as overcooked noodles. "Your ego hardly needs any encouragement."

His smirk widened into a wolfish grin. He stood, gloriously naked and utterly unashamed, scooped me effortlessly into his arms, and strode toward the bathing chamber. A startled laugh escaped me. I instinctively wrapped my arms around his neck, pressing my cheek against the warm skin of his shoulder. Ridiculous. Being carted around like a spoil of war by a terrifying Dark Lord shouldn't feel this . . . comfortable. Safe, even. Gods, I was ruined.

He deposited me gently onto a bench near the enormous marble tub that could probably host a small naval battle. He fiddled with ornate taps, pouring in oils that released a heady scent of spice and something dark and floral. The steam swirled around him, obscuring him like his own shadows.

I couldn't help it. I grinned.

"Care to share?" he asked, turning back toward me, one eyebrow raised.

My grin widened. "Just enjoying the domestic image. The Scourge of Azroth, fussing over bath salts."

He flicked a spray of water droplets at my face. I shrieked, half laughing, as he reached for me again. "Don't you *dare* drop me!"

He pulled me flush against his chest, his grip firm. "I just went to all that trouble with the bath salts. It'd be a shame to waste them by splashing all the water out."

I clung to his neck anyway, preparing to be dunked. But instead of tossing me in, he lowered me carefully into the steaming water. A long, contented sigh escaped me as the heat seeped into my aching muscles, melting the tension. Bliss. He slid in behind me a moment later, his body fitting against mine like we were carved from the same stone. His legs bracketed mine, his chest a solid wall at my back. Pure, decadent comfort.

We soaked in silence for a while, the only sounds the lapping water and our quiet breathing. His arms rested loosely around my waist, his stubbled chin settling on my shoulder. It was almost normal. Which, for us, was wildly abnormal.

He finally broke the quiet, his lips brushing my ear. "I'm proud of you."

I turned my head, blinking. "Proud?" That wasn't a word I associated with Kazimir. Possessive, yes. Impressed, occasionally. Proud?

"You fought," he stated simply, his eyes holding a rare, unguarded intensity. "Like a cornered shadowcat. And the Lifeweave . . ." His grip tightened fractionally. "Reckless. Godsdamned, suicidally reckless." A beat. "But you did it. You survived harnessing that kind of power. Alone." He shook his head, a flicker of awe warring with the lingering disapproval. "It's staggering."

Heat flooded my cheeks. Annoyingly, a part of me preened under his assessment. "I—" I floundered, sinking lower in the water. "It all happened so fast," I admitted quietly. "I didn't exactly have time for a risk assessment."

I felt the rise and fall of his chest behind me. "I know," he said, the words rough. "And I'm . . . relieved you're still here to assess anything at all."

My heart gave a painful squeeze. That kind of vulnerability from him was rarer than a snowstorm in the desert.

He reached for a soap and sponge and began lathering up my back. "Did you study the ritual on your own?"

"Yes." I quickly told him how I'd been memorizing everything in secret, even as he was pushing me toward learning the control that I so desperately needed. "In the end, I wasn't alone, though," I said as he ran the sponge over my chest. I turned for better access, but also so I could lock eyes with him. "Without your magic helping me, I wouldn't have been able to complete it."

I placed my hand over his heart, fingers splayed. "You could have died."

"Unlikely," he murmured. "I had unfinished business."

With a smile, I took the soap and sponge from him and began massaging his chest and abdomen. "Skyspire?" I prompted, needing to focus on something other than the way he looked at me.

"A mess," he confirmed, his voice regaining its sharp edge. "The eastern tower is gone, of course. Collateral damage in the adjacent corridors." He paused. "But the citadel holds. Mostly."

"And the Guild?"

Shadows flickered at the edge of my vision, Kazimir's power stirring with his anger. "Thorne is handling the interrogations. He took Sims's death . . . personally."

I swallowed hard. Kazimir placed his hand over mine, to stop it from moving lower.

"There was a spy," he continued, his tone hardening. "Feeding them information."

My stomach plummeted. "Who?"

"Unconfirmed. But Pip vanished during the attack, with no trace."

"Pip?" The image of the nervous, earnest young servant flashed in my mind. The one who'd seemed genuinely terrified of Kazimir but still tried to be kind. "You think *he* betrayed us?" It felt wrong. Impossible.

Kazimir's hand tightened around mine before he released it. "I don't know yet."

Worry warred with a sudden, icy suspicion. "I can't believe—"

He cut me off with a low exhale. "We'll find out. For now, the Heirloom is secure. Hidden here, in our private tower. Warded to hell and back. Only you and I will know its location." His voice dropped, possessive and absolute. "I'm not taking chances until I know who to trust."

"Always the strategist," I teased, trailing wet fingertips over the runes on his chest. "Even midbath?"

"Strategy has served me well," he murmured, a flicker of that danger returning. "It led me to you, didn't it?"

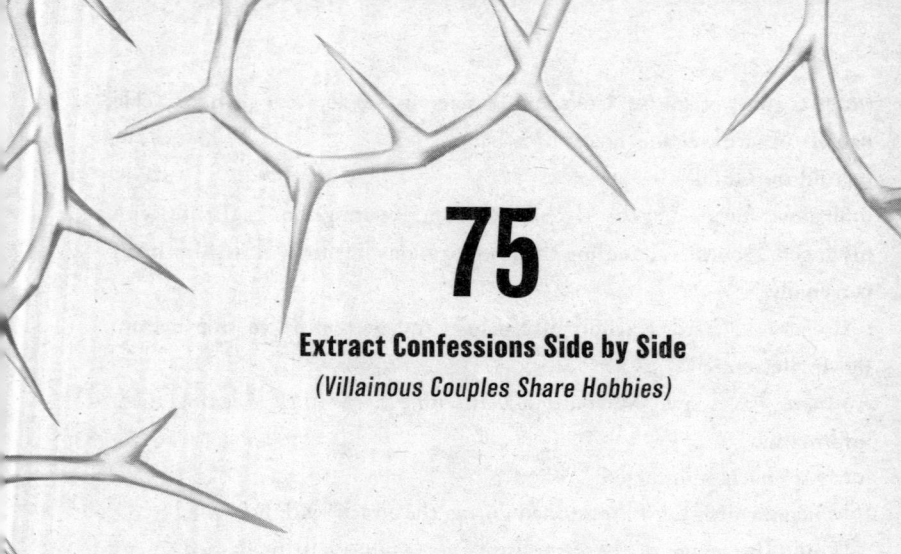

75

Extract Confessions Side by Side
(Villainous Couples Share Hobbies)

Kazimir

I was still grappling with the phantom heat of Arabella's skin against mine, which reality was doing its damnedest to exorcise. Three days lost to the kind of deep, bone-weary recovery that blurred waking and sleeping, tangled limbs and shared silence. It had been . . . satisfying. Immensely so. But the sharp tang of ozone from the Guild's attack, the vacant space where Sims used to stand, and the undeniable rot of betrayal somewhere within these walls clawed their way back into focus.

Contentment was a fragile beast.

Thorne had begun processing our captives—efficiently and brutally, as needed—but I wanted Sir Darian Lightbringer, the golden-haired poster boy for heroic delusion, all to myself. My magic felt frayed. My battle overload made compulsion impossible. Still, I needed answers, and I didn't care how ugly fetching them became.

Arabella had insisted on attending this little show. By rights, she could have claimed dibs on Lightbringer, but she'd been content to observe. She was calm beside me, her posture betraying none of the ferocity I knew simmered beneath that exterior. She was also a distraction, occupying a corner of my mind that should have focused on the battered knight bleeding out on the floor. I couldn't help being drawn to her, but a man could multitask.

Sir Darian knelt on slick stone, face already punished by fists, torment etched into bruises and cuts.

"I'll ask one more time." I let my voice drop to a bored monotone, something that wracked an enemy faster than theatrical rage. "What does Auremar want with my wife?"

He spat a stringy mixture of blood and saliva near my boot. Solid defiance for someone who couldn't move half his body. "She's not your wife," he said. "She's a prisoner. A toy."

Prisoner, toy, bride—*call her what you like, you drooling hypocrite.* My left hand flexed, and shadows gathered at my command, coiling around his throat until he made a strangled noise. "That's still not an answer."

I should've been able to break him faster, but his mind was shielded by a vile mix of holy conviction and something else. Possibly Auremar's new brand of magic, or my own magic's post-battle drag. Either way, I tamped down a sliver of frustration.

Darian's face went red as the shadows tightened. "The king . . . peace . . . restore Lady Evenfall . . . ," he rasped, voice strangled.

I released his throat so he could attempt a real explanation. Another shadow twined up his arm instead, sliding beneath his ragged tunic and burrowing beneath his skin. His choked gasp ripped into a raw scream that echoed off the cold, uncaring stones. Arabella watched him, her expression masked in dispassion. She didn't bat an eye.

"Propaganda again?" I said, letting the shadow retract slightly. "I'm tired of the kingdom-approved script. Spare me the heroic drivel and give me something I can use."

I pulled a melted sliver of blood from him, a thick droplet glimmering with an oily sheen. Corruption clung to it, humming with dissonant power. It was disturbingly familiar, like a warped reflection of my own shadows, which told me it definitely wasn't standard-issue Guild bravado.

"You've been feeding on something interesting," I remarked, flicking the globule in idle fascination. "Dark magic? It tastes foul, especially for a 'hero.' Auremar's doping his knights now?"

Fear finally won over his battered pride. He choked on a plea. "Please."

Progress. I crouched down to meet his eyes, ignoring the stench of panic. His entire body trembled, withdrawal etched into every twitch. "Your heroic blood is tainted, Lightbringer. Did you know? Or did you suspect it all along and take it anyway, hoping for a power boost?"

I conjured a thin thread of shadow, imbuing it with a faint shimmer mimicking the corruption in his blood. The illusion of relief.

"I could probably give you what you need," I said casually. "That power you crave."

Hope, raw and ugly, flared in his desperate eyes. He swallowed hard, eyes darting to the flicker of corrupted essence spinning at my fingertips. "He promised . . . it would make us strong. Then the pain . . . it's too much when it fades."

I let the swirl of black shimmer drift closer. Lightbringer shuddered, ready to debase himself for another taste.

"Small wonder you attacked us like a pack of rabid wolves," I said. "Tell me about the spy, knight. Someone inside Skyspire gave you a way through. Who was it?"

He started, "We didn't—" I jammed the needle-sharp shadows back, and he shrieked. "Tokens! Enchanted tokens. We activated them when we reached your ascension platforms. They let us in before your wards fully recognized . . . But we weren't expecting you . . . to be there."

Access tokens.

Griffin's intricate system, perverted and turned against us. Standard guest tokens wouldn't bypass the Inner Sanctum wards or grant access that deep without multiple alarms triggering. Which meant someone with high-level clearance had provided them. Someone who knew about the emergency ascension protocols, the linked portal network, the lightning bridges.

Someone who could issue or duplicate a token cleared for the Inner Sanctum. Pip? No, a servant was seeming less and less likely. A guard captain? One of the senior staff? The list of suspects narrowed considerably.

I met Arabella's stunned gaze. She'd clearly reached the same damning conclusion.

Darian was trembling, eyes locked on the illusion of corrupted magic I still held. "Please," he begged. "Just a scrap . . . I can't stand the emptiness . . ."

It was pathetic, yet informative. The king had given the Guild something they couldn't live without, and now they were tethered to him through magical dependence. Brutal, but not particularly clever, considering Lightbringer had just given up everything for a taste.

"Viscountess Morana," Darian blurted, tears streaming. "She let us march through Arvoryn Pass . . . no patrols . . . We had a deal."

Of course, the jealous bitch. Another loose end dangling, waiting to be snipped.

I dismissed the conjured darkness. My compulsion, when it returned, wasn't likely to glean more from a mind half-rotted by addiction. I stepped away from him, turning to Arabella. "He's broken. He might babble more once the withdrawal really digs in. Your choice: kill him or store him for later?"

Cool, pragmatic resolve flickered in her expression. "Lock him up. He'll beg for relief soon enough, and maybe we'll learn something else. Let him contemplate his choices for a few more days."

I shrugged. Two black-armored guards emerged from the deeper shadows to drag Darian off. His boots scraped the bloody floor, leaving a trail of misery behind.

Arabella and I left for the exit, but as we passed one cell, another voice howled, "Arabella! Daughter! You have to listen—Blackrose has poisoned your mind!" Atticus Evenfall, disheveled and half-crazed, flung himself at the iron bars, a pale, wretched ghost of a father. "He's the *villain*!"

She didn't spare him a glance. I saw the muscles in her jaw tighten, but not a single word slipped out.

I gave Evenfall a lazy smirk as I passed. Let him rot. She and I had more important business.

When we reached the next corridor, Arabella finally spoke. "Arvoryn, then. Morana helped kill Sims. She tried to kill us. I want to be there when she answers for it."

"Yes," I said, eyeing the determined set of her chin. That unstoppable edge only made me want her more. "We'll pay the viscountess a visit and remind her exactly who she betrayed."

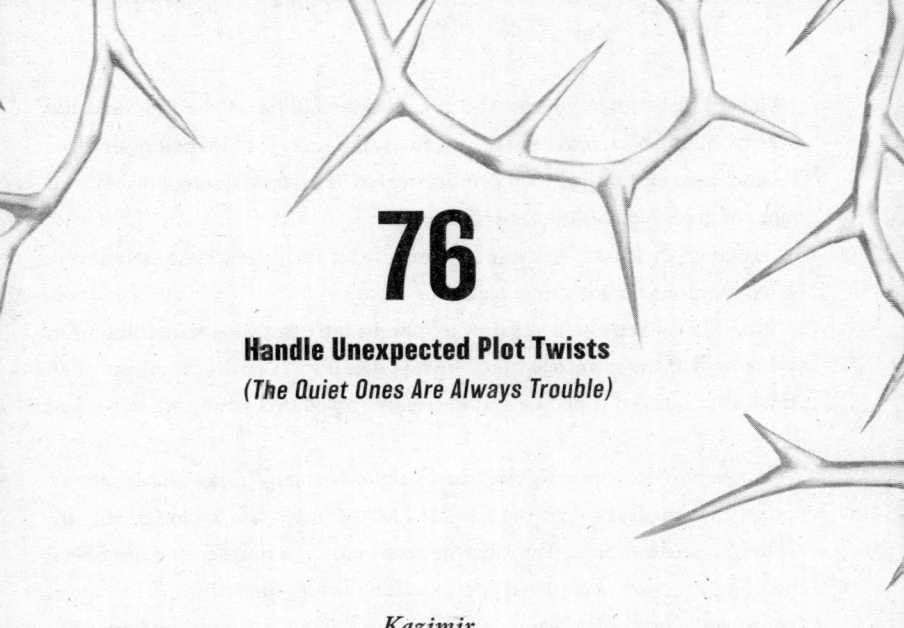

76

Handle Unexpected Plot Twists
(The Quiet Ones Are Always Trouble)

Kazimir

The corpse at my feet still twitched, the last vestiges of life fleeing Edmund's body where it sprawled on Arvoryn Manor's wooden floor. I hadn't been the one to kill him. That honor belonged to my wife, who stood beside me with her palm still glowing from the concentrated burst of death magic she'd channeled through it. Her expression was stone, but her eyes blazed with satisfaction.

"That was for Sims," she said, her voice unnervingly calm, almost like she was commenting on the weather.

I studied her for a moment, more intrigued than surprised. The ruthlessness with which she'd executed Edmund had been swift, efficient, almost beautiful in its economy of movement. One moment he'd been babbling his pathetic confession, the next his heart had simply stopped. No mess, no drawn-out torture, just the clean finality of judgment rendered. As executions went, I'd give it a solid ten out of ten.

"I will never lie to you again," I promised, unable to keep the appreciation from my voice.

Arabella flexed her fingers, the golden light fading as she absorbed the residual energy back into herself. "I actually felt sorry for him before all this," she said, her voice tinged with genuine regret. "He seemed so oppressed, and then you had to go and sleep with his wife."

I raised an eyebrow. "Are you blaming me for his treachery? Surely I can't be held responsible for every one of her affairs."

"No." She looked down at Edmund's body, her expression hardening. "I'm saying he had my sympathy until he revealed himself as the architect of an attack that killed our people and nearly destroyed everything we've worked for."

Our people. We've worked for. The casual ownership in her words sent an unexpected thrill through me, almost like I'd just taken a swig of the finest brandy instead of confronting the aftermath of a murder. It hadn't been that long ago that she'd been my unwilling bride, unleashing a torrent of venom while holding a dagger to my throat. Now she stood beside me as a true partner, executing my enemies as if they were her own. Which, in this case, they were.

I nudged Edmund's body with the toe of my boot, confirming what I already knew—he was thoroughly, irrevocably dead. "I didn't expect this particular twist," I admitted. "The henpecked husband revealing himself as the mastermind."

We'd arrived at Arvoryn Manor expecting to find Morana cowering or plotting her next move. Instead, we'd been greeted by Edmund in widow's black, spinning a tale of betrayal and abandonment—how Morana had fled the moment news of the Guild's failed attack reached her, leaving him to face our wrath alone.

He'd played the part well—the grieving, abandoned husband, throwing his treacherous wife to the wolves to save his own skin. I might even have believed him if not for Arabella's truth-sense.

"What do you think happened to Morana?" Arabella asked, breaking into my thoughts.

I surveyed the grand hall of Arvoryn Manor, noting the absence of any signs of struggle. "Two possibilities," I said. "Either Edmund eliminated her to tie up loose ends, or she discovered his betrayal and fled before we arrived."

"Which do you think it is?"

I shrugged. "Edmund would have gloated if he'd killed her. It's more likely she realized what was happening and ran. After all, Morana has always had a keen sense of self-preservation."

Arabella nodded, stepping away from the body. "What now?"

"Now?" I smiled grimly. "We leave this mess for one of my minions to clean up and return to Skyspire. There's a crown waiting for us . . . and possibly some overdue paperwork."

The journey back through the portal was swift, but my mind was racing faster than our travel. The king was moving his pieces across the board with increasing desperation.

And according to Edmund's final confession, one of those pieces remained hidden within Skyspire itself—a spy with access to our most sensitive areas. The description he'd provided matched no one in our ranks, suggesting whoever it was used a magical disguise. We'd neutralized one threat only to confirm another lurked much closer to home.

Arabella's hand found mine as we emerged onto Portal Isle, her grip tight as if she thought I might bolt. "How much did the Alchemist know?" she asked, voicing the question that had been nagging at me since we'd discovered Edmund's treachery.

"I've been wondering the same thing," I admitted. "Was their warning about your father a genuine attempt to elicit a favor, or a calculated move to draw us away from Skyspire at a critical moment?"

Arabella's expression darkened. "I don't like being indebted to anyone, especially not someone from the Syndicate."

"Neither do I," I agreed. "And debts to the Alchemist have a way of coming due at the most inconvenient times. We'll need to be prepared when they call it in."

Vex was waiting for us on the other side of the lightning bridge, her expression grim. "Morana?"

"Gone," I replied. "Edmund, however, won't be a problem any longer."

Vex's eyes flicked to Arabella, noting something in her posture or expression that gave away her role in Edmund's demise. "I see," she said simply. "And what of Auremar's forces?"

"Retreated back through the pass," I said. "The Guild's failure at Skyspire has forced him to reconsider his strategy. It buys us time, but not much."

Vex's expression shifted slightly. "And the Heirloom?"

I exchanged a glance with Arabella. Vex didn't know where it was, only that it was safe. "Waiting for us to take full control."

"You think it's ready?" my wife asked.

"I think we're ready," I corrected. "The Lifeweave ritual repaired the damage, and our bond has only strengthened since then. It's time to wield its power."

Vex looked between us, her expression carefully neutral. "And then what?"

"Then it won't matter what Auremar or anyone else is plotting," I said with grim satisfaction.

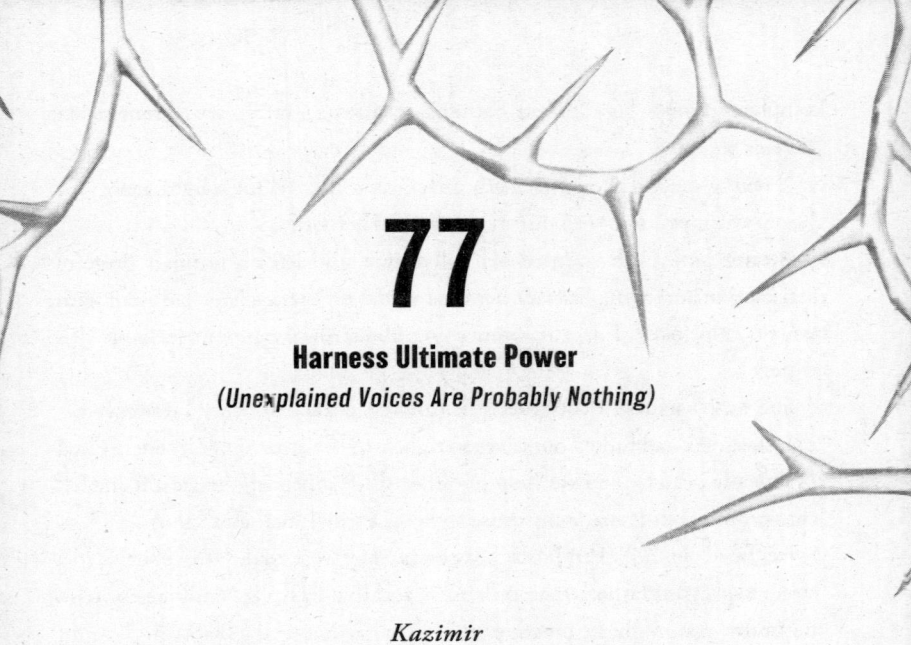

77

Harness Ultimate Power
(Unexplained Voices Are Probably Nothing)

Kazimir

The Heirloom pulsed on its makeshift pedestal—a dull, rhythmic glow that grazed my senses like the slow pound of battle drums. I'd chosen this cramped, mostly forgotten antechamber in our tower to hide the circlet until Arabella and I were ready. Now, though, its power flooded the space with dancing gold light and shadow, the two energies swirling together in an almost sentient conversation.

I circled the pedestal, trying to ignore the slow churn of dread and excitement in my chest. "It's stronger than it's ever been," I murmured. Dust motes trembled in the artifact's glow. "The resonance changed again after the Lifeweave."

Arabella lingered near the door, arms locked tight around herself. Her shoulders looked tense enough to snap. "Are you sure," she asked quietly, "that pushing straight into another ritual is a good idea? Especially after all of this?"

I stopped my prowl and faced her. The flickering light carved stark angles into her face, creating hollows beneath her cheekbones. She didn't look simply cautious—she looked haunted in a way I rarely saw, even in her darkest moods.

"Having second thoughts, Lady Blackrose?" I tried for a light tone. "Or have I worn you out with our more physical activities?"

A faint pink flush warmed her collarbone, and I felt a familiar surge of satisfaction at stirring her. Yet her eyes stayed on the circlet, shadowed with worry. "No jokes, Kazimir. Something about the Heirloom feels off this time."

She wasn't wrong. I could feel the difference too. After the Lifeweave ritual, she and I had linked ourselves so tightly to the crown that its energy had practically become an extension of our souls. But hearing her admit she felt that ominous shift made my pulse spike in a way I loathed to show.

I stepped closer. When I took her hands, they were cold. "We've survived a siege, a spy, your father's manipulations, and that fiasco at Morana's estate—naturally, you might be on edge."

She lifted her gaze to mine, searching my face for a moment. "You're not? You look like it's all just a standard Tuesday of villainy."

I tried for a dismissive grin. "Let's just say chaos is my default setting. Maybe you'll learn to enjoy the adrenaline rush."

Her answering attempt at a smile was small and fleeting. "What does that make me, if I'm enjoying it?" she asked, voice hushed.

"My queen," I said simply, raising one of her hands to my lips. "My co-conspirator in all forthcoming war crimes."

She didn't smile this time. Concern pooled in her eyes, a tension I recognized far too well. "Kaz," she repeated, more insistently, "I'm serious. Something—"

"I know," I cut in, lowering our hands. "So am I. But we can't avoid it forever—the Heirloom is ready, and waiting only makes it more dangerous. This is what we've built everything toward."

I felt her squeeze my fingers, the defiance creeping back into her posture as she straightened. "All right. Let's do it."

So we positioned ourselves, the crown at the center, its restless light flickering like some hungry beast waiting to be fed. I brought my palms close to it, letting my magic skim its surface until I felt the runes in my bones stir to life. Arabella mirrored me from the other side. In that moment, my awareness of her was painfully tangible: the pale line of her throat, the determined set of her jaw, the exhausted fear she was valiantly pushing down.

"Focus on the ley lines," I reminded her, locking my gaze on hers across the artifact. "They're there, right beneath us. Raw power we can funnel wherever we want."

She nodded, placed her hands near the gold-and-shadow circlet, and exhaled. I matched her breath, the air thickening with tension as we began the incantation. The words were older than most living languages, lost to time until I dug them up from forbidden texts. Our voices entwined in the cramped room, pouring the syllables into the artifact, coaxing a response.

It didn't take long. The Heirloom flared, gold and shadow twisting violently, merging in an almost hypnotic pattern. My runes burned under my skin as I unleashed more of my dominion magic, channeling it toward the circlet. There was that wild, reckless surge I craved. I felt unstoppable, primed to devour entire realms if I wanted to.

Arabella's power joined mine with a ferocious jolt, bright and pure. She'd once been all about healing; now, she wielded a lethal mix of creation and destruction. Our combined might pounded against the artifact.

Then came the psychic scream—like the crown unleashed every ounce of tension I'd ever felt in my entire life and hurled it back at me. The air throbbed with a high-pitched ringing, the kind that made my teeth ache.

"It's working," I managed to choke out. My heart pounded with brutal excitement. This was it. A lifetime of searching and scheming, and I was seconds away from absolute dominion.

Before Arabella could respond, everything fractured.

In one blink, I was no longer in the tower chamber. Instead, I stood on a stark plain under a sky devoid of stars. The ground looked like cracked obsidian, and the air felt saturated with old magic that prickled deep, right in the marrow of my bones. An echo of something I *knew*.

A massive shadow spread across the plain—impossible to map in shape or scope, more a devouring void than a tangible creature. But the most jarring part was my own sense of recognition. I didn't just see the darkness. I felt its hunger. Its rage. Its crushing loneliness. Because they were *mine*.

I was the darkness.

Then the vision whipped me to a different scene. A man stood in front of me, his expression carved from something stoic and annoyingly noble. He held a golden rose, shining painfully bright.

"This ends now," he said, voice ringing with authority. "You've devoured enough, Shadow King."

I felt a harsh laugh tear from my lungs, but it was foreign, unlike my usual cynicism. More chaotic and brutal. "You think you can stop me, Soriven? I am eternal. I am the void that remains when all else fades."

He lifted the rose. Its radiance ripped through me, an explosion of agony that tore my essence to ribbons. There were binding chains next—golden light twisting around me, forcing me into a prison. I screamed without a mouth, raged without form. Torn asunder, remade, sealed away.

But not destroyed. Never destroyed.

Ages blurred. I slept. Dreamed. Occasionally, a shard of consciousness broke free. Sometimes I latched onto a child born under unlucky stars, brimming with the right shade of darkness.

Always the same cycle. Growth. Awareness. The slow dawning of ancient memory. And then—death. Swift, violent ends snapping me back to the void. Again. And again.

Until my mother, her hands slick with my blood as she carved runes into me, unknowingly unraveling a portion of the chains that contained the Shadow King. I understood now that each cut was part of a monstrous puzzle, forging me into a more perfect vessel. They didn't break my golden chains but cracked them just enough.

Skyspire appeared in my mind. My seat of power before Soriven and his cursed rose. Always mine, across countless attempts to reclaim it.

The knowledge scalded me. I was the Shadow King. Reborn countless times, inching closer to remembering, to reclaiming what was stolen. The Heirloom itself was the artifact Soriven made to contain my darkness. And now, ironically, I was about to unleash it.

I felt something stir inside—an ancient presence, uncoiling with lethal fascination. It peered through my eyes and saw *her*. Arabella . . . Soriven's *descendant*. The rightful inheritor of that rose magic, the bloodline that bound me. The enemy.

Hatred, immediate and inhuman, roared through my veins.

Destroy her. Consume her with your vengeance.

But I forced that voice aside—hard. I pictured Arabella's face, her feral grin when she bested me at golf, her quiet vulnerability when she'd told me she wouldn't leave my side. *My* Arabella. Not Soriven.

She isn't my enemy—she's . . . everything. She's my . . .

The word surfaced, shocking in its raw unfamiliarity. *Love.*

The Shadow King hammered back, protesting that attachment as a pathetic weakness. My skull felt like it would split. Ribbons of darkness scythed through the air, gold fragments of heroic magic entangled with them. I heard Arabella shouting my name, though I couldn't say if it was in the vision or in real life.

Then everything snapped to black.

When clarity returned, I was on the stone floor of that cramped tower space, the tang of raw power still stinging my mouth. Groaning, I blinked up at Arabella. She knelt next to me, her hand pressed firmly over my heart. Her eyes were big, her lips parted in anxious relief.

"Kaz," she breathed, voice frayed with worry. "Are you all right? Do you remember . . . anything?"

I swallowed, pushing myself upright. My head throbbed—an echo of something enormous. "I—" My words caught in my throat. "The Heirloom started the process. Then I blacked out. Did . . . did we succeed?"

She didn't answer right away. She studied my face, a swirl of thoughts behind her steady gaze. "You honestly don't recall any of it?"

Bits of memory hung just out of reach. "I remember light. A surge. Then a storm of shadows. Why? What did I—?"

"See for yourself." Her voice sounded too careful.

I turned my head to discover the Heirloom glowing with a perfect union of gold and shadow. The hum it gave off vibrated through the floor, up my spine, making me feel both electric and slightly nauseous.

"It's . . . fully activated," I realized, staggering to my feet. Arabella moved to steady me, but I waved a hand, too hyped on raw adrenaline to care about any weakness. "Look at it. It's—this is what we wanted."

I approached the artifact, reached out, and let my fingertips graze the warm metal. Energy jolted up my arm with an intensity that was almost too much. But I felt something else too: a link that reached from the Heirloom into me, and from me directly into Arabella. Our bond roared back to full strength, an intimate exchange of power and breath.

I turned to find her staring at me, eyes still brimming with confusion and maybe unspoken fear. "Can you feel it?" I asked, voice low with barely contained excitement. "The ley lines. They're right there. We're standing in the center of a living map."

She swallowed, nodding slowly. "I can. It's almost . . . too big."

"Too big?" A hungry laugh burst from me. "It's magnificent!" Impulsively, I grabbed her waist, spun her around, only putting her down when she gasped. "We can do anything. Reroute the magic running beneath entire kingdoms, cut off water supplies, starve armies. The Syndicate can't touch us now. And Solandris . . . you know what we're capable of."

She went still at my words. Something fluttered across her expression. "And the Shadow King?" she asked softly. "My father thought—"

"Legends," I scoffed quickly, an involuntary chill crawling under my skin. She hadn't said one word about her father since leaving him in the dungeons. And now she was asking about his ramblings. "But if some ancient force is lurking, we'll handle it the same way we handle everyone else who tries to stand against us. We own the Heirloom now."

She kept looking at me. I couldn't place the emotion in her gaze. Not quite trust, not quite mistrust, but a wary acknowledgment of something she wasn't ready to say. I hated the uncertainty there. I wanted the entire world to quake at our approach, and here she was, giving me reservations I didn't want.

"Cheer up," I told her, even as a flicker of restlessness warred inside my chest. "This is a victory. It calls for celebration, not . . . this." I waved a hand at her solemn face.

She pressed her lips together, evidently deciding not to push the topic. "Fine." She exhaled shakily and placed her hand over mine on the circlet. Energy leaped from her touch. "At least we did it. The Heirloom's ours."

Yes, I thought, ours. But what had happened to me in that vision? Why couldn't I remember important parts? My mind refused to latch onto the details, swirling them away like leaves in a storm. I swallowed my frustration. The only thing that mattered was the artifact's new stability.

Arabella guided me to sense the ley lines. Luminous webs crossed the dark beneath our feet, miles below the fortress. She and I held a single vantage now, a vantage of unstoppable dominion. The entire Western Realms spread out before us, waiting to be claimed.

"It works," I murmured, letting the raw triumph coat my words.

Her hand slipped away from the Heirloom and went around my waist instead. "Of course it does," she said, subdued but resolute. "We make a dangerous team."

I flashed her a grin that felt a tad sharper than usual. "Dangerous indeed." I tugged her closer, drawn by the need to taste that soft mouth and bury any lingering whispers of that ominous presence. For a split second, I saw our merged shadows flicker on the wall behind us. The shape seemed too large, bat-like wings unfurling before collapsing into a normal silhouette. I blinked, and it was gone.

Arabella caught my tension and slid a hand up my chest, probably to distract me. Her lips brushed mine, dissolving my doubts in a surge of heat. I let myself fall into it, ignoring the tingling dread at the base of my skull. We had power, we had each other, and unstoppable dominion was ours to command. Whatever nightmares lurked, I'd face them on my own terms.

Pulling back, she breathed, "We should tell the others. And then we'll tighten security around the tower, keep the Heirloom hidden. The Syndicate will sense this surge."

I released her, my pulse still hammering. "Yes. Let's not pretend they'll be thrilled to see us with an artifact powerful enough to warp the entire map. More wards, more guards . . . and if they come looking for trouble, they'll find it."

A flash of her usual defiance lit her face. "For now, let's share the good news with Vex, Griffin, and Thorne. And figure out how to keep the Heirloom stable if we push it further."

No mention of the Shadow King again. I was more than content to let the subject remain buried. With renewed confidence, I offered her my arm.

She accepted, sliding in close. That steady hum of energy rolled through my bones, echoed by the warmth of her body against mine. One unbelievably powerful relic, one unstoppable union, one conquest at a time. Whatever had happened in that vision was secondary. We'd risen from the rubble before; we'd do it again and again.

I led Arabella out, the glow of the Heirloom pulsing behind us. Let the rest of the world brace itself. We had unstoppable chaos to unleash.

But as we walked through the damaged corridors of Skyspire, I shoved aside the nagging certainty that I was forgetting something vital.

Acknowledgments

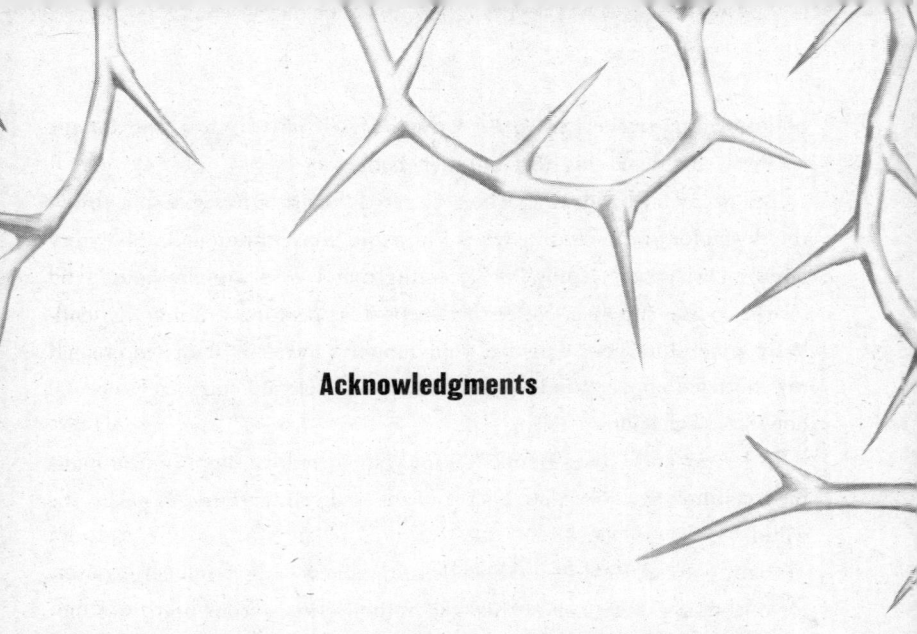

Writing about villains with boundary issues and the women who survive them takes a village—preferably one that doesn't flinch at deranged shenanigans.

This book found its way into your hands thanks to the passionate team who championed it. First, to my incredible agent, Lauren: Thank you for believing in this story's unique brand of chaos and for finding it the perfect home. I'm so incredibly grateful for your guidance and I don't know how I got so lucky to have you in my corner.

To my brilliant editor, Sarah, and the entire team at Scarlett Press and Simon & Schuster: Thank you for seeing the potential in this story and giving it such a wonderful home. Your enthusiasm for Kaz and Arabella and their sidekicks made the entire process a joy. Thank you for welcoming me and my unhinged villains so warmly.

My deepest gratitude goes to my family. First and foremost, to my sister Nicole, who looked at the romance landscape and said, "You know what's needed? More cute villains." When I boldly declared, "I could write that!" you probably didn't expect me to actually follow through. Thanks for believing in this chaotic story from the very beginning, for late-night brainstorming sessions when I'd written myself into corners, and for the feedback that made this story infinitely better.

And to my husband, Eric, who's mastered the art of living with a writer: thank you for understanding when I stop mid-conversation to scribble story notes on whatever's handy, for accepting that I keep vampire hours, and for the endless supply of coffee that keeps this operation running. I'm endlessly grateful for your patience, your support, and your ability to pretend my muttered conversations with imaginary people are completely normal household behavior.

To Jeremy and Catie: Thank you for your incredible support. You make me feel infinitely cooler than I actually am, and your enthusiasm means the world.

To my parents, Robbin and Dennis, and the rest of my family: Thank you for celebrating every step of this wild author journey. Your pride and support are amazing . . . even though I must formally request that you never, ever read this book. Seriously. It's filled with swearing and spice. Just admire the cover, nod, and tell people you're proud of me. I'm so grateful for you all.

This story also wouldn't be what it is without the crucial help of Brian and Nina, who repeatedly told me I had a hit on my hands. (I didn't believe you, sorry). Brian, thanks for helping me untangle plot threads. Your ability to ask the right questions at exactly the right moment saved this book from several narrative disasters (and from unnecessary changes). Nina, thank you for graciously beta reading this manuscript with feedback that was both timely and encouraging. I'm so grateful to you both for your time and willingness to engage with all this chaos.

To every reader who picks up this book: Thank you from the bottom of my heart. When I first wrote this story on a whim, I genuinely wasn't sure if what I thought was funny would work for anyone else. I have been completely and wonderfully overwhelmed by the flood of reviews, comments, and messages. To everyone who has shared this book in reader groups or tagged me on social media, your enthusiasm has meant the world. You make this wild career possible.

TIFFANY HUNT writes all things fantasy romance with salty characters, action, kick-butt heroines, and spice. If it has castles, magic, and hunky, irresistible men (or elves, etc.), she's down for it. Her favorite tropes are enemies-to-lovers, one bed, fake dating, arranged marriages, and forbidden love.